A NOVEL

# Bill Flanagan

RANDOM HOUSE

NEW YORK

Library of Congress Cataloging-in-Publication Data

Flanagan, Bill.
    A&R: a novel / Bill Flanagan.
        p.      cm.
    ISBN 0-375-50266-1
    1. Sound recording industry—Fiction.    2. Music trade—Fiction.    I. Title: A and R.
    II. Title.

    PS3556.L313 A62 2000
    813'.54—dc21    99-056309

Random House website address: www.atrandom.com

Printed in the United States of America on acid-free paper

9  8  7  6  5  4  3  2

First Edition

Thanks to John, Jeff, and all at VH1 for giving me support and time off to write. Thanks to Candida, Sheila, and all at Principle for the help and accommodations. Thanks to Ned, Maurice, and Dreamchaser for hot meals and the use of the machinery. Thanks to Tom and Kathy for the research field trip. Thanks to Susan, Kate, Sarah, and Frank for all they gave up so the book could get done. Thanks to Scott for getting me to finally do it.

—B.F.

*For my brothers, Jack and Jim*

A&R

# 1

Cantone got in the car and closed the door and Booth went into his pitch: "Jimmy, I want you on my team. I appreciate your loyalty to Barney. He's been good to you. But let's be honest. You have been very, very good to him. You found Metric Sect, you found Planet Fish. I won't embarrass you by asking if Barney even heard those albums before they went platinum. But it's his picture in *Vanity Fair* with his arms draped around them at the Grammys and a headline, 'The Man with the Golden Ear.' I saw that and I said to Lois, 'Barney's got a golden ear, all right— but it's attached to Jimmy Cantone's head!' Don't misunderstand me. I love Barney. The guy's fifty-four years old, claims he's fifty-two, and is still crawling around the carpet on all fours vacuuming up the last bits of Bolivia. No one's told him it's not the nineteen hundreds anymore. You're up all night pulling hits out of whining hopheads and Barney's taking the Concord to Paris to sample some new pastry and try to hump the busboy. How many times have you had to break the news to one of his lambchops that there will not be a record deal in his future? Never mind. I won't put you on the spot. I can imagine.

"Someday you'll look back on that and it will all seem funny. Bottom line, Jimmy, you've gone as far as you can go with Barney. You've outgrown that situation. I can offer you an opportunity to play at the top of the game. At WorldWide you'll have the authority to oversee your projects from beginning to end. You'll have a say in how your acts are marketed, promoted, the video budget, where the ads are placed—every aspect from development to reissues. Bill DeGaul is a very big fan of yours. I told him I was going to make you an offer and he said, 'That guy's got it. He belongs here.' I think all three of us know that. The only thing we have to discuss is, how much it will take to make you feel at home."

Jim was listening to Booth like a radio. He was startled he had to talk back. When he did, he said more than he should have. "I'm making one-fifty now, which with bonus and profit sharing ends up at about two hundred, two twenty-five."

Booth smiled too quickly. Jim felt like a sap.

"We can do better than that. I want you to come in as a vice president. You start out at two-fifty plus a minimum bonus of thirty percent. Within two years, you'll be at three hundred and forty percent. That's the base. You're going to earn your real money on points on all the albums you're going to make for us. That's where you're going to get rich, Jimmy. You have kids, right?"

"Two boys."

"How old?"

"Almost three. They're twins."

"Imagine what it's going to cost to send two kids to Harvard at the same time in another fifteen years! You better take this job, Jimmy."

Booth laughed and the driver, who Jim had not noticed listening, joined in.

"It's real tempting, J.B.," Jim said. He wanted to regain a little leverage. "But you know, I've had a lot of offers. I like working with Barney. He is a nut, but he's a nut who lives for music. And it's home to me. I really like what you folks are doing. My wife sure wants me to make a move. I just need a few days to look at all the possibilities." He tapped the driver's shoulder. "I get out just up there on the right, behind the police car."

Jim thanked Booth for the lift and said so long. As the car pulled away Booth lowered his window and called back, "Jim—listen to your wife!"

Jim walked through a crowd of punks and college kids into the Mercury Lounge. He was thirty now, but he believed he still looked like one of the fans. He had shoulder-length hair, no longer as red as it used to be, and he was very thin. His skinniness exaggerated all his other features—his roman nose, his heavy brow, his big hands—and made him look taller than his six feet.

Jim leaned down to tell the rat-faced kid on the door that his name was on the guest list but before he opened his mouth the kid said, "Go ahead, sir," and waved him in.

A *Rolling Stone* writer Jim knew was leaning on the bar, smiling at this display of deference.

"I guess he could tell I'm important," Jim said.

"No," the writer said. "He took one look at you and thought, 'This guy's too old to be here for fun.'"

The band Jim had come to see was called Jerusalem. He had been watching them for more than a year, giving them advice on songwriting and how to carry themselves on stage. He had seen them through three drummers, the bassist's suspended jail sentence, and the keyboard player's divorce and remarriage. He had helped them get publishing money so they could afford decent equipment and a van. He watched them grow from a promising local group to a confident band ready to record. Along the way other labels began sniffing around. Jim did not want to lose Jerusalem, but Barney held back from letting him sign them. They had an ambitious lawyer who wanted big money and Barney said to let them sweat.

Jim ordered an orange juice to take into the back room, where the band was playing. When he paid he looked down the bar and saw Zoey Pavlov, a talent scout for WorldWide Music. That spooked him. Did Booth know that one of his A&R people was here when he dropped Jim outside? Maybe not. Zoey was out in some bar somewhere seeing some band every night. There was no reason to be paranoid.

Zoey picked up two drinks and carried them to a table near the stage. She set them down in front of William "Wild Bill" DeGaul, the CEO of WorldWide Music, Booth's boss and maybe soon Jim's own. There was reason to be paranoid.

Jim banged through the ugly possibilities. First: *Booth was only pre-*

*tending to court him to get Jerusalem for WorldWide.* That made no sense. Big shots like Booth and DeGaul don't need to stoop to conquer small-label A&R men. They step on them without wiping off their shoes.

Second: *DeGaul had arranged to be here to bump into Jim. Booth set him up with the flattering car ride and now the big boss was waiting at the other end to close the deal.* Well, it would be sweet to believe it. Jim's ego was not grand enough to seriously consider that these giants of industry designed their movements to seduce him into taking a job he would be nuts to turn down anyway.

Third: *Zoey Pavlov got wind Jim might be coming into her department and was trying to (a) make friends with him, (b) scrutinize him, or (c) steal his next signing out from under him.* Maybe Zoey heard Jim was close to signing Jerusalem and she convinced the boss to come see them, pretending they were her discovery. It would be a way of saying to De-Gaul, "My ears are as good as this guy's. What do you need him for?"

Fourth: *Zoey and DeGaul are just here because they like music.* It would be sweet to believe it.

Zoey spotted Jim staring at them and vaguely waved hello. She leaned over and said something to DeGaul, who turned and smiled and motioned for Jim to come sit down. There were no free seats, but by the time Jim got to the table a lackey had vacated his chair and disappeared.

"Hello, Zoey," Jim said. She mouthed hi and returned to looking bored and breathing through her mouth. Jim turned his head to De-Gaul. "Bill, who's watching the empire?"

"I got people to do that for me!" DeGaul announced. "Siddown, Mr. Cantone! I want to get your read on this next band!"

Jim sat. Wild Bill DeGaul always spoke a notch louder than he had to. Slight hearing loss, Jim figured, a common liability in this business. DeGaul was in his middle fifties but looked right at home in the rock club. His hair was thick and had turned white so evenly that you could figure him for a blond. His skin was tanned, his white collar and cuffs were starched, his khaki suit jacket was perfectly draped over his broad shoulders. He looked like a man who had arrived at his fifties feeling right at home. The world was designed for people like DeGaul. He was happy holding the lease.

"I just got back from Africa!" DeGaul said in Jim's ear. "Dakar! What a place! You been? You gotta go. We hired camels! I drank some bad moonshine and woke up with a swollen colon and a shrunken head! The music is incredible there! Mbalax! I brought back some CDs, you gotta hear it."

DeGaul fished in a leather satchel under the table, pushed aside a couple of stacks of what looked like fifty-dollar bills wrapped in rubber bands, and hauled out several compact discs with Xeroxed paper covers and French titles. He handed one to Jim. "Take this home and tell me what you think of it! It's great!"

Well, Jim figured, DeGaul is a cowboy, all right. The only way you'd ever get Jim's boss, Barney, up on a camel would be if he ran over it in his Bentley on the way to pick up a cheesecake.

An MTV executive came up behind DeGaul and squeezed his shoulders. DeGaul turned and sailed into a conversation about whether one of WorldWide's big acts would headline the next Video Music Awards. Jim was relieved to be off the hook for a minute. He wasn't sure if he should mention the job offer. He wasn't sure if DeGaul's outgoing manner was part of the mating dance. He looked at Zoey Pavlov, who regarded him as if he were standing on her foot.

DeGaul made some halfhearted wisecrack and the MTV exec fell over laughing. Gosh, Jim thought, what must it do to a man's ass to be constantly kissed?

DeGaul's legend was the stuff of *Billboard* Spotlights. His father was a naval officer and Wild Bill grew up at different bases around Latin America and the Caribbean. He was, famously, kicked out of military school for knocking out the commandant after being caught drunk. Shamed, he packed his kit and spent the next two years roaming Brazil. When he came out of the jungle he set up a small export business for bossa nova and mambo albums. He made money at it, and in the mid-sixties opened a record store in New Orleans. He ran back and forth to Brazil and the Caribbean, buying records for his store. He got a mail order business going. He set up a little label of his own. He recorded local New Orleans R&B and shipped it up north and overseas. He licensed foreign recordings for the USA. He was one of the first entrepreneurs anywhere to record reggae.

In 1967 DeGaul expanded his record-exporting business into England and Europe. He got the U.S. rights to some second-level British rock bands and scored a few hits. His import and R&B sales kept climbing. He bought a couple of small radio stations in New Orleans and Florida, and pushed his own records on the air until the FCC came after him for conflict of interest. He then sold the stations at a big profit, which he put back into his record company.

By 1970, DeGaul's Tropic Records was a money mill. He had produced seven Top Twenty pop records and three dozen R&B hits. He sold the company to the conglomerate now known as WorldWide Entertainment for five million dollars and a pile of stock. He stayed on to run things as he always had. He acted like he still owned the joint. He rose through the ranks of WorldWide Music until he was in charge of the whole show. In 1995 WorldWide was bought by a Swedish multinational called NOA, which did not pretend to understand music and left DeGaul alone. By now, Jim figured, he must pull down ten million a year, and he still gave every appearance of being in it for the music and the adventure.

As the house lights went down, DeGaul leaned over to Jim. "So—are these guys gonna roll my socks up?" Jim smiled and turned toward the bandstand.

The four members of Jerusalem slunk out onto the stage and began switching on amps and tapping microphones. Jim looked around to see if Barney was there yet. Tonight was the night Barney was supposed to finally sign off on giving Jerusalem a contract. If everything went as planned, Jim would introduce Barney to the band, they'd have a nice chat, and then Jim would take Jerusalem out for a meal and make the formal proposal they had all been dancing around for twelve months. Jim searched through the faces in the half-dark room until he landed on the one he was looking for. There by the soundboard stood Barney Whippet, the father of Feast Records, looking like an imp.

Barney's hair, dyed roadwork orange, stood straight up like the spikes of a crown. His eyebrows came to a sharp arch and his pointed ears stuck out from his head like little red wings. Barney was a smart and powerful middle-aged Englishman who looked as if he should be making toys at the North Pole. He winked at Jim. If he was rattled to see his top A&R scout sitting with a rival, he did not show it. Barney looked like he always looked, like a happy delinquent. He looked like he was about to give someone a hotfoot.

Deciding if he should leave Barney to sign up with DeGaul would be tough, but Jim was grateful for the choice. The music business was more and more dominated by bean counters and corporate opportunists. Jim appreciated the older guys who had gotten in out of love. They might be pirates, they might be reprobates, they might have picked the pockets of poor bluesmen and ignorant English kids, but at least they were dedicated to music. The MBAs and Hollywood lawyers who began infiltrating the industry in the eighties did not care if they were selling records, deodorant, or breakfast cereal. They wanted to make their names fast, build their résumés, and move on. In such a world there was no loyalty down, so there was no loyalty up.

What Jim knew for sure about Barney and suspected about DeGaul was that they weren't leaving the record game until their corpses were dragged off the field. What other kind of boss was worth following?

Jerusalem began playing and to Jim's relief sounded great. They were a real rarity—a four-piece band with three solid singers and good original songs. The guitarist and focal point was a twenty-two-year-old woman who called herself Lilly Rope. Lilly was short and striking, with big brown eyes circled with dark makeup, thick black hair, and pale white skin. When Jim met Jerusalem, Lilly was pudgy and uncomfortable in the spotlight. In the last year she had lost her babyfat, found her cheekbones, and become confident on stage. Jim figured Lilly for a star.

Dick the bassist and Anthony the keyboard player wrote songs as good as Lilly's and supported her musically. Dick and Anthony had spent years in cover bands. That would be left out of their press bio, but the apprenticeship made them good players and helped them understand songwriting. Tonight their lessons were paying off. By the end of the week Jerusalem would have a few hundred thousand dollars and the promise of a recording career. Jim was proud of them for performing so well with their future riding on it.

"They're good!" DeGaul said when the group went into their third song. "I love the drummer!"

That was Mack Toomey, a Scottish kid Jim had recommended when the band's previous drummer missed a gig because he got drunk and snorted Ajax. Mack was a strong musician with a great attitude and the bonus of being shockingly handsome. James Dean, Brad Pitt—Mack invited comparison to all the himbo icons. Women followed him down the street. His Scottish-by-way-of-Brixton accent and a genuinely happy, open manner added to his charm. When Jim fixed up Jerusalem with Mack, he knew they had everything.

The set ended, the band walked off, came back and did an encore, walked off again, and came back and started packing their gear so the next act could set up. Jim excused himself from the table. He went to find Barney.

"What do you think, B.?"

"That last song was good. Did she write that?"

"The bass player wrote that one. Barney, this group has three writers. They're bullet-proof. We have to get them signed now or World-Wide is going to grab them."

Barney's pixie eyebrows shot up. "I saw you fraternizing with Zoey Pavlov. I hope you washed."

"You've got to come say hi to the band. You're with me on this, right?"

"I would dig to China with a spoon, Jim, if you told me it was the way to go."

"I want to offer them three hundred up front, a hundred when they deliver the album, and two hundred for each of the next three, okay?"

"Hold on to that as a fallback. Watch Daddy work this."

That made Jim shake. Barney's nickname at work was "Mr. Mxyzptlk" after the mischievous imp in Superman comics. There was no end to the havoc Barney could wreak when the impulse took him. Barney was off to meet the band. Jim hurried after him, praying that he would not queer the deal.

The small dressing room was buzzing. It smelled of new sweat and old beer. There were too many people crammed in the small space, all congratulating Jerusalem and trying to grab a corner of their coattails. The *Rolling Stone* writer looked like he was composing an "I-Knew-Them-When" scenario to pull out when they were platinum. A couple of Lower East Side girlfriends were mentally counting the rooms of their honeymoon mansions, ignorant of the sad inevitability that by the time those mansions were bought, their places would be taken by fashion models and actresses. Jim surveyed the scene like Santa peeking down a chimney.

He grabbed the Jerusalem member closest to the door. "That was a great one, Dick! You know Barney Whippet, my boss."

Dick took the cigarette out of his mouth to say hi and Barney loomed up against him, gazing into his eyes. "You wrote that song 'Daytime Nighttime Girl.' That is a great, great song. I could hear Madness or the Specials doing that."

"Oh, thanks, Barney. Yeah, it's got that bluebeat thing in it." And with that they were off. Jim tuned out Barney telling Dick about his involvement with the Sex Pistols, Stiff, Chrissie Hynde, Joe Strummer. The old ringmaster would wow the boy with his proximity to history and inside gossip about the giants of yore. Yore was 1978. By the end of Barney's rap Dick would beg to log his band's name in Barney's Big Book of Rock Stars I Have Touched. Jim panned the room looking for Lilly and was bugged to see her crouched over a bottle with her lawyer and Zoey Pavlov. At least DeGaul wasn't there.

Mack, the beautiful Scottish drummer, stuck a beer in Jim's hand and smiled. "Are we partners, then?" He asked.

"We're partners," Jim said.

"Yeah!" Mack punched the air. Anthony joined them in a huddle. Jim and Mack nodded to him like secret agents exchanging signals.

"Can we get Lilly out of here and go talk?" Jim asked. The two musicians said they'd take care of it fast. Jim went back to Barney, who was telling the bassist a horrible story about a famous pianist who had to play a whole tour standing up because a Dr Pepper bottle broke off in his ass. Jim cringed, but the young musician was appropriately impressed with Barney's historical depth.

"We're going to go somewhere and talk," Jim told Barney and Dick. "Mack and Anthony are getting Lilly. Where do you guys want to go?"

"My place on Christopher," Barney said. "Come on, I've got a stretch!"

The boys separated Lilly from Zoey and steered the singer toward the door. Jim said to Catalano, Jerusalem's lawyer, "I'm taking the band over to Barney's house."

"Give me the address, I might catch up with you in a bit," Catalano said. "I have to finish up with Zoey."

Power play, Jim thought. The lawyer's taking a risk by not being there when the band sits down with Barney. But letting me know he's hobnobbing with Zoey is a warning that if we don't make a strong offer tonight, we'll blow the deal. Jim shrugged it off. They were going to make the deal. Barney was into it, he'd turned on the charm. If the lawyer didn't make life a little more miserable than it had to be he wouldn't be a lawyer.

The band and Barney were already in the limo. On the way out of the club Jim bumped into DeGaul again. He was talking into a cell phone but he stopped when he saw Jim. "Cantone," he said. "I'm going to Odeon for dinner! Want to eat?"

"I can't," Jim said, gesturing toward Barney's car. "I gotta work."

"I'll be there a while. Come by later if you get done."

Jim smiled and got in the limo. Barney had a hip-hop CD blasting and was pouring brandy into crystal glasses and passing them to the laughing musicians for the short ride to his brownstone. Jim needed this deal to work out. He needed to justify sticking with Barney in the face of WorldWide's offer. Feast Records was as comfortable as an after-school job at the soda shop. As long as he stayed there Jim could tell himself that he was a free spirit, outside the mainstream. He could hang on to the belief that his destiny was still unwritten. If he moved to WorldWide and up the corporate ladder there would be no denying that he had turned into a man who made his choices based on assessing his professional options, taking the long view, building his résumé. He'd be admitting he had not a job, but a career.

At the house, Barney switched off the alarms and led the band through the basement door into his big kitchen with oak tables, industrial stove, and overstuffed couches. The house was elegant and uncharacteristically understated: Barney's wife's influence. It seemed weird to Jim that Barney had a wife. Alice Whippet still lived in England. She and Barney treated each other like grown siblings. They came together each winter for the Grammys, the Rainforest, and the Rock and Roll Hall of Fame—the high holy days.

Barney put on a Miles Davis CD and laid out sandwiches, wine, beer, caviar, chocolates, and Fritos for the band. He praised them lavishly, recalling lyrics to songs he had just heard for the first time and remembering facts Jim had told him when Jim thought he was paying no attention. Barney speculated about producers the band might want to work with, exotic studios, and the possibilities of pulling a few strings to get them the opening spot on the next R.E.M. tour. He compared the decisions they would face with dilemmas he had solved for his friends Oasis, Radiohead, and Björk.

The band were flattered, it was all going fine. Jim kept slipping into listening to the Miles record. It summoned memories of his college dorm, his old girlfriend, driving across country after graduation. Then he'd snap back and force himself to focus on the conversation.

Handsome Mack was keeping his equilibrium in the face of all Barney's compliments. He asked some tough questions about promotion budgets, ad buys—all the things most bands don't think to ask about until their record comes out and no one buys it. Good for Mack, Jim figured. He wondered where the group's lawyer was. Was Zoey a real rival? Was this a test by Booth and DeGaul to see if Jim could be tackled at the goal line?

A psychic alarm went off and Jim's attention jerked back to the conversation in front of him. Barney was pulling his off-to-Britain move.

"Listen, Jerusalem," Barney said, waving a flute of wine in the air like a man flagging down a plane, "I want to sign you to Feast and Jim wants to sign you to Feast. But we have a problem."

Everybody sobered up fast. Jim felt his face flush. Barney went on: "I have to leave for Britain first thing tomorrow. No, look at the time. *Today.* The car takes me to the airport in five hours. I will be gone for four months. Feast cannot sign any act in the States until I get back. I had figured we'd pick this up again then, but after seeing you tonight, I don't want to wait."

Barney pulled an envelope from his breast pocket. "This is a standard Feast recording contract. I am going to cross out all the standard parts." Barney whipped out a Sharpie and began slashing and scribbling. "I am changing the term from seven years to . . . what do you want? More? Less? Let's make it five, I don't want to tie you up for life. In five years I'll be crawling to get you to re-sign and Columbia, Warners, and WorldWide will all be offering you millions to betray me."

This was the side of Barney that Jim hated. No one was as shameless when it came to bullying insecure musicians and pinching pennies. Barney's crowning glory—still whispered about among managers and music lawyers—came during the disco era when a singer called Valentino, Feast's one true superstar, demanded to renegotiate his miserly record deal. Barney had signed him when he was Vinnie Mastratano, singing to backing tapes at New Jersey dance clubs, and Barney refused to increase Valentino's royalties when he began selling millions, making movies, dating screen stars, and adorning the cover of *People*. Second album multiplatinum, third album multiplatinum—Barney would not budge. He had Valentino for seven albums, he was his bird in the hand. It became a professional embarrassment to Valentino and his managers that he was earning dimes on his records while stars who sold far less earned dollars.

Finally, Barney could keep him at bay no longer. So he played his greatest scene. He said he would talk about a new deal for Val, but only to Val, no lawyers, no managers, no intermediaries. That led to another round of screaming threats, but Barney said, "Here I stand." He said none of those white-shoe shysters was around with his hand out when he found Val singing at wet T-shirt contests, and if Val was going to drag Barney over broken glass now, let him do it to his face. Valentino was no pushover, he wasn't afraid of a fight; part of him liked the idea of personally choking a decent royalty out of Barney. So he spent a week getting prepped by his advisers on what to say, which were the key points, how much to demand, when he could compromise. Then he put on a business suit and went off to negotiate with the B-man.

Valentino did not find Barney in his office. Barney had checked himself into Lenox Hill Hospital complaining of chest pains. Val had to negotiate with him through an oxygen tent, Barney gasping and wheezing the whole time. When Val told the Englishman he was making millions off him while holding him to a rotten deal Barney wept real tears about the ingratitude, and when Val asked for a retroactive adjustment in his royalties Barney screamed and grabbed his heart and set off all the alarms. The nurses ran in and jumped on his chest and shot adrenaline into him while Valentino stood there turning white. This went on for two hours. Val never got his new deal. For seven albums one of the biggest stars in the world was held to the same royalty rate as a first-time hair band. By the time his deal with Barney was done, so was disco. So was Valentino.

Compared to what he was capable of, the bullshit Barney was now spraying at Jerusalem was fairy dust.

"The standard advance is sixty thousand dollars for the first album and fifty for each album after that," Barney lied with schoolmarmish sincerity. "Let's double it across the board. This contract says you get paid a third on signing, a third on acceptance of your first album, and a third on release. I don't want you to have to wait—let's give you half on signing. That's sixty thousand dollars in your bank tomorrow morning. What else? Let's put in an obligation on our part to pay for ads in *Billboard*, *Spin*, and *Rolling Stone*. Nonrecoupable. That should take care of your points, Mack. Good going, no one ever thinks to ask for that. Fair play to you. Anything else? I wish Barrister Catalano had been able to be here with us. Where did he go, Jim?"

"He said he might come later," Jim mumbled.

"I guess he has some other clients who need his attention at"—Barney looked at the clock—"one in the morning. Well, what else? I want you four to feel great about signing with Feast tonight or I don't want you to sign. I will be back in April and if I am still alive and nothing has changed we could pick up the conversation, then. Lilly—you've been very quiet. Do you want to go through with this?"

"I want to make records," Lilly said. She was slouched back on the couch with Anthony and Dick on either side of her. Her eyes were sleepy but her voice was strong. "We've been flirting with Jim for a year, trying to get to this point. It's a little strange that now we have to make a decision on the spot or go back to the end of the line." She looked at Jim. "I didn't realize we were up against such a deadline."

Jim felt lousy. He didn't want to lose the band, and he might if he pissed them off or pissed Barney off at them. He hated this unnecessary scam. Barney was not going to England tomorrow, and the band did not have to sign the lame deal he was offering. But there was no way to tell them that without causing a fistfight.

"Barney," Jim said, "Catalano's going to have issues. We could spend all the months from now until you get back haggling over the fine print." He looked at the band. "How this is supposed to get done is that Barney puts the contract in front of you and you take it to Catalano and he makes a hundred changes, then we change fifty of them back and after six months and twenty thousand dollars in lawyer bills, we end up where we all knew we were going to end up anyway. So can we do this? Barney, don't shoot me. Here is the furthest we could ever go: a million dollars for four albums, with a three-album option after that." Barney shot Jim a look like a blowdart.

Jim avoided the evil eye and laid out for the band the fallback offer Barney had privately agreed to. "We pay you three hundred thousand dollars to sign. Remember, the album budget comes out of that. Don't think you're going to be buying new cars. When you deliver the album we give you another hundred grand. I can't write tour support into the contract, but I promise I'll fight to get some. We pay two hundred thousand for each of your next three albums but we do have an option to drop you after album number two. I hope that doesn't happen. I don't think it will. I think you guys are great. You have become everything I hoped you'd be when I first heard you play. But I'd be a liar if I said we might not fail. You and us. But even in that worst case, we'd have fronted you six hundred thousand dollars and put out at least two albums. Now, if you can live with that, I can promise that there is nothing more you would get from us by holding out. There is nothing more Catalano could squeeze in six months of squeezing. One million for four albums is our best offer, that is our only offer, and I hope you take it."

No one spoke. Barney looked at the clock and emptied a glass of wine, filled the same glass again, popped two pills in his mouth, and swallowed.

Lilly leaned across the table, picked up Barney's pen, and signed her name at the bottom of the contract. She pushed it toward Jim. She said, "Will you write in all those figures?"

Jim smiled and looked at Barney, who shrugged. Jim scribbled in the numbers he had promised, and pushed his luck by crossing out several of Barney's sneakier subclauses, including ownership of the band's T-shirt licenses, soundtrack rights, and name. He passed the contract back to the musicians, who signed it with jokes and nervous laughter. Anthony fed Dick some caviar, which he washed down with beer. The tension in the room gave way to giddiness.

Amid the laughter and high fives, Jim saw Barney putting the contract in his coat pocket. He did not sign it himself, or give anyone in the band a copy. As the musicians got up to put on their coats and say goodnight, Barney pulled the handsome drummer aside.

"Could I ask you to stick around for a few minutes, Mack?" he said. "We really didn't resolve these issues you raised about promotion. Can we get that out of the way, too?"

Mack was tickled. He liked the notion of taking care of business details that might elude his less-sophisticated bandmates.

"That caviar made me hungry," Dick said happily. "Let's go get some breakfast."

"Sure," Jim said. "There's a diner on Sixth." He looked over his shoulder at Barney, whose tufts of hair were taking on the aspect of horns. "See you in the morning, B.," he said.

"You forget, Jim," Barney said with a pointed grin, "I leave for Britain in the morning."

• • •

For the next half hour Jim sat in a diner booth with Lilly, Dick, and Anthony, fiddling with his french fries and worrying that Barney was going to figure out a way to snatch defeat from the mouth of victory. Jerusalem chatted happily over their omelets and coffee, oblivious to Jim's mood.

When Jim saw Mack hurling himself down the sidewalk outside he thought he was, in his anxiety, imagining things. He watched through the window as the drummer staggered out into Sixth Avenue. A taxi slammed on the brakes just short of hitting him and then slammed on the horn. Mack wavered in the street, pounded his fist on the hood of the cab, and threw in the air what looked like Jerusalem's record contract. Jim said, "Oh hell," and ran from the diner into the avenue.

By the time he got to the furious Scot and hauled him back onto the sidewalk the rest of Jerusalem were there, too.

"You arsehole, Cantone!" Mack shouted. "Do you run this pimp routine on every musician your boss fancies?"

"What happened?" Jim asked.

"Your great leader there locks the door after you and asks me to sit down and smoke some pot. I did. Then he brings out a clothes box with a ribbon on it. He asks me to put it on while he goes in the other room."

"Put it on?"

"He farts off and I open this . . . box. You know what's in it? A cowboy suit."

Dick laughed. Lilly and Anthony looked confused. Jim felt sick.

Mack continued: "A cowboy hat, six-guns, leather chaps, and a lasso. I didn't get it. I thought it was some sort of memento, like, 'Elvis wore this in *Flaming Star,* I want you to have it.' I put on the hat, for a laugh. I pick up one of the six-guns. I twirl it around. And then the man comes back in dressed as an Indian."

Lilly asked what Mack meant.

"I mean he's all done up as a bleedin' Red Indian with a feather bonnet and war paint and moccasins on his feet and nothing over his nuts but a little cloth flap—which he proceeds to raise aloft as he comes at me doing a war dance."

Dick was the only one laughing, but he was having a jolly time. "Gee, Mack, I hope you did what you had to do for the sake of the band's relations with the record company!"

"Ain't our record company anymore, mate," Mack sneered. "I shot the pink bastard with his own pistol."

"Oh, Mack," Lilly whispered.

"I didn't think it was a real gun! But the big poofter was coming at me with his snorkel out and I freaked. I pulled the trigger and hit him in the toe. He starts screaming and cursing and calling me every name in the Bible. He jumps around the room on one foot, saying he's dying. He calls 911 and says he's been shot by an intruder and to send a rescue and some sharpshooters to take out this mad burglar in a cowboy hat. Then he hangs up and tells me to run for my life and takes out the record deal and says, 'Here's a souvenir of what you flushed away to look at when you're working in the prison laundry.' "

Jim Cantone stood on the sidewalk with Jerusalem, a band he loved and into whom he had poured his work and heart for more than a year. They looked at him as if they had never seen him before. He said he was very sorry, and went in and paid the diner tab. When he came out Jerusalem was gone, already on the phone to their attorney, no doubt. Already running into the arms of WorldWide Music.

Jim thought about going back to Barney's house, to hold his hand until the ambulance came and ask him why he had to screw things up in such an elaborate way. But he couldn't look at Barney right now. He didn't want to hear the hysterical lunatic monologue. He was sick of Barney.

He walked downtown until he was at Odeon, a restaurant that still served dinner all night, years after New Yorkers stopped doing cocaine and starting their evenings at midnight. A waiter was clearing plates from a table in the back of the room. Bill DeGaul was still there, talking on his cell phone and writing a check. Everyone else had left. Jim sat down with him. DeGaul put the phone in his pocket.

"Catalano and Zoey just left in a hurry," DeGaul said. "I guess there was a shoot-out at the O.K. Corral."

"Jerusalem is a great band," Jim said sadly.

"You want to work them for us?" DeGaul said. "I told Booth, if we can get a guy like Jim Cantone, give him whatever he wants."

"I appreciate that," Jim said. "Bill, I don't need to report to you, but I do need to know I'll be reporting directly to Booth. I need to be a senior VP, I need four hundred thousand base to start, I need to be head of East Coast A&R. If you can do that for me, I'm yours."

"Let me call Booth when I get home. We'll make it happen. We have a lot of fun at WorldWide, Jim. You're going to love it."

"Thank you, Bill. I think I will, too."

• • •

It was quarter to three in the morning when Jim put the key in his apartment door. He heard the whistles, crashes, and shouts of the Cartoon Network on the other side. He came into the living room to find his wife, Jane, under a quilt on the couch and his son Mark bouncing up and down in front of the TV. "Daddy! Daddy! Daddy!" The little boy ran over and Jim scooped him up.

"What are you doing up, Cheetah? Don't you know your brother, Luke, is asleep, and your cousins are asleep, and Uncle Jack and Aunt Ellen and Izzie are asleep? And Superman is asleep and Peter Pan is asleep and Aladdin is asleep? Why isn't Mark asleep?"

"Mark has to wait up for Daddy," Jane said, sitting up. Her eyes were half closed. She looked beautiful. Jane always looked beautiful. She was wearing Jim's hockey jersey from college and nothing else. She padded into the kitchen and asked Jim if he wanted her to make him some food.

"No, I ate," Jim said. He put Mark on his shoulders and followed her. "Jane, I told WorldWide I'm taking the job. I said I needed four hundred thousand a year and they didn't blink. I think we're in the money."

"That's great," Jane said. "We'll be able to move." She began heating up some milk for the baby. "What did Barney say?"

"I haven't told him yet. Barney pulled a real horrible move tonight. He tried to attack Mack from Jerusalem and got shot in the foot."

"Mack shot him? Is he going to be okay?"

"I'm sure he will be. He'll use this to renegotiate his distribution deal or something. He'll end up getting himself on a postage stamp."

"It seems like a bad time to quit on him. He's going to be hurt. Will he think you're kicking him when he's down?"

"Jane, I'd like to kick Barney when he's down. I'd like to kick him regardless of his posture. He acted like a real jerk."

"If acting like a jerk is a shooting offense," Jane said, taking the baby from Jim's shoulders, "everyone you work with will end up in front of a firing squad."

Jim checked on Luke: sleeping soundly. Jane gave Mark his bottle and let him lie between them; pretty soon wife and son were asleep. Jim lay in the dark with his eyes open.

Jim had been with Feast Records, with Barney, for five years—most of his professional life. He was thirty now, he was a father and a husband. And from here on he was going to be a senior vice president of a major record label making upwards of four hundred thousand dollars a year.

So far so good.

# 2

Wild Bill DeGaul and his number one, J. B. Booth, ate breakfast in De-Gaul's fifty-fifth-floor office. They had some muffins and watched the winter sun come up over Times Square. They finished talking about the Knicks and closing the Hamburg office and some trees DeGaul was having moved. "When does Cantone start?" DeGaul asked.

"He started Monday. Tried to get a corner office. I think we'll make him wait a little for that. I told him, 'Well, Jim, I know what we said when you were up here before and I could give you that space. But if I do, everyone will hate you. Why come in with that burden?' So he thought about it and took Katz's old office."

"With Katz's old couch?"

"Yeah."

"That'll be full of earrings and torn stockings."

"I think Zoey might bolt. She's not happy about reporting to him."

"Which one's Zoey?"

"Zoey Pavlov, the girl with the nose ring, you went with her to see Jerusalem."

"Oh, yeah. She's funny. Do we want to keep her?"

"Maybe not. She's smart, but she's got a big mouth. Nothing damaging to WorldWide, just to promote herself. It's one reason I wanted

Cantone over her. Last month she slips a little item to *Airplay* magazine: 'Talk among the rock crowd is that several big acts won't re-sign with WorldWide until they see if respected exec Zoey Pavlov jumps to a rival label. Neither Pavlov nor WorldWide would comment.' "

"You sure it came from her?"

"I called one of the ad guys at *Airplay* and he went and dug out the original copy. It had her phone number on the fact-check notes."

"You're Columbo! You're Ironside!"

"Remember that when you break my balls about why we're buying full-page ads in *Airplay*."

"Did you bust her?"

"Yeah. I called her in and said, 'Zoey, I hear you're getting a lot of big offers.' She said, 'J.B., my first loyalty is always to you.' I said, 'Zoey, I don't want to stand in your way. I think you should accept one of them.' "

"Holy cow! You roasted her ass! What did she do?"

"What could she do? She turned white, she stammered, she slid off. Now she sits at the end of the meeting table and doesn't talk. She resents reporting to Cantone, but what can she say? She's got her résumé all over town. She might hang on just to keep her thumb on Jerusalem. It itches her that she snatched them from under Cantone's nose and then he shows up here."

"Look at that rainbow!" DeGaul was out of his chair and standing at his great window, scanning the sky above Manhattan. "It's going to be a lucky day." Booth went and stood beside DeGaul and they studied their kingdom.

The two men were so high up that Zoey Pavlov, standing in Times Square looking straight up, could not see them. She squinted at the top window, trying to make out if anyone was there yet. It was a useless exercise. The reflection of the morning sun in the glass made it impossible to see in. She looked up and down Forty-seventh Street. She looked at her watch. She had been up all night, seeing bands, shaking hands in dressing rooms, and eating toast and jelly with small-time managers. Jerusalem had agreed to meet Zoey for breakfast at Hugo's coffee shop when they got back from a gig in Philadelphia. They said they'd be there by five-thirty. It was already nearly seven. Zoey regretted not having gone home for a couple of hours' sleep. She had spent the little time between getting in and going out again on the phone to England, where it was mid-morning. She was going to be dragging all day. She looked back at the building where she worked and shuddered.

. . .

The New York headquarters of WorldWide Entertainment shot up from Times Square like a mushroom. The big, black, T-shaped building rose in the construction boom of the 1980s. During the Reagan goldrush skyscrapers appeared like oil wells from Sixth Avenue in the fifties, moving west and south in what seemed to be an unstoppable procession toward the Hudson River. You looked out one day and St. Patrick's was gone, obscured by an obelisk. Delicatessens, shoeshine stands, tuxedo rentals, and flophouses were trampled by building after building. The strip joints and porno shops of Times Square fell under the shadow and trembled. The kung fu theaters of Forty-second Street emptied out to await the wrecking ball.

Then the stock market crashed in October 1987 and all construction froze. The new skyscrapers of Times Square stood vacant. If you went up to survey space in one you could look clear through the next three. They were all empty, not only of tenants and curtains but of interior walls. Each was its own *Titanic,* upright and ready to sink. The new skyscrapers stayed hollow for the entire Bush administration, while Wall Street waited for the other shoe to drop.

When Clinton was elected, the economy boomed because people believed it would. In Times Square the skyscrapers marched forward again, plowing over the X-rated bars to plant Bugs Bunny stores and TV theme restaurants and golden showplaces for multimillion-dollar live-stage reenactments of Walt Disney cartoons.

During the pause in the progress, Booth had secured the Black Mushroom, the best new building in Times Square, at the lowest price for the longest lease. Two months after the crash of '87, when the landlords were sliding on their bellies to grab the heels of fleeing corporate tenants, Booth went up and down the elevators of the new empty buildings with thousand-dollar bills hanging out of the corners of his mouth.

When Booth first inspected the great tower in which he and DeGaul now loomed, the wind was whistling down its unused corridors. Booth had dragged to the top floor (the very floor on which he and DeGaul now buttered their muffins) the overmortgaged junior partner of the venture company that had sunk all its investors' life savings into constructing this starving white elephant. Once up here, Booth asked detailed questions about the window coating and the air-filtering systems and the number of circuit breakers and then, just when the junior partner was trembling with the possibility that he might actually be about to rent his space and save his job and keep his bosses from being dragged off in chains to S&L prison, Booth looked across into the empty building next door and said, "Gee, that one looks closer to the subway. Do you know who's renting that?"

By the time the junior partner regained bladder control, Booth had choked out of him the promise of a twenty-year lease for the top fifteen floors. The deal was so tilted that it would in the long run make the landlords no money at all, but it would in the short term give them an infusion of cash to keep the banks at bay. It could be rationalized as a loss leader to draw other high-rolling tenants to the premises. And in fact, having WorldWide's corporate HQ here in the helmet of the Black Mushroom probably had helped to fill the stem with big-ticket law firms and a talent agency and a radio syndicate. Perhaps it had even helped lure the Beacon Superstore to the basement and enticed John Wayne's Western Beefhouse into the ground level. By Clinton's second term the building, like the neighborhood, was back in the bucks, though the venture company for which the junior partner had labored had long since collapsed and the building's deed had been grabbed by a Hong Kong trust that got in hot water of its own in 1997 and had to sell the block cheap to Hartford Properties, a subsidiary of NOA, mother company of WorldWide Entertainment.

"I'm having lunch with Stupid from NARAS," DeGaul told Booth as they walked away from the window toward the office door. "You want to join us?"

"I can't, I have an offsite all day."

"Gonna figure out how to make me some more money?"

"You don't need any more money. You need love."

"If I have money, everyone loves me."

"That's called executive compensation."

On the way to his office Booth took a detour down the A&R corridor. No secretaries were in yet, but some of the VPs were. Cantone was unpacking boxes of books and records and putting them on his shelves. Zoey's office was still dark.

. . .

Across Times Square, Lilly and Dick of Jerusalem finally lumbered into Hugo's. Zoey was more relieved that they had showed than angry that they were two hours late. They said the gig in Philadelphia didn't start until 1:00 A.M. and the club owner tried to screw them on the money and the van broke down in New Jersey in the rain. The others went home to bed, but Lilly and Dick dragged themselves over because it was really important that they work out this issue with Black Beauty.

Lilly started in. "Zoey, Black Beauty says they still don't have a real deal offer. You can't dick me around on this. You said if we signed with WorldWide, you'd sign Black Beauty, too. Jerusalem is not signing until Black Beauty is taken care of."

Zoey was weary and stressed but she stayed even. A little voice inside was begging her to tell Lilly that she was lucky to have the chance to sign to WorldWide and, since she had broken ties with Feast, was in no position to bargain. But the angel on Zoey's other shoulder whispered that Jerusalem needed only a tiny excuse to blow her off and go back to dealing with Cantone, their old champion and Zoey's new boss.

So Zoey bit her lip and said calmly, "I can't sit here and tell you that WorldWide wants Black Beauty as much as WorldWide wants Jerusalem. They don't. They look at a seven-piece band made up of very unglamorous black women playing Woodstock-era folk rock and they see problems with radio, problems with MTV, and problems with concert bookers. The black audience will not understand why these sisters sound like an old Neil Young record. The white-male rock audience that likes that kind of music will have a hard time relating to a posse of radical black lesbians. No matter how good this music is—and some people at WorldWide will admit it is very, very good—no one knows how to sell it. If it does not sell, it is a failure. Not just Black Beauty's failure. It is the failure of whoever in the company stood up for Black Beauty and got

WorldWide to invest half a million dollars in a hopeless cause. That person will see her own ability to get bands signed and maybe her own job go out the window. And as very few of the support people you need to break a record will want to risk going out the window behind her, Black Beauty's chances may be ruined by indifference within WorldWide before they ever get the chance to be rejected by the outside world."

Zoey could filibuster like Winston Churchill when she was sleep-deprived and zipped up on cappuccino. She did not let Lilly or Dick get a word in. She rammed on, "I need you to understand that I believe in Black Beauty so much that I am risking everything I have to get them signed. If their record comes out and it flops, you've made a nice gesture to your friends and you can go on with your own career with your heads high. But I will be taking the fall along with Black Beauty. I will be out. So please don't punish me because the deal I am shoving through to get these women signed is not as good a deal as you're getting, or not happening as fast as they'd like. It's happening at all because I'm putting everything I have behind a group I love, even though I know that sticking up for them may cost me my job."

Lilly stared at Zoey, impressed enough to keep her mouth shut. Dick said, "Wow. Zoey, it's so cool that you are doing this. We'll explain to Black Beauty."

"No," Zoey said. "Don't tell them anything except that the deal's coming along and Zoey will push to make it happen faster. I told you this in confidence. I love Black Beauty. I don't want them to worry about anything but making a great record. And if worse comes to worst and I lose big on this, I will always have that record to listen to, and I'll know I did the right thing."

As soon as the last bit came out of her mouth, Zoey knew she'd overcooked it. But Lilly seemed pacified and Dick was so impressed that Zoey was scared for a minute he was going to ask her out. She explained she was late for work and got the check.

Zoey paid for the breakfast and bought some breath mints and ate them on the way to her office. When she got out of the elevator she walked the long way around, turning three corners, to avoid passing Jim Cantone's office and have him see her coming in after he did.

Jim was lying low himself. He was slumped behind his desk, hiding from Helga, the sour, hulking temporary secretary who had been assigned to tend to him until he could hire an assistant of his own. Helga had been part of the WorldWide system forever. She knew which strings to pull to get Jim's pictures framed, his stereo hooked up, and his speakers hung. Helga presented Jim with a calendar chock-full of meetings with people he had not yet met. It felt like the first week of school. It was nothing like his old job. Feast had operated in a state of creative chaos. Meetings were not planned, they formed spontaneously in the corridor, the bathroom, the stairwell. When Jim wanted to do something at Feast, he chased Barney until he got him in a headlock. At WorldWide, there was a meeting for every number on the clock and a companywide standard of proper memo form.

Jim was confident he could learn all the lingo and master the protocol, but he could not decipher the designation on his calendar for today, his fourth day on the job. The other days of the week had been algebra equations:

|       |      |
|-------|------|
| 8:30  | T&E  |
| 9:00  | Budg |
| 9:45  | JBB  |
| 11:00 | A&R  |

Easy enough to follow. But today there was only one entry: "8–6 Offsite."

He asked Helga what it meant. She looked up annoyed from *Travel & Leisure* and said, "You have an all-day offsite at the Century Hotel on Forty-third Street. It starts at eight."

"Helga, you know I'm from Maine. What's an offsite?"

"All the executives go out of the building to have a monthly planning meeting."

"Why do we go out of the building?"

"So you won't be interrupted."

"Why don't we just go into one of the nine conference rooms here and say 'hold all calls'?"

"Because executives can't control themselves. They end up running out of the room to deal with make-believe emergencies. The only way to get them to focus on one thing all day is to march them across the street and lock them in a two-thousand-dollar hotel room."

"Seems like a waste of money."

Helga glared at him. "I make thirty thousand dollars a year. Don't talk to me about the money this place wastes on perks for douchebags."

"I'm going to go to the offsite now, Helga."

. . .

Zoey saw Cantone heading out the door and seethed that he would be cozying up to Booth while she was stuck on hold with those Soviet bureaucrats in the legal department. Finally she got through.

"Marta. Zoey. Listen, I need the Black Beauty contract put through today. Why are you dragging your ass on this? It's nothing, it's a low-level, short-term deal with a band who will never sell a record. It is a favor. It is an add-on to another band's deal! Let Black Beauty keep their publishing! It's worthless! Marta, don't tell me about precedent. What is the precedent for you losing Jerusalem, who DeGaul personally courted and won in an intense bidding war, because you are fighting over imaginary future points with Black Beauty, a group that will be dropped and in the cutout bins by this time next year? Please! What if, what if. What if Jerusalem—who got me out of bed at six this morning to say they are walking away from WorldWide because we have not kept our promise to sign Black Beauty—drop this mess on DeGaul before you have a chance to clean it up? Marta, I cannot protect you if you sink this one. Fix it!"

Zoey hung up, yelled at her assistant, shoveled a stack of papers from her desktop into her work bag, and ran out the door to the Century Hotel.

. . .

Jim was sitting at the bottom end of a large U-shaped hotel conference table when Zoey stormed into the room and took the empty seat farthest from him. The sixteen WorldWide vice presidents had finished the continental breakfast of sticky rolls and mineral water and now an outside consultant, the tallest Asian man Jim had ever seen, was making his 9:30–10:15 presentation of New Direct Marketing Opportunities Through the Internet. Jim struggled to pay attention to what the consultant was saying, but he seemed to be spouting a kind of double-talk, paragraphs full of propositions and colorful assertions that never reached any conclusion.

He'd been circling for fifteen minutes already and had now doubled back, for no apparent reason, to 1945:

"When World War Two ended, the military industrial complex emerged. In order to make sure they benefited from the huge accounts being handed out by the government, corporations began hiring admirals and generals as company presidents. These new industrial leaders reorganized American businesses along a military model. They spoke of advertising *campaigns, targeting* a new market, acquiring new *divisions*, media *blitzes*. If you understand this evolution of modern business techniques, you will see what we can adapt and what we must abandon as we seek to bring our own experience to bear on the emerging megamarkets."

Jim fought to focus, but trying to find this consultant's point was like trying to keep melting butter on an ear of corn. He studied his reflection in the shiny tabletop, its polish being punished by all the little bottles of Pepsi and Evian, dripping ice pails, and tiny tubs of butter. Someone, probably the junior executive who'd booked the suite, had slept in the bed on the other side of the open French doors and eaten out the minibar. Back at the table, each place was set with a cheap writing tablet emblazoned with the hotel's logo and a dull pencil. Jim found himself wondering what erasers were made of. He turned his attention back to the consultant.

"How many of you own four-wheel-drive vehicles? Quite a few. How many own conventional sedans? Aha. You folks with sedans need the back wheels to power what the front wheels steer, right? I look around this room and I see a university of steering talent, but if you don't spend as much time maintaining your rear tires you will end up just spinning your wheels."

On and on and on, like a junior high school teacher who had given the same lecture on Napoleon to so many classes for so many years that he no longer heard himself talking.

Jim searched the room for some sympathetic eye contact, and realized he was the only loser even making an effort to listen to the lecture. A couple of VPs were writing away on legal pads as if they were taking notes, but seemed to actually be scribbling correspondence. A balding black man knocked numbers into a pocket calculator. A couple of his comrades were tapping away at portable computers, tethered by long cords to the wall sockets like astronauts afloat from their capsules. Everyone else in the room was half turned away from the table and the speaker, crouching with a finger in one ear and a cell phone pressed to the other. They were all intense and whispering.

Jim turned in his seat slightly and leaned back to eavesdrop on the fellow next to him, who was almost under the table, red-faced, muttering into his phone, "Well, he can't be the only pool man in Westchester. . . . Leaves get into drains, that does not mean tearing up all the pipes. . . . He's crazy, he's lying, the kids can't get electrocuted swimming in an ungrounded pool!"

How remarkable, Jim thought, to spend so much money and effort to get all these overpaid executives into a hotel room to force them to concentrate on a single topic, only to have them whip out portable phones and thwart the attempt. These were people who shared nothing voluntarily, least of all their attention.

Zoey looked up from her phone and saw Jim's half-smile. Look at that idiot, she thought, gloating because he's a senior VP and he got here early enough to grab a seat at the head of the table. He won't last six months.

Booth looked at Zoey out of the corner of a squint. He was listening to a phone message from Marta, a company lawyer, complaining that Zoey Pavlov was hysterical and abusive, demanding that they push through a contract for a hopeless band called Black Beauty because she said DeGaul wanted it. DeGaul's assistant checked and came back and said Wild Bill had never heard of Black Beauty. What did Booth want Marta to do?

Booth rolled his chair away from the table, swiveled around, called back Marta's extension, got her voice mail, and said in a harsh whisper, "J.B. here. Go ahead and offer them fifty grand for two albums. Set it up to maximize our benefit and minimize our exposure. And don't bother DeGaul with this sort of trivia again."

Booth scrutinized Zoey, slumped low behind the table looking like she needed a shower and shampoo. He studied Jim Cantone, hanging on every word the pinhead consultant said like they were directions to Chuck Berry's video collection. He wondered if in a couple of years

Cantone would be as miserable and used-up as Zoey was now. He hoped not, but you never know. The business drags down more than it raises up.

Booth was bored enough to check if the consultant might be saying something worth hearing, and opened his ears. The consultant said, "You have to let go of the in box/out box mentality and replace it with a *constant now* box." Booth sunk down in his chair. Beneath the table he punched in the phone number of his barber.

First thing Monday morning Booth, Cantone, and WorldWide finance chief Al Hamilton—the bald black man from the offsite—stood in a row at the urinals staring straight ahead. Booth, in the middle, said to the wall, "You're from Maine, Jim, you must hunt."

"I don't," Cantone said. "I used to shoot when I was a kid but I haven't touched a gun in years."

"Well, then I'll make sure I don't stand in front of you when you fire. This Friday afternoon you and I are sneaking out early and flying up to Vermont to hunt some geese. Pack your rubbers!"

"It's the wrong time of year, J.B., and, anyway, I don't hunt."

"It's a private reserve, the laws of nature and man don't apply. If you can afford the price you can hunt anything up there. Zebras, baby seals. I hear for ten thousand they'll arrange for you to shoot a Frenchman."

"It's winter," Jim said. "The geese are still down south."

"It's stocked, Cantone. It's business. We're going with Asa Calhoun."

Hamilton whistled. "The Kingfish! Attorney to the stars. Someone's hunting for back catalog."

Booth translated for Cantone: "Asa Calhoun wants to add Emerson Tory to his client list. Before Tory was a superstar for Warners, he made two flop albums for a small label that is now part of our WorldWide family. Asa will be negotiating to buy back Tory's masters and publishing."

Cantone zipped up. "Can't we meet in an office? Why do we have to go hunting?"

"Asa's a pal," Booth said. "After all, he's on retainer to WorldWide, too."

"Isn't that a conflict?"

"Think of it as a fraternity. Artists, executives, and labels, we're all in this together."

Booth flushed and turned to Hamilton, who was pissing away with the force of a horse in a monsoon. "What about you, Al? Want to spent the weekend shooting geese?"

"I'm a gay black man from the West Village," Hamilton said. "I only hunt for bargains."

. . .

And so on Saturday morning when he should have been in bed with his wife, his babies, and the crumbs of a corn muffin, Cantone slogged through a muddy patch of Vermont woods, carrying an open shotgun on his arm, in the company of Booth and lawyer Asa "Kingfish" Calhoun, a Louisianan six feet five inches tall with round shoulders and the stooped posture of someone who spent his formative years trying to sink into the crowd.

"Hard to see geese in this mist," Booth said. "The bastards'll be on top of us before we can make 'em out."

"I'd hate to shoot a seagull by mistake," Calhoun mumbled. He had sunken eyes and an elaborate comb-over that rested across two support walls of hair that rose from the sides of his head, above his ears. It looked absurd from any angle except straight on, the only angle at which the attorney ever saw himself, in the shaving mirror and in music business trade shots.

"I wonder if that's what happened to the *Hindenburg*," Booth said. Steam came out of his mouth. "Some drunk hunter thought it was a fat goose."

"Imagine his chagrin," Calhoun said.

Jim had forced down half a Thermos of coffee. He still could not wake up.

"It's not the kind of thing you could tell anybody about," Booth continued. "They'd give you the electric chair. You'd just have to go home and shut up."

Jim studied the shotgun on his arm. It was British, a Purdey 12-gauge engraved with a gold inlay rendering of a fox and a hound, teeth bared, squaring off against each other. Jim figured a gun like this could cost forty thousand dollars. Had Booth ever even fired it, or did he buy it because it looked good on the wall of his Connecticut den?

Booth had selected for himself a Holland & Holland 12-gauge with a specially made thirty-two-inch barrel. When they started out in the morning he had held it out to Jim and announced, "Gunmaker to the king!" The Kingfish had shown up with a very expensive Belgian Browning thirty-ought-six hunting rifle with a scope. Such a weapon would be useful against a goose only if the bird were seated in the back of an open car in a slow motorcade. The Kingfish didn't know that, Booth wasn't going to tell him, and Cantone, whose sympathies lay with the birds, kept his mouth shut.

"Where I grew up," Cantone said, "they now have hunting packages where they promise you'll bag a bear. You know what they do? They tag the bear with an electronic beeper. All the hunter has to do is follow the signal and shoot the animal while it tries to cover itself. Great sport."

"Hey!" Calhoun whispered. "I hear geese."

Jim heard nothing, but sure enough, a moment later a cluster of flapping shadows appeared in the fog above the trees. Booth and Calhoun raised their rifles and waited. "You go first," Asa whispered. Jim stood with his neck craned and his shotgun still open. Four lost ducks appeared and the two guns let loose a blast of noise and smoke. The ducks dived and dropped and disappeared.

"I think you got one," Calhoun said.

Booth said, "Let's go have a look."

Calhoun sighed. "We need a dog."

They tramped through the wet leaves searching for their game. Cantone studied the gun Booth had provided him. He once would have trembled with joy just to hold a shotgun like this. As a child he had loved guns—toy guns, pop guns, water guns, air rifles. When he was ten he got his Christmas dream, a Daisy BB rifle. He loved everything about it. He loved walking up the train tracks to the hardware store to buy a cardboard tube of gold BBs. He loved loading his gun, cleaning his gun, and shooting his gun. He shot branches, crows, and weather vanes. He set up a shooting gallery in the hayloft of his family's barn and spent hours in the stuffy summer heat, getting better and better. When he ran out of ammunition he would scrape spent BBs out of the cracks between the planks, reload, and start over.

That summer he won a pair of sunglasses and a straw cowboy hat at the shooting gallery of the Skowhegan Fair. At eleven he traded a box of X-Men comics for a pellet pistol. This was a meaner weapon, heavier. If state troopers saw it, they'd take it away.

When Jim was twelve his dad told him he was old enough to handle a shotgun. They went out and learned to shoot by firing across a pond. The echo felt like a mountain falling down. The recoil was so hard that Jim woke up the next morning with a stiff shoulder. It was worth it. He and his father had entered the awkward age, too old to kiss goodnight or, in the Cantone family, even hug. Jim felt that his dad had introduced him to hunting as a replacement. They had lost the intimacies of childhood, but they could be close as men are close.

In the seventh grade Jim won two blue ribbons in marksmanship from the 4-H club. That summer his father died of a heart attack while swimming. In the autumn of eighth grade his two uncles invited Jim to join them hunting, taking his father's place.

Jim's great moment of clarity occurred in the fall of ninth grade. He had a weekend job sweeping a local shoe factory. He worked with a nasty old Quebecer named Jo Clem. In spite of Clem's antagonism toward all human beings, he impressed Jim by the fact that in his lunch bucket he always brought something extra for a doe that peeked out from the woods in back of the building. Over the course of the late summer and early fall, the deer began to wait for Clem's treats. It went from sniffing at the edge of the yard to wobbling out and eating the food Clem spread on the grass. By the end of September Clem could whistle and the deer would eat from his hand.

It touched Jim that even this hard character could find kindness for an animal. The first Saturday of hunting season Clem showed up at the factory with a shotgun. At lunchtime he went out and stood in his usual

place at the edge of the woods and whistled for the deer. The doe hobbled out of the trees and nudged Clem's outstretched hand. He lifted his
gun and shot it.

From that day on Jim decided that he would not kill animals for
pleasure. With great solemnity he sold his rifles and fishing pole. He
bought his first Walkman with the money.

Jim's reverie was broken by Asa the Kingfish crying, "God damn it to
hell!"

Calhoun had found Booth's duck. The bird's right wing was blown
off, and it was limping, tilted, through the wet leaves toward the cover of
a bush. Booth and Calhoun stood looking at the pitiful duck in confu-
sion. What was the etiquette here? If they shot it at this range there'd be
nothing left but feathers.

Jim swallowed his disgust. He handed Booth his shotgun, stepped
forward, and lifted the duck into his arms. He stroked its feathers for a
moment, cooing. Then in a single quick motion he wrung its neck.

Booth and Calhoun were startled. Jim held out the dead bird and
said, "Here's your dinner."

The fun had gone out of the hunt. The three men wandered for another half hour, then Booth said, "It looks like it might rain soon. Let's
head back to the cabin and talk a little business."

Jim smiled for the first time all day when they got back to their
rented house and he saw Booth trying to figure out what to do with his
kill. Booth draped the duck's neck over the clothesline and tried to secure it with two wooden clothespins. The bird's throat was too thick.
Booth grunted around the porch and finally tied the duck to the line
with a ball of twine.

The hunters left their boots by the door and lit the stove to warm the
cabin. There was a fireplace, but a dawn attempt to light it had filled the
house with smoke. They sat in the kitchen and broke out a box of plain
doughnuts and some cans of beer. It was a horrible lunch.

"So Emerson Tory," Booth said to Calhoun.

"Yeah," the lawyer said.

"He's doing great. He's a big star."

"We're very satisfied. Warners has done a good job."

"We screwed up. We never should have let him go."

"Who knew?" Calhoun said gravely. "Emerson's matured a lot since he made those early records. Never tell him I said so, but if I were a label and he'd given me those first two records, I'd have dropped him too."

"Of course, it wasn't WorldWide who dropped him."

"You had nothing to do with it."

"We picked up those records when we bought HiFo."

"Hidden treasure!"

"Too bad Emerson wasn't on WorldWide from the start, we could have made it happen quicker for him."

"It happened quick enough. If he'd gotten big then, he might be dead now."

"So it's for the best."

"I think so."

Booth suddenly banged a hard, stale cruller on the edge of the table like a judge calling a courtroom to order. Jim snapped to attention. Booth bit off a piece of the cruller and talked with his mouth full: "Emerson wants to buy back the masters of those old albums."

"It's sentimental." Calhoun smiled. "He owns all his new songs, his hits, and he wants to tie up loose ends. We'll pay you a million for the publishing and masters on those two LPs. I told him, 'Emerson, you're crazy! Those old records will never earn that money in a million years.' But it's not logical with him, it's emotional."

Booth brushed some crumbs from the table into his hand and got up and dropped them into the stove. He offered to heat up some of the leftover coffee. Calhoun and Cantone said no thanks. Booth went back to the table and sat.

He said, "Asa, I feel bad about this, but it's a no. I talked to the lawyers, I talked to our catalog guys. I was surprised. Everyone feels like it's good for us to have some Emerson Tory in the attic. He's a big name, it impresses the stockholders. It's good for our budget line. There's a lot of eighties nostalgia, we might license some of those tracks to movies. And you know, if Emerson's plane should go down, there could be value there that we don't see today. I feel bad about it, but my hands are tied. I can't do this deal."

Asa Calhoun was gobsmacked. He did what show business attorneys do when they are shut down. He threw more of his client's money on the table.

"J.B., I can't believe we have to play this game. How much do you want?"

"It's not about money, Kingfish. A million is more than generous. Those records are not for sale at any price. We own them, we're keeping them. Tell Emerson it's actually a mark of WorldWide's respect for him that we don't want to let his music go."

"Look, I think it's insane of him, but I have to be frank with you. Emerson told me to go to two million if I had to. I feel like a fool even saying that because it's so much more than any attorney should allow his client to pay, but you are really putting me on a spit here. So let's cut to the money shot—Emerson Tory will pay WorldWide two million dollars for the publishing and masters on two flop albums."

"Don't, Asa." Booth put up his hand as if shielding his eyes from the sun. "Please, I'm not pulling your wick here. You could offer ten million and it wouldn't matter. I tried to sell this internally and I was shut down. It's a no. Now let's go fishing."

"Fishing!" Calhoun shouted, red in the face. "You take me up here into the forest to screw me? Is this *Deliverance*? Why didn't you just shoot me in the back when you had the rifle?"

"Come on," Booth said, standing and smiling. "Let's go pluck that duck for dinner."

"Fuck your duck!" Calhoun shouted. "This is a humiliation!" And with that the slope-shouldered lawyer stormed out of the cabin.

Booth turned to Jim and smiled. "I got the car keys. Let him blow over for a while."

"How come you brought him up here to tell him no?" Jim asked.

"'Cause we're not done yet." Booth leaned over and spoke in a whisper. "Let me explain something about Asa. Asa doesn't care about his client's interests. That's why all the labels like to work with him. Musicians come and go and they're all stupid anyway. But the corporations are here forever. Asa knows that. He's just got to figure out some way to fool his client into thinking he's taking care of him while really taking care of us. That way he stays in business and collects his big fees."

"No conflict of interest?" Jim asked.

"Kingfish Calhoun's interested in what's best for Kingfish Calhoun. No conflict. If Emerson Tory is such a choirboy that he believes anything else, he shouldn't play in this ballpark."

Booth and Cantone sat at the table playing chess until Calhoun came back, found a beer, and slumped down next to them.

"Look," the lawyer said sadly, "I need to do this deal. I don't care how it gets done, I don't care what it costs, but I need to do this deal."

"How come?" Booth asked.

Calhoun looked at Booth sadly. He looked at Cantone, weighing whether he could trust him. Then he said, "Cone of silence, right? Okay. I do this deal for three million, I get a three-hundred-thousand-dollar fee from Tory. That's first. More important, I do this deal, he puts me on a monthly retainer. I've been after him to put me on retainer for two years. This deal sinks, I lose that. So what will it take?"

Booth shot Cantone a look that said *Keep your mouth shut.* Then he offered Asa a terrible deal with a straight face. He said, "I'll sell you the masters for three million. WorldWide keeps the publishing."

Cantone had to look away. It was embarrassing. The masters, the rights to the records themselves, had very little value. Emerson Tory had made eight or nine albums since these two early flops, all of which sold more and always would. The only value in this deal was in the publishing, the ownership of the songs Tory wrote for those albums. Three million was a very generous offer for the combined masters and publishing. To ask for three million for the masters without the song rights was insulting.

Cantone had a lot to learn. He saw Calhoun study Booth, who was holding a bishop. Cantone expected the lawyer to turn over the table and storm out, but he said, "Okay, I'll do it."

He and Booth stood up and shook hands and popped open cans of beer. Calhoun, suddenly laughing, turned to Cantone and said, "Hey, farm boy, why don't you go pluck that duck for us?"

· · ·

Two hours, three hamburgers, and ten beers later, a sweaty, wet-eyed Asa Calhoun sat on the cabin's porch between Booth and Cantone and said damply, "You guys must think I'm a real sucker to pay three million for the masters and not get the publishing."

Jim looked at the floor; Booth grinned. Calhoun kept talking, "But you're wrong. I'm the big winner here."

"Explain that to Jim, Kingfish," Booth said.

Asa looked at Jim and talked as if to a remedial student: "I'll go back to Emerson and tell him, 'Great news, Em! We got back all your masters for only three million bucks!' I'm gonna make it sound like his mother just baked him a birthday cake. And he's gonna hug me and thank me and kiss my hand. And he's gonna put me on retainer and pay me my big fat fee."

The lawyer accidentally kicked over his beer, cursed, and reached for a new can. He continued spinning his scenario while he struggled with the pop top. "And then, six months from now, I'm gonna say to him, 'Emerson! Great news! I think I can make a deal to buy back your publishing, too!' And he's gonna say, 'Cool! How much?' And I'll say, 'Another three million!' He'll say, 'Wow! Great!' And I'll come to you bastards and you'll ream me for another three million and Emerson will pay it and I'll collect another three-hundred-thousand-dollar fee. Instead of getting paid once, I'll get paid twice. And my client will love me for it."

The lawyer lay back his head, closed his eyes, and after a moment of silence let out a long, loud, foghorn of a belch. Then he drifted into the sleep of the satisfied.

Jim looked over at Booth, who seemed to be taking tremendous satisfaction in the clouds blowing over the lake. "I like nature," Booth said.

4

On Tuesday morning Zoey called a special breakfast prayer meeting for the New York A&R department, minus Cantone the usurper. Officially it was a chance for all the A&R stringers WorldWide kept on retainer to come in and trade information with the staffers. Zoey oversaw a loose network of semi-employed talent scouts who collected small stipends and free records from WorldWide in return for wading through demo cassettes, checking out local bands, and writing wordy reports that Zoey's assistant boiled down into quick summaries of what was going on and who was worth watching in Austin, Tacoma, St. Louis, and Cleveland. This crew of nitcombs, fanboys, and wanna-bes included ambitious student directors of college radio stations, a couple of badly ironed music editors of alternative weeklies, and two or three self-improving secretaries from WorldWide field offices in secondary markets.

Once a month the label sprung for economy airfares and train tickets and let these hungry trail scouts come to New York for a free meal in the conference room. There they were joined by as much of the rest of WorldWide's East Coast A&R staff as could be dragged out of bed early. Zoey leaned on everyone to show up this time, as she wanted to discuss how life would work now that Jim Cantone was running the department. Not foolish enough to say anything directly against him, Zoey decided to adopt a rueful "I'm your big sister and I'm here for you" attitude regarding Cantone that she hoped the stringers would swallow and regurgitate as loyalty to her.

She studied the knights of her round table. They were pathetic. The perma-lancers were a mixture of the sort of boyish avarice often personified on screen by Michael J. Fox and record-collector nerds excited to be allowed to eat as many free rolls as they wanted. Her coworkers on the WorldWide A&R staff were not much more impressive; they just had better haircuts.

Zoey took inventory of the WorldWide professionals seated around her. Rick Finkle was slouched in a black leather jacket and the same Ramones haircut he'd worn since he was fifteen. He was a rock purist who refused to have any part of the corporate culture or socialize with anyone who did. He had a bad attitude but good ears, and as he held the system in such contempt, he did not mind passing his discoveries down the corporate food chain where others could handle the details and take the credit. His small, windowless office looked like a cave full of old records and CDs. Finkle's only attitude was irony, his only expression a sneer. He would never advance within WorldWide and he made it clear he did not care.

Far more friendly but equally useless was Flute Bjerke, who had been an A&R director for five years and never signed anyone. It was a company record. Bjerke came into WorldWide as secretary to a long-since departed VP who was determined to mentor his young assistant into a position from which he could grow. That Bjerke had no desire to grow never occurred to the motivating boss. Under his mentor's guidance, Flute was promoted to talent scout, and held on to the job after his boss was sacked. Flute knew that to sign acts that fail was how A&R men lost their jobs. That he might sign an act that would succeed never occurred to him. Flute flew around the country seeing bands and listened to tapes in his office from the time he arrived at work at eleven until he left at five, except for the two and a half hours he was at lunch and the gym. That he was paid ninety thousand dollars a year to sit around and say "I don't hear it" about whatever he heard struck Flute as a wonderful blessing, and he was not about to blow it by liking something.

Sharon Walpole was the envy of all the college stringers, a student rep who had moved up to the show. In her Princeton radio days Sharon was an early and vocal advocate of a couple of local hip-hop acts that went on to make it big in the majors. Her gift for prognostication and the gratitude of those acts brought her to the attention of WorldWide. She still brought in unsigned music she liked, but if anyone on the staff disagreed she would fold up like a pup tent. Sharon had good ears but no backbone. All it took was one loudmouth to stand up in a meeting and say, "This is garbage," and she'd never mention the act again.

Finally there was Boris. Boris Verger was forty-eight years old and had not signed a successful artist in a decade. A failed musician himself, he talked a great game, but could not deliver. Time had abandoned Boris. Every act he brought in was a young version of the kind of music he'd had success with in the seventies. He tried to get WorldWide excited about good-looking blond kids who played bad imitations of Allman Brothers songs, or young fusion bands in dashikis and Afros, or the half-breed sons of weird old bluesmen no one but Boris ever heard of. Boris was one of the sad cases who believed in his heart that kids today would surely love the music he did more than the crap they listened to, if only he could dress it up in cool clothes. Boris went back with Booth and De-Gaul, which was the only reason he had not been put out of his misery.

Looking at the sad company around her, Zoey understood why Booth brought in Cantone when the old A&R chief left. But she was damned if she would be lumped in with these losers. Most of the black music had already been allowed to slide to the West Coast and a separate A&R kingdom. Zoey was not going to be left in the tar pits with these mammoths.

She called the meeting to order. "Thanks for coming in, everyone. Welcome. No sense waiting for Bruce Gilbert—if he ever opened his eyes before noon he'd be struck blind. First order of business: I want to raise a glass to our departed friend and boss Andy Kasdan. We will miss Andy's wisdom and leadership, but we can't blame him for stepping into management. I think we all look forward to the day when Andy sits across from us with the tape of a new band, and we get to look him in the eye and say, 'Sorry, man, I don't hear a single.'" This got a knowing laugh around the table.

Zoey turned serious. "Now I know some of you are upset with the decisions upper management has made about filling Andy's place." This was news to the room, but each figured he was out of the loop. "Let me say this. This team has never been about one person. It is about all of you, each and every one. Executives come and executives go, but the work we do together is what matters. Jim Cantone is not a bad person. He might be a little new to our culture, but I am sure that if we all do our best to help him, he can learn."

Flute Bjerke glanced at Boris Verger with eyebrows raised in alarm. Was Cantone bad? Boris made a stoic, been-there done-that face and nodded slightly as if to say, Keep strong, brother.

Zoey continued: "We are a team. We are the guardians of World-Wide's future. You around this table decide what America hears. I am sure that if we give him time and the benefit of our experience, Jim Cantone can make it." Now she turned quiet and strong: "But if any of you, staff or freelance, should find yourselves in a situation where you are angry or hurt or frustrated, come to me. I don't care if it's Sunday, I don't care if it's New Year's Eve. You all have my cell phone number. I beg you, no matter how angry or resentful you get, no matter how unfairly you are treated, hold your tongue. Count to ten. If you run into a situation that seems intolerable, call me. I will help you. And I hope I will be able to help Jim, too."

One of the alternative-press stringers started clapping and most of the others joined in. A little college rep with too many teeth for his mouth interrupted the moment to say, "So what's wrong with Cantone? He seemed okay to me when I met him at South by Southwest last year."

"Yeah," an aspiring secretary said, "my girlfriend interned at Feast and she said he was nice."

"That's right," Zoey said, covering her tracks. "Jim is a good, good guy and I think when you all get to know him, you'll see that. Don't go by first impressions."

Zoey's kite was spinning in the wind. Cantone walked through the door and yanked it out of the sky.

"Hey, I heard there was a confab going on in here!" he said, grinning. He grabbed a bagel and took a big bite. He circled the room until he landed on the arm of Zoey's chair, to her horror.

"Listen," Jim said as he chewed, "anytime you guys are in town, let me know. I wouldn't have heard about this meeting if I hadn't been looking for Flute. I'm really glad I did, because I want to tell you all, as far as I'm concerned, every single person at this table has the power to sign an artist to WorldWide."

There was the sort of happy gasp usually heard on grand prize night at bingo.

"Hear me out. I'm not giving away the ranch here. But anyone working for WorldWide A&R should know they have the authority to sign an act to the label, for reasonable money, one time. One time. I'll tell you what. I think a lot of record companies miss big opportunities because they try to filter passion through a corporate system. Passion doesn't filter."

Zoey looked around the table at a roomful of puppies, lapping up their master's drool. She was disgusted. How could he possibly allow these idiots to sign acts to WorldWide without any checks and balances? This guy was going to be an even bigger disaster than she had expected.

"I promise you each one shot," Jim said. "If you do well with that, you get more. But before you run off and sign whoever you're sleeping with"—appreciative chuckles—"I want to give you a few guidelines.

"One. Don't sign your friends. I know that each of you has at least one old pal whose cassettes you listen to at night and who you know is just as good as anyone out there. Maybe he is, but I'll tell you what—you would be the last person to know. Because when you know someone too well, when you're invested in their lives and you know who the songs are about and where they came from, you can't possibly hear the music as the public would hear it. So save yourself a lot of grief. If you really believe your buddy is the next Madonna, give the tape to someone else in this room and let them A&R it. If they share your enthusiasm, you're probably on to something big. If they don't, they saved you and your pal some heartbreak.

"Two. Take the best recording of your discovery's best song and put it on a mix tape between some really great records. Before you sign anyone, see how their song sounds between Lauryn Hill and Led Zeppelin. Then give the mix tape to your sister and your roommate and your hip uncle in Miami and see if they think your new discovery stands up. Remember, if you have to explain it or make excuses, it's not ready for primetime.

"Three. Ask yourself if it's something WorldWide can sell if it's not priority number one, but—say—priority number ten on a list of twelve. What's going to make your act break through if there's no dough for advertising or tour support? Are they great live? Are they so good-looking they'll get in all the magazines? Will they be irresistible to TV? How are we going to connect them to a mass audience? How are we going to get the word out?

"If you think you have any act who's great and you can get them through all those hoops, bring 'em on. I can't swear we'll make superstars out of them, but we will give them—and you—a shot. Just remind yourself, 'I get one chance to do this. Who do I want to risk it on?' "

When Jim was done the staff was impressed and the freelancers would have lined up to lick him. Zoey was disgusted. Jim asked if he could steal Flute Bjerke for a few minutes and you would have thought Flute was the lucky bachelor on *The Dating Game*. When Cantone and Bjerke left, the toothy college kid said, "I knew he was a great guy."

"Clean up your mess," Zoey announced, and vowed to herself to discontinue these monthly meetings.

# 5

Helga, the scary giant secretary, buzzed Jim's hotline. "DeGaul's office just called to ask if you have your visa for Brazil. Do you?"

Jim grabbed one of the four remote controls on his desk and tried to stop the CD that was playing. Instead the TV came on. "Why do I need a visa to go to Brazil? I'm not going to Brazil."

"DeGaul's office thinks you are."

Jim punched in DeGaul's assistant's number and said, "Hi, this is Jim Cantone."

"Just a minute, I'll get him."

Before Jim could protest that he didn't need to bother the big boss, DeGaul was on the line.

"Cantone! Get your sunblock! First time you cross the equator you gotta shave your head! Get a hat!"

"Bill, this is the first I'm hearing of it. When are we going? Why are we going?"

"The only day of the year that's an order! March fourth! You're pals with R.E.M. and Counting Crows, right? They're all playing this Rio Rock Festival. You, me, and Booth are gonna go schmooze the stars."

"Are any of our acts on the bill?"

"Some Portuguese rock bands from the Latin division. We'll have our pictures taken with them, inspect the South American operation, and get into some heavy voodoo! We're going down early so we can cut the heads off some chickens! We'll hire a chopper to take us into the rain forest. It'll be wild!"

"I'm not saying no."

"Okay! I gotta run! I got some Chinese diplomats here!"

Jim hung up and looked through his calendar to see what he had to cancel. He asked Helga to check into the visa situation. His phone buzzed again. He grabbed it before Helga could. It was Booth.

"Yeah. Jim. J.B. I'm going down to Brazil for this Rio Rock Festival and I'd like you to come along. We'll take the company plane. It's nice, you'll like it. I want you to meet some of the people in our South American operation. You should have a dialogue with them, see if they have any acts we should pick up. We're weak in the Latin market here in the States, maybe you can help fix that."

"I don't know much about it, J.B."

"You'll learn. I'm going to see if DeGaul wants to come along. I think he should."

Jim said nothing. Booth wanted him to think this was a Booth operation and that was fine with Jim.

Booth said, "One thing. You must back me on this. If DeGaul says anything about hiring helicopters, say no. The guy's a maniac in a whirlybird and the pilots down there are blind, born-again idiots who think if they die they'll go right to heaven. I spent a hundred hours in choppers in Vietnam and I have never been as scared as going up with DeGaul and his lunatic stick monkeys. If Wild Bill even mentions helicopters, you refuse."

Jim said okay and goodbye. He wandered out into the corridor. Finance chief Al Hamilton came toward him, trailing a long computer printout.

"Al, hey. I never knew Booth was a Vietnam vet, did you?"

"How could you not? He mentions it all the time. 'Want peanuts, J.B.?' 'No thanks, I was in 'Nam.' "

"You've seen the film of him a hundred times," Helga put in. Jim was getting used to her inserting herself into his conversations. "He was one of those Marines on the roof of the embassy when the last helicopters left Saigon."

"Really? Booth was at the fall of Saigon? With the overcrowded heli-copters lurching off the roof and refugees hanging out the doors and Viet Cong tanks rolling up the road?"

"Yes," Helga said, "that fall of Saigon."

Boy, Jim considered, and he's scared to go up with Wild Bill. I better make sure the company life insurance has gone through.

• • •

Jim told his wife about the trip at dinner.

"That sounds like fun," Jane said. "I went to Rio, once. I had a great time."

"Oh, who did you go with?"

"Some friends. *Girl* friends."

"That's good."

"I met all the boys when I got there." Jim grimaced and his wife laughed. "One boy's family owned silver mines and hotels. He tried to get me to stay there. His mother thought I was the one."

"You met his mother?"

"Well, she'd been asking him about me."

"How long were you there?"

"A couple of weeks. I was making a commercial and I stayed on."

"I thought you went with your girlfriends."

"Sure, other actresses. They were in the commercial too."

"What was it a commercial for?"

"Some diet drink. It only ran in Mexico and South America."

"Why am I scared to ask what you were wearing?"

"Because you're a pig."

"Well?"

"You don't want to know."

"You're not mad with me about going on this trip, are you?"

"No, I want you to go. And you have my permission to wear a thong on the beach."

Jim and his wife had observed, from day one, a policy of total truth-fulness. Anything he asked her, she would tell him. It was a mixed bless-ing. Jim came at his Honest Abe attitude from a provincial background. Growing up in Maine he went to church every Sunday, got good grades, lettered in three sports, and played in the school band. Jim was deter-

mined not to let New York or the music business shake his sense of himself as a straight shooter.

Jane came at her honesty from a more urbane angle. She was
brought up in Manhattan, the daughter of a psychiatrist and a scientist.
She had been raised to value truth as an absolute, lying as a pathology.
Jane was honest to the point of discomfort; if she did something wrong
she would own up and make amends. If she hurt someone's feelings un-
intentionally, she would knock on the door and apologize. But Jane's
straightforwardness sometimes bruised Jim's Puritanism. If they were at
dinner with a group of people and someone made a bigoted joke, Jane
would bust him in front of the whole table. And her guiltless attitude
toward sex occasionally caused Jim to fold up. Jane once, over Thanksgiving dinner, told Jim's mother and sisters about an affair she'd had as
a college freshman with a fifty-year-old professor.

Most of the time, though, Jim took delight in his wife's ethical rigor.
She gave him a standard to shoot for.

When Jim met Jane she was working as an actress in soap operas
and Off-Broadway plays. Jim was quietly grateful that her feminism
caused her to reject movie roles in which she'd be cast as a bimbo or sex
object. At the same time, she had no objection to appearing nude if a
theatrical role required it, or doing art modeling for quick money when
the rent was due.

When the twins came, Jane dropped acting like an empty can. Her
attitude was that it was not her identity, just something she could do to
earn money. Now that she had two babies and Jim was making a good
salary, she had no reason to do it.

Jim leaned forward to give his wife a kiss and Luke jumped in between them. He waved a Darth Vader doll at his dad and said, "Don't
kiss my girl!"

"She's my girl too."

"No, she's my girl! Go away or Darth Vader will hurt you!"

"Darth Vader doesn't scare me. I think he's pretty."

"No, he's scary!" Luke screwed up his face and made a growling
noise.

"No, he's sweet. Darth Vader wants a kiss."

"HE'S SCARY!" Luke shook the doll in Jim's face.

"He's cute."

Luke slammed the doll across Jim's face. Jim reeled back, hurt and surprised. He put his finger to the bridge of his nose and came away with blood. Jane grabbed the doll, swept Luke up, gave him a kiss, and then fell back laughing at Jim's stunned expression. "No, Daddy," she said, "Darth Vader *is* scary."

• • •

J.B. Booth, WorldWide Music president, Harvard graduate, and Vietnam veteran, was less than a block away from the Cantones' apartment. While Jane and Jim were wrestling their kids into bed, Booth was squatting in the coat-check booth of a chic cigar bar down the street, trying to hear his wife on a cell phone over the blasting beep-beep-beep of an electronica CD on the house PA.

"I am going to have to stay in town tonight, Lois," he shouted above the din. "Rod Stewart's agent is insisting we go to some reception at Ahmet's for some Turkish painter and I have to go. I can't get out of it. By the time I leave there it will be midnight and I have to be back in for a conference call with Germany at seven. It makes no sense to drive home. Yes. . . . Yes. . . . I know, I'm sorry about that, I'm not doing this for fun, believe me."

He closed his phone and straightened up. He apologized to the coat-check girl for crowding into her small space.

"That's quite all right," she said. She had a slight southern accent. "You're in the music business?"

Booth was about to be offended at the presumptuousness, but he softened. The girl was chestnut-haired, brown-eyed, and guileless. Her manner suggested she had just stepped off the bus from Hooterville.

"Guilty," Booth said. "Where are you from?"

"Gainesville, Florida."

"I've been to Gainesville. How long you been in New York?"

"Four months."

"Well, welcome."

"Thank you."

Booth went back to his party. "If we're going to Ahmet's we better go," he announced to the group, but the gibbering cluster around Rod

Stewart's agent got up, sat down, went to the bathroom, came back, asked for the check, ordered more drinks, and looked for cigarettes for another half hour. Finally Booth said, "I'm gonna start uptown. I'll see you there." He got his coat, went outside, and waved over his car.

"Back home, boss?" the driver asked when Booth sank into the backseat. When it was just the two of them buzzing around town, Booth usually rode in front. That he slumped into the back meant it was either time to head back to Connecticut or he was in a rotten mood.

"Nah, Randy, I gotta go meet some more morons. Head up Park Avenue. I'm gonna stay in town tonight after all."

He felt in the pocket of his coat for a smoke. Old habit. He quit years ago. Instead he found keys, a pen, and a cassette. He pulled out the tape, trying to remember who gave him homework for the ride. It wasn't a WorldWide act, it was a demo with a hand-printed label, "Cokie Shea Band," and a phone number. He handed it over the seat.

"Here ya go, Rand, let's see what my crack A&R staff wants to sell me now."

The tape hummed and snapped and singing filled the car. The first thing Booth noticed was the poor fidelity. This was not a professional demo, it was homemade. It was unusual for the staff to give him something this raw. He tried to remember where he got it. Not from his assistant, not from anyone at dinner or the nightclub. The woman singing had a pleasant voice, young but with a little blues edge, like Bonnie Raitt. The lyric was some sappy greeting-card sentiment about "leaving the love on." Booth's attention drifted out the car window. There were hookers rolling their tongues and freezing in their hot pants. There was a big billboard of a wasted teenage girl wearing boys' undershorts. There were bus-stop posters for a new Mariah album.

The singer reached the last chorus and suddenly swelled up like Barbra Streisand on a sinking ship. She wailed the hook line, "leave the love on," over and over, louder and higher until Booth thought the speakers were going to pop out of the car walls.

"Hey, boss, that's a hit," Randy said. "Who is it?"

Booth trusted Randy's taste more than anyone's on the WorldWide staff. He relied on his driver's ears to help him decide who to push and who to pass on. Randy was Booth's real talent scout.

"Cookie something," Booth said. "Let's see if she's got anything else."

The next song was up-tempo, a country-rock bounce with another strong hook, another cheesy lyric ("The High Cost of Lovin'"), and another powerful vocal performance. Booth was intrigued. The third song was a heartbreak ballad about a single mother describing to her young child the daddy he never knew. Randy thought it was lovely.

They were getting close to their destination. "Randy, drive around for a while. I want to hear the rest of this." Booth popped out the cassette long enough to check the name and then phoned Zoey and Cantone and his secretary at home to ask where this tape came from. No one knew. Booth listened to the first song again, then the second and third and fourth. He tried the phone number on the label. He got an answering machine. A southern woman's voice said, "This is Cokie, if you have a message for me, Lynn, or Lauren, please leave it at the beep. Bye!"

Booth said nothing. He turned off his phone and sat with his eyes closed like Kreskin for five seconds. Then he got it.

"The coat-check girl at the club!" he said. "Randy! The coat-check girl at the club put this tape in my pocket! Let's go back downtown!"

The entourage attached to Rod Stewart's agent was still orbiting their table when Booth returned to the nightclub. He went straight to the coat check. The woman with the big brown eyes flinched when she saw him, then smiled bravely.

"You're Cokie?" Booth said.

She nodded.

"Did you write those songs?"

"Yes, I did. Well, one—'How It Really Was'—I cowrote with my former organ player. I had the melody and words but he changed some of the chords. But the others are all mine, one hundred percent."

"And you did all the singing."

"Yes."

"You're talented. Where did you record it?"

"At home, I have a little Portastudio. I played the keyboards and guitar and did the vocals on Sundays when the neighbors don't complain so much. We added the bass and drums at a rehearsal studio."

Booth was happy with everything he was hearing. He was also glad

to see that she was as young as he'd thought and prettier than he'd noticed. Unless she was married to a jerk who wanted to manage her, Cokie
Shea was the full package.

Two drunks from Rod Stewart's agent's party flopped across the
coat check waving claim tickets. "Let's go, J.B.," they squawked. "Let's go
to Ahmet's and meet the genius."

"I have other plans," Booth said. "I'm meeting with Cokie Shea."

He and the coat-check girl maintained eye contact as one of the
drunks said, "I know Cokie very well! Tell her to call me tomorrow."

. . .

Booth treated Cokie to late dessert at a little hole in the wall he knew in
Soho. She talked about her songs, quoting her own lyrics as she went,
and he warned her that the record business was a rocky river on which
she would need an experienced guide. He told her that he wanted to
hear a lot more, but based on his first impression of her cassette, she had
the most important gift a singer could have, and the rarest—a unique
voice.

She blushed. Booth thought he had not seen anyone blush since
high school. He sent Randy home and he and Cokie began walking up
Broadway.

Ahead of them were three drunk boys of about twenty, with hob-
nailed boots, studded leather jackets, metal buttons in their lips and
noses, and high, spiked mohawks. They were acting up for one another,
banging trash cans and shouting obscenities. Booth did not register
them at all until he and Cokie passed them, lost in conversation, and one
of them muttered an obscene insult.

Even then Booth only glanced up before turning his attention back
to Cokie. But the kid wanted trouble. He said, "What are you looking at,
creep?"

Booth did not stop walking. He looked back and grimaced with an
expression that said, Don't be an asshole.

But the spiked kid loomed forward and got in front of Booth and
demanded again, "What are you looking at, creep?"

Booth stopped. He stared at the punk. A metal stud was stapled to
the kid's nostril. It hung from his nose like a silver snot. Booth said, "I'm
lookin' at Fonzie."

The punk sputtered and pawed the pavement with one boot, like a horse. His two friends—both of whom Booth measured to have skinny arms and awkward posture—came up beside him. They were trying to look tough, like little boys in front of a mirror on Halloween.

Booth repeated, "I'm lookin' at Fonzie. Some little homo playing dress-up like it was twenty years ago. See, Fonzie, I was there in 1977. I was at the Chelsea with Sid and Nancy. I took Sid's smack and flushed it down the shitter and slapped his mouth when he tried to take my money and he whimpered like a little dog. I've seen tougher punks than you coming out of my ass. Little dress-up Barbie doll trying to scare your mother! You got big gonads coming into New York after dark! If you don't step back I will put your eye out." He turned to the two nervous sidekicks and said, "You can be real friends to this turd and get him home before he gets hurt, or I will blind him and cut his throat."

The punks strutted away, kicking sideview mirrors down the street as they went and, once they were at a safe distance, hollering insults back at Booth.

Cokie did not seem terribly shaken by the confrontation, but she took Booth's arm as they walked on up Broadway. "Listen," he said, "if you're not too tired I'd love to hear some more of your songs."

"I've got roommates," Cokie said evenly. "Can we pick up the tapes and my boombox and go somewhere else?"

"Just get the tapes. I have a stereo system in my suite."

• • •

Jim Cantone was awakened by shouting and crashing in the street below his apartment. Another minute and it would wake up the kids. He got up and made his way through the dark living room, trying not to step on any trucks or toy soldiers. He found his wife leaning out the window with a brown lunch bag full of water.

"Going to bomb them?" Jim whispered.

"Um-hum. I'm just waiting for them to move a little closer." The bag began to split. Jane let fly and she and Jim jumped back from the window so they wouldn't be seen. A horrible scream went up from one of the three mohawked punks, who had been punishing trash cans and sideview mirrors all the way up the road.

"Direct hit," Jane said with a smile.

Usually such a shot was enough to drive loudmouths away from their window, but these three started wailing for whoever dunked them to come out, banging on garbage can lids and jumping on the hoods of parked cars.

Jim looked at his wife and sighed. No recourse now but escalation.

"I'll get the eggs," he said.

# 6

Jim Cantone, J. B. Booth, and Wild Bill DeGaul were living high on the hog. They were watching an Oscar-nominated movie and listening to a Grammy-nominated CD and drinking champagne and eating prawns served by their personal steward on a private Gulfstream jet over the Amazon rain forest on their way to Rio.

They had been flying above the rain forest for two hours and it was still going strong. When the clouds opened and they got a look at the trees there were no roads or shacks or radar stations such as break up the natural monotony when you fly over Greenland or the Mojave Desert or any of the other wastelands one has to cross in the usual course of doing big business. There was no sign of the fires the size of Delaware one hears about at celebrity cocktail parties. DeGaul peered out the window as if searching for a landmark and observed, "No sign of Sting."

"I was hoping to see more of the jungle," Jim said, turning away from the window. "It's almost all clouds."

"It's a *rain* forest," Booth laughed from the couch behind him. "What did you expect?"

Booth was not paying much attention to the view. He was refilling the champagne glass of his unexpected plus-one, a pretty young woman named Cokie Shea whom he had introduced to DeGaul and Cantone as WorldWide's next star. Cantone figured maybe it was routine to impress

The party passed through double security doors. There were a few Latin travelers dragging luggage behind them in slow motion. It seemed to Jim they were walking in broad circles.

"You okay, Cantone?" Booth said.

"I'm discombobulated," Jim answered.

"Be careful of hepatitis," Booth whispered. That gave Jim something new to worry about. He followed DeGaul, upright and confident, and Booth, stone-faced and impassive, and Cokie, excited as a Munchkin in the Emerald City, through the airport and onto the street, where DeGaul flipped open his leather appointment book with his left hand while punching numbers into his cell phone with the thumb of the right.

After a minute he turned to Booth and said, "I don't know where the car is."

"Don't bother," Booth said. "Get a cab."

Booth went over to a taxi stand and put some money in the hand of the attendant on duty. By the time he walked back to DeGaul, Jim, and Cokie, two taxis were racing to reach them. The one that drove up on the sidewalk won.

"Demolition derby!" DeGaul said with a smile as he climbed in.

The driver popped the trunk for the luggage, which Jim and Booth loaded. Cokie got in the middle of the backseat, between DeGaul and Booth. Jim rode in front with the driver and his hatchet.

They barreled through the night, in and out of civilization, until they came to a ten-floor concrete top hat rising from the crest of a hill surrounded by a moat.

"The Hotel Managua!" Booth declared as if he were regarding Camelot.

The cab drove too fast over a stone bridge, scattering beggars and bead merchants as it ricocheted up twenty feet of Z-shaped road to the check-in entrance. They got out of the car and Booth walked to the edge of the driveway and looked down.

"This is not a hill," Booth announced. "Look how it rises straight up. This is a landfill. It's like Staten Island."

"Staten Island's nice," Cokie said.

At the front desk Booth made a great show of ordering separate rooms for Cokie and himself while DeGaul translated the requests into a Spaniard's idea of Portuguese. There was a lot of exchanging of passports and Amex cards and trading of dollars for Brazilian cruzeiros.

When the four room keys were finally produced Booth grabbed two, hoisted his bag and Cokie's over his shoulder, and strode toward the elevator like a poobah in his palace. The elevator door opened. He stood back and gestured gallantly for Cokie to precede him. Before she stepped forward, the doors began to close. Like any New Yorker, Booth stuck his arm into the doors to stop them.

Two metal slabs smashed into his wrist. He let out a howl like a dog under a train.

Cokie screamed a perfect two octaves above him. DeGaul stuck his shoe into the slit between the doors and cranked until they snapped open again. When they did, Booth yanked out his arm.

"I think my wrist is broken!" Booth bellowed.

DeGaul tried to get a look but Booth turned and stalked toward the dark end of the lobby, jabbering obscenities like a busload of Tourette's patients sliding over a cliff. He cursed and stammered and kicked a cat, after which he started sneezing like a choo-choo train. Jim took a few steps toward him and saw fluid streaming from his nose, mouth, and eyes. He dropped back. Cokie went to the front desk and demanded that the clerk summon medical help. The clerk stared at her without any sign of comprehension or caring.

Booth came back into the light, rubbing his wrist furiously while wiping his nose on his sleeve with his clawed right hand.

"If you can move your fingers it probably means nothing's broken," DeGaul said.

"Flknstcktzkrtshtfrzkknfskr," Booth replied.

"Concierge!" DeGaul called to the empty foyer, "this man needs codeine! Quick!"

Booth was opening and closing his fingers with an exaggerated display of concentration and forbearance. Having already acted like a big baby, he could look cool only by making a retroactive show of stoicism.

"It hurts like hell," he said grimly. "But I took worse most weekends when I was a kid."

"And gave back twice as bad," DeGaul said happily. He was glad the drama was over. The elevator opened again. The four travelers stepped inside and as they did an English-speaking porter appeared in the lobby and said, "Is the gentleman all right, then?"

Booth began to raise the middle finger of his wounded hand, but the elevator bell rang and he got scared and pulled it in fast before the doors closed.

"Let's meet in the bar in thirty minutes," DeGaul said as the party headed for their rooms. "We don't want to be late for the conga line."

"Why do you assume there's a bar?" Booth muttered. "There's probably a big stew pot."

. . .

Booth found his door and twisted the key until the lock gave in. His room looked like a cell at a minimum-security prison. He put his bag on the bed. The single blanket was as thin as a handkerchief. He went straight to the little security safe in the closet, dumped in his passport and about six hundred dollars, and shut the door. But no matter how he punched the buttons and wiggled the lock, it would not close securely. "I'm not leaving my money here," he muttered, and shoved the bills back in his wallet.

His passport caused him more concern. Losing a passport in the Third World was, he knew from experience, a portal to being dunned, abused, and humiliated. Booth unzipped his shaving kit and poured out onto the bed a toothbrush, comb, deodorant, Band-Aids, mouthwash, shaver, toothpaste, shoelaces, scissors, aspirin, cold pills, beta carotene, soap, razor blades, shampoo, melatonin, shaving cream, and gum. He pried up the cardboard liner at the bottom of the kit and stuck the passport in. Then he covered it with the liner and put all the little containers and plastic bottles back in on top.

This activity was helping him to keep at bay his embarrassment over making an ass of himself in front of the others when the door closed on his arm. He was glad to see a bruise forming, proof that he really did sustain some kind of injury. He'd behaved like a jerk in front of Cokie and the others. Maybe Cantone would pass it around over drinks at an A&R retreat. Maybe it would make him seem foolish to DeGaul. Maybe it made Cokie think less of him. Booth felt the incident at the elevator bubble between his consciousness and his memory, forming itself into a small, hard anxiety deposit that slipped down his throat like a quarter in a coin slot and lodged in his gut, where it would quietly gather interest until the opportunity appeared to jump up again some night when his defenses began to fall on his way toward sleep.

Booth picked up the hotel phone and called home. He got a machine. He told his wife he'd arrived in Brazil and he was fine, but he was not in Rio, DeGaul had diverted them to the provinces. He did not yet know where he'd be staying. He'd call back later with a number.

He went to brush his teeth and was startled by his reflection in the three-sided bathroom mirror. He looked pale green in the shuttering light, flabby and old. Hotel mirrors caught him at his most vulnerable, from unexpected angles. He approached familiar mirrors from rehearsed positions, and knew what to expect—but to walk exhausted into any rented bathroom was to be confronted with a debauched caricature of how he told himself the world saw him.

Booth locked on the image staring back at him with black-ringed eyes. Who was this stooped minotaur, this Caliban, this Piltdown man? Not the 1973 party king of URI! That was a beautiful boy with thin hips and a smile no girl could resist. Not the handsome Marine marching back from war! That was a broad-shouldered hero with flat belly and firm jaw. And surely this was not the thoughtful Harvard grad, the soldier-scholar who had lived and loved and bled in the world his classmates knew only from books! No, none of those—this was some monkey.

Booth ripped off his clothes like he was tearing off the years that concealed his lost beauty. Then, in his shorts and socks, he fell to the floor and puffed his way through two hundred push-ups. Red-faced and gasping, he rolled over on his back and began racing toward a hundred sit-ups, too, but at twenty he felt a stab in his spine, and at thirty-two he stopped and lay sweating on the dusty floor. He could not afford to throw out his back again. If he did he would be in pain for the rest of the trip, and bent as a Neanderthal to boot.

So he lay still for a minute and then began the dainty, ladylike exercises his chiropractor had prescribed, raising his head and legs together at a forty-five-degree angle until he tiptoed up to a hundred. Then he snorted and found his feet. He showered and emerged again into the scrutiny of the ugly mirror with his gut sucked in and his head erect. He had beaten back the beast once more. He was ready to perfume himself and greet the world.

• • •

In his room DeGaul was calling California. His ex-wife's third husband answered the phone and passed it along to DeGaul's younger daughter with a grunt.

"Helen? Hi, honey, I'm in South America. . . . Yes, Brazil. I'm here with J.B. and some other friends from work. We're going to see R.E.M. and Counting Crows in Rio. Did you get that grade change you were looking for? . . . Good for you, don't let those eggheads push you around. When do you go back up to school? . . . Oh, boy, you better get packing. . . . Yeah. . . . Okay, sweetie, I'm sorry to interrupt dinner. . . . Yeah. How's your sister doing? She hasn't been returning my calls. . . . Well, I'd like to but I can't get her to pick up the phone. . . . I know that, Helen, we're all busy, but I worry about her. . . . I'm not prying at all. I just want both you guys to know you can always call me if you need anything. . . . Okay, I'll let you go. Say hi to Mum. . . . Okay, sweetie, I love you. Okay. Bye-bye."

• • •

Three doors away Cokie Shea washed, hung up her clothes, and sat on the corner of her bed looking at the clock.

• • •

Cantone called his apartment collect. There was a ruckus as one of the boys picked up the phone and dropped it and Jane tried to grab it and he tried to get it back. She won, and above his squealing protests said hello. Jim said, "I made it," and Jane announced, "It's Daddy!" which set loose more pandemonium at the other end.

Jim took turns with both of the twins and then managed to talk to his wife. They had agreed that he would call once when he arrived and again just before leaving. Jim had no idea what it cost to call collect from South America. He was not yet so relaxed in his new circumstances as not to care. But he and Jane had come up with a plan to bridge the distance.

"Has the special delivery arrived yet?" he asked her.

"We're expecting it after bath time," she said.

"Oh, good. Remember, they all have the dates on."

"We're all set."

"Okay, great. I guess I'm going to go meet the others for a drink. I'd like to just go to bed."

"Don't drink too much. Coke is the safest thing down there."

"I only drink tequila."

"Whew, glad I'm not with you."

"Okay, don't forget the special delivery."

"I won't."

"I love you."

"Hubba hubba."

Jane hung up and got the kids bathed and into bed. Then she went to the hall closet and withdrew the first of six sealed envelopes. Each was addressed to the twins and covered with Jim's drawings of them. Jane ran into the bedroom and announced, "Boys! Look what just came! A special delivery from Daddy!"

The twins jumped up, grabbing for the letter. They tore it open and out poured a handwritten note, two plastic whistles, and a cassette tape. The note told the boys Daddy missed them. It was decorated with a drawing of an airplane and a palm tree and pictures of the boys and their mom. Jane put the cassette into the tape player and Jim read his kids a bedtime story, "The Seven Chinese Brothers." The twins demanded to hear the story twice more. By the last time, they were asleep.

· · ·

Jim, Booth, and Cokie sat in the hotel bar drinking rum and cokes. DeGaul rolled in looking fresh and happy. "I sent the plane on to Rio," he announced. "We'll have a big day here tomorrow and I've hired two helicopters to fly us out to the concert on Sunday!"

Cokie seemed delighted. Jim looked at Booth, who made a pistol of his forefinger and thumb, pointed it at his temple, and pretended to pull the trigger.

# 7

At breakfast DeGaul presented Booth, Cantone, and Cokie with his plan for the day. He had retained a local woman called Frat Marie to drive them around town and act as a guide. Frat Marie worked for some rich friends of DeGaul's who lived in São Paulo. They were in Miami for the winter and Frat Marie was up here visiting her people. What good luck!

They'd spend the morning shopping, the afternoon sightseeing, have a nice dinner, and then—once the moon rose—head off into the jungle to catch some black magic.

Jim had enjoyed a good night's rest, so he was all for it. Booth was neither in nor out. To him it was simply another itinerary. Dinner with lawyer in London; meeting with producer in Los Angeles; voodoo ceremony in Brazil—all deductions, different receipts.

Cokie kept her opinions to herself. They would make themselves known as the day progressed.

. . .

The shopping was a disappointment. Frat Marie, who drove like a New York cabbie, hauled them all to some warehouse filled with market stalls. Cokie bought a scarf; Jim bought some puppets for his boys; Booth bought a banana, ate half, and gave the rest to a dog.

Jim said, "That dog must be hungry, to eat a banana."

Booth said, "Down here dogs eat what they can get."

After an hour they admitted to one another that the market was a drag and asked Frat Marie to speed up the schedule. DeGaul was especially eager to get through the day and on to the voodoo. Marie led the company through a series of remarkable old Portuguese churches. One seemed to be made entirely of green glass. Another was bronze from the baptismal font to the belfry.

"Amazing, isn't it," DeGaul said. "These are some of the poorest people in the world, they don't have indoor plumbing. One of these tabernacles could pay to inoculate all their children."

Booth and Jim nodded but Cokie said, "That's true, but the beauty of their churches might be the only hopeful thing in their lives. I can't begrudge them that."

"If they had better lives they might not need the church," Booth said. "Bill's right."

"You know," Cokie said to DeGaul, taking his hand, "if you sold that private jet of yours you could build them a new hospital."

"But how would we get home?" DeGaul said. Everybody laughed more than the line was funny, hoping that was the end of it.

In a chapel that seemed to be carved out of melted wax Booth declared, "I don't have a lot of use for institutional religion, but I value spirituality."

"Oh, not me," Cokie smiled. "When some people talk about spirituality I wonder if they mean they're interested in what makes them feel good. It's kind of a self-help thing. 'Religion' seems stronger to me, it doesn't bend. It says, 'This is right, that is wrong. Do what's right even if you don't want to.' I know I need to do more of that."

"So you figure religion is like doing push-ups," DeGaul said. "And spirituality is liposuction."

Over the course of the afternoon's sightseeing, the subject kept coming back. Booth blamed it on Frat Marie's church parade. The May Procession, he called it. He was beginning to worry that the guide was some kind of undercover nun. He took off his watch and waved it at her and said, "Frat Marie, I'll give you this watch if you take us to a whorehouse."

She took out her bandana and blew her nose at him. Booth didn't like what the whole holy atmosphere was doing to Cokie. He had a sexual as well as professional interest in her; it was no time for her to grow scruples.

Frat Marie led them to a cathedral completely covered, top to bottom, inside and out, in Christmas lights. DeGaul looked around and said to Cantone, "Who climbs up the steeple to screw in a new bulb? They must lose a lot of altar boys."

Booth planted himself in a pew, took off his shoe, and shook out a stone. Cokie came up beside him, studying the stained-glass windows. "Don't you believe in anything bigger than us, Jack?" she asked.

"Sure I do," Booth said. "My problem with most religion is that it's based on guilt."

"And I think that's so valuable," Cokie said brightly. Booth saw she was one of those women who ratchet up the cheerfulness when they lob one across your bow. "The world would be a better place if more people felt guilty when they did something wrong. I wish rich people felt guilty when they passed the homeless on the street. I wish the companies that run sweatshops in the Third World felt guilty. I have friends who are proud of themselves for getting rid of their guilt. It seems like a feeble accomplishment."

Booth was getting annoyed.

"A lot of wars have been fought in the name of religion," he said.

"That's true," Cokie said. "But look at the atrocities done in the name of antireligion: Stalin, Mao, Pol Pot. Look at the Chinese in Tibet."

Cantone loomed out of nowhere and said, "Look at Hitler! He wanted to replace Christianity with some weird Nietzsche-Wagner-Viking civic belief system."

Cokie beamed at Cantone. Booth glared. Was Cantone putting the moves on her? Booth would strangle him. "I don't think the Christians had it so tough under Hitler," Booth muttered. "I think the Jews maybe had it a little worse."

He stalked outside, pulled Frat Marie aside, and told her they'd made their stations of the cross, could they go somewhere else now? Frat Marie said, "Do you want to see the drummers?"

Booth smiled. "Bingo!"

They walked over cobblestones, down a steep street that ended in a broad plaza that continued down the hill at a severe angle. DeGaul walked around, doing reconnaissance. "This square," he announced, "is a triangle."

It was a funnel. Two streets poured into it from the west and east at the top, where the square was broad. The rows of buildings on either side narrowed to another single street at the bottom. Across the top of the triangle was a large raised stage. Young men, many of them shirtless, were leaning on buildings, sitting in doorways, and drinking something from little plastic cups. Whatever they were having, DeGaul decided to try. He strolled over to a vendor who looked like a Mandingo warrior and had a card table set up in the doorway of an abandoned church. Cups full of the liquid were laid out on the card table. The drinks were all different colors—baby blue, bright green, dark red, urine yellow. DeGaul pointed to the red one and the vendor told him how much. Booth came up beside him. DeGaul said, "And a yellow one for my friend."

DeGaul stood there holding the red drink. He handed Booth the yellow one. Booth said, "You first."

DeGaul shot it down. He gasped and coughed. "My God! I've drunk some pretty rough stuff, but what is this poison? And how do I get some more?"

"Take mine," Booth said.

"No, no, don't be a Mary."

Booth squinted at the piss-colored compound and raised it in a toast. "Up yours."

He swallowed, shook, and laughed. "Oh! There goes the liver. What the hell . . . ?"

DeGaul called over to Cokie, Cantone, and Frat Marie, who were watching a dozen teenage drummers assemble on the stage. "Marie, we need a chemical analysis here!" DeGaul bought two more drinks, green and blue. "What am I drinking here, Marie, and how long have I got?"

"Phewww," Frat Marie said with contempt. "This is sugarcane alcohol with food coloring. Very bad. Use it to clean sink, disinfect cuts. All the men who drink that end up bleeding from rear end. Very bad."

DeGaul held out the two cups to Cantone. "Jim, you can't ask for a higher recommendation."

"It'll take the rust off your rib cage," Booth said.

"I'll pass," Jim said.

"Sister Bertrille?" Booth asked Cokie.

"Did you guys try it?" Cokie asked. Booth and DeGaul nodded.

"I'm game." Cokie took both cups and downed them in two quick gulps. She stood there like a wine taster, examining her palate. "It's not as good as tequila," she said. "But it's better than light beer."

Everyone was impressed. "What a gal!" DeGaul said. "She writes great songs, she sings like an angel, she looks like a movie star, and she drinks like a lumberjack! She's got it all!"

"Yeah," Booth said. "If not for that morality thing she'd be perfect."

The drummers at the top of the plaza began pounding out a beat, and two local boys with sweatsuits and hand mikes appeared from the side of the stage, rapping in Portuguese. The young men milling around the square came to life and formed rocking knots in front of the stage. The Americans watched for a while. Different rappers and singers came and went, some from among the drummers, some from the crowd. There was a system to it, but that system was unclear to the outsiders.

"How long does this go on?" Jim asked Frat Marie.

"All day and night," she said. "This is junior division, young kids. When the sun goes down the real drummers come out."

"No kidding," DeGaul said. "Is it worth seeing?"

"People come from all over the world," Marie said. "Famous musicians come to see the drummers."

"Oh, man, but we have to go see the voodoo tonight, the black magic."

"I feel funny about that, Bill," Cokie said. If the alcohol had any effect on her she didn't show it, Booth thought. Or maybe she was about to. Cokie said, "I don't feel great about the idea of taking part in something like that. I don't want to gawk at someone else's religion for kicks. And if it turns out to be any kind of black mass or sacrilege, I'd be ashamed."

Booth figured this was the opening Frat Marie had been pushing for all day. The guide suddenly started throwing her hands in the air and shouting, "Magic very bad, very dangerous. You should not go! Not go! Bad people out in woods, hurt animals, kill cats. Not safe for lady. Not something good people want to see."

Booth had no moral compunctions about going. It wasn't his cat. But neither did he particularly want to drive out in the woods to be with a bunch of freaks with machetes. Still, he had no intention of raining on DeGaul's parade. They had come all the way to Far Armpit, Brazil, so the boss could see some black magic. Booth's attitude was, Bring on the zombies.

Cantone spoke up then. "You know what? I'm with Cokie. Fun is fun, but if these are bad people doing cruel things, I'd just as soon skip it and hear the drummers."

"Okay," said DeGaul, always a gentleman. "But we got some time to kill. Marie, is there anything to do around here that does not involve consecrated relics?"

"Good cafes!" said Frat Marie. "Just beyond the plaza."

"Now you're talkin'," said Booth.

"Okay," DeGaul announced, "but I want everybody to have one more shot of Liquid-Plumr as penance for denying me my Third World Don Juan experience."

Booth went and bought five more nuclear cocktails. They all drank, Frat Marie burped, and everyone fell over laughing.

As they walked out of the northwest corner of the plaza, the kid drummers got wilder and soldiers set up barricades and big plastic barrels along the streets leading in.

The Americans climbed the steep street until it split in two. In the V of the intersection was a cafe with outdoor tables. "Party of five!" De-Gaul said to the waiter, who spoke no English but could count. The group settled in and ordered wine and shrimp and rice and beans and hot bread. Everyone was glad to get off their feet.

Frat Marie knocked back some wine and began talking too much. She was worried that DeGaul, who was paying her bill, resented her speaking up against his voodoo excursion. She went on and on about how bad it was, what a ripoff, how likely it was they'd have been brained and beaten. The wine kept coming but the meal was nowhere to be seen. Frat Marie talked about candomble and Yoruba and other subjects that meant nothing to the North Americans. She began talking about indulgences.

"Frat Marie," Booth said. "How many rolls can you fit in your mouth?"

He decided the waiter had gone off to the voodoo ritual and taken their dinner along. Probably going to bring the shrimp back to life.

It was getting dark. Lights were coming on. Down the hill, at the entrance to the square, soldiers were stopping local kids at the barricades. They shook them and out fell knives, chains, pistols, and straight razors. The soldiers tossed the weapons into the big trash barrels. Then they let the kids proceed into the plaza. There were young men coming from everywhere now. It was as if the buildings that walled in the area were false fronts, a Hollywood set, and hundreds of extras were pouring through the doors and into the plaza. And those extras were armed.

DeGaul had polished off a bottle of wine and was now thinking he wouldn't mind trying another of those sugarcane shots—the one with chocolate syrup. He sat back in his chair magnanimously and declared, "So everyone's up for going back to the plaza!"

"If we ever eat," Booth declared loudly, slapping both his hands down hard on the table as if it were a Ouija board on which he might conjure a waiter.

As if answering Booth, a rumbling syncopation began to swell behind them. The two narrow streets on either side of their outdoor table filled with dancing children, swaying teenagers, and—driving the procession down the hill and toward the plaza—a legion of men pounding drums. They were beating congas, rattling traps, slapping bongos. They wore the drums over their shoulders, under their arms, on their belts. There were dozens of drummers, flowing around the outdoor tables on their way to the plaza, carried along by the polyrhythms and the dancing feet of the crowd around them, kids circling and beating their bellies and chests and waving flags made of shirts and bedsheets. A river of rhythm and flesh flowed over the whole neighborhood.

Jim stood up. "I gotta go see this. Anybody coming?"

"Dinner's about to arrive," Booth said.

"I'll be back in a minute," Jim told them. "I just want to get a look."

He fell in with the crowd, rocking as he walked, carried along by the kids pushing and dancing. As they approached the barricades the soldiers formed a line. They let the drummers pass through the open intersection of the sawhorses without interruption but the others, the kids, the young men, the few hard-looking girls, were roughly frisked, disarmed, and shoved through the barriers. Jim took the treatment and followed the crowd.

The plaza was filling. The drummers proceeded onto the raised stage, where they made formation in the spotlights. The people in the square pushed forward. Jim swam through the bodies like in a mosh pit, until he was in front of the stage. It was Mardi Gras, it was New Year's Eve. He let himself be carried on the crowd. The drummers shifted and changed rhythms without ever losing the thread. Jim heard everything in the beats, from James Brown to Johnny Cash. After fifteen or twenty minutes he realized he should go back to the others, to eat his supper and collect whoever wanted to come down.

He started to make his way back toward the northwest corner. Pushing against the pulse of the crowd was much harder than riding with it. He moved a couple of steps to the left and someone shoved him forward. So he went forward, then moved left again and felt fingers on his back, tugging him. He put his hand on his wallet. The crowd was getting really tight, really fast. For the first time Jim was aware that his red hair and pale face stood out in this mob of black skin. He kept moving toward the left, where he came in. He swam against the bodies. If someone resisted letting him through, he stepped back and tried another path. Slowly he made progress.

When he got away from the stage he found a second human stream, this one flowing toward the barricades. He fell in and let it carry him. Someone was shoving him from behind. He ignored it. Someone punched him in the back. He kept moving forward. At last he was carried to where the soldiers had their sawhorses. He struggled through. There were five people squeezing into the plaza now for every one pushing out. The barrels of weapons were overflowing.

Jim climbed up the street against the crowd. DeGaul and the others were still at their table outside the cafe. The food had arrived. Jim joined them soaked with sweat, his long hair matted to his forehead.

"What happened to you?" Booth laughed. "You get up and play a bongo solo?"

"It's wild," Jim said, grinning as he fell into a chair. He picked up an almost-empty bottle of wine and drank what was left. He wiped his mouth on the back of his hand. "It is like the maddest crowd-surfing at the biggest punk club you ever saw. Those guys who've been drinking that colored liquor in the hot sun all day are going nuts."

Jim had intended to cool out and eat before returning, but Cokie said, "Will you take me in there?"

Jim said sure. He asked if the others wanted to go too.

"Lemme finish this shrimp," Booth said. "I waited for it long enough."

"You two go," DeGaul said. He was mixing some kind of paste into his rice and beans. "We'll catch up in five minutes."

Jim and Cokie stood up. Frat Marie insisted Cokie hand over her bracelet, earrings, and billfold. "I'll hold this for you," she said. She took Jim's wallet, too.

"You're not joining the boogaloo, Marie?" DeGaul asked her. She shook her head like it was the stupidest idea she'd ever heard.

Jim led Cokie down the hill and to the barricades. Something had changed. The men the soldiers were frisking now were older, bigger, meaner. There was more shoving and threats. The soldiers slapped at the men and were slapped back. Jim had been to enough rap shows and heavy metal concerts to know the smell—the scene was turning ugly.

The soldiers frisked them both, pinching and stroking Cokie. She shouted, "Knock it off!" and they did. As soon as they passed into the plaza, Jim's radar screamed. He grabbed Cokie's hand and pulled her along behind him. A scrim of teenage boys came barreling toward them, backward, slapping and slugging one another. Jim got in front of Cokie just as the rolling mob slammed into him. At the center of the huddle was a fight, and as always happens when a fight breaks out in a crowd, people were trampling one another to get out of the way of the swinging fists. The back of one of the fighters rammed into Jim, who pushed him away while trying to stay in front of Cokie. The fighter spun around, showing his back to his opponent, and slugged Jim in the side of the head.

Jim wobbled, but he didn't go down. He didn't understand what was happening. Both fighters seemed to have spontaneously decided to join forces against him and Cokie. Their hands reached out to her face. Jim slapped them away and shoved Cokie behind him. He could not tell who in the mob was attacking him and who was just trying to get out of the way. He reached for Cokie's hand. She was being pulled away. In trying to stay in front of her, he lost his footing. A teenager punched him in the chest. Jim's sunglasses, hanging from his shirt collar, broke in half. One of his legs was in the air; he worked to keep his other foot on the ground. If he went down, it was over for him and for Cokie, who was throwing some punches of her own.

Jim began falling in slow motion because the people around him were packed so tight. He saw a hand grab Cokie's hair. The crowd was closing over him.

And then, through the arms and faces, he saw Booth come plowing through the mob, mad as he would be at a bad busboy and no more intimidated. Booth made short jabbing motions and thugs fell back before him. Jim found his feet and righted himself. He was taller than the crowd; he could see what was happening.

DeGaul was with Cokie, shielding her with his arms, offering his back to the mob as he moved her toward the barricades. Booth was a rabid wolverine. He jabbed with both hands, poking everyone near him in the eyes. People screamed and jumped away from him. Two fingers stuck out on each hand, like a gunfighter, like Moe in the Three Stooges, Booth the Marine was drilling 'em new sockets, he was blinding the baying banshees, he was smiting the infidels. Jim imagined the thugs and thieves sharing a sudden epiphany—Booth wasn't trapped in the pit with them; they were trapped with Booth. He rolled through the throng jabbing and poking any eye that crossed him.

He turned to Jim with a crazy expression, his eyes wide and his skin tight over his skull. Jim thought for a minute that Booth was going to poke his eyes, but instead he grabbed Jim's arm and said, "You okay?" Jim said yeah. "Geez, what a stunt! Next time, let's go for the voodoo, right?" Booth was grinning madly and breathing hard. Jim nodded and tried to smile. "Okay, get your ass back up to the cafe," Booth said. "See if Cokie's okay. I'll be right behind you."

Jim pushed his way through the mob, back past the barricades. He turned, looking for Booth, and saw him coming up the hill behind him. A tall black man appeared and stuck a hand in Booth's jacket pocket. Booth slugged the guy hard in the mouth and they both went down under the sea of excited faces. Jim tried to go back but a soldier stopped him. "You blood!" the soldier said. "You blood!" Jim shouted that his friend was being attacked but the soldier shoved Jim back from the barricades and yelled again, "You blood!"

Jim stepped back, trying to get enough height to find Booth. He touched his forehead and felt warm stickiness. He was bleeding from his scalp. He did not want to go toward the cafe and desert Booth, but he knew that even if the soldiers let him back in, he would not find Booth in the rolling mob. He took off his T-shirt and mopped his forehead. There wasn't that much blood, he'd live.

He saw a rumble of activity and Booth popped out of the crowd like a volcano. "J.B.!" Jim shouted. He leaned on a different soldier and pointed. "Help that man! Let him pass!" The soldier shrugged. Booth steamed through the crowd. One skinny six-foot-six kid in a track suit stuck out his leg in front of Booth, to trip him. Booth punched the kid in the balls and he fell over like a tree.

The soldiers stepped back and let Booth pass. Jim, now shirtless and with streaks of blood on his face, put his hand on Booth's shoulder, gently. Booth looked like he might bite off the hand, then recognized Jim and smiled.

"Haven't seen a mob like that since Hanson played the Jingle Ball," Booth snorted.

"I saw you go down. I couldn't get to you," Jim said. They walked quickly up the hill to the cafe.

"Yeah, some wipehole put his hand in my coat pocket..." Booth slapped up and down his chest and thighs and screamed, "Shitdamn! The suckers got my wallet! Shit! And they got my watch! Shit!"

Booth was twirling in circles. Jim was afraid for a minute he was going to leap back in and fight the whole mob.

"Oh, those punks! Those bastards! I was rolling around with the one who put his hand in my jacket and I felt fingers all over me. I was up in the air and all I was thinking about was kicking the face of the first one. I fell for it. While I was swinging at him, the others were going through my pockets! Bastard!"

"They got your watch, too?"

"Right off my goddamn wrist! Can you fathom it?" He turned and shouted at the whole multitude: "You bitches! You bastards! Cheap pickpocket pricks!"

They made it back to the cafe. DeGaul and Cokie were drinking wine and giggling. They gasped when they saw Jim, bare-chested and bloody, but he assured them he was okay. He dipped his shirt in a glass of water and dabbed his wounded forehead.

"Booth saved me," Jim said. "But he got robbed. They got his billfold and his watch."

All the attention shifted to Booth. DeGaul said, "You okay, J.B.?"

"Yeah, yeah, but guess who's paying for dinner now? I had five hundred bucks in that wallet and all my credit cards. Driver's license, IDs. Oh, and my phone numbers. Shit. Some little turd's got my Diners Club and Garth Brooks's direct line. He can call Mick Jagger in Mustique and put it on my phone card."

"Passport?" DeGaul asked.

"No. No, thank God I left my passport in the fleabag. In my shaving kit. Hey, my hotel passkey was in the wallet—you think these punks are smart enough to go over there and rob my room?"

"We gotta call the hotel," DeGaul said.

"Tell you what," Booth said. "You call the hotel, I'm gonna go report this to the cops."

Frat Marie made a noise and a face that indicated he might as well put a message in a bottle. Booth didn't want to know. "Frat Marie," he said, "all I want to hear from you is directions to the police station. Go ask the waiter. Please. You don't give me any more advice and I won't mention whose idea it was to go see the drummers—on account of the voodoo ceremony might be violent."

Frat Marie skittered away. She came back with instructions that the police station was up the hill about five blocks and across the street.

"Maybe the thieves will take the cash and throw away the wallet," Booth said. "I could at least get back my license and pictures and the Blockbuster card. I bet they go through that plaza in the morning and sweep up strongboxes and false teeth and wooden legs."

Frat Marie started to say something but Booth glared at her and she clammed up.

"If I'm gone more than an hour go back to the hotel," Booth said. "Give me some cruzeiros so I can get a cab home." DeGaul peeled off some bills and handed them to Booth.

"You want me to go with you?" Jim said.

Booth laughed. "Cantone. You got no shirt on and your head's split open. You walk into the police station like that, you ain't coming out."

Booth left them and strutted off to find the cops. His bad night was just getting started.

# 8

In New York City, Zoey was depressed. Lilly Rope told her it was no hard feelings, but Jerusalem would be dopes to let Zoey A&R them with Jim in the picture. Jim was Zoey's boss, right? So she'd have to go to him for everything anyway. Why would Jerusalem want to deal with—no offense—a middleman? Jim and Jerusalem went back a long way. Hell, Jim brought Mack into the band. And when the chips were down, Jim quit his job with Barney to stick with Jerusalem. That proved his loyalty! That Jim ended up head of A&R at WorldWide just as Jerusalem signed—well, it just goes to show that everything happens for a reason.

Zoey left before Lilly told her nice guys finish first. She thought she heard that idiot Dick's words coming out of her mouth. Maybe they were having an affair. Dick struck Zoey as just the kind of insecure creep who would try to grab power by sleeping with the star. Why did beautiful women fall for these jerks? Zoey had a theory: it was because jerks and psychos were the only ones who went up to beautiful women and demanded their attention. The normal guys stood at the back of the room, gawking. The normal guys. Zoey was still waiting to meet one. She decided Dick should drop the intrigue and work on his bass playing.

She walked backward with one foot on the sidewalk and one in the street, trying to flag a cab to get downtown for another meeting. It was

Saturday night. She should be on a date or watching a play or at least eating a pizza in front of the TV. But she was A&R, she had no life. A cab on the other side of the avenue saw her at the last minute and jumped four lanes to meet her. She got in and said "Fifteenth and Union Square West." She had to shout it three times to be heard over the tape recording of a celebrity weatherman telling her to buckle up for safety.

At Union Square she found Joe Precious reading *The Stranger* and drinking a tiny cup of exotic coffee. Joe was, by title, the head of West Coast A&R at WorldWide, but his real job was overseeing black music. He was in town to meet with some young African-American moguls who had been making hip-hop hits in their bathroom in Brooklyn. He had also expected to meet with Booth and Cantone. Zoey figured he had to be sore to arrive in New York and find that the white boys had flown off to South America and left him behind with a girl.

Zoey had one motive in meeting with Precious tonight. She needed to get him to take Black Beauty, the radical black lesbian band, off her plate. Bad enough she had lost Jerusalem—to be stuck with their hopeless contract rider was more than she could stand. She and Precious stood and kissed awkwardly and sat and chit-chatted until the waitress left. His look hadn't changed: shaved head, a patch of black hair on his chin, an Italian suit over a black T-shirt, slippers without socks, little round sunglasses on the end of his nose. They got down to business.

"Zoey," Precious said. "I'm sure you appreciate that I have no truck with sexism, homophobia, or small-minded ignorance of any kind."

Here it comes, she thought.

"But I have to be mindful of my constituencies. I am assembling alliances with artist-producer-auteurs of enormous potential but limited sophistication."

"You're making deals with gangster rappers."

"Among others. Among others. Now, I appreciate the historic connection between Black Beauty's music and the entire Ma Rainey–Big Mama Thornton–Odetta tradition. I wrote papers on that tradition at university."

*At university.* Zoey got a bang out of that affectation. He went to UCLA. She said nothing.

Precious continued: "But at the level where my projects are con-

ceived and considered—on the street—I'm afraid that Black Beauty will
be dismissed out of hand as big dykes on stools."

Zoey got steamed. Precious held up his hand. "I know. I'm being
callously blunt. Because, Zoey, that is the world in which I operate."

"Maybe you should expand your world a little, Precious."

He smiled sadly. "If you said to me, 'Precious—this is the only way
for Black Beauty to get a shot,' I would take them and suffer the conse-
quences. But, Zoey, that is unnecessary because *you* can take them on.
You signed them! And I applaud you for it. Market them through New
York, through the pop division, and we'll have our cake and keep our
diets." He laughed. "It's actually wonderfully progressive. You need a
little chocolate sauce in that vanilla refrigerator where you all work.
Shake up the redhead a little, Zoey. That boy's from Maine—he's never
met an African."

Zoey smiled tightly. She had wondered if Precious resented Cantone's ascension as much as she did. Apparently so. Well, he should. Although they were technically equal—Cantone heading East Coast A&R,
Precious West Coast—everybody knew that a white A&R chief running
pop and rock from a label's New York headquarters carried a lot more
weight than a black man running R&B from a field office three thousand miles away. Precious and Zoey could share an unstated contempt
for Cantone's undeserved promotion, just as they could share a belief
that Black Beauty was a boondoggle that would drag down whoever got
stuck with it, and never say either out loud.

# 9

Booth had spent lots of time all over the world. He knew that most places people knew a little English, even if they pretended they didn't. But as he walked around the side streets of this old slave haven in northern Brazil asking drunks and whores and soldiers which way to the police station, he realized they really didn't understand a word. This was a long, long way from Rio. A longer way from Lisbon. These people didn't even speak any kind of Portuguese anyone from Portugal would understand.

The soldiers were leaning on their guns flirting with the prostitutes. They didn't want to be bothered. "Police?" Booth asked. They shrugged. "I been robbed, I been robbed," Booth insisted. The soldiers looked annoyed. They waved him toward a dirty stone building up the hill.

That place turned out to be a barracks. Booth went inside. There was the kind of municipal paint job and lowest-bid furniture you'd see at a bad junior high school or Registry of Motor Vehicles. Little groups of soldiers—half in uniform, half in T-shirts and sneakers—were smoking cigarettes and picking through cardboard boxes of confiscated pistols and knives.

Booth asked if anyone spoke English. No one cared. Finally a young woman in short shorts and a soldier's shirt pointed him toward a clerk behind a counter.

"Excuse me," Booth said to the clerk. "Do you speak English?"

The clerk held up his thumb and finger to indicate "an inch."

"I was robbed in the square," Booth said. "Beaten and robbed. All my money is gone, all my papers. I want to file a report."

"Police," the clerk said.

"Yeah."

"Not here. Police up mountain, by church."

"Which church? You people have more than a couple."

"Up mountain, this road. Big field? Big plaza. Plaza with church all lights."

Booth knew where he meant. The Christmas-bulb cathedral where the Holy Ghost goosed Cokie. He thanked the clerk and went back outside. The streets were jumping with young men floating up from the plaza. Some were puking, some were singing. One of them had his money.

Booth found the police station. He must have walked by it during Cokie's sermon on the mount. He laughed when he went inside—the place was full of the only white people he had seen all day. It was like Babel. An old German couple were weeping and bleeding. A Japanese man with a ripped suit and his shirttail out jabbered like a burning parrot. Two French girls were crying and holding ice to the jaw of a dazed boy. A fat blond lady missing one shoe was sitting on a bench with an expression of exertion on her face like she was trying to lay an egg.

This is fantastic, Booth thought. The fool tourists stroll into the center of town, the soldiers seal them in with a thousand impoverished thieves, and let the feeding begin! It's like the town square is a big turkey shoot and we're the turkeys.

He remembered the old people sitting in the balconies above the plaza, fanning themselves and watching the evening's events. He had thought they were enjoying the music. Now he knew they were watching the foreigners get thrown to the sharks. Booth decided it was funny. And with a real-world attitude that put Cokie's piety in its place, he decided that if that's what these poor starving bastards had to do to survive, more power to them. Hell, this is a place where bored soldiers drag those street kids out and shoot them. For them, robbing the tourists was worth risking their lives. For Booth it was five hundred bucks he could afford to lose. He decided to treat his wallet as the price of admission.

Still, he wanted back what he could salvage. He pushed to the woman behind the desk and said he wished to report a stolen wallet and watch. She said, "English?"

"American, yes."

"Wait for English."

Booth sat down and waited. A lot of the white people crawling in here were pretty beat-up. He'd been lucky. A couple of bloody black kids stumbled in. They were really messed up—bleeding eyes, ripped ears, missing teeth. The woman behind the desk shouted at them and they went and sat in the back.

Finally a tiny woman with cat's-eye glasses came out of the back and called, "English?"

Booth jumped up ahead of the one-shoed blond woman and said, "Me! I was beaten and robbed in the square."

"Come back, please."

Booth followed the cat woman into the back. The one-shoed lady slumped down in her seat as if she would never rise again.

Cat woman led Booth into a cell and told him to sit down. He sat on a cot, she sat on a stool across from him. She had a clipboard with about twenty-five sheets of paper stuck to it. She asked him his name, first, last, and middle.

"Booth. B-O-O-T-H. John B. 486 East Avenue, Greenwich, Connecticut, USA. President, WorldWide Music, 1616 Broadway, New York, New York 10036, USA."

He gave the woman his Social Security number, his wife's name and address and phone number, the hotel where he was staying, the purpose of his visit, what he was doing here, his birthdate, his place of birth. Now he wanted to describe the wallet and the watch. She wouldn't let him.

"No, please," she said. "We must fill out the form in order."

"Look," Booth said. "I don't expect to get my money back."

"How much money?"

"About five hundred dollars. I don't expect to get my money back."

"Five hundred U.S. dollars?"

"Of course U.S. dollars. Look, I don't expect to see the money again but if the wallet itself shows up, I'd really like to get my personal effects and phone numbers and . . ."

"How much in cruzeiros?"

"I don't know, a hundred bucks' worth maybe? How much is that in cruzeiros? I thought you people were going on the dollar anyway."

"Religion?"

"What?"

"Your religion, please?"

Holy Mary, Booth figured, they're all in on it. It's all a big plot to get me back to confession. "Episcopalian."

"Mother's maiden name?"

"What could that possibly matter?"

"Please, sir, we must fill out the form completely." She had turned to page two of her documents. Was she going to ask Booth to fill in all of them?

"My wallet was stolen, lady! I want to describe it to you so if someone brings it in you can return it to me! My mother died twenty-five years ago!"

"We must fill out the form, sir."

"Mother: Constance Sayles of Natick, Rhode Island 02887, USA. Born 1926, died 1972. She didn't take it!"

"Father's profession?"

"Barber! What do you care?"

"Political party or union affiliation?"

That's when Booth realized what this was about. He relaxed.

"These forms," he said. "You been using these for a while."

Cat woman nodded and smiled cautiously. Booth said, "Like, you've been using them for twenty years."

"I have worked eight years here."

"But the forms were here before you."

"Yes."

"And they have not changed."

"No."

"Because, until not so long ago, the military had a lot of power here. Yes? Ruled this part of the country with a strong hand. Rounded up the bad guys and took them out in the woods. Bang bang. Got the wallets back."

The woman seemed to be paying no attention to Booth at all. She held her pencil over the second page, waiting to resume.

Booth continued: "Anybody who came into the police station for any reason got a file opened on them. Yes? And that file said who their father was, who their mother was, what church they went to, how they voted, where they kept their money. Everything the generals might want to know."

Cat woman was getting impatient. There were other victims to debrief. She tried to get Booth back on the program. She said, "Brothers or sisters?"

"Fidel Castro and Che Guevara," Booth said, standing. "They changed the family name when they went into show business. Miss, I have to go now, my armored car is waiting to take me back to the base. Can I ask you to write down a description of my wallet so it can be returned to me if it is turned in?"

"Must finish filling out form."

"But I have to go, I have to catch my ride. See, my wallet was stolen."

"Finish filling out form Monday?"

"You want me to come back here?"

"Yes, you come back Monday, finish form."

"Monday I will be far, far away from here."

"You will be gone Monday?"

"Yes."

"When did you arrive?"

"Last night."

She wrote that down.

"You only stay three days?"

"Hard to imagine, I know. It's been like a trip to Epcot Center. Will you please, if my wallet should by any miracle show up, call the Hotel Managua or—even better—call my office in New York?"

"Take forms with you and send them back?"

Booth gave up. He took the pages from her. "Sure I will," he said. He put the forms in his pants pocket and walked out to look for a cab. Some drunks sat on the edge of a fountain smoking cigars and swearing in Portuguese. Booth ignored them. He walked toward a row of bright lights. Maybe there was a restaurant or a hotel where he could find a taxi. His adrenaline was wearing off. He felt he could lie down on the sidewalk and sleep for twelve hours. He should have had DeGaul wait for him.

When he got close to the lights he saw it was an empty lot, some kind of ball field. He tried to decide which way to go. Not back toward the police station. He saw cars circling a roundabout beyond the ball-park. He headed that way. As he walked he was aware of someone walking behind him. He did not look back. He figured he had nothing left to rob. The person walked past him and glanced back. He was young, tall, skinny. He wore a brown leather jacket and a wool hat and glasses. He was trying to grow a mustache. Booth stepped out into the street to cross and someone kicked the back of his knee. He stumbled. A clumsy hand reached around his neck, dragging him. Booth looked up toward the skinny kid for help. The kid ran toward him while Booth tried to reach back and grab the face of the one behind him. He thought the kid would help him, but the kid pulled his wool hat down over his face and Booth saw it had eyeholes cut out of it.

"Hey," Booth said, "it's Zorro!"

The man behind him got hold of Booth's arms and the skinny kid belted him in the belly. Booth groaned. It was unfair. He had already had a big fight tonight, and come out okay. He should be poking these goons in the eyes, but his hands were behind him.

A minibus pulled up alongside them. Good, Booth thought—help. He kicked at the masked kid and got one of his hands loose. He grabbed the hair of the man behind him and ripped. The man screamed. The car door opened. Booth thought, I'm saved. Someone in the minivan reached out and pulled Booth in. Booth went with it. He was getting away. Then the two he was struggling with climbed in after him. Booth didn't get it. He turned and looked at the men in the van. They were wearing masks, too.

"I don't believe it," Booth said out loud. The backseat was too small for four of them. Two sat on Booth. The car lurched forward. Booth gave the man who had pulled him in a sharp elbow in the neck. The man shouted.

The driver screamed orders. All three of the men in the backseat with Booth struggled to get some kind of scuba mask over his face. Booth kicked and spit and bit. He smelled something he associated with bad childhood memories. Getting his tonsils out. His dog and the vet. Chloroform?

This cannot happen to me, Booth said. Then, with strange fingers running like spiders over his face, something hit the back of his head and he went to sleep.

Booth was aware of being in motion. That wasn't unusual, he often slept on airplanes. But, man, he thought, I must be flying Delta and I must be in coach.

He forced his eyes open. He was leaning against a car window. There were palm trees going by, and signs he couldn't read. A big billboard by a construction site had text in three languages. The English said, COMING SOON! SUPER FUN WATER PARK!

Booth went back to sleep.

He woke to find himself being carried. His ass was scraping the ground. This was wrong. He remembered the men in masks and the van and the chloroform. He opened and closed his fingers. He pretended he was asleep. He was put on a table on his side. He smelled disinfectant. Someone was leaning over him, cutting his jacket and shirt off with scissors. It took all his willpower to not open his eyes. Men were speaking softly. Someone laughed. Someone else spoke an admonition. The voices receded, a car engine turned over and drove away. Something damp was swabbed on Booth's bare torso.

He thought, Wait a minute!

He felt an incision being made along his side. He snaked out his hand and opened his eyes. A woman in hospital scrubs was cutting his skin. She drew back in panic. Booth seized the wrist that held the scalpel and bent it backward. She dropped the knife with a little squeak. Booth grabbed it. He slashed the air in front of her and she jumped. Now she shouted. Behind Booth a door opened and the skinny kid from the street came in and froze. Booth plowed toward him with the scalpel. The kid backed out of the room. Booth followed him onto a screened porch. The kid ran to a shelf and pulled down a baseball bat and held it before him.

"You sucker," Booth growled. "My old man was a barber. I can do more damage with a straight razor than you could with a hand grenade."

He slashed at the kid, who stumbled over backward. Booth sliced a line down the kid's leg. He wailed and dropped the bat. Booth picked it up with his free hand and swung at his head, catching him on the shoulder.

The woman was screaming now. Booth turned and smashed whatever was in reach of his bat—a pitcher, a lamp, a table covered with flower pots. Dizzy, but coming more to his senses each moment, Booth howled like a maniac, club in one hand and bloody scalpel in the other. "VIETNAM! VIETNAM! I KILLED YOU IN VIETNAM, I'LL KILL YOU HERE!"

His intentions breached the language barrier. The kid on the floor pulled down his pants to see the damage to his leg and cried like a baby. The woman in scrubs implored Booth to leave.

"CAR KEYS!" Booth screamed. He made a driving motion with his occupied hands and said *vroom vroom*. "CAR KEYS!"

The skinny kid ran out the door. Booth thought of the other two men from the car. He thought of guns. He ran after the kid, who was running toward the minibus. Booth caught up with him at the van and swung the bat at his back. The boy fell on the ground, covering his head. Booth put his knee on his victim's neck and pressed the scalpel against his ear. "CAR KEYS."

The lady doctor ran outside and threw a ring of keys at Booth. He made a thrust like he was going to cut her. The kid on the ground covered his eyes. Booth said, "And your wallet."

The skinny kid shivered and twitched. Booth started slicing at his pockets with the blade. The woman shouted something to the kid in

Portuguese. The kid pulled out a roll of money bound with a rubber band. Booth shoved it in his pants and hit the kid in the ear with the bottom of the bat. Then he got in the van and locked the doors and found the ignition key. He rolled off down the road with no idea where he was going.

In minutes he came to a wider road that ran along the ocean. There was a big, beautiful white beach in the moonlight. Booth was pretty sure they were north of town, so he turned right, heading south along the coast.

He felt he was outside his body, watching himself in a movie. He spoke out loud: "Hey, Lois! WILD WEEKEND!"

He was cold. His shirt and jacket were shredded. He tried to cover himself with what was left and realized he was wet. He recognized a sharp sting in his lower back. Oh no.

He looked at the scalpel on the seat next to him. Blood was running from the incision in his side.

He wiggled out of what was left of his jacket and shirt and bunched it into a pillow that he pushed against the incision. He could feel himself fading in and out. He might faint. Headlights were approaching on the other side of the road. It was the first car he'd seen. He slowed down and turned the van sideways, straddling the two lanes. He knew it was a risk. He rested his head on the steering wheel and waited. The other car swerved and honked and passed. He lay there, looking at its taillights. Then its brake lights. It backed up.

A man with a beard came to Booth's window and peered in. Booth could not even raise his head. He tried to smile. The man shouted and a woman in a white straw hat came running. Booth used every bit of willpower he could summon to reach up and unlock his door. Then he went back to sleep.

• • •

DeGaul got the call at the Hotel Managua. He woke up Cantone and said Booth was found on the highway north of town bleeding to death. That made no sense to Cantone, but he got downstairs fast. DeGaul was already there, talking in his portable phone a mile a minute in English, Spanish, and Portuguese.

"I got half the country out of bed," DeGaul said. "They're going to take us to the hospital." Within minutes an armored limo pulled up outside escorted by two soldiers on motorcycles.

"Did you call his wife?" Jim asked.

"Not yet, I want to find out what's really going on."

"What about Cokie?"

"I left a message at the desk for her to sit tight. She can call Frat Marie if she needs to find us. I'm not sure Cokie should be there if it turns out to be really bad. Lucy Mercer, you know?"

Jim had no idea what DeGaul was talking about, but he guessed it meant that if Booth died, it would not be cool to have the babe he picked up for the road trip at his bedside.

They reached the hospital in no time. A doctor and a policeman met them at the door.

"How is he?" DeGaul asked in Portuguese.

The doctor answered in English. "We stitched him up and gave him some blood. Your friend is lucky, they did not get his kidneys. He must have woken up and run away."

The policeman said something in Portuguese and DeGaul laughed. He turned to Jim and explained, "It looks like some kidney thieves grabbed J.B. off the street and tried to cut him open. He must have kicked their ass and stolen their car. He was driving back when he passed out from loss of blood. A judge and his wife found him on the road. How's that for luck?"

"Good or bad?" Jim said.

"Pantloads of both."

"How did they find us? He didn't have his wallet."

"That's a good question." DeGaul asked the soldier in Portuguese. He smiled at the answer and told Jim, "J.B. had a three-page police report in his pocket. It told everything about him, including where he was staying. The hospital called the hotel."

DeGaul asked if they could see Booth. The doctor led them up a flight of service stairs and down a corridor. Booth was lying on his belly in a green room with a tube in his arm. DeGaul crouched down next to his face and said, "Hey, man."

Booth opened his eyes slightly and grunted.

DeGaul said, "Is it true that you are ruthless?"

Booth smiled and closed his eyes.

DeGaul asked the doctor a lot of questions. As long as they were there, he had them check Jim's scalp wound. The doctor offered to put in a couple of stitches. Jim said no thanks.

"Okay," DeGaul said, "we're getting J.B. out of this pisspot tomorrow. I'm going to have the plane take him back to New York. I won't call Lois, I'll wait until he can talk to her so she doesn't flip. It's bad enough as it is. This doctor's okay, his brother is a big publishing mogul in São Paulo. He's going to find a good private nurse with big jugs to go along and make sure Booth takes his medicine."

"Next time we go to the black mass," Jim said.

"I'll say. Frat Marie's going to crap herself when she hears about this one. Hey, maybe she did it! We better find out if she has an alibi."

"What about us?" Jim asked. "Should we fly back with him?"

"I think it would be bad form for Cokie to be on board when Lois Booth meets the Gulfstream. She'd finish what the banditos started."

"So we're staying?"

"Cantone! Our vacation has barely started!"

# 11

They unloaded Booth from Brazil on a stretcher and slid him into a wheelchair to be rolled through Teterboro Airport. He protested the whole way but the airport and the airport's insurance company and his doctor and his doctor's insurance company and his wife all pecked at him until he lay back and took it. He was borne by private ambulance to a sterilized hospital room near his house in Greenwich, Connecticut, where his physician gave him the once over twice and declared that he'd seen better sewing on a Halloween costume. The doctor said Booth had a minor infection that could turn major and he didn't like his yellow eyes at all. He was looking at at least ten days in the hospital, gallons of antibiotics, and let's rip those stitches out and start over.

Booth said okay to all that but he wanted to be laid up in the city, not in Connecticut. The doctor bitched a little but Booth said, "I'll pay your mileage," and he shut up. Lois Booth made more of a fuss—he was already here, he was close to home, this was a better hospital, what possible reason could he have for being back in Manhattan? She said, "This is all about getting better as quickly as possible."

Booth insisted that the only way he could be laid up for two weeks was if he could run the company from bed, and for that he had to be where the people he needed could get to him. It was not negotiable. He would do what the doctor wanted as long as he was not cut off from his job. If he stayed in Connecticut, he was on sick leave and the staff would be panting to tell him how great the place ran without him. If he stayed in New York and summoned people to his bedside, he was the wounded general commanding from his tent.

Booth had Al Hamilton find out which hospital was most in hock to WorldWide. The tendrils of corporate charity were wrapped all around the city. The best deal was struck with a good hospital on the East Side. WorldWide had run a couple of company blood drives for the place, Hamilton had cochaired a fund-raising campaign, and DeGaul had boated with half the board. Hamilton pulled strings and landed Booth a private room in the middle of flu season. The catch—probably stuck in by some resentful bureaucrat—was that his room was off the maternity ward. That turned out to be okay, as that was the one part of the hospital where chaos reigned night and day. People having babies came and went at all hours and security was used to stepping aside to let the panicking father, dilating mother, or exuberant out-of-town in-laws plow through. No one was much bothered if Booth had guests parading in outside visiting hours. When one vengeful old nurse turned away two product managers coming for a 7:00 A.M., Booth told them by phone to go buy teddy bears and come back. It worked. From then on, executives coming to see Booth on WorldWide business at odd times carried rag dolls, Furbys, and used Beanie Babies.

For the first day or two Booth almost enjoyed his convalescence. He liked that while DeGaul was still off partying in Latin America, he was seen taking charge and barking orders through a haze of gauze and pain. But being in bed for days is boring, and Booth could not get himself on any kind of normal sleep schedule. He lay awake at night, listening to the murmur of the maternity ward outside his walls. He heard the low panic of fathers, the muted cries of labor, the exhausted gossip of nurses, and the petty tyranny of doctors. He heard laughter and delight and weeping and recrimination. Often he watched dawn come up through the cold blue windows, unsure if he had slept at all.

His anxieties took a hundred shapes, but by the fifth night they had all begun to form themselves around one swollen resentment: that his colleagues had shipped him back home from Brazil and continued their vacation.

Cantone had no reason to be there at all. If he were made of anything he would have climbed on that plane with Booth and followed him home. He was knifed in South America for God's sake. The kid had no brains, Booth decided, and worse, he had no class. He had been given a big job, a job he maybe wasn't ready for. He better show something soon.

Cokie disturbed him more. He could rationalize that she genuinely did not know what to do. Booth had, after all, swept her off her feet and carried her into a world in which she had no bearings. But she should not have stayed there without him. You dance with the one that brung you, Booth believed, in business and in matters of the heart. He could forgive Cokie being overwhelmed. He considered a mental picture of her now full of regret and desperate to get home. But she had not phoned or attempted to reach him. Perhaps, he told himself, it was because she was not sure if she should. Perhaps she feared that she was a secret that could not be exposed. Maybe she was afraid that if she left a message expressing concern, Booth would be angry with her. She didn't know how his organization worked. Perhaps, he promised himself, she felt guilt, maybe shame. She might even worry that what happened to Booth was a punishment on her for falling for a married man. After all, she had a spiritual side.

It better be that, Booth thought. She better be tied into a knot of guilt and concern and not flopped on some topless beach drinking mud slides with Cantone.

DeGaul loomed largest in Booth's bad dreams. The two kids were hicks, they didn't know how to act, but there was no excuse for DeGaul. It was his trip, it was his plane, it was his call. Let's look at this dispassionately. DeGaul let Booth, cut open, be shipped back home alone so he could go to a rock concert. So he could bunk work. And here lay Booth, the loyal dog, the faithful blowboy, the stooge, with tubes in his arm still doing DeGaul's work for him, covering his absent ass. For what reason? So the old ingrate could spend the company's profits chasing chicks through the tropical underbrush.

Booth knew his job. His job was to make DeGaul look good. As long as WorldWide's stock price kept climbing and the records kept selling and the margins looked healthy, DeGaul could fly around the world smoking ganja and drinking champagne and riding racehorses up and down the aisle of the Gulfstream. But one day the stocks would slip or

the hits wouldn't come or the margins would contract. It might be a natural market adjustment, it might have nothing to do with anything in
WorldWide's control. Some schmuck in Taiwan could have a hard time
taking a dump and set off a panic in Hong Kong that could shake up the
markets in Germany and a twenty-five-year-old chickenshit on Wall
Street could get nervous and shift all the old ladies' retirement funds out
of entertainment and into adult undergarments. Then the board of directors of NOA, the conglomerate that owned WorldWide, might look
up from their strudel and ask DeGaul, "What are you doing wrong over
there?" And DeGaul would recite the magic incantation: "Well, I'm
afraid I relied too much on J. B. Booth. It's time for me to take back the
tiller."

Like DeGaul could find the tiller with both hands.

Booth knew what happened to middle-aged men thrown overboard
in such circumstances. At best he would be given his own imprint. The
honored music-biz fig leaf! He would get a fax machine and a secretary
and a small office close to the mail room. Corporate would put out a
press release saying that J. B. Booth had started his own label within the
WorldWide family where he would actively pursue and sign new talent.
But any act he signed would be buried in the bottom of the cardboard
mailing box, underneath the soundtrack to the flop movie and the re-
released classic comedy album. There would be no money spent on promotion, no whisper to retail or radio, and after a year or two the senior
staff would look at one another across the conference table and agree
with mock sadness that poor old Booth's signings were really pretty
lame, he'd lost touch, it just wasn't fair to the corporation to keep this
vanity label afloat any longer. And then, his worthlessness demonstrated
and ratified, Booth's secretary would be reassigned and his fax machine
unplugged and his little office locked up. The entire charade would last
just as long as the nonmitigation clause in Booth's contract.

And that was the best scenario! They could do worse! They could
put him in on-line!

Booth sat up in his dark hospital room. Outside sirens were con-
verging, wailing louder as they approached. A parade of submerged
anxiety deposits shot up from his gut and erupted across his brain like
Fourth of July fireworks, and like fireworks they illuminated the night.
Booth suddenly saw his position with cold clarity. He realized that he

had been sentimental. He had deluded himself that his relationship with DeGaul was a genuine friendship, that it transcended the bottom line. This abandonment had opened his eyes. If DeGaul would desert Booth when his life was in jeopardy for no reason at all, there was no sense pretending he would be loyal when only Booth's job was in jeopardy, when loyalty meant DeGaul putting himself at risk. That would never happen. Booth felt like a chump for having ever thought otherwise.

DeGaul was, Booth decided with the moral certainty of a monk, the most selfish man he had ever known. It was funny for a while, but his self-centeredness had gone on so long that WorldWide itself might not withstand it much longer. If Booth were gone, DeGaul would let this once-great company go the way of Asylum and Island, Mercury and Motown, Geffen and A&M. All great labels. All models for what a record company could be. All hollowed out and abandoned by the appetite of the market and the incompetence of their inheritors.

Booth knew he was tough enough to build a fort around himself. He had already laid the first stones. Now he saw how in protecting World-Wide he could also protect himself. He stared at the cold dawn light coming through the window and was satisfied he had the map he needed. He heard a newborn crying. He lay back into his pillow and for the first time since Brazil fell into a deep and dreamless sleep.

· · ·

Booth was vivid in the thoughts of Jim Cantone. Jim was pale and shaking, looking through the glass floor of a helicopter shooting up and down, left and right, over the rich hotels and beautiful beaches and abrupt hills and poverty shacks of Rio de Janeiro. It was already mid-morning in Brazil, another shining sunny day, and Jim was digging his fingernails into his seat cushion as the pilot beside him jerked the stick this way and that, making the helicopter do tricks nothing made of metal was ever meant to do in the air. DeGaul was in the seat behind the pilot, egging him on to greater stunts while Cokie, sitting behind Jim, whooped with the delight of a teenager on a roller-coaster. In his head Jim heard Booth's warning over and over: "Never get in a helicopter with DeGaul." In these circumstances that sentence took on the gravity of "Beware the Ides of March," "Never get involved in a land war in Asia," and "You won't come back from Dead Man's Curve."

"We probably should head out to the concert," Jim called to DeGaul, trying to sound chipper.

The pilot glanced at Jim and said something to DeGaul in Portuguese. DeGaul laughed. They were approaching the great statue of Jesus that stands, arms outstretched, on a peak above the city.

"We gotta buzz the statue!" DeGaul shouted.

The pilot said something to protest. DeGaul went to his wallet and waved a hundred-dollar bill over the pilot's shoulder. It blew out the window. DeGaul laughed and pulled out another. "That'll have to go on my T&E!" he said.

The pilot took the bribe. He dive-bombed toward the concrete Christ, sailing right under one of the outstretched arms. Jim saw tourists at the base of the statue ducking and falling on their bellies. The pilot pulled up and circled for another pass. Jim closed his eyes. Behind him he heard Cokie laugh and clap. DeGaul said, "That was great! We gotta go under the other arm! It's a special indulgence!"

The pilot careened even closer this time. Jim opened his eyes, still looking down through the clear plastic floor, and saw nothing but the face of the statue. The helicopter, he realized with terror, was almost on its side. The pilot found level again and Jim struggled to keep quiet.

DeGaul's voice came from the backseat. "Okay, that's enough fun! Let's go to the concert!"

It took no more than twenty minutes for the helicopter to sail above the miles of traffic jam that crawled out to a racetrack in the southern part of the city. In a section of parking lot fenced off from the rest, a man in a yellow slicker was waving a flag for DeGaul's pilot and several other men were moving red traffic cones to mark off a landing pad. The helicopter tilted in against the wind and bounced to the ground. Jim was out of his seat belt and onto the asphalt before the runners settled on the pavement.

He followed the man in the yellow slicker toward a backstage hospitality suite. He was shaking. As he walked, an Asian girl was hanging backstage credentials around his neck like leis. Jim heard DeGaul behind him telling Cokie, "Wait'll we fly back! The pilot will have been drinking for eight hours by then and it'll be night!"

Of all the petty humiliations Zoey suffered in reporting to the dolt Cantone, this assignment on her voice mail was the lousiest:

"Zoey, it's Jim. I'm going to be stuck down here for a while yet and I need you to cover something for me. We're paying for a demo session by a guy named Mick Nahod, who plays bass with Kelvin Burner. Nahod's written a really good song called 'Lose the Uniform.' I said we'd pay to record it and two others on spec. I need you to meet him at S.I.R. downtown tomorrow at six. He's rehearsing with Burner. I have time booked from seven to midnight at Electric Lady. Can you go meet him and make him feel comfortable and just keep an eye on things? I really appreciate it. Thanks."

This message offended Zoey in a number of ways. It treated her like a servant. It showed no respect for her schedule. It was a baby-sitting job. But Zoey was most appalled by the prospect of having to be anywhere near Kelvin Burner—a man's name, a band name, a brand name—or anyone associated with him.

Kelvin Burner (real name Kevin Burns) was a Texas-born pretty boy who had a string of arena rock hits in the late eighties and early nineties and had been hanging on to fame any way he could since the hits stopped coming. His success had been built on big power ballads for fifteen-year-olds and very tight pants. His signature songs—"One More Road Ahead," "High-Ballin' Man," and the romantic prom classic "Nobody Loves You (Like I Do)"—were everything Zoey got into music to destroy. In the last six years Burner had kept the illusion of success alive in the face of a procession of flops by selling his songs to car commercials, showing up on every TV awards show that would have him, making cameos in popular prime-time soap operas, and licensing his songs and any oldie any producer wanted to remake to any big-budget movie that needed an all-star soundtrack at a cut-rate price.

"He's not a rock star," Zoey said whenever she saw Burner's great white teeth lighting up another People's Choice Awards or American Music Awards broadcast, "but he plays one on TV."

Now Cantone was going to force her to sit in a rehearsal room and listen to this Ken doll emote like a dying rhino close up. It was horrible. When she got to Studio Instrument Rentals and the shrunken hippie behind the counter waved her into the big room, it was as bad as she expected. She took a seat on a road case as far from the rehearsal stage as she could manage and tried to hide behind the beat-up coffeemaker, but it was no use. Kelvin Burner, his hair weave flowing to his shoulders, spotted a new face, a *female* face, amid the bored techs and road crew who had heard him sing a thousand times and pumped up the charm wattage with the aim of projecting all his sticky charisma right at her.

"It's the power—it's the *power*—it's the POWERRRRRR OF MY LOVVVVVVVVE," he bellowed toward the corner where Zoey cringed, his voice amplified by walls of speakers and all the veins on his neck and forehead bulging. When the song crashed to its cymbal-ringing coda Kelvin grinned like he had just won a decathlon and all his band members congratulated him, with forced smiles and beaten eyes, on really nailing that sucker.

Rehearsal was over. Mick Nahod made his way over to Zoey and introduced himself. He spoke softly, with restrained excitement, about the songs he was going to cut and how a couple of the other guys in Kelvin's band were going to help him. Zoey was struck by the kid's whipped-dog demeanor. It must be awful playing behind this creep, Zoey thought. If Nahod has any taste at all, he must suffer whenever Kelvin turns up the Vegas. Still, it's a job. It's the big time. A player can get hooked on the nice hotels and regular paychecks.

Nahod introduced Zoey to the drummer and keyboard player, who were joining him on the session tonight. They shook hands and exchanged small talk. Zoey asked Nahod if he wanted to grab an acoustic guitar and run through the songs for her now. He looked nervous. He clearly wanted to get away from Kelvin Burner as quickly as courtesy allowed.

It wasn't to be. Burner came striding and grinning across the room and inserted himself into the little circle. He stuck out his hand to Zoey and when she went to shake it, he grabbed her by the wrist and yanked her forward to plant a kiss on the cheek. She recoiled so fast he ended up kissing her ear.

"I'm Zoey Pavlov from WorldWide," she said, wiping it off. Kelvin grinned and stood back with his hands on his hips.

"Hello, Zoey!" he said. "I'm Kelvin!" He smiled and looked at his backup band as if that were quite a joke.

No one said anything; it got awkward. Finally Nahod said, "I'm doing a demo session tonight of some of my songs, Kev. George and Rufus are going to play on it. Zoey's coming along."

"No kidding? Hey, let's hear your song, Mick! Come on! Maybe I'll sing backup on it! What do you think, Zoey? You wouldn't mind having me along to do a little harmony, would you? That wouldn't hurt Mick's chances much, would it?" He winked.

Zoey grinned. What a baboon, she thought. It was kind of great when celebrities lived up to their clichés.

Nahod and the other musicians had the look on their faces Zoey remembered getting when her mom would want to join her and her teenage friends for a night out. Kelvin started walking around the room, calling out orders to the roadies like the captain of a bikini beach volleyball team. "Hold up, boys! The crew and I are going to try something different! Mick's got a song and we're all going to learn it!"

The other musicians limped back to their places. Kelvin handed Nahod a guitar and insisted he stand in Kelvin's stage-center spot, behind the microphone. Nahod looked embarrassed. The others looked as if their night out had just been ruined. Kelvin Burner looked over his shoulder at Zoey and then strode across the open rehearsal room back to her. He stood too close and put a hand on each of her shoulders.

"Zoey, I gotta ask you something," he said in a low voice, still twice as loud as it had to be given that he was an inch from her face. "You and I slept together, right?"

"Wrong."

"No kidding?" He studied her. She could not bring herself to look at him. "Cool, then. That's a relief."

He dropped his hands from her shoulders and strutted back toward the stage. "Okay, boys, let's hear this rocker! One, two, three . . ." He had no idea of the tempo, so his count-off was inappropriate, but the band seemed used to that. Mick Nahod began to strum some power chords and sing in a pleasant voice. The drummer and keyboard player joined in.

The song, "Lose the Uniform," was not to Zoey's taste, but it was not bad. She heard what Cantone liked in it. A big riff in the classic rock style of "Jumpin' Jack Flash" or "Money for Nothing" echoed around a smarter-than-you'd-think rhythm out of Bowie. The lyrics were slightly rebellious, but nothing any parent would worry about, and the melody bored right into your brain. It was not a song Zoey would put on in her own home, but she could imagine millions of teenagers turning it up on the car radio.

As the band winged its way through the tune, Nahod's confidence grew and the drummer and keyboard player threw themselves into the song. Kelvin Burner stood just to Nahod's side, strumming an acoustic guitar, prancing around like a stripper, and—once he got the hang of it—leaning into Nahod's mike on the chorus to add off-key harmonies.

As soon as they made it through the song once, Burner shouted, "Again! Rufus—you kick it off!" and the group played the song with confidence. Nahod still recoiled a little when Burner loomed in to share the mike with him, but he was clearly relaxing as his song took shape. When the second version ended Nahod did not wait for Burner to shout orders. He immediately asked the keyboard player to repeat a little melodic phrase on the build to each chorus. They churned through the song a third time.

This time even the roadies enjoyed it. When the song ended the soundman and instrument techs cheered and clapped. Zoey thought it was time to get these guys down to the recording studio, while it was still fresh. She said, "Let's go to Electric Lady now."

The other musicians climbed down from the stage, but Kelvin

Burner stayed where he was, strumming the riff on his guitar and shaking his head from side to side with an exaggerated smile on his face. He was laughing loud and fake, and he would keep it up until someone noticed and asked him what was so funny.

Nahod and the other musicians were excited. They asked Zoey what she thought, proud that they had won her over. But finally they had to respect their employer. The drummer turned to Burner and said, "What's so funny, Kev?"

Kelvin shook his furry head back and forth three times, pretending to laugh. Then he said, "Well, it's just such a coincidence. It's really wild."

Zoey saw Nahod's whole body clench up. The other musicians looked frightened. She said, "What?"

"Well, this song . . ." Burner strummed the riff a couple of times on his acoustic guitar. "It's so weird. I have a new song with the same title and almost exactly the same music."

He demonstrated, playing the song he had just learned and singing the title phrase and the few other lyrics he could remember. The musicians stared at him. The roadies looked at the floor. Zoey did not get it and she said so.

"This song," Kelvin laughed. "It's just like my song. I was going to teach it to the band tomorrow. Mick, you must have heard me working on it."

Nahod was fighting back either rage or tears. He said, "I wrote the song at my parents' house last fall, Kelvin. I have a cassette."

"No bullshit? Really. Wow. Must be a crazy coincidence, then. You've just been spending so much time playing my tunes and watching me work you really picked up my style. Almost like telepathy, huh? Isn't that something?"

The musicians stared at Nahod and Burner. The roadies moved away. Burner said, "Well, the thing is, I did write the song and I plan to rehearse it tomorrow and record it real soon. So I need to make sure you guys understand that."

Zoey was flabbergasted. Surely this creep could not get away with stealing his backup musician's song so blatantly—words, music, and arrangement—right in front of everyone. She said to the musicians, "Come on, guys, let's go downtown," but no one moved.

The drummer and keyboard player looked at Mick Nahod. His face had gone pale and empty. The drummer took a step forward and stopped. Mick swallowed. He said to Zoey, "I can't do the session tonight." The other players relaxed. Kelvin Burner smiled and shrugged as if to say, What can ya do?

Zoey watched everyone start to pack up and put on their coats and she shouted, "What is going on here? Mr. Burner! Please tell Mick that this is a gag—he can go ahead and record his song as planned!"

Burner looked back at Zoey with no charm at all. He looked at her like she was a pickup still in his hotel bed when breakfast arrived. He said, "Mick's made his decision, lady."

She went over to Nahod, who was polishing his bass and pushing back tears. She grabbed his arm and said, "Come on, Mick. WorldWide wants to hear your other songs."

"I got kids," the bassist whispered. "I need this job."

"But this is unfair! I can't believe you guys."

"It's not fair to the other guys to ask them to risk their gigs for me. Please, just leave before you get him mad."

Zoey saw the drawbridge go up and she was left staring at the castle. She walked to the studio door, turning when she got there to give Kelvin Burner the finger. He saw but did not react at all.

Out on the street she cursed Jim Cantone for making her party to such dishonesty and sleaze. She damned the Kelvin Burners of the world, and all the Cantones, Booths, and DeGauls who made them possible.

# 13

The day they were leaving Brazil, Jim got up early to swim in the hotel pool. After the flophouse Hotel Managua, their luxury lodgings in Rio felt like Buckingham Palace. Jim was sorry they couldn't stay longer, but DeGaul had announced at 3:00 A.M., at the height of a postconcert party, that rather than hang around Brazil for the next three days they would take the Gulfstream up to the Caribbean and visit his favorite place in the world, the secluded beach town of St. Pierre.

Cokie, sharing a couch with three South American teen idols, said, "Yippee!"

Jim asked about the meeting with the representatives of WorldWide Latino. DeGaul waved his arm around the party at several drunk men balancing young women on their shoulders and pretending to be polo ponies. "This is the meeting!" DeGaul declared. "WorldWide Latino is looking good!"

When the party was over Jim gave his seat on the helicopter to one of the polo ponies. He drove back to the city with a young Irishwoman who worked for the concert promoter. They left the main road when they found some big rocks blocking the lanes of a highway tunnel.

"Bandits," the woman explained. "They wait in these tunnels like trolls. We stop the car and you get out to move the rocks, they pop up and knock you on the head."

"You like it down here?" Jim asked her.

"I love it," she said, backing the car the wrong way down an on-ramp. "The weather's fantastic, the money is good, and the people are straight ahead. I'd rather deal with thieves who come up and hit you on the head than those who pretend to be your friends while they pick your pocket."

With their late start and long detour, it was dawn when Jim and his driver got close to his hotel. To his surprise she said to him, "My place is right over the road if you'd like to come up." Jim blushed and said, "I've only got three hours to sleep and pack before we take off."

She smiled and said nothing. When Jim got out she leaned over and kissed him goodbye. He got his key and made his way to a beautiful white suite of rooms on the top floor, with the balcony doors open to dawn on the ocean. He promised himself he would get up and swim in the morning, no matter how tired he was. His suitcase was in the living room. He took out his bathing suit, sandals, and a travel alarm and set it for 9:00 A.M. He took off his shirt, shoes, and pants and lay down on the couch to watch the sunrise. An ocean breeze fluttered over his skin. He closed his eyes for what he could swear was five minutes and his alarm buzzed.

He forced himself to pull on his trunks and go to the pool. He was in the air leaving the diving board when Cokie appeared on the cement lip of the pool in skintight red hiphuggers and a rubber halter top, sucking a banana-colored beverage through a straw. She shouted hi and licked her lips. Jim opened his mouth to answer just as he belly-flopped into the pool. He swallowed what felt like a gallon of water and came up spouting.

"You okay?" Cokie asked as Jim clawed for the side of the pool. Her toenails were bright red.

"Slipped coming off the board," Jim gurgled. He hauled himself out of the water. He stood next to Cokie, dripping. Her perfect skin was already turning brown. Jim was not so blessed. Laminated in sunscreen, he knew he'd end up with red and white streaks anyway.

"You packed?" he asked. Cokie had the body of a teenage track star, smooth and strong. She had thin legs, small hips, tiny waist, long neck, high cheeks, chestnut hair, and, in the vivid words of Firesign Theatre, a balcony you could do Shakespeare off. No wonder Booth went for her. Jim just hoped she could sing.

"Ready to go," she said. She offered him her straw. "Last sip?"

Jim leaned forward and sucked in some horrible combination of coffee-milk and coconut. It landed in his stomach like a bomb. He suddenly wondered what swallowing a swimming pool would do to him in a country where you don't drink the tap water.

He went to his room to dress and felt a cold shiver. He told himself it was from too much sun. Twenty minutes later he was kneeling before the toilet, sweating and gagging.

The phone rang. DeGaul—it was time to go. Jim pulled himself together and joined DeGaul and Cokie at the checkout desk, damp and shaking. DeGaul took one look at him and said, "I got some pills for you. Saved my life in Uganda in the seventies. They seal your every orifice with cement. No shits or pukes for three days."

Jim shook his head. Whatever parasite was swimming through his system was nothing he wanted locked in. "Let me try to tough it out," he said. "After all, we have our own plane, right? If it gets bad I'll try your medicine."

"Suit yourself. But this stuff is like concrete. It'll close you up like the Baghdad USO."

Once the plane was airborne Jim locked himself in the head like Nero in the vomitorium. The plane hit choppy air. Jim clung to his porcelain life preserver, his insides heaving.

After a couple of hours of misery he was strong enough to limp out of the washroom. DeGaul and Cokie were playing cards. Jim muttered a few brave words, forced a smile, and collapsed on the couch in the front of the cabin where he lost consciousness to one of DeGaul's Dylan CDs. "People just get uglier," it said, "and I have no sense of time."

• • •

When he woke the cabin was filled with red sunlight. He checked his watch. He'd been out more than six hours. He sat up cautiously and decided he felt okay. He turned. DeGaul was asleep in the captain's chair with a book in his lap. Cokie looked up from a magazine and smiled. "He is risen," she said.

"I'm gonna go clean up," Jim said. "How long till landing?"

"Minutes."

There was a little shower in the washroom. When the water hit him, he felt alive again. As he rubbed perfumed liquid soap on himself, he thought of the Irishwoman inviting him upstairs. Then he felt guilty and thought of Jane and the kids. He came out smelling like lilacs. At the back of the washroom was a little hatch into the luggage room. Jim found his bag and dug out his toothbrush. He got a clean T-shirt and socks, dressed in the tight space, and rejoined the others. DeGaul was awake.

"Wait till you see St. Pierre," DeGaul promised. "You'll never want to leave."

The Gulfstream landed at a large airport, which Jim took as a good sign. The pilots helped the three passengers with their bags and walked them up to the main terminal, where a tall woman with a walkie-talkie took over. She escorted them to customs, chatting happily with DeGaul all the way. As soon as she left them in line, DeGaul turned to Jim and whispered, "Come on—we can take a shortcut."

DeGaul led Jim and Cokie out a side door and between two aircraft hangars. He was looking for something. He tried one screen door; it was locked. He tried another; it opened, and he went through. He went up to a black man with red hair who was wearing a whistle. DeGaul said something about needing to catch a charter. The man tried to send him back to the customs building but DeGaul said no, no, I have to get these people to St. Pierre, Paulo's taking us. The man with the whistle shrugged. A fellow in a uniform with short pants said to follow him and led the three Americans down another corridor and out a back door. Two young rastas in jeans and sweatshirts were sitting on the ground against the building, drinking Pepsi.

"Paulo!" DeGaul said happily.

"Mista Bill, Mista Bill," one of the men said.

"Mista Bill—OOOH NOOOO!" said the other. DeGaul and the two young men laughed.

"Jim, Cokie—this is Paulo and his brother Chris. They're taking us to St. Pierre."

"Driving?" Jim asked hopefully.

"Driving in the clouds!" Paulo said, and DeGaul laughed.

"It would take hours to drive," DeGaul said. "It's all the way around the other side of the island. But it's just a quick hop over the mountains. Where's your plane, Paulo?"

Paulo pointed across the runway to a sixteen-seater. "Just over there," he said, finishing his Pepsi and tossing the bottle onto the tarmac, where it shattered.

Oh, well, Jim thought, that's not so bad. I've been on small planes like that before, going to Cape Cod. That's not so bad.

"That's your plane?" DeGaul said.

Paulo and his brother laughed. "No, no. Our plane is *behind* that plane."

The company walked across the runway. Behind the sixteen-seater stood a tiny aircraft, a single-engine go-cart. Jim looked in. There was no way they could all fit—it was two pilot seats in front with a board shoved in behind. Chris pulled open a little trap door in the side of the plane, under the backseat board, and began jamming in the luggage. Then Paulo opened the pilot's door, tipped forward the seat, and invited Cokie, Cantone, and DeGaul to climb in. DeGaul swung up like John Wayne mounting a stallion. Cokie stepped up like Cinderella getting into her pumpkin coach. Jim shuddered and climbed after them like Buddy Holly.

Brother Chris stood out in front of the plane doing God knows what—tying new rubber bands around the propeller, Jim imagined—while Paulo got into the pilot's seat and flooded the engine. Jim wiggled his butt, trying to get comfortable on the board. Cokie put her hand on his knee and squeezed it. Jim looked at her. She was smiling. "You feeling any better?" she asked. Jim nodded.

"We're going through the mountains, right?" DeGaul shouted above the noise of the engine coughing and sputtering.

"Too foggy today," Paulo shouted back. "Can't go through mountains, can't see. We'll have to go around the island, over the beaches."

Jim shivered with relief. Flying low around the outside of the island, over the edge of the water—that sounded okay. If this matchbox went down over water, they'd have a chance. People would see them, the impact might not be so great, the plane might glide into the waves. Thank God for the fog in the mountains.

DeGaul shouted, "Come on! We want to get there before the sun is completely down! Take us over the mountains, it'll be fun!"

Jim couldn't believe it. Surely the pilot would not consider such . . .

"Too foggy," Paulo said again. "Can't see. Too many peaks."

"I've got a hundred bucks says you can do it," DeGaul shouted. Chris got into the plane. Paulo looked at his brother seriously and said, "We're gonna go through the mountains. You gotta look out for obstacles." Chris nodded and started fishing around under the seat for a map and a flashlight. Jim could not believe this was happening.

The little plane putted down the runway, turned around, and started back. Big aircraft were zooming into and out of the sky above them. As far as Jim could tell, these bozos were not even in radio contact with the tower. Chris asked Paulo if he'd closed the luggage door. Paulo looked concerned and then said sure he had.

The little plane took a left-hand turn off the runway and drove over a grassy hill, like a rider mower. "Tell me we're going to get a bigger plane," Jim whispered to Cokie. She smiled and squeezed his knee again. They came down the other side of the hill and rolled onto a smaller runway, not much more than a single-lane road. Paulo gave it the gas and after a very short burst the little go-cart was up in the air, climbing away from the airport and the ocean at a ridiculous angle, rattling like marbles in a washing machine.

"This is the life!" DeGaul said. "The farther you go the better it gets!" From somewhere in his jacket he produced a Red Stripe beer. He popped the top and took a swig, passed it to Cokie, who took a tiny sip and passed it to Jim, who said no thanks and gave it back. Wild Bill took another drink and handed the beer to Chris, who spilled it all over the map in his lap. Jim wanted to jump out and get it over with.

The plane was leaving behind the city, the suburbs, and then the farms as the land below rose up and turned rocky. In no time the plane was struggling to rise faster than the hills beneath them. Mountains appeared, stony and rough. Clouds gathered all around the plane, and the windshield was washed by drops of water. Paulo told his brother to stop mopping up beer with the wet map and pay attention.

For the next twenty minutes Jim remembered prayers from Sunday school, prayers from infancy, genetic-memory caveman prayers to bison gods. Chris, who was apparently working for his brother because he'd been fired from his old job as village idiot, actually leaned out the window at one point and motioned for Paulo to turn right. The clouds around the plane opened just in time for stone peaks and ledges to make themselves known. Paulo reacted by weaving to port or starboard or—in one case—climbing as fast as he could and sailing over a summit. It was getting dark fast, which threw big shadows on the ground and on the clouds. The little plane passed between two peaks, sailing through a gully. Below them Jim saw a little house on a patch of grass with no sign of any road. Who could live there, he wondered. It's like Butch and Sundance's hideout, it's Hole-in-the-Wall. If the plane crashed here, would the people in that house help us? Or would they take the luggage and bury the wreckage?

He was jolted by a sensation of sudden weightlessness. "We're not *that* high," he thought. He looked up and saw that the plane was floating backward, passing between the two peaks again, in reverse.

"We're fighting a headwind!" DeGaul shouted as Paulo pushed his whole body forward, leaning on the controls, and Chris held up the wet map like a sail. "The plane's being blown back! This is fantastic!"

Jim did not have the nerve to turn around and look behind them. He barely had the nerve to keep his eyes open. He fished in his pocket and pulled out his wallet and studied a photograph of his wife and children. Cokie leaned into his ear and said, "Let's make a deal—when we get on the ground you're going to give me a big kiss. And then we're going to say the Our Father and forget this ever happened."

Boy, Jim thought, this is my day for exotic propositions. The plane abruptly shot forward and out of the mountains. There was the ocean—they'd crossed to the other side of the island. Jim folded his wallet and put it away. Chris and Paulo exchanged secure smiles. DeGaul started rolling a spliff. The plane continued to buck in the wind, but now they were flying low, just over the beach. The sun was down, but there was enough lingering light that Jim could make out a few great hilltop homes carved out of jungle, a one-lane blacktop winding above the shore, and little clusters of shacks and cabins. Big waves were breaking over empty beaches. A couple of waterfalls peeked out of the jungle hills and became streams into the sea. It was as beautiful as DeGaul had promised, although it would have been just as beautiful if they had taken the long way around.

Chris and Paulo scrutinized the landscape. Jim was anxious to get down. Every time he saw a signal of some civilization he told himself it must be St. Pierre, and each time the plane sailed on past it. Finally Paulo touched his brother's arm and motioned toward what looked like a farm. The plane swung out to sea, made a big circle, and turned toward the land.

"Get a load of this," DeGaul smiled. He had the unlit spliff in his mouth. It was hard to see in the fading light, but a man dressed in black was holding a flashlight at the end of what looked like a short gravel driveway. A woman was standing in the driveway, tugging on a rope around the neck of a cow.

"We got cattle on the runway!" DeGaul shouted, delighted. "What do you figure, Paulo? If you got a gun on here we can try to shoot it from the air."

"Then you'll never get it off," Paulo said, as if it were a serious option. "Let Mrs. Mac get it out of there. We'll go around again."

Jim was past being scared or annoyed or surprised. He had decided to become a fatalist. Go on, he said to himself, let the cow win. We've eaten enough hamburgers.

The plane zipped down over the waves like Lindbergh and came around again. The cow had at least two legs off the runway now. That was probably as good as they were going to do. The man with the flashlight was waving like a cheerleader. It was almost completely dark. The little plane bounced and shivered and spat gravel as it clattered down the runway. Jim looked out his window and saw a goat passively looking back at him, chewing. The plane sputtered to a halt and the motor burped and farted. Jim watched the propellers *swoop swoop swoop* slower and slower around. He was in no rush to move.

Paulo climbed out and started talking to the man in black about going back for another passenger. They argued about whether it was too dark. Cokie said to Jim, "Can you believe these fellas do this every day?"

Chris climbed down from the plane and spread his beer-soaked map on the ground. DeGaul stood on the runway in the dim light, his white hair blowing back from his bronzed face, smoking his spliff.

Jim nudged Cokie in the direction of Paulo and Chris and whispered, "The Wrong Brothers."

"Wait," she said. She was moving her lips. "Deliver us from evil, Amen." Then she took out some gum, flicked it to the ground, and gave Jim a big kiss on the mouth. He leaned into it. He put his arms around her waist as she put her hands behind his head. She tasted like coffee milk and coconut. She tasted great.

They smiled at each other and then Cokie turned and hugged both Chris and Paulo, who unloaded the luggage and passed it to the man in black and his heifer-herding wife. Cokie picked up her bag and went over and linked her arm around DeGaul's and strolled with him off the runway.

Jim took his bag from the cow lady and followed the others off the gravel airfield, past a little concrete bunker that served as the office and granary, and toward a waiting rental car. A big black man got out of the car and shook hands with DeGaul, who signed a yellow paper and took the keys. The bags went in the trunk. DeGaul stubbed out his joint and got behind the wheel. Cokie got in front next to Wild Bill. Jim got in back by himself.

They drove like maniacs down the bumpy, winding, potholed, single-lane road. DeGaul had a cassette on already. Bob Marley, of course. "No Woman No Cry," of course. He was singing along. Cokie looked over the seat at Jim and smiled. She said, "We made it."

Jim took out his wallet and studied the photo of his family. "Lead us not into temptation," he said, but not so she could hear him.

# 14

Booth called Al Hamilton to his bedside. Hamilton was short, pudgy, and losing his hair. He was also black and homosexual. What Booth liked about him was that he was a cold-hearted bastard. Most people didn't see that side of Hamilton. They saw an amiable joe. Al played piano at parties. Gilbert and Sullivan and Billy Joel songs. He was quick with a joke and to light up your smoke. He was always smiling. Everyone liked Al.

But Booth had seen Hamilton chop up numbers like lines of cocaine. When it was just the two of them, hunched over a desk in the middle of the night, Hamilton was heartless. Second-quarter earnings down, Hamilton consolidated three regional warehouses into one, fifty people thrown out of work in the boondocks—chop, like that, gone. September one year, profits steady but word comes that the label's best-selling diva is on the pipe and won't have her album in for Christmas—not a tragedy, but it probably means the top execs won't make their bonus goals. Nothing can be done? Wrong. Al Hamilton knows that three of the highest-paid hog rubbers in marketing and two past-their-prime product managers are out of contract. A word here, a nod there. Reorganization time. Those jobs go and with them five secretaries and a couple of burned-out acts. Three of those people were in the same regional office? Shut it down. Three or four little moves like that, a Greatest Hits package from Diva Crack Pipe, and the fourth-quarter bonus goals are magically met.

What Booth liked best about Hamilton was that he never talked about it. He never paid lip service to pity or pretended he wasn't going to do what he had to do to make the numbers work. Hamilton didn't dance around. And he could read a spreadsheet like tarot cards. Some blowhard in the Nashville office had been cooking the books, fiddling with the figures, burying overages and dispensing petty cash from the bottom of his cowboy boots. Three different review teams went down there in two years and he buried them in bullshit, unfolded telephone books of computer printouts and double-talked the bookkeepers blind. Each review team came back promising there wasn't a problem, the profits were being deferred for good reasons, it was all square. But the money kept flowing out.

Finally Hamilton stepped in. He never left New York. He had the blowhard put all his printouts in boxes and ship them up to Manhattan. Then Hamilton loaded the boxes into a station wagon and drove off to Fire Island for Memorial Day weekend. On Monday afternoon Booth went out to see him. Hamilton was sitting on a porch by the bay in his short pants drinking lemonade and reading those reams of computer paper like it was Tom Swift.

"What this knucklehead is doing," he told Booth, "is paying commissions before profits. See?" He had circled several tiny lines of hieroglyphics from several different pages and stapled them together. "Look. He's tried to hide it, but what he's done is get his staff hopped up by paying them on orders placed, not payments received. So they are filling orders like crazy, loading up the retailers, shipping out mountains of product. But we're not *selling* it. The retailers are sitting on the CDs, probably not even putting them out. Because we do our bookkeeping by quarters and annums, nobody's been correlating the commissions out with the money in. He always makes it look like the billing will catch up next time, but it never does. It never will. This guy dug himself into a hole three years ago and he's been digging deeper and deeper to cover it up."

Hamilton looked at the spreadsheets and laughed appreciatively.

"When our guys come in to look at the books they can't get a straight answer out of anybody. No wonder! His staff is loyal! They're making double their salaries in commissions!"

Booth asked, "Is he taking kickbacks from his team? Are the retailers getting paid under the table to play along?"

Hamilton adopted a Buddhist calm. (He was also a Buddhist. One thing Booth was sure of, Hamilton never had to worry about being drafted.) He said, "There's no way to know that and it doesn't matter. This might be a straight scam or it might be a well-intentioned motivational process gone wrong. We're not going to see this money again. Accept that and let's close the leak."

Booth parked his ass on the railing and looked out at the kayaks and catamarans. He put three spoonfuls of sugar in a glass of lemonade and stirred it up and drank. He said to Hamilton, "What I don't get is, why did we let this pork chop pay spot commissions at all? Bonus incentive, sure, but that's once a year. Who let this get started?"

The truth was, Booth had, but Hamilton didn't put it like that. He said, "We all thought it was worth letting Nashville hang on to consignment after everyone else got out of it, because Knucklehead claimed that so much of the country business was selling cassettes to truck stops and gas stations and mom-and-pop stores. He said it was the only way to keep our product in those places. And he made the case for letting his crew work on commission so he could hire cheap help and lay them off during slow periods. I think he said something about, 'This ain't Manhattan, gentlemen, and these ain't superstores. I'm still getting orders for eight-tracks out here.' "

Booth nodded. He remembered. He appreciated Hamilton not saying out loud that Booth fell for the lying hillbilly's Li'l Abner routine. Well, let's see who falls now.

That Nashville knucklehead howled and cursed and threatened when Booth lowered the boom on him. Hamilton went down there and laid down the law. He let Li'l Abner know exactly what WorldWide knew and implied that the investigation involved the FBI, IRS, and hidden videotapes of money changing hands. By the time Hamilton was done with him, Abner was weeping. Hamilton gave him his handkerchief. He told him he should let his people know their jobs were over, but he did not have to tell them their jig was up. "Tell them as much or as little as you like. Tell them this is an inevitable corporate restructuring that you have held off for months already. Have a little party. But every person who took part in these misdealings must be out of this building and off the books by three weeks from today or—don't tell them this—the feds are looking for jail time."

Abner nodded. Then he had the stone balls to ask Hamilton if he could keep his stereo and office furniture, among which sat an antique electric chair.

Hamilton acted like it was a perfectly regular request and he gave him what he made sound like an answer from the WorldWide Human Resources Manual: "Whatever you can carry in two wheelbarrows."

When Abner and his furniture were gone, Booth put Crash Cronin, one of his old allies, in charge of the Nashville office. Ever since, the place hummed.

Booth had let Hamilton name his own reward for cleaning up cowboy town. Hamilton's request made Booth laugh hard and like him even more. Hamilton wanted his name to be the signature on all the World-Wide paychecks. So it was done.

Most people looked at Al Hamilton and saw a jolly fat black man who laughed first and loudest at homo jokes and Amos 'n' Andy routines. People said, isn't Big Al a regular guy? Booth was smarter. He saw Hamilton totting up accounts on every racist wisecrack, every homophobic quip, every fat and bald joke. He hooted and kept score. He drank ginger ale while those around him got sloppy drunk and said more than they meant to. Al remembered every word. Booth knew something the others did not: Al Hamilton might be very friendly, but he wasn't very nice.

So it was that Booth called Hamilton to his hospital room after visiting hours, after all the babies were asleep, after the English-speaking nurses had gone home and the immigrant night shift offered privacy from eavesdroppers. Booth called in Hamilton because he knew Hamilton would immediately understand the ramifications of what Booth wanted to do, but he would say nothing about it out loud.

"You look better," Hamilton said as he pulled up a chair by Booth's bedside.

"All my misery has moved to my anus," Booth said. "I got piles from lying here all day."

"What do you want to talk about?"

Hamilton was wearing a suit and tie. Booth appreciated that. Booth said, "I've been thinking about how that shake-up in Nashville helped the whole company. That situation got out of hand because I let it. I did not care about Nashville the way I cared about the rest of our domestic operations, and as a result WorldWide suffered."

"You didn't screw up Nashville. Knucklehead did. You saved Nashville when all of the accountants said nothing was wrong."

"Thanks, that's not important. I've been thinking about other operations I may have neglected. Most important—our foreign divisions. The world is getting smaller and we've still got twenty separate fiefdoms, each with their own rules, their own accounting, their own policies. God knows I got enough on my plate without having to worry about whether the Krauts are taking off Mondays for Oktoberfest. But what I have put off admitting to myself for too long is that our international operation needs to be consolidated, and I need to take a more active role in supervising it."

"You're not talking about stepping away from WorldWide domestic?"

"The opposite. I intend to retain all my duties as president of WorldWide USA, but also assume the title and responsibilities of COO of WorldWide International."

Booth waited to see if Hamilton said that that was stepping on De-Gaul's toes. DeGaul was CEO of all WorldWide operations, foreign and domestic. For Booth to take COO—a half step below DeGaul's title— was a way of assuming DeGaul's duties outside the USA. Hamilton said nothing, so Booth kept going.

"Al, I need you to quickly and quietly see how we can consolidate European operations. Who over there should run things? Or is it someone from here? Cronin's done a hell of a job in Nashville."

"Crash should stay in Nashville. His is not a European sensibility."

"Fine. Figure out who the right people are, and then see where we can combine operations and save money. They're all going to the euro, right? That should make it easy to see which operations are most efficient. We can finally look at apples to apples."

"Absolutely. Our European cousins have used exchange rates to disguise monkey business like our beloved Knucklehead used spreadsheets."

"It's a painful amount of dishonesty we deal with, isn't it, Al?"

"This will take a few months. More if we don't want to make them nervous."

"Do it as fast as you can doing it right. We need to build something here that will last a long time. Who knows? Down the line some World-Wide chief of the future may want to spin off some of these operations. It could be that in a couple of years we'll want to unload foreign divisions, put a few hundred million in our pockets, and then go after the same markets by other means, right from New York."

"Internet commerce."

"Can't ignore it. Wouldn't it be funny if we sold off all our foreign trucks and warehouses and pressing plants just before they all became worthless—and then we kept the music anyway."

"Careful, J.B., you could start World War III." Hamilton smiled.

They were quiet for a minute. Then Hamilton spoke carefully.

"There is one impediment we're going to come up against right away. Although more and more of our revenues are generated internationally, the acts selling over there are mostly American, or at least signed by the American company. So the bulk of the profits are recorded with WorldWide USA. The British do okay, but if you isolate the French or German or Benelux operations, not one of them will show a profit. They are carrying the expenses of running record companies, and they bring plenty of money back to the mothership. But as long as they only peel off a small piece of the profits they make for us on American acts, they will be—on paper—in the red."

This was the opening Booth had hoped for. Good old Hamilton. Smartest bastard in the company.

"Good point," Booth said. "Well . . . looking at it long-term, we have to make these operations attractive on paper. And you could sure make a case that the operation that presses, markets, and sells the music in its region ought to get the credit for the profits made in its region."

"You sure could."

"What's the downside?"

Hamilton took a breath. He said, "In real dollars and cents, none.

And if we ever did decide to spin off any of the foreign operations, it would certainly make them more attractive to potential purchasers."

"Which we might never do, but it makes sense to be in shape if we ever want to."

"Sure. The hit, of course, would come—on paper only—on the domestic side. WorldWide USA would account for less and less of the company's total profits."

Both men sat quietly for a minute. As if this were news.

"Of course," Booth said happily, "that's just on paper. We'd be making as much money as ever. More, as this foreign reorganization rolls out."

"That's right."

Hamilton and Booth looked at each other. Booth was proposing a redistribution that would make WorldWide's money flow away from DeGaul and through Booth. Booth not only wanted titular control of the foreign operations; he wanted bookkeeping to move huge profit lines from the United States to Europe. With a little reshuffling of paper and no change in the actual money coming in, it would look like Booth had revitalized all the foreign labels. Anyone reading single-page year-to-year profit-and-loss sheets would see Booth's areas growing as the house DeGaul built broke apart.

Booth waited for Hamilton to say it out loud. This was speak now or forever hold your peace.

Hamilton leaned forward and said, "I don't think it makes sense for you to ask DeGaul for the COO title over there."

Booth felt his gut clench. He said nothing. Hamilton continued: "If you take on these new responsibilities, you should be CEO of World-Wide International. DeGaul will understand that. I don't think he'll mind."

Booth almost laughed out loud. He didn't, though. He just nodded. Hamilton asked him, "When is your contract up?"

"June."

Hamilton grinned with his lips pressed together. "Let me see if I can finish this study and have my recommendations ready by the end of April. Are you planning to ask for a big raise?"

"Not out of whack with my worth."

"If I were you I'd ask for a really big raise, and use these new responsibilities to justify it. Then if you have to fall back on salary, they'll
be happy to appease you with the CEO title."

"It's worth more to me than money," Booth said.

"I understand."

"It's what the company needs."

"For the future."

"Exactly. For the future."

Hamilton pushed back his chair. "I'm going to start on this tomorrow. I'll probably drop in on our German brothers first. They love
pulling out the paperwork. They have the souls of accountants. Wonderful guys."

"Don't tell me you speak German, Al."

"I get by. I have relatives there."

"There are black people in Germany?"

"Turks. My mother is part Turkish."

"Geez, Al, what minority are you not?"

Hamilton got to his feet and said, "Stupid."

Booth stretched and lay back on his pillow. "Don't kid yourself,
buddy. Stupid ain't a minority."

"I have to hand it to DeGaul," Jim said to Cokie. "This place is the cat's pajamas."

They were standing at the edge of a private beach, along a series of small lagoons divided by hills thick with palms. They had the whole place to themselves. Scattered over a hundred green and rolling acres were a dozen stone and glass bungalows, as well as an old colonial hotel. Cantone, DeGaul, and Cokie each had their own bungalow. They were the only guests.

"I'm going to put on my bathing suit," Cokie said. "You want to swim with me?"

Jim said, "You bet."

DeGaul came strolling down the road like Lawrence of Arabia. He was walking with his British friend Royal Nightingale, who ran the place.

"Did I exaggerate?" DeGaul asked Cokie and Jim. "Is there a better place in the world than right here?"

"How do you do it, Mr. Nightingale?" Cokie asked. "I see people cutting the grass and watering the gardens and washing the windows, but there are no guests."

"Consider this a preview, Miss Shea," the Englishman said. "I have been here since 1997 supervising the restoration of Webster's Retreat. By the end of this year we will be complete. The hotel will be returned to its early glory, the golf course and tennis courts will be finished, and the world's most discerning travelers will be making their way to St. Pierre."

"So we better live it up now," DeGaul said, "'cause by the time Roy and his partners are done, this remote corner of the Caribbean is going to be jam-packed with fat Americans riding mopeds in Bermuda shorts."

"Far from it," Nightingale chuckled. "My partners and I wish to revive the old tradition of the secluded baronial hideaway."

"This spot has a fantastic history," DeGaul said. "It was a sugar plantation until the early nineteen hundreds, and then it became a superposh resort. A thousand dollars a week when that was real money. Noël Coward and George Gershwin used to hang out here with nude cabana boys. Old Joe Kennedy would pull up his yacht and make Gloria Swanson swoon. Cary Grant, Bogart and Bacall. As late as the fifties, Ava Gardner hid out here with her lovers. If these walls could talk, man."

"They'd sound like Kitty Kelley," Jim said.

"I feel so grateful to be here," Cokie said. "The beaches are incredible. I have waves crashing at my bedroom window."

"It's all good," Nightingale said. "Now you nice people go get into the water. I'll send Mr. Jay down with some champagne and mango. I have to go make sure the workers lay the clay properly for the courts."

"What a nice man," Cokie said when Nightingale left.

"He's a great guy," DeGaul agreed. "I've known Roy since I was twenty. His father was a diplomat in Jamaica. Real Graham Greene Sun Never Sets on the British Empire stuff. In the late sixties, early seventies this place was completely abandoned. We hippies used to sneak in here and have pot parties. You could live here for days and never see an outsider."

Jim considered that DeGaul was already a rich man in the early seventies. That clearly had nothing to do with it.

"Does Mr. Nightingale own this whole place?" Cokie asked.

"Him and about six banks. This has been Roy's lifelong dream. While the rest of us were sitting around stoned and naked on the beach he was figuring out how to buy the Retreat and restore it. It's occupied his whole adult life. He finally put together a group of British and Australian investors and did the deal. He has about half the parish of St. Pierre working for him."

"I suppose they work pretty cheap," Cokie said.

"Cheap is relative," DeGaul said. "Thirty bucks a week for cutting the grass here can be a hell of a windfall to a guy with one room, three kids, and six chickens. And if the resort happens like Roy hopes, everyone in St. Pierre will be rolling in dough."

"The sun never sets on British colonialism," Jim said.

"It's free-market economics, Jim," DeGaul said. "And I promise you, the folks around here want in on it."

"Let's go swimming," Cokie said.

The rest of the afternoon was spent riding big waves and floating down the tributaries that snaked in and out of the cove. Mr. Jay, Nightingale's majordomo, arrived with champagne and shrimp and set it out on a long table in the shade of a palm.

Around four o'clock they dragged themselves back to their houses. Jim fell asleep with the glass doors open and the surf crashing. He had taken the photos of Jane and the boys out of his wallet and stuck them in the corners of the living-room mirror. He wanted to bring them here.

He woke after sunset to Cokie standing in his open doorway, rapping on the glass.

"Mr. Nightingale has a big dinner planned in about twenty minutes," she said. "They sent me down to rouse you."

"We're going to eat again?" Jim said.

"Look what I have," Cokie said. She held up a small acoustic guitar. "You get dressed for dinner. I'll be in the living room."

Jim washed up and put on a clean shirt and slacks. He could hear Cokie singing. He was relieved that she had a nice voice. He sat on the edge of the bed and listened. She sang a song with the refrain "I never could believe I wouldn't see you anymore." In this place corniness felt okay. Jim knew he had to broaden his taste if he was going to oversee all pop music for WorldWide, and he imagined this song appealing to millions of ordinary civilians, people who did not live in big cities, go to nightclubs, or care what was hip. Sitting here listening to Cokie by the ocean, what he might have called mundane working for Barney sounded sweet and sincere.

He went into the front room. "That's a nice song," he said.

"Oh, thanks," Cokie said. "It's not finished. It doesn't have a real chorus or a middle part or anything. Just three four-line verses and the last line is the same each time."

"But it works," Jim said. "Play something else you wrote."

"Okay," Cokie laughed. "Is this my official audition?"

"No, no. I just want to hear what J.B.'s so excited about."

"Sure thing. Okay. This is called 'Fast Asleep' and it's kind of different from the others, it's a little more rock in the chords but I think the lyrics and melody feel pretty country. It's . . ."

"Cokie, don't spoil it for me. Sing it."

Jim decided the song was very good. The second verse was a little obscure, but Cokie had a real gift for writing with a kind of melancholy strength—more stoic than self-pitying. Jim had never gone for the Lilith types, the folkies, the Joanies and Judies. But Cokie avoided the usual traps. She sang a song called "Responsibility" about a high school graduate left behind in a small town after the smart kids went away to college. Then she sang one she said Booth had really liked. Jim liked it too.

"You're good, Cokie," Jim said. "And I can't tell you how happy I am. It would have been a big drag if you stunk!"

"Oh boy, Jim, I am so glad you like it. I was getting worried."

"Were you?"

"Yes, I was scared that . . ." She shut up and considered her words. "Jim, I need to ask you something in complete confidence, okay? I feel like we're friends."

"Go ahead."

"I don't completely understand the division of responsibilities between you and Jack and Bill. I don't exactly know who does what."

"Bill's the big boss. He founded the company. He's a legendary figure in the music business."

"Does he own WorldWide?"

"No, he started the label and used to own it, but he sold it years ago. He is the head of the record division."

"Who is his boss?"

"The chairman of the board of NOA, who also oversees movie divisions and book companies and magazine publishers. Bill is the kingpin of WorldWide Music."

"And Jack works for him."

"Cokie, you may be the only person alive to call J.B. Jack. Yeah, J.B. is president of the record company. He runs things day to day and he oversees all the hirings and firings and business deals and strategic issues. DeGaul is the face of the company and the spirit of the company. He interacts with all the other parts of the NOA empire and has to think about the stock price and stuff. It's like DeGaul is FDR and Booth is General Eisenhower."

"What's your job, Jim?"

"I'm the head of rock and pop A&R. I'm responsible for finding acts and signing them and working with them to build careers and make great records. I work with the head of marketing and the promo guys and product managers to try to make sure that artists make the best music they can and that it gets to as many people as possible."

"That's a big job."

"Well, I don't do it alone."

"How long have you been with WorldWide?"

"What day is it now? Wednesday?"

Cokie laughed.

"About three weeks."

"No."

"Yes. Cokie, you've been with the label about as long as I have."

"Oh my God, that's so funny. I thought you guys were like the Three Musketeers."

"Yeah, well, I'm the young musketeer. I'm Michael York."

"You're Charlie Sheen."

"I'd rather be Michael York."

"What does A&R mean?"

"Talent scout."

"What do the letters stand for?"

"Artists and Repertoire."

Cokie laughed. "My dad used to be a policeman. When I told him I was going to Brazil with some A&R men he got all upset. 'A&R men' is what cops used to call muggers, 'Assault and Robbery men.' I'll have to tell him it's . . ." She looked at Jim for help.

"Artists and Repertoire. In the old days songwriters wrote and singers sang and arrangers arranged and musicians were hired for the gig. The A&R man coordinated all that. He found a hit song and brought it to a singer, booked the studio, brought in the arranger, paid the orchestra, filled out the time sheets. Everything changed after the Beatles. Musicians became self-contained. They wrote their own songs, played their own instruments, and ran their own recording sessions, usually far away from the label. Independent record producers rose up. The label became less involved in the creative. The label became the bank, the distributor, and the copyright holder. A&R changed into something else—the people who find the acts and serve as the link between the label and the artist."

"So the title has sort of outlived the original job."

"Yeah. Like 'record company' outlived records."

Jim was sure Cokie was beating around the bush.

"Okay, now—this is just between you and me, right?" she said.

"Yes."

"Please, please, Jim. Don't say I asked you. I have to know. What is the situation with J.B. and his wife? Are they together?"

Oh hell, Jim thought. This is bad on so many levels.

"I don't know much about Booth's personal life, Cokie. You probably know more about it than I do. He's been married a long time, I think. No kids. I believe they broke up for a while and got back together. What the situation is now, I couldn't say."

"See, Jim, I didn't even know he was married until the plane ride down to Brazil. Not that we're involved or anything. But—you won't repeat any of this, right? But I wasn't really clear on what he was thinking. I mean, I really felt he liked my music. He said he did and I believed him. But then I began to think, well, you know. Maybe he wasn't completely sold."

"Cokie, I'm glad I heard your songs. They're real good. Booth wouldn't have brought you along and introduced you to Bill and everything if he was . . . if his intentions were shaky."

"I can't tell you what a load off my mind that is." She looked around awkwardly and brightened when she saw the photos stuck in the mirror. "Are those your kids?"

There was another rap on the glass. DeGaul said, "Hey, come on, you two! Supper's on the table!"

"Okay," Cokie said. She put down the battered little guitar. Jim picked it up and strummed it.

"Ow! Cokie, these strings are about an inch off the fretboard! Your fingers must be shredded!"

"I put the pain into my work," Cokie said, and made a goofy face to show she was kidding. Jim followed her out the door and up to the hotel for dinner. He shook his fingers. She must have calluses like a deckhand, he thought.

Dinner was one more pleasure in the St. Pierre parade of high living. Mr. Jay served dumpling appetizers, some kind of succulent fried fish in wine sauce, and tubes of chocolate filled with ice cream and blueberries that could have stopped a plump man's heart. They dined on the upper porch of the old hotel and then drank brandy and studied the stars.

When the conversation turned sleepy Mr. Jay appeared with the guitar Cokie had left at Jim's bungalow and Nightingale prevailed on her to perform. After a lot of clapping and whistling Cokie sang a sad, beautiful love song called "Power Over Me."

Oh my God, Jim thought, get me out of here before I turn into Booth. She's got everything.

Nightingale clapped longest. "So, DeGaul, this is the next Joan Armatrading. Miss Shea, how can I entice you to swear you will come back and sing for us again when you are famous?"

"You got me, sir," she said. "I'll come back here forever. Show me where to sign."

"Cokie, that was the best one yet," Jim said, standing. "But I gotta go to bed or I'm going into a coma. Bill, Roy—what a wonderful day. Thank you."

"I'm pooped, too," Cokie said. "Will you walk me home, Jim?"

Sure, Jim said. He wasn't sure if he wanted to or not.

Nightingale waved. "See you in the morning." Everyone said it back to one another. DeGaul said to Jim and Cokie, "You two are the future of my company."

Jim and Cokie walked down the path from the hotel in silence. In the trees a bird was whistling. The ocean was lapping the beach. They turned off at the walk to Cokie's cabin and she said, "Thanks for tonight, Jim. And thanks for keeping my secrets."

"No sweat," Jim said. They stood awkwardly for a moment and he kissed her on the cheek and stepped back and said goodnight. She held on to his wrist. She said, "You have smooth arms." She smiled and turned. She let herself in and switched on the lights. He heard the lock turn and went down the path to his own stone house.

He looked back once at the great hotel at the top of the lawn. On the balcony the glow from two cigars hung in the dark like red eyes.

. . .

"She's a knockout," Nightingale said to DeGaul as they watched the curtains close in Cokie's bungalow.

"Yeah, she's good. J. B. Booth found her. Man, I gotta call and check in with him. I spoke to his wife, he's gone to a hospital in Manhattan. The maniac."

"Bill, I have to talk to you about the banks. The Australians are okay but the Brits are being horrible. I had to go into Martha's money to pay for the clay for the courts."

"Hell, Roy, we could have skipped the shrimp on the beach. How much are we short now?"

"Forty grand. I could get by with thirty, but I want to pay back Martha quickly. It's unfair to her."

"Yeah, yeah. I know. Well, you spent all the dough I sent you at Thanksgiving?"

"Remember, that was for the furnace and the roof. There was no discretionary money in that. I was very careful to spell out all of it."

"I know, I know. I'm not being tight, I just . . . You know, I'm flush, but not that flush. My ex-wives have lawyers going over my books with fingerprint powder. And the girls are both in school. I can't be completely reckless."

"Willie, your recklessness is your most endearing quality. If you help me out this time I insist on adding your name to the deed. God knows you've earned it. Anyway, I always wanted you to share in the place. It's your dream as much as mine."

"I'm not the one who's been living here for three years, dealing with the day-to-day. How's the help holding up?"

"Well, Mr. Jay is impeccable. The man can rewire a chandelier, carve a gargoyle, or baste a goose. John Peatracioz runs the grounds and he's very caring. You remember Buster Odo? He's the fellow who believes the earth is flat and Neil Armstrong walked on a set in a TV studio in Texas. But he can make any flower bloom. They are my main officers, and they command a dozen to twenty troops, some of whom demand a lot of supervision, but the work is progressing."

"I'm in for an awful lot already, Roy. I don't know if I can keep doing this."

"You won't have to. And anyway—once we open, this place will be a bonanza for all of us."

"I just want a bungalow by the cove and a big bag of herb."

"You won't get off that easy. I want you as my partner in name as well as deed."

"Tell you what—I'll get you the thirty grand, but I never want to have to chase a tennis ball. I want a native girl with a dozen cans of yellow Wilsons to follow me at all times."

"Done."

"And then she has to wash my back."

"Done."

"And you don't get to sleep with her."

"Oh dear. That could be a deal breaker."

. . .

Jim had his glass doors open, letting the salt air blow his bedroom curtains. It was only March; at home it was still cold. He heard the murmur of DeGaul and Nightingale laughing on the porch. He watched the light from Cokie's house. She was still up. He allowed himself to call up a picture of her in silhouette standing in his doorway, tapping the glass. He twisted on the bed. He was exhausted, but it took a long time to fall asleep.

# 16

Cantone was sleeping. Someone kissed his fingers. Then his cheek. A hand tugged at his hair. A second hand brushed his forehead. A third hand rocked his shoulder and a fourth tickled his ribs. He opened his eyes, laughing. Luke and Mark were climbing over him like a sandpile, following Mommy's orders to get Daddy out of bed.

"Wise guys, huh?" Jim grunted. He rolled over and grabbed the boys, who squealed and wiggled and tried to get away. "Oh no, you don't!"

Jim and the twins tumbled over one another in a tangle of sheets and swinging pillows.

Jane appeared in the doorway. "Come on," she said. "I made pancakes. You said you had that big meeting this morning. You can't be late."

"It's summer, Daddy!" Luke announced, pulling open the curtain. It had been a year with no spring. One day New York was buried in snow, the next it was eighty degrees. Spring was the day the puddles evaporated.

"What time did you get in?" Jane asked when they sat down to breakfast.

"Four, I think," Jim said. "Do we have any Coca-Cola?"

"For breakfast, Jim? I wish you'd go back to coffee."

"Coffee's bad for you. Very habit-forming."

"You want Coke at seven A.M. for health reasons."

"I've got to be awake for this meeting."

"The kids have chocolate milk."

Mark ran to the refrigerator and came back with a half-empty bottle of Yoo-Hoo with a defeated paper straw hanging from its rim.

Jim looked at it and said, "Maybe I'll try some tea."

"Luke, let Mommy pour that!" Jane said. "How did the recording go last night?"

"Pretty good. Jerusalem is having a little trouble making the adjustment to the studio, but they'll be okay. Lilly is learning a lot faster than the band, which causes tension. Dick and Anthony are having some issues, I think."

Jane seemed to listen as she served the waffles. Jim kept talking: "I encouraged them to spend last night just playing all their songs live, vocals and everything. To loosen things up. Macnie, the producer, wants to keep working on that song 'Hard Hearted.' That feels like the hit. But I convinced him that if we didn't get the whole band feeling confident it would take twice as long to get 'Hard Hearted' and the album would become a misery. So I think for a couple of nights we'll just play."

"You have to find some time to look at these schools this week. They're all getting ready to close for the summer."

"Are you sure the kids have to start school this September? They're only three. I didn't start school until I was six."

"You grew up in Dogpatch. Kids start school younger now. This way they'll be able to fly spaceships when they grow up."

"Yeah, I fell for that one," Jim said. " 'By the year 2000 day trips to Mars will be routine.' What did we get instead? Laptops and cable TV."

"Count your blessings," Jane said as she cut up Luke's pancakes and put the syrup out of reach. "My seventh-grade teacher told us that by the end of the century there would be so many people we'd all have to sleep standing up."

"Those were the days," Jim said. "You boys ready to go to school and make lots of friends?"

"I don't want to go to school!" Mark shouted.

"School is fun," Jane said. "If you don't go to school you'll grow up to be an ignoramus."

"You'll love it," Jim said. "You'll play games and draw pictures and learn numbers. And when you grow up you can be anything you want. An airplane pilot or a scientist or a baseball player or anything."

"I want to be a pirate," Luke said.

"How about you, Mark?"

"I want to be an ignoramus."

. . .

Jim was the last one into Booth's conference room. It was the quarterly all-hands-on-deck meeting to report the state of the big fall albums and assign priorities.

Zoey was there, along with the other New York A&R reps and the SVPs of press and marketing. Precious was in from Los Angeles. Crash Cronin was up from Nashville. Al Hamilton sat primly against the wall with a laptop and a folder full of files. Jim had not expected to see Roger Rose, head of WorldWide UK, at the meeting, and he had never met David Knopft of WorldWide Germany face to face.

Jim felt like a slouch that people who flew thousands of miles arrived on time and he, who lived thirty blocks away, was late. He should not have stopped for that bottle of Jolt.

"Close the door, please, Jim," Booth said. "Thanks. Okay, we're all here. Bill DeGaul is going to stop in a little later, but we should get started.

"First, it's great to have all of us in one room. I wish we could do this more often. You people are the ones who make WorldWide run. You are the brain trust. We have no success, we have no reason to exist, without the talent the people around this table discover and develop and market. Looking ahead, I feel we have some extraordinary opportunities. I'll get to them in a minute, but I want to say on the record and in front of everyone that Jim Cantone"—Booth saw Zoey looking at him—"and his staff are working with a young woman named Lilly Rope and her band, Jerusalem, on what we all believe will be a rock act of major importance, critically and commercially. How are the sessions going, Jim?"

"Really great, J.B. I was down there until five this morning. This could be big across the board, I think. These guys are very young and very talented. Jerusalem has the potential to make important music and build the kind of audience that increases from album to album for years."

"Don't rush them," Booth said. "This is the kind of band that has to develop and grow their audience at their own pace. We want to cultivate this just right with press and the right kind of radio. Maybe not make a video right away. Nurture the buzz, people. I've seen these kids and they got it. This girl Lilly Rope is the whole nine yards." Booth turned to Jim and grinned. "By the way, what's her real name?"

"Susan Roper," Zoey said.

Booth looked at Zoey. "Zoey has also been very involved in signing and working with Jerusalem," Booth told the table. "This is a team effort all the way. Check 'em out. Get on board.

"Now let's look to the big Christmas releases. What the hell is wrong with Loudatak? Bruce? I heard the demos, they sound like Neil Diamond. What the hell?"

Bruce Gilbert was an A&R director who had been with WorldWide more than ten years and never made vice president. He was an old rocker who dyed his long hair black to mask the gray. He sold T-shirts for Led Zeppelin in the seventies, comanaged some prominent heavy metal acts in the early eighties, moved into A&R with some moneymaking hair bands at the end of that decade, and signed a couple of momentarily successful grunge acts in the early nineties. He spent all his time on the road, roosting at whichever WorldWide office was convenient.

Loudatak was a heavy hair act that made a last-minute turn toward Seattle in 1991, just in time to save their credibility. They had enjoyed a good run, moving into big rock ballads and movie soundtracks as the decade wore out. They had hung on longer than most of their peers by their willingness to do whatever it took to connect with their demographic, horny teenage boys and the girls who love them. Like Bruce, Loudatak had managed to remain in the racks past their sell-by date.

Given that symbiosis between band and A&R man, it was hard for Bruce Gilbert to say what he said to the room: "J.B., they all went into detox and cleaned up and, I don't know, they're having a hard time getting back into that headbanging head."

"Huh. What I heard is a long way from rock and roll. Do you think they can bring off a turn like that? Who's going to buy this record?"

"The Germans might," Roger Rose said brightly. He grinned at David Knopft.

Knopft shrugged. "We would have to hear it. Loudatak has a follow-ing in Europe, yes, but I don't know. If this is limpy, maybe not."

"It's not limpy," Gilbert protested. "They're moving toward power ballads. I think it may be age-appropriate. Their fans are growing up."

"I don't think MTV is going to want them," the head of marketing said.

Gilbert glared at him. "I'll tell you what," he said emphatically. "Loudatak has run up a lot of favors with MTV. They played the beach house, the European awards, the opening of MTV Indonesia. Same thing with radio. These guys have done every Christmas party, every spring-break blowout, they know the programmers, they pose for pic-tures. We sent out almost a thousand platinum albums on *Eat Um Up and Spit Um Out.* You go into any big rock radio station in the Midwest, the South, the Northwest, you'll see a picture on the wall of the station manager with Loudatak."

"They don't mean shit in the UK," Roger Rose said.

"Yeah, well, you drive out to Detroit and see how many Portishead records they're selling, okay, Roger?" Gilbert snapped. "Ask the retailers in Pontiac if they're moving a lot of Blur this season. Then I'll worry about what England thinks."

"Gentlemen," Booth said. "WorldWide serves many constituencies. Room for everyone. Maybe marketing could get research to do some call-outs on the new Loudatak songs. Don't say who it is, just play the hook and see what kind of response you get. Perhaps Loudatak can tap into a new audience. If not, there's always Branson."

Everyone laughed except Bruce Gilbert. Roger Rose said, "Have you heard what's the difference between Branson, Missouri, and Jurassic Park? At Jurassic Park the dinosaurs were alive."

Booth smiled. "Moving on, what is the current status of Lydya's record?"

Lydya Hall was WorldWide's best-selling artist, a crossover pop diva who had missed her last five album delivery deadlines owing, it was whispered, to a substance abuse problem.

"Is she still sucking the crack pipe?" Roger Rose asked.

The SVP of press shivered and flapped her hands and said loudly, "That is not acceptable from anyone in this room, Roger! That is a slan-der! Lydya has been going through some emotional ups and downs because of the end of her marriage and a brutal custody battle over her children. As she was married to her manager, the situation is incredibly demanding and complicated. She is working at the same time to evolve her music to the next level. She is still a young woman, she does not want to go to Vegas. This is a time when this whole company should be supporting Lydya and cheering her on. I have a hard enough time dealing with these sick rumors in the gutter press without having World-Wide executives propagate them."

No one spoke for a minute. Then Roger Rose said, "I only ask because the last time I saw her in London she asked if I could get her some crack."

Bruce Gilbert broke up laughing. The SVP of press broke her pencil.

"What you're all telling me," Booth said, "is that two of what should be our biggest Christmas albums are in jeopardy. We gotta get Lydya off drugs and Loudatak back on. Anybody got anything that's going to help us make our bonuses?"

"I do." Joe Precious looked out from behind his little round sunglasses. "As most of you know, I have been assembling a deal for World-Wide to buy fifty-one percent of the hip-hop label Solidarity. Solidarity is two young entrepreneurs who have written and produced a series of singles, cassettes, and CDs that have sold upwards of eight million copies in the last two and a half years. With WorldWide distribution behind them, I believe Solidarity can be the garden for a whole new crop of platinum artists. The first major release on the new WorldWide Solidarity imprint will be ready in August. It is by a rapper called Brute Apache. He has already established his bona fides with guest appearances on albums by other Solidarity stars. I predict that by Christmas of this year Brute Apache will have a number-one album and we will all earn our full incentive packages."

"Thanks very much, Joe," Roger Rose said. "I'll be off, then."

"That's great, Joe," Booth said. "You all have the release schedule. Anything else we need to talk about while everybody's here?"

Zoey sure wasn't going to mention Black Beauty. Last time she brought up that project to Booth, he suggested she talk them into using as their producer a Manhattan studio owner to whom WorldWide owed a big bill. Booth thought the studio owner would drop the debt in ex-

change for getting a chance to be a record producer. Zoey tried to sell
Black Beauty on the plan, telling them it would mean unlimited studio
time. They said no because he was straight, white, and male. Booth
never asked about it again and Zoey did not tell him.

"Come on, people," Booth said. "This is your meeting."

Crash Cronin painted a rosy picture of Nashville's projects. Roger
Rose gave a quick summary of the British division's plans. David Knopft
talked about the club scene in Germany. Cantone noticed that Al Hamilton had stopped tapping on his laptop. No one cared about the club
scene in Germany.

The door to the conference room opened and DeGaul came in and
took a seat by the wall. Roger Rose grinned and waved to him. Everyone
sat up a little straighter. Knopft wrapped up his summary of what shook
the Hun's tailfeather.

"Welcome, Bill," Booth said.

"Hello, you all," DeGaul said. Everybody said hi. "Go ahead with
your meeting."

"We're talking about our fall priorities," Booth told DeGaul. Then
he addressed the table. "Most of you have already met and heard Cokie
Shea. People, I cannot overemphasize how excited WorldWide is about
this artist. The work Crash and his team in Nashville have already done
with Cokie delivers on every promise I heard in the demo tape she
slipped me in the coat-check room of a cigar bar last winter."

There were appreciative chuckles all around. Booth was polishing
into myth the legend of how he discovered Cokie. The SVP of press was
forming headlines in her mind.

Booth went on: "The Cokie Shea campaign is going to involve every
person in this room. This is not about subtlety or creating a low-level
street buzz. This is about Garth numbers. This is our *Thriller*. I'm not
kidding. Expectations are that high. Of course we are coming out of
Nashville and we want to cultivate and protect that base." He turned to
Crash Cronin and smiled. "We know how jealous country radio is.
Cokie's at Fanfare, Cokie's doing Nashville Network and CMT, Cokie's
cutting a song for a Tammy Wynette tribute album, Cokie's frying cat-
fish on some Birmingham cooking show. Crash is also working over-
time to get her a duet on Alan Jackson's next album."

Everyone murmured approvingly.

"At the same time we are looking at the right film soundtrack to introduce Cokie to the mainstream without pissing off the country community. But we must protect the base. People, I want each of you to think, regardless of your regular constituencies, 'What can I do to help Cokie Shea happen?' Is Regis looking for a guest host? Is *The View* broadcasting from Nashville? Is Oprah doing something on single girls chasing their dreams in the big city? Get Cokie in there!

"David, is there a track on Cokie's album that you could take to one of your German remixers and turn into a European club hit? Joe—think about this for a minute—is there some bit on Cokie's album that could be a sample on Brute Apache's CD? Think out of the box on this.

"I don't want this to feel like a hype, but I do want every mom, dad, and child in America—and Europe—to wake up over the next six months and learn about Cokie Shea in a way that makes them feel like they discovered her on their own. I want all of this to be perfectly coordinated to feel spontaneous. Now, let's hear what I'm talking about."

Booth went to the stereo and tried to get a DAT to play. Several highly paid music executives joined in to no avail. Booth's secretary appeared out of nowhere and hit the right buttons. Cokie's voice filled the room. The song was "The High Cost of Lovin'," nicely played and slickly produced. While Booth tapped his pen on the table, his assistant lowered the lights and pulled down a white screen, onto which were projected expensive *Vanity Fair*-style photographs of Cokie in a variety of sexy, friendly, and exuberant poses.

The song ended and everyone clapped. Booth held up his hand. Another track began. It was a slowed-down version of "How It Really Was," Cokie's song about talking to a child about the dad he never knew. Now the projections of Cokie on the wall were moody black-and-white shots of a serious artist strumming her guitar. People applauded again. The final number was a big, string-arranged version of "I Wouldn't See You Anymore," the ballad she sang for Jim in St. Pierre. The song still didn't have a chorus or middle section, but now it went up a step with each new verse and Cokie's vocal built from a whisper to a chandelier-shaking crescendo that escalated at the end to a sustained high note such as would break all Ella Fitzgerald's china.

Everyone at the table clapped and said wow and oh boy are we in the money while the lights came on and DeGaul stood up and walked around to stand behind Booth.

"Pretty good, huh?" DeGaul said. "And let's not forget that to secure, sign, and protect this act, your president, J. B. Booth, fought off a mob of mad Brazilians, got kidnapped, escaped, and beat up four guys with his side slit open! And he's not even taking points on the record."

Everyone laughed and applauded. The SVP of press was making notes like a court stenographer on Judgment Day.

"That's typical J. B. Booth," DeGaul went on. "Harvard lawyer, Vietnam Marine, ass-kickin' street fighter. I said to Lois Booth after the kidnapping, when J.B. was laid up, 'The scariest part of this whole thing is the thought of Booth in bed with time on his hands.' "

Everyone laughed except Al Hamilton, who was studying J.B.'s expression. It gave away nothing. DeGaul would place in Booth's hands the means for Booth to someday destroy him and laugh about it. Hamilton wondered what Booth was thinking, and if when the time came he would have the will to seize power from the man who had made him.

DeGaul continued: "Of course, J.B. refused to take any time off. He set up an office in a hospital room in town and kept you all jumping. Now some of the work J.B. devoted himself to in that hospital is coming to fruition. Cokie Shea is going to be one of the biggest, brightest talents WorldWide has ever had. And I know J.B. will continue to work closely with Crash and the Nashville cats and with Cokie herself to make sure she gets all the success she deserves. Jerusalem and some of the other new signings are proof that WorldWide will never rest on past accomplishments. We are always looking for the next thing. The deal with Solidarity and so many of the new urban projects Joe Precious and his crew are pulling in is proof of that.

"I have an announcement to make. I know you've all noticed that Dave 'the Rave' Knopft is with us today from Hamburg. And no one can ignore my old friend Roger—I call him 'the English'—Rose. Let me tell you why they're here. And it's not just to make the secretaries miserable."

Someone chuckled politely.

DeGaul said, "On Wednesday we are going to announce the restructuring and consolidation of all WorldWide's foreign divisions into a single company, WorldWide ILG. International Labels Group. The companies on the continent, including free-standing imprints like Filu and VDVC, will all be brought under the WorldWide ILG umbrella and headquartered in Berlin. Copresidents of WorldWide ILG will be Dave Knopft, in his fancy new digs by the Brandenburg Gate, and Roger Rose, maintaining the current WorldWide operation in London.

"I don't have to tell you all the opportunities that are available to us in the new Europe. The changes going on over there almost month to month are just unprecedented. It's appropriate to go into the twenty-first century with a fresh approach to what's going to be a whole new international business landscape.

"Now, I know what you're all wondering. How will these two brilliant, aggressive, ambitious characters run a company together without killing each other?"

"No," Bruce Gilbert said, "I just want to know if I can watch."

DeGaul said, "Here's how. I got the greatest ref in the world. Because in the same announcement on Wednesday, it will be made public that the chief executive officer and top dog of all of WorldWide ILG will be—who else could it be?—the fighting Marine who wears the scars of battle, J. B. Booth!"

Everyone applauded. Booth stood and made a little half bow and shook hands with DeGaul, who put his arm around his shoulder and squeezed him.

"Thanks, Bill," Booth said. "Thanks, guys. Now, let me make one thing clear. Just because I'm gonna be spending a lot of nights sleeping on those Virgin Airlines barber chairs, it doesn't mean I'm going to be any less in your shit than I ever have been."

Booth the regular guy! People said ha ha ha.

"I am still going to function as president of WorldWide USA. But while I am marching through Europe, I am honored to announce that many of the oversight duties for U.S. operations will revert to the man who really does it all anyway—our leader, our pope, our big kahuna—William DeGaul."

More clapping, DeGaul raised his hand.

Booth continued: "My hope is that over the next five years we are going to integrate everything that's best about all our operations, while respecting what's particular to each individual country and corporate culture."

"Is WorldWide Latino part of this?" Jim Cantone asked.

"Eventually," DeGaul said. "It will function as part of WorldWide ILG, but we are going to give J.B. a little time to get all of Europe humming before we send him back to Brazil." DeGaul put his hand to the side of his mouth as if telling a secret and stage-whispered, "He tends to get a little violent down there. The locals are scared of him."

All the people around the table agreed that this was big news, indeed, and certainly the greatest alliance since Simon met Garfunkel. Roger Rose said he had not seen so promising a blend of goodwill and shared resources since the Hitler-Stalin pact. Cantone made a mental bet with himself that Knopft would be running his hemisphere alone within a year if Rose didn't learn to clam up.

"There's one last piece of this scenario I want to lay out," Booth said. "Although I intend to remain in touch with American operations, and although Bill will make the big decisions, I will need to let go of some of my day-to-day domestic duties regarding numbers, contracts, meetings with lawyers—all that fun stuff. So with Bill's blessing, I will make official what has always been true in fact. Brother Al Hamilton will assume the newly created title of executive vice president of WorldWide USA, with responsibilities for all the internal operations of this company. So from now on if you don't like your car allowance, leave me out of it! Go bitch to Al!"

More clapping. Hamilton stood up, smiled at everyone in turn, and sat down.

"That's the news, people," DeGaul said. "I don't have to tell you all how much J.B., Al, Dave, and Roger deserve these promotions. World-Wide has had a fantastic run these last few years, and with executives like these at the helm—and good, talented folks like you all at the top level—ya ain't seen nothin' yet!"

There were celebratory toasts and admonitions not to tell the lesser staff until Tuesday so that the press announcement could go off unhitched. Booth and DeGaul eventually made their way to DeGaul's office for some private back-rubbing. At 6:00 P.M. the whole party reassembled at an Upper East Side restaurant for drinks and war stories.

Cantone was ordering an orange juice at the bar when Roger Rose sat down on the stool next to him and ordered a gin-and-lemon. Rose made a great ceremony of unscrewing his wedding band and dropping it into his shirt pocket. He smiled at Jim and said, "Let the holidays begin!"

. . .

An hour later Cantone came out of the subway and around the corner toward his apartment as the sun was sinking in the new summer sky. Daylight savings was back; these were the longest days of the year.

At the top of the block he greeted an old man called Captain Tim who lived in a shelter nearby. Captain Tim's one possession was a folding lawn chair on which he sat all day long, greeting his neighbors as they passed. He did animal impersonations and little magic tricks for the twins, who insisted he was related to Santa Claus.

"How are you today, Daddy?" Captain Tim asked Cantone.

"Everything's shipshape, Cap'n," Cantone answered.

"Your missus and the little ones have been out working on the trees all afternoon."

As Jim got closer to his building he saw Jane and the boys digging earnestly at the small square of earth around the base of one of the elm trees planted in the sidewalk in front of it. Walking along, he saw that fresh flowers had been planted at every tree on the block, and brave little fences erected to discourage dogs and litterers.

It was a hopeless enterprise, Jim thought, but it moved him beyond all proportion that his family was out there trying. He watched his beautiful wife and perfect little boys spading and spooning the black Manhattan soil, positioning their flowers with care and confidence.

Mark saw him first and came running. "Daddy! Daddy!" Both little boys flew toward him and wrapped their dirty arms around his legs. Jane stood up and collected her garden tools.

"What do you think?" she said. "I don't know how much good these fences will do, but we have to try."

Jim was carrying a kid in each arm. Luke wiped his hands on Jim's shirt.

"It's great, Jane," he said. "It's summer, it's warm, and you guys are making our street bloom. I'm proud of the Cantone family."

"How was the big meeting? Were you late?"

"Nah. It turned out to be nothing, really. Just moving the chess pieces around. What do you guys want to do for supper? Want to go out for pizza?"

"Don't you have to go to the studio with Jerusalem?"

"I'm bushed. I want to be with you guys."

"If you think that's relaxing," Jane said, "you're in for a shock."

"Daddy, Daddy," Luke said, pulling at Jim's collar. "Can we bring some pizza back for Captain Tim?"

"Sure, Bobo."

Luke screamed, "HEY, CAPTAIN TIM! WE'RE GONNA BRING YOU PIZZA!"

Down the block Captain Tim smiled in his lawn chair and waved. Jim unlocked the door to the building and held it open for his family.

As she squeezed past him he whispered, "Hey, Jane—you want another baby?"

"Hey, Jim," she said, "you want another wife?"

Cantone pulled his easygoing subordinate Flute Bjerke into his office and asked him to translate some arcane bookkeeping gobbledygook between A&R and product management. It looked to Jim like double-billing, and Flute's signature was on a pile of odd documents. Flute kept smiling and repeating that this was just how it always worked, the forms were filled out by the product managers and sent to A&R for signatures before going on to accounts payable. Jim backed up and walked through what was wrong—or at least confusing—about the system as he read it. Jim went through his entire thought process three times, holding up the forms to illustrate each point as he did. Flute smiled and nodded.

Finally Jim gave up and said, "So who would know?"

"Business affairs, I guess," Flute said. Then he smiled inscrutably at Jim and said, "I know where you got that shirt."

"What?"

"That shirt. You had that made at Veston and Arles, didn't you?"

"My shirt? No." He looked at his shoulder. "My wife gave me this for Christmas."

"She got it made at Veston and Arles. Very nice."

Jim let Flute go back to whatever he did all day. He knew his shirt came from the Gap. It was pressed, which set it apart from the combat gear he wore most days. Jim was inclined to khaki T-shirts under loose, military jacket shirts. He often wore army pants with multiple pockets, or imitations from the secondhand stores on St. Mark's Place. He wore sneakers in the summer and work boots in winter. He had been dressing like this as long as he'd been in New York. It was only a slight variation on how he dressed in college. Bjerke's comment brought to the top of Jim's mind a feeling that had been creeping up on him since his first day at WorldWide.

This was a place where people judged you by what you wore. Flute Bjerke, a bit of a traditionalist, still dressed in the classic middle-period David Geffen ensemble aped by aspiring music honchos since the early eighties: short hair, pressed jeans, loafers without socks, a simple but expensive T-shirt, and a thousand-dollar jacket. Most of the WorldWide brass had moved on with the times to a slick but comfortable post-ICM elegance.

Jim did not want to be shallow or give in to some unspoken corporate dress code. Neither did he want to be one of those sad cases who keeps trying to dress like a kid years after it stops being appropriate.

I hope I'm not turning into one of those lingerers, Jim said to the ghost of his reflection in the window. Oh, those lingerers were sad cases. He had seen them in rock clubs as long as he could remember. Middle-aged men squeezing into tight pants and then walking like cowboys from the pain. Bald men growing long ponytails. Men with expanding melon heads who wrapped desperate goatees around their double chins. Squat gnomes in faded tour T-shirts and black jeans with baggy asses and even—the saddest sight of all—the Levi's label with the waist measurement ripped off.

Jim had long ago promised himself that when the jig was up he'd know it, and he'd make smooth the midlife transition from beauty to dignity. He realized now that no man ever thinks that day is here, which is why those poor pony-tailed baggy-assed melon-headed gnomes keep combing their hair forward to fool only themselves.

Is thirty too young for a midlife crisis? Or, Jim wondered, is a midlife crisis what happens when a man keeps doing what he's always done but starts to look ridiculous doing it? A twenty-four-year-old who buys his first motorcycle just came into some money and can finally afford to satisfy a dream. A forty-year-old who buys his first motorcycle is battling menopause.

Jim was thirty. He wasn't sure what that meant these days. It still felt young, but maybe that was self-deluding. When he was nineteen he worked summers with a thirty-year-old guy who thought he was one of the kids. It was pathetic.

Like many of his friends, Jim had extended his teenage years through most of his twenties. His job at Feast had been an extension of adolescent interests. The last three years had been a series of shocks and adjustments: Jane getting pregnant; the decision to have the baby; the baby being twins; getting married; Jane quitting work; leaving Feast and moving into the high tax bracket at WorldWide. This career he had stumbled into out of college without consideration was now a necessity.

Jim had to work out how to become a man. How much of your youth were you meant to keep, and what should a man let go? He wished, in a new way, that his father were alive to talk with. For years after his dad's death Jim had taken comfort in being able to know what his father would say about most big issues that faced him. But now his father had been dead for more of Jim's life than he had been alive, and on these middle-aged matters, he had no idea what the old man would think. This next bit Jim would have to work out for himself.

He picked up hints like an illegal immigrant learning English from the radio. When the other male SVPs were in public they'd make small talk about sports or investments or the opening figures on the latest movie. (Sex was not generally on the agenda, as the wrong word in front of the wrong person could plant a red flag in your personnel file.) But in private groups of no more than two or three, when there was no one around to overhear, they would whisper about hairdressers, tailors, and personal trainers like second wives at the country club social. Jim learned that if he played along a little, if he asked where one of his buddies got those shoes, or mentioned that he was worried about a strand of gray, he would be invited into a brotherhood of secret enthusiasm and shared passion. All around him, he came to understand, high-powered middle-aged heterosexual men were enhancing their complexions with creams and whitening their teeth, trading diets, comparing strategies to thicken and color their hair, poking in contact lenses, sharing tips on

cleansing scrubs and worrying about—no other word for it—their figures.

It was as if every boy who dreamed of growing up to be Keith
Richards had decided as a man to become Felix Unger.

Jim noticed that among the well-groomed, there was a subtle exclu-
sion of those who remained off-the-rack. On three different occasions
Jim heard executives with expensive dental work and beautiful skin
choose to pass over qualified Oscar Madisons for important assign-
ments or, in one case, a promotion with the same subtle dismissal: "He's
a talented guy, but he's not really buttoned-down."

Jim studied himself in the mirrored wall as he rode up the escalator
and wondered if those *GQ*-groomed arbiters considered him suffi-
ciently buttoned-down, figuratively and literally.

Had Jim been a wiseass or a finger pointer he might have mocked
these conceits and become cocky about his own good looks and athletic
health. But he was by nature a joiner, and so he overcame a reluctance
born of years of low budgets and went out to buy some new clothes.

He went to Emporio Armani but he couldn't handle the salesman
telling him to have a drink at the little Armani bar and "Put it on my tab"
while he rang up two hundred dollars' worth of cummerbund.

He went to Barney's and saw a nice brown sport coat and a blue
Sunday go-to-meeting suit. He tried them on, got his inseam measured,
and felt pretty good about it. But when the clerk said, "Two thousand,
eight hundred dollars," Jim could not let go of his credit card. He could
afford it, but he could not stand it. He could buy a jacket and suit indis-
tinguishable from these at Sears, and give the three-thousand-dollar difference to PETA.

He went home a failure.

"I don't see any bags," Jane said. "Getting alterations?"

"I bought two pairs of black wingtip lace-up shoes," Jim said. "One
with little airholes for summer, like my grandfather used to wear. But it
was, like, three grand for a blue suit with one pair of pants. I couldn't do
it, Jane."

"Then don't do it. It's only clothes. What do you care about the
opinion of anyone who would judge you by what you wear?"

"I feel like some kind of arrested adolescent that I can't get this together. The senior staff at work all dress a certain way. And the people who dress the way I do now are sort of the rank and file. I don't want to look like I'm copping an attitude toward the other executives and I don't want to seem like I'm condescending to the staff."

Jane turned away and started going through the bills. "No one but you is thinking about this. You should forget it."

Jim felt foolish. He went to work the next day in his old army pants, with a starched white shirt and a tie. One of the guys who brought the mail around said, "Court date?"

At lunch he heard the head of business affairs say to the head of human resources, "I like his policies but I can't vote for a man who wears a Timex watch. What will Wall Street think?"

In the restroom Legal advised Marketing, "If you tuck your undershirt in your underpants your shirt won't bunch up at the waist."

That afternoon Jim went to Mano 2 Mano, a reasonably priced clothing store on Sixth Avenue, and bought two suits, six blue dress shirts, eight pairs of socks, cuff links, two blazers, and three pairs of dark blue slacks—for a total price considerably less than what the suit and jacket cost at Barney's.

He was so hopped-up from his breakthrough that he even bought some workshirts at Abercrombie & Fitch that were exactly like the ones he usually bought at the Salvation Army except that these cost seventy bucks. Home and triumphant, he wrote a two-thousand-dollar check to People for the Ethical Treatment of Animals and put it in an envelope and stuck on a stamp.

Jane kept her feelings to herself.

On his third day dressed for success, he learned a lesson about cost-cutting. He stopped for a pee on his way to a staff meeting. He flushed, closed up, and the zipper came off in his hand. It did not just snap or break—it lifted right off his pants like the skeleton coming out of a split fish.

He gathered his pants together as well as he could, belted up, and closed his jacket to try to disguise his open fly as he walked stiff-legged down the corridor and sunk into a chair and under the table. Al Hamilton, who paid no discernible notice to fashion, came and sat next to him, and in the moments while the others at the table were rustling papers and making small talk, Jim whispered, "Al, whatever you do, don't ask me to stand up in front of the group. The zipper just came off my new pants."

Hamilton glanced down at Jim's suit and said matter-of-factly, "What did you do? Buy from Mano 2 Mano?"

That's how Cantone, a simple boy from Maine, ended up in Prada.

DeGaul and Booth were in the back of Booth's car on their way to a fund-raising dinner the New York Public Library was throwing for a Sicilian opera singer.

"You going to the Vineyard for the fourth?" DeGaul asked.

"I don't think we're gonna make it this year. Cokie's playing a showcase in Austin and I need to be there."

"You're practically managing that girl. You should take a commission."

"I got Garth Goes at Edgewater looking after her."

"Don't tell me about it, I might get subpoenaed."

"Just play Sergeant Schultz."

"I know nothing."

Edgewater was the publishing company in which Booth had been a partner before joining his pal DeGaul at WorldWide. He had been required to cut his ties with that company when he joined the WorldWide team. On paper, he had.

"I have to talk to you about something serious," Booth said. "This situation with Lydya is not getting better."

"She still sucking the glass snorkel?"

"She was supposed to do a ribbon cutting for some women's health center yesterday. She was almost incoherent. They did a photo op with some little kids and she was scaring them, she smelled bad. She stood there scratching herself. I gotta tell you, Bill, it's this close to making the papers."

"Intervention?"

"There's nobody around her who's not scared of getting thrown off the honeypot. She's got her sister and brother on staff. She's divorcing her manager husband. He's using custody of the kids to blackmail her into screwing herself over on all the business. The lawyer's gone over to his side. It's goddam horrible."

"What can we do?"

"Okay, that's what I need to talk to you about. I'm playing good cop on this one because I have to make her feel she has a safe haven. I want her to believe I am her one true friend among all the turncoats."

"You want me to be bad cop?"

"How do you feel about that? I've been telling her I would be happy to wait forever for her next musical masterpiece, but I'm getting big pressure from up top. Well, she knows there's only one guy big enough to scare me. I hate to put you in this position, but I don't know how else to work it."

DeGaul stared out the window. "That's okay. You've been the villain to make me look good enough times. Do I need to do anything? You want me to send her a nasty e-mail?"

"Lookit, what I need you to do . . ."

DeGaul and Booth's cell phones began beeping at the same time. Booth answered first. "Yeah," he said. "He's right here. We're in the middle of something, what is it?" He said to DeGaul, "It's Royal Nightingale from St. Pierre."

"Jeez," DeGaul said. He answered his own phone. "What is it? He is? He's on Booth's phone, too. Yeah, right now. Okay, give him to me. I got him here, J.B. Sorry about that. Won't take a minute.

"Roy! What's up, man? You caught me about to drive into the tunnel, I may lose you. . . . Yeah. . . . Jeez, Roy, can this wait? I'm in the middle of three things and I got people here. . . . Yeah . . . yeah . . . yeah, all right. Look, I can't think about that right now, but I'll tell you what. Call back my office and ask for Cindy. Tell her I want her to cut you a check out of my canoe fund. She'll know what that is. Make sure you tell her it's the canoe fund, okay? Roy, we need to figure out if we're throwing good money after bad here. . . . I know, man, but maybe we can't afford the fine white pea stone. Maybe we just pour some cement and paint it yellow. . . . Yeah, I'm about to drive into the tunnel, Roy. . . . Okay, man, I love you, too. Don't go smoking up the profits. I'm losing you, Roy! I'm paying the toll now, I gotta go."

DeGaul clicked off. "Sorry, J.B. Childhood friend. His mother needs a new iron lung. What were we talking about?"

"I need you to put the fear of God into Lydya. You up for that?"

"Sure. What do I do?"

"How long we got? Hey, Randy, go up Madison and come back down through the park, okay?" Booth reached in his jacket pocket and unfolded a typed call-sheet. "I want you to call her now and show her visions of holy hellfire. You up for that?"

"I'm Marjoe, pal."

"Remember, I'm the poor schnook who's sticking up for her. You've had all you can take."

"Yeah, I can be a mean bastard. I'll pretend I'm you."

"I need you to be meaner than you've ever been, Bill," Booth said quietly. "I need you to reach right through her inebriation and slap her. No one expects Bill DeGaul to be cruel. It will shock her and I hope it will infuriate her. But I think it's the last chance to reach her. If you can't blow a hole in her defenses, we'll be going to Lydya's funeral."

Lydya's phone rang twelve times. Her sister finally answered.

"Ruth? Bill DeGaul from WorldWide. How are you?"

Booth sliced his finger across his neck, warning DeGaul not to be nice. DeGaul nodded.

"I need to talk to Lydya right now. It's an emergency. . . . Yeah, well you better wake her up for this."

Muffled voices argued in the background. DeGaul held his hand over the mouthpiece and looked around. They were passing a movie house. "Have you seen the new Woody Allen?" he asked Booth. "I hear it's pretty good."

Lydya Hall came on the phone. She sounded normal. "Wild Bill, how's the king of the western world?"

"Right now I'm pretty pissed off. I got four lawyers trying to stop the editor of *People* magazine from going with a cover story about your cocaine addiction, of which they have irrefutable proof including hidden movie footage. We're going to keep that out of print, but it's going to cost us a fortune. I'll probably be served with a writ taking me to court to testify about how many times you missed your album deadlines. And believe me, these guys know the answers before they ask the questions. I have every reason to believe that you are on the road to losing all your money as well as your future royalties to your husband. And no matter what he tells you now, once *Inside Edition* starts running film of you freebasing, he won't have to take the kids away from you. The courts will declare you an unfit mother and give them to him.

"I don't know if you can save your career or your reputation, Lydya. It's probably too late for that. But it might still be possible to keep you out of jail."

There was silence on the other end. DeGaul thought she had hung up. Then he heard voices shouting at each other in the distance. Someone picked up the phone. There were footsteps and Lydya came on the line again.

"Who do you think you are, DeGaul?" She tore off the words with her teeth. "I thought you'd be too much of a mensch to lie like that. You windbag. You pompous tick. You don't know one thing you're talking about."

"Bullshit, Lydya. Everybody knows. Look around. Your sister Ruth knows, she's just too scared to tell you the truth. I know you love that drug now but there's no question you are giving it up. The only question is if you're going to do it by your own choice, with doctors to help you, or if you're going to withdraw in jail, with some dirty prison guard videotaping you puking to sell to the news."

"You don't scare me. You've done more drugs than I ever will."

"You can't handle it."

"You don't scare me, Big Bill. I've been attacked by real men. You're just an old blowhard. Talk to me about people laughing behind my back. You're a clown, a relic. You screw yourself, Wild Bill."

"I don't care what you think of me, Lydya. But when this phone call is over you better think about what I said, because it's all true. Think about how you want your children to remember their mommy. Because you have to choose now if you will be a dead junkie, a destitute ex-con, or a successful woman who went through a bad time and beat it. Today you have those three choices. In a couple of days it'll just be the first two."

"You don't know anything about my situation."

"I do. One more thing you should know. J. B. Booth has put his own job on the line for you. He has made so many excuses for your inability to deliver an album anyone wants to hear that at this point I would say there is a good chance he will be fired when you fail. You have one real friend left in this company, and in your selfishness you're going to destroy him, too."

Lydya hung up. DeGaul sat listening to the dial tone and then folded his phone and put it in his pocket. He looked at Booth and said, "How's that for a bad cop?"

"Call Serpico! That was perfect, Bill. You might have saved that woman's life."

"Yeah." DeGaul was distant. "I don't think I'll be going to the Hall house for dinner, though."

"Someday she'll thank you, man."

Booth's phone was beeping like a heart attack. He turned it off. They arrived at the library and got out of the car.

"You go on without me for a minute," Booth said to DeGaul on the sidewalk. "I gotta check in with Lois."

DeGaul went up the steps and into the library, greeting people the whole way. Booth got back into the car and turned on his phone. His assistant was looking for him.

"Yeah, I'm back. . . . Okay, put her through on the car phone." The car phone buzzed. "Hi, Lydya, what's cookin', beautiful?"

He listened to a tirade. He told his driver to cruise. WorldWide's mightiest diva could hold a single note for a long time. When she finally took a breath, Booth spoke slowly and firmly.

"Okay, sweetheart. You listen to me. First of all, my job is in no danger. Believe me. The board knows who's carrying their water. Okay? So don't you worry about me. Now I'm going to tell you some things and I want you to listen very carefully. Hear what I'm saying.

"Number one. There is no *People* magazine story. That's bullshit.

That's a little game DeGaul plays to scare artists into doing what he wants. I'll bet he told you he had three lawyers working round the clock to keep it quiet, right? Four? Unbelievable. Inflation. Yes, he's run that con before, believe me.

"Number two. There is no secret videotape. That's another lie. I swear to you. I told him if he played that game with anyone ever again, I would resign in protest. Oh yeah. Yeah, he's done it before. He did it with Loudatak, he did it with a lot of people. Lydya, he tried it on his ex-wife when they were breaking up. You know what happened? Her lawyer subpoenaed the tape! Yes! That shut him up for a while.

"Number three. You will never, ever, ever go to jail. That cannot happen and that will not happen. Telling you that, that's low even for him.

"Look, sweetheart, this situation has really gotten awful. I can't stand by and watch people hurt you anymore. Let me tell you what's going to happen now. You know Asa Calhoun, my lawyer? I'm bringing him into this. Tonight. I want you to pack a little overnight bag. I'm going to get Asa to come out to your house and pick you up. I got a doctor friend runs a little place in Pennsylvania. Used to be a convent. No, listen to me. It's a retreat house, you check yourself in and out. You can leave whenever you want, go out to supper, come back. It's a hundred percent voluntary.

"You gotta do this, Lydya, it's our only defense. If—God forbid—it ever gets to the point where we have to show you don't have a problem, we get a note from my doctor friend saying you checked into his place and he treated you and everything's A-okay.

"Listen, my love. You have to do this for me. I need you to help me make sure the old snake doesn't have an opening to move against you. Now I'm going to go out to Connecticut and pack a bag of my own and I'm going to meet you in Pennsylvania later tonight. Yes. Yes. I just need a couple of hours to get out to Greenwich and get down there. But I'm going to call my doctor friend—his name is Doctor Golub, you'll like him, he's like Jimmy Stewart—I'm going to call Doctor Golub and tell him you're coming and I'm going to call Asa Calhoun and have him pick you up. Okay? Okay.

"No, don't you thank me. I thank you for being so strong. I take strength from your example.

"Yes, he is. Yes, Bill is a real rat. I don't know, he didn't used to be this bad, he's getting worse. But he can't hurt you and he can't hurt me. We're tougher than that old bastard. We're street kids."

Booth coddled Lydya for another minute and then hung up and dialed Asa Calhoun. "It's me. The bird is in hand. You all set? Where are you? Oh, you're kidding, I just left DeGaul there. Do you see him? Asa, come on. You got the directions to her house? Okay, her sister's name is Ruth. I told talent I'd meet you two out at the animal hospital around midnight. Yeah, I got a suitcase in the trunk here. I gotta go to this thing you're at for a couple of hours. So why don't you get your ass out of there and let me come in and you go pick up the talent. Hey, she's going to be a good client for you, Kingfish. She's going to make you mucho qwan. Yeah, we do well by doing good. Now get out of there, I'm coming in."

"Back to the party, boss?" the driver said.

"Yeah. What do you think, Randy? Who's the best bad cop?"

"You are the bad lieutenant, Jack. You remind me of me."

"Omerta, brother, omerta. You listen to that last bunch of tapes I gave you?"

"Yeah. I liked that one song by that new group you got with the chick singer."

"Jerusalem."

"No, not them. The other one."

"Who?"

"Wait, I got my notes here. Black Beauty. They had a nice one."

"Find it for me, we'll listen on the way to Pennsylvania. Here—pull up over here. I want to scope the perimeter before I go in."

Booth and his driver sat in front of a hydrant and watched the rich people going up the steps. "Here comes Asa. Okay, Randy. I'll meet you right back here in ninety minutes. Can you please not nail any women in the car between now and then?"

"No way. I'm spending tonight in a convent."

• • •

Booth joined DeGaul at their table just as the chicken was being served.

"You just missed the Kingfish," DeGaul said. "He bolted out of here. Must have heard an ambulance go by."

"That's good," Booth said, snapping open his napkin. "I'll eat his Jell-O."

They had the bad luck to be seated across from an agent for a has-been seventies singing duo. He tried to sell Booth and DeGaul on a re-union album. It took twenty minutes to convince him it would never happen. When that sank in the agent banged right into his next gear and started crowing about his wife's business. The wife, blond as a pancake and just as appealing, sat beside him beaming and passed a copy of her business card to everyone at the table.

"What Judith does is, she organizes your photo albums," the agent said.

Booth and DeGaul nodded. The agent said, "I'll bet both of you have dozens and dozens of pictures in envelopes all over your house, right? Sure! Each of us does! Who has time to put them in albums? Ju-dith has an incredible eye. She's really an artist. What she does is, she goes through all your photos and arranges them by theme, by subject, by year. She'll juxtapose a snapshot of a daughter with a portrait of her mom at the same age. It's really something. She takes all your stray pic-tures and assembles them into a beautifully conceived one-of-a-kind unique rare first-edition book of *you* and *your family* and *your life*. She did some for the Rockefellers, she did one of the Dillers, she designed a special book as an anniversary gift from a certain world-famous super-model to her boyfriend."

"We can't say who," Judith giggled.

"No, we can't, but it was a *magical* gift."

"How much do you get for a job like that?" Booth asked, knifing his sweet roll.

"She could do your family's album for thirty thousand," the agent said.

"Ha. I'll say she could. No, really, Judith. It sounds like something my wife might like for her birthday. What do people pay you?"

"Thirty thousand," Judith said.

"That's including everything," the agent said. "Time, transporta-tion, and a beautiful album. You should see the paper Judith uses. All watermarked. It's exquisite."

"Sounds like it," DeGaul said, looking at Booth. "J.B., I think Lois would go ape over a thoughtful gift like that. You should go for it. Maybe a whole series, the Booths through the ages. Multivolume, like *The Story of Civilization*."

The agent and his Judith beamed.

"I dunno," Booth said. "The kid who cleans our pool would probably do it for twenty-nine-five."

· · ·

Collecting their coats later, Booth and DeGaul shared a laugh.

"Can you believe Donny and Marie there with the photo albums?" Booth said. "Holy cats! Thirty grand to stick my pictures in a book! You think she gets many takers?"

"Hey," DeGaul said, "if she only makes one sale a week . . ."

They walked out to the street together. DeGaul said he was going to fly out and spend the Fourth of July with his kids. "Good luck with Cokie, say hi to Lois," he told Booth. "Don't blow your fingers off with those firecrackers."

· · ·

Randy had the car where it was supposed to be. He drove Booth out to Pennsylvania. When they got to the clinic, Asa Calhoun had already been and gone. Lydya and her sister Ruth were in the kitchen having tea with Dr. Golub. The doctor was in pajamas and a bathrobe, eating crackers. Ruth looked anxious. Lydya looked like she'd smoked enough rock to carry her through a year in the convent. The doctor smiled politely when Booth joined them. He suggested a mild sedative to help Lydya get to sleep. Better make it a mild sledgehammer, Booth thought.

After they put Lydya to bed, Booth huddled with Ruth and the doctor about her treatment. "Whatever it takes," Booth said in front of the worried sister. "I want you to send the bill to my house, Doctor. I don't want anyone at WorldWide to know she's here."

The doctor went to bed and Ruth said, "I thank God you're in Lydya's life, J.B. I never saw her like she was after DeGaul called her. How could he do that to someone? Never mind that it's Lydya Hall. How could the man do that to another human being, say those awful things about jail and losing her children? It was all just lies?"

"I'm afraid it was, Ruth. DeGaul only sees profits and losses. He doesn't realize these are fragile human beings. What can I tell you? He's old school."

"How can you work for a man like that?"

"Did you ever see that movie *Mister Roberts*? Henry Fonda played a naval officer who protected his men from the crazy captain. When I feel sorry for myself, I think of that movie. Not that I'm Henry Fonda by any stretch. My job is to be a buffer between the artists and that kind of corporate bottom-line, take-no-prisoners attitude. I'm sorry I wasn't there to protect Lydya this time."

"Well, as soon as Lydya's better she's going to skin that evil sucker. It's all she could talk about on the drive out."

"Now listen, Ruth. I need you to be very clear on this and I need you to make sure Lydya's clear. The best defense we have against DeGaul is that he does not know Lydya knows he's bluffing. Understand? That's our secret weapon. He does not know Lydya and I are sharing information. We must keep it that way. If the cat gets out of the bag, well, Lydya could survive it but I'm afraid I couldn't. I would be asked to depart the fifty-fifth floor without benefit of the elevator if you catch my meaning."

Ruth nodded without blinking.

"I think that within the year it may come to a head between DeGaul and me over what kind of company WorldWide is going to be. I want Lydya healthy and strong when that day comes. Because I know she is going to kick this thing, and keep her kids and her money and her reputation. And I believe she is going to finish an album that will prove to the world that Lydya Hall is the number-one female artist in America and the most important single act in the WorldWide family.

"When that day comes, I may need a friend in my corner. Until that day, I don't want DeGaul to know how close the three of us are. Yes?"

Ruth said she understood. She went off to check on her sister. Booth found his room and unpacked.

He lay in the dark with his thoughts. There was nothing to read except a Bible, so he stared at the ceiling. He had to be ruthless, he told himself, to get through this. He took no satisfaction in setting DeGaul and Lydya against each other. Bottom line: Lydya was now voluntarily in a place where she could get help. What else could have got her here?

Time wore on in the dark. Booth became aware of a distant whistling. It was soft and steady. He tried to place it. Was someone making tea? No, it was not in the kitchen, it was not in the building. But neither was it outdoors. He fixed on the whistle. It faded and returned. It was not inside or out.

In time he knew. It was in his head. Not in his mind, in his head. He drew in his breath sharply and felt a pain between his eyes. He let the air out and—sure enough—the whistling returned, pitched high before settling into a long, sustained note. There were tiny holes in his head somewhere, he thought. Sinuses, he figured. Perforated membranes, he supposed. The frail walls that held him together were dried up and cracking.

Was it the result of narcotics he snorted years ago? Or the scars of childhood allergies, primitive nasal sprays, pre-recall airplane glue, secondhand smoke, firsthand smoke. Or was it just the warning whistle of impending age, the starter gun for the coming collapse of all his insides? These were thoughts he would not even remember tomorrow during his working day, but tomorrow night when he finally put his head on his pillow and closed his eyes they would return. It would keep him from resting, it would give him another thing to sweat about, it would trouble his dreams.

Booth tried to shut out his anxieties by force of will. He thought about money and sex. Neither moved him. He thought about the smells of his father's barbershop when he was a boy. It was almost a comfort, but it led to bad memories: his father's business disintegrating in the early seventies, when everyone grew long hair. Booth flinched, remembering the embarrassment his old man felt when he gave in and turned the barber shop into a *styling salon,* and the shame when it made no difference.

Booth's father used to stand in the shop window and watch the long-haired kids walking past him, laughing, on their way home from high school. The same kids he gave first haircuts. The same kids he gave lollipops, and buzzcuts in summer, who sat next to their dads and got men's regulars for fifty cents. As teenagers they grew their hair down their backs and let their girlfriends trim their bangs.

All through that period, the late sixties and early seventies, Booth let his father cut his hair every three weeks. White sidewalls and Wildroot. A little Clark Gable swish in the front. The only other boys with haircuts like that in 1972 were the dweebs, the dorks, the pocket protectors. Booth felt like a dipshit. He felt ugly. He imagined the girls laughed at him. Once a new boy, a surfer from California, made a joke about Booth's haircut in the lunch line. Booth pounded out the beach boy's front tooth. Got suspended and never told his parents what the kid said that set him off.

But they still made cracks behind his back.

Booth watched his father slip an inch at a time from the middle of the middle class to the lip of losing it. There were calls during dinner from the finance company. His mother sat at the kitchen table clipping coupons and licking green stamps not for extras, for the necessities. And the unspoken cruelty was, it needn't have been that way. Booth's father was smart. He had the grades to go to college back when almost nobody went. He dreamed of being a doctor. But it was the depression and his own father was dead. So Booth's old man went to work cutting hair to support his mother and his two younger brothers. And because Booth's father passed on the chance to go to college, because he worked as a barber all day and unloaded fruit at the market at night, he was able to send his two little brothers. The middle brother became a lawyer and moved to Chicago and after their mother died was only good for a Christmas card. The youngest became the doctor Booth's father dreamed of being and then was killed in the Pacific War.

So Booth took a little abuse at school to spare the old man's feelings. And although he was not much interested in going to college, he knew he was sure as hell going to go. He enrolled at the University of Rhode Island and drank beer and went out with a lot of girls and had a great time for a semester and a half. In April he looked up and saw that while he was doing okay in his afternoon courses, he was flunking every class that met in the morning. He went to the dean to ask for a chance to put it right. The dean said he was out of luck. His professors didn't stick up for him. He was told that if he stayed in, even if he aced his finals, he would flunk out of college. His only shot was to withdraw from school now so the semester wouldn't count, and reapply in a year or so.

Booth's father did not understand. He was distraught that his son had partied his way out of the university. Booth's mother had died the year before. His father said his grief from the two tragedies was equal. He all but disowned him. When an aunt tried to intervene on the boy's behalf, his father said in front of the whole family, "So you want me to keep him as a pet."

Booth was ashamed and enraged. He saw one way to prove his father wrong and redeem himself. He went and signed up for the Marines. This was the kind of penance his old man had to respect. It was 1974, the depth of the armed forces' post-Vietnam inability to recruit cognitive men who could walk upright. The recruiting sergeants licked their lips and tucked in their bibs when Booth walked through the door.

Hell, he already had the haircut.

The great joke was, Booth would not even have considered signing up if the war had not ended in January 1973, when he was a senior in high school. He'd sweated the draft like everyone else, for all the years of promises that the war would be over by Christmas and never was. So in early '73 when the United States signed the Paris Peace Accords and all the churchbells rang and the draft was officially ended, Booth poured beer on his head with the rest of them. It was the week he turned eighteen! The draft was over, the war was over, and the drinking age was lowered. Booth and his buddies thought they'd won the pools.

So when Booth enlisted in June '74—angry and resentful though he was—it never occurred to him that under any circumstances he would end up seeing action. Everyone knew the United States would not go near another war for many years.

When in 1975 he found out he was heading to Saigon, it didn't shake him. Two years after Kissinger got a Nobel Peace Prize for ending the war, Booth no more expected to end up in a combat situation in Vietnam than he would have expected to fight Nazis if they'd sent him to Germany.

Even when Saigon was falling and Booth was herding desperate Vietnamese into the basement room where they stored the soda cans and trying to get a straight answer out of any officer in charge, it hardly sank in that the Vietnam War, that monster he'd grown up watching on TV, had caught up with him. It was only when he got back to the States that he realized he'd been part of it, he'd been in it. In the eyes of Americans, the end of the war had been moved forward from January '73 to April '75. In the eyes of Americans, Booth was a Vietnam Vet.

He played that card for all it was worth. In the fall of '76 URI took him back and all but saluted as he marched into class. He was a war veteran going to school on the G.I. Bill. The professors either deferred to him or tried to debate politics with him or looked like they were scared he'd beat them up. He stood out. He worked hard. He took easy courses. He got great grades.

He began going out with Lois that year. She was a Harvard leftist; opposites attract. He was sitting around her kitchen in Cambridge with a bunch of her Harvard friends, listening to them flap on about subjects he knew more about than they did, and it struck him: he could compete with these people. He could hold his own. In the spring of '78 he applied to Harvard as a transfer student. Lois helped him fill out the forms and write his essay. Harvard's undergraduate college was big on diversity. They were delighted to get one blue-collar Vietnam vet who'd come back from combat and dragged himself up to a 4.0 at URI. It balanced the three thousand rich kids from prep schools who couldn't lift a cricket bat.

Harvard accepted only half his credits. Booth didn't mind. He was in. And for the next three years he stayed in. He and Lois lived in a tenement on Rindge Avenue. She sold fishcakes at Legal Seafood and worked on her thesis. He spent all his time studying, cranking it out. He held on to a C average. Good enough.

His old man hung up his Marine picture in the barber shop so when people asked he could tell them, "Yeah, that's my son. He's up at Harvard now." Booth even let his hair grow a little, but by then everybody was cutting it off.

He finished in 1981. He was accepted to Suffolk Law School that fall. He and Lois married. They had bad luck with kids. She had complications from an abortion in the seventies and now she had trouble carrying a baby to term. The doctors said it wasn't related. Booth didn't care that much. Lois said she didn't either.

When he passed the bar he took interviews all over. The best offer came from a firm in New York that handled a lot of personal services contracts. That's how Booth began hooking up with record executives and managers and musicians. He made plenty of new friends. DeGaul was one of them. It was the last days of the big discos, the velvet rope at Area, wild sex, drug parties, and bands going on at 3:00 A.M. Booth got a kick out of it all. Lois had a hard time making the adjustment. He screwed around on her. She left him for a while.

When the junior half of a music publishing company went out on his own and took a couple of clients along, Booth came in as his partner. The other guy was a moron. Booth had to do everything and he was good at it. His partner eventually burned out and left. Booth changed the name of the firm to Edgewater. He brought in Garth Goes and some other drones to help out. They were all like him, blue-collar kids hungry to turn WASP. They signed some big talent.

Booth and Bill DeGaul saw eye to eye on almost everything. When the two of them got in a room and closed the door, they could cut any deal. They drank together, they fished together, they chased women together. It wasn't a big surprise when DeGaul came to Booth and said, "Look, I need someone I can trust running this company with me. Every screwhead I've had in the top job has either messed it up or tried to stab me in the back. I need you to be president of WorldWide. What will it take to make you say yes?"

Booth thought about it and named a figure. DeGaul said, "Hell, man, if you're gonna work for me you better think bigger than that."

Booth and Lois eventually reconciled. She didn't get pregnant again. He bought the house in Greenwich as evidence of his new maturity. By that time it had turned out that cocaine was dangerous, free sex could kill you, and nobody had ever really wanted to watch rock bands at four in the morning. Booth was wealthy, settled, and secure.

Secure. Funny word. His old man thought he'd be secure as a barber, 'cause after all, people always need haircuts. His uncle the young doctor must have felt secure before he got sent to war and shot. Booth was secure that Vietnam was over when he joined the Marines. His father was secure when he married a much younger woman that she'd outlive him, but Booth's mother died when she was forty-six. Booth would be forty-six soon. He was the age now his mother had been when she got sick.

Booth resolved to start tomorrow to clean up his diet. He started counting the years until he could cash in his 401(k). He counted the same number backwards to see how long that was. He thought of Lois in college, trudging up the stairs with her books and his supper. He thought about finding Cokie a house near Nashville; she had to establish residency down there before the album was done. He thought of DeGaul and him laughing about the agent with the photo albums. He thought about how much grief would break open if Lydya couldn't keep her mouth shut. He thought this bed must be broken.

Finally Booth dropped into a troubled sleep, still whistling.

Labor Day weekend Jim took Lilly Rope for a long ride from Manhattan to Maine in his new car. It was a ten-hour drive and they spent half of it listening over and over to the finished Jerusalem album. Dick, the bass player, had shown up at the last minute and invited himself along. Jim didn't mind. His mom had room. Jane and the boys had been at Jim's mother's house for the whole month of August. It was time to collect them and get ready for the first day of school. Jim, Lilly, and Dick drove up through New York State, took a ferry across Lake Champlain, and crossed the width of Vermont and New Hampshire listening to Jerusalem's recordings and talking about the future.

"When will I be able to buy a car like this?" Dick asked. Lilly curled her lip but glanced at Jim from the side of her eye. She wanted to know about money but didn't want to say so.

"I wouldn't expect any CD royalties for a while," Jim said cautiously. "Remember, we're not looking for this album to sell Alanis numbers. This is a foundation, this is a starting place. Jerusalem is going to do it right and stick around a long time."

"Hell, Jim." Dick was leaning over the center of the seat, his elbows nudging Jim and Lilly. "Listen to this! This is better than Alanis! If we did sell a couple of million, how long before I could buy a car like this?"

"The record royalties might take a year, realistically. You'd see songwriting money sooner. And of course, your live price would go up right away. Concessions might be the first money. Jerusalem sweatshirts. That's cash right in your pocket."

Dick bounced against the backseat, delighted. Lilly stared out the window, imagining her face riding up on some fat frat boy's belly.

They wound through the White Mountains with all the windows open, eating ice cream cones and listening to an album that sounded better every time they played it.

"How about your parents, Lilly?" Jim said. "Are they excited about your coming fame?"

"I don't see them," Lilly said. "They don't see each other, either. Our nuclear family exploded a long time ago."

"She's a stray atom," Dick said from the backseat. "The band's her new molecule."

"Where do they live?" Jim asked.

"My mother's in either Oregon or Alaska. My father's Australian but he could be anywhere."

"Lilly was raised by hippies," Dick said. "It's why she has no morals."

They listened to the tape for the thirteenth time. " 'Hard Hearted' is a hit," Jim said. "I don't know if we come with it right away or start with 'Jean Baptiste' to establish a base at alternative and then hit them with 'Hard Hearted.' "

"I think of 'Hard Hearted' as almost a joke song," Lilly said. "It's fun to play in a bar but I don't think it represents the band."

Dick said, "I want to slip a couple of cassettes to writers I know. People who supported us early on. I've been getting a lot of calls."

"Boy, Dick," Jim said, "I wish you'd hang off on that a little while. All these songs might not make it to the album. Anything you let out now will be bootlegged as soon as you're famous."

"I just mean one or two copies for real friends of the band."

"Let's wait until we're sequenced and mastered."

They took a break from the tape and turned on the radio. Lilly found a Boston station playing the British band Pulp. She turned it up.

"That's my old station!" Jim said. "That's where I worked right after college!"

"We're making a journey backward through the life of Jim Cantone," Lilly said happily.

"James Cantone—Behind the Music!" Dick proclaimed.

"Listen, that was a great time for me," Jim said. "When I was in high school I hung around a little college station in Farmington, up in Maine. When I got to BU I got a job at the radio station and ended up program director. It was a great, great time to be in Boston. The Pixies were around, Throwing Muses. The Lemonheads and Blake Babies and all these fantastic bands. Everybody hung out together, everybody was getting signed. It was really amazing to me to be part of it. When I got off the bus I was, like, wearing overalls and chewing on a piece of straw."

"Now you're a slick corporate mogul with two passports, four bank accounts, and three wives!" Lilly put the back of her hand to her forehead and sighed. "Where is my simple farm boy?"

When they crossed into Maine they began to lose the Boston station. Lilly fiddled with the radio dial.

"Heart of Gold" came on.

She turned it again. "Down By the River."

She kept going. "Helpless."

"Did Neil Young die?" Dick asked from the backseat.

"Welcome to Maine," Jim said. "Where the seventies never stopped."

"And you don't mean punk rock," Dick said.

"Predisco. This is the stuff I grew up on. It's *Wayne's World* up here."

They drove past farms and fields. Jim and his guests played count the hippies. Dick tugged Jim's long hair and said, "Don't forget the one behind the wheel." They pulled over to get sandwiches. There was a poster for a Livingston Taylor show. The jukebox was playing Carole King. There was a sign that said, "You are now at the exact halfway point between the equator and the North Pole." Jim thought of the endless plane ride from equatorial Brazil to the Caribbean. He thought of how far it was from the Caribbean to New York and how long it took to drive from New York to here. And all that was only halfway to the North Pole? Canada must have endless miles of nothing.

They wandered into a paperback bookstore and heard the Youngbloods—Jim was the only one who could identify that one. Lilly studied a magazine rack. It was filled with local-press earth-shoe womyn's-issue hemp-promoting nonviolent Trotskyite organic vegetarian solar-powered goddess-worshipping holistic self-help publications, one rack away from the rifle & ammo/dirt bike/snowmobile shelf. They got back in the car, laughing, and when the radio came on, so did Jonathan Edwards.

"That store looked like a Phish concert," Lilly said.

"Hey, hey," Dick said in a low, excited voice. "Dig the earth mothers in moccasins and flannel shirts. From the first time!"

"Up here, when a hippie calls his girlfriend his old lady," Lilly said, "it's frighteningly accurate."

"You guys haven't met my mom yet," Jim said. "Moonshadow."

They got back in the car and wound up mountain roads on two-lane blacktop. As they got higher into the fir trees and long views, Jim saw his friends were impressed. He was glad. He could take a joke, but he was sensitive about his home.

They listened to the radio—Joni Mitchell—and Jim noticed Lilly softly singing along. They passed a sign selling nightcrawlers that was stuck to a trash can from which was sticking out the bottom half of a dummy, dungaree legs and rubber boots.

"Look," Dick said from the backseat, "someone threw away a perfectly good Deadhead."

"We're almost there," Jim said. "You guys mind if I take a scenic detour?"

"I thought the last nine hours was a scenic detour!" Dick said.

"Go ahead, Jim," Lilly said. "It's pretty here."

Jim veered off the blacktop and drove around the lake where he had his first teenage summer romance with a vacationing girl from Boston. The father had been married twice and had about eleven kids from both wives in two cabins on the lake. They took Jim water-skiing. They let the kids drink wine with dinner. They seemed like the most sophisticated people in the world. He wondered now if that planted the seed of his wanting to go to Boston to college.

"It must have been nice growing up here," Lilly said.

"Yeah, but you couldn't do what I do and make a living here. There are no A&R men in Maine. It's funny, isn't it? Something that isn't even a job in one place, you go someplace else and they pay you a lot of money to do it."

"I want to be a rodeo clown," Dick said. "But there's no openings in Manhattan so I have to be a rock star."

"I always remind my mom," Jim said, "that all the school subjects she told me I was going to need when I grew up and went to work—algebra, chemistry, trigonometry, conjugating Spanish verbs—never came up again. I have never used one of those skills. Not once! But all the stuff she warned me I was wasting my time with—listening to records, thumbing to concerts, working at the radio station, reading rock magazines—turned out to be how I make my living."

"Of course," Dick said, "maybe she hoped you'd be a doctor, rather than a record-biz weasel."

Jim stopped the car. They had come to a flat open clearing from the lake into a wide field. A red and white house with a broad front porch and a red and white barn stood back from the road in the center of the meadow. The mountains rose straight up behind it. A thrasher was moving through the high green grass and spitting out bales of hay. Two children, a boy and a girl about seven and eight, swung from a tire hung from a tree in front of the house.

"We're here," Jim said to Lilly. "That's my sister's kids. My favorite days were when we'd bale hay and pick it up in the dumptruck. A bunch of us would ride way up on top of the stack, swaying this way and that as the truck bounced over the bumps. We'd drive to the hayloft and load it in. It was about two hundred degrees up there. You'd get all sweaty and bits of hay would stick to your skin and itch. After doing that all day we'd jump in the lake and wash it away. Jumping into that cold water at the end of a hot day was the best feeling I ever had."

They got back in the car and drove up to the house. The two kids on the tire swing shouted a greeting to Uncle Jim. Jane came to the door and said hi to Lilly and Dick. Jim stood back and gestured to his new car.

"What do you think?"

"It's a rental, right?" Jane asked.

"It's a purchase," Jim said. "It's our car."

"You bought it?" Jane walked toward the automobile. "It's a Mercedes! Jim, we don't need a Mercedes. We live in Manhattan, it will sit in a garage ten months a year."

"It's a station wagon. I read up on all of them. It's the best-made, roomiest, safest station wagon you can buy. And it will run forever." Jim opened the door. Jane stared but did not get in.

"We don't need a sixty-thousand-dollar car. I thought we talked about a Volvo."

"It will run forever! This car will still be on the road when the kids are in college. Jane, I know it's kind of gross but believe me, as an investment and for safety this is the wisest choice."

"An investment." Jane looked at her husband. "We don't even have life insurance, Jim."

"I do, through my job."

Lilly and Dick tried to blend in with the lawn. Jim's mother appeared at the door and called his name. He ran up and kissed her on the cheek and introduced Dick and Lilly and his new Mercedes, which Mom walked around and smiled at as if her boy had brought home a frog in a can. Sarah Cantone, despite Jim's tall stories, was no hippie at all. She was the lady on the oatmeal box, a white-haired, fine-boned yankee.

"You're dressing like a real dude," his mother said to Jim.

"He's gone corporate, Sarah," Jane said from the far side of the new car. "Maybe you can remind him how he was raised."

Jim opened the hatch and took out the bags. He was bugged by his wife's tone but he didn't want to kick off the weekend on the wrong foot. Sometimes Jane seemed to want to keep him in a box, and greeted with sarcasm any attempt he made to break out of her picture of him as a sweet-natured yokel.

"So," Sarah said, turning to Lilly and Dick, "will you two rockers be sharing a room?"

Lilly laughed. "Not in this life."

Dick said, "She doesn't trust herself alone with me, ma'am."

Lilly said, "The only man here I want to sleep with is your son, Mrs. Cantone, and the best woman already got him."

Jim was embarrassed from all angles. What was with his mother saying "dude" and "you two rockers" and asking his friends if they slept together? She was like the with-it teacher you dreaded in high school. He thought bringing Lilly and Dick up to stay with his family would be fun, but it already felt awkward. To these musicians he was a patron and a mentor. In his mother's house, he'd always be a kid who looked silly in grown-up clothes.

"Where are my sons?" Jim asked. He found the boys in the backyard, flooding the sandbox with the garden hose. They greeted him with high screams and muddy hugs.

Jim's mother showed Lilly and Dick to neat little bedrooms on the third floor with flowered wallpaper and white lace curtains.

Dick was saying, "It's a heartbreaker for me, Mrs. Cantone, the way these women all swoon over your son."

Sarah said, "Jim tells me that at this time next year screaming girls will be chasing you down the road. You'll be a regular Ringo."

"That's what we call him," Lilly said. "Irregular Ringo."

Sarah Cantone put out lobster-salad sandwiches and pumpkin pie. Jim's sister Ellen came to collect her kids and started right in on the Mercedes.

"Well, I guess some of us are prospering from the bull market," she said, floating into the house and sliding some pie onto a napkin. She waved the pie in the direction of Lilly and Dick without introducing herself and shouted, "Ticky! Dougie! Get your shoes on, we're going!" and then said to her mom and Jane, "A Benz! I love it! I guess we've gotten over the trauma of Kurt Cobain's suicide, then?"

Jim put down his sandwich. He was tempted to mention her new frosted hair and Sally Jessy Raphaël glasses but he stopped himself. What was this capacity his family had to reduce him in ten minutes to the mentality of the seventh grade? How come no matter what you accomplished in the greater world, when you came back home they still put you in the baby seat? And what in the lonesome world made his wife laugh loudest?

"Hi, Jamie," his sister finally said in greeting. "So you've gone Hollywood. Good for you. Doug says in the future all cars will be exactly the same but New Yorkers will pay thousands of dollars more for impressive hood ornaments. Isn't that a hoot? We have had a ball up here, the kids. I don't know how they handle being in the city all year, they're so athletic."

"They like the city," Jim said.

"Oh, I think it's great. So much culture." His sister suddenly turned to Lilly and Dick. "I'm Ellen, the boring sister from the suburbs. Don't mind me."

"I'm Dick, the swinging musician from the city. This is Lilly, the sensitive beatnik songstress."

"Oh my God," Jim's sister said, turning back to him in wonder and delight. "You're not wearing black lace-up shoes with no socks! Oh, Ma, get a load of JFK Junior!"

Jim's neck burned. Were they going out of their way to act like jerks in front of the musicians? Had they rehearsed this?

"Where are your socks, darling?" Jane asked with phony sweetness.

"It's not Labor Day yet," Jim said quietly. It brought down the house like Bob Hope. It brought down the house like Samson.

"We're not laughing with you, babyface," Ellen said with a mouthful of pie. "We're laughing at you."

It got worse later on, when Jim slipped and mentioned Booth's having a two-million-dollar apartment. As soon as it came out of his mouth, he knew it sounded ridiculous. His mother said, "But, Jim, if he can afford two million dollars, why does he live in an apartment?" His family made Jim feel like the world he was in was the most trivial, superficial place in the universe.

That night in bed Jane said to Jim, "I met an old friend of yours up here this week. Micky Cowls? He was cleaning the storm drains."

"Oh yeah, he's a great guy. We were really close in high school."

"I thought I'd met all your high school friends."

"Yeah. Micky got expelled in tenth grade. The week he turned sixteen. As soon as he was old enough that they didn't have to take him back."

"Really. He didn't seem like a hood."

"He wasn't. He was a really smart kid. Grew up in a commune or something. The teachers hated him because he was smarter than they were and gave them a hard time. Big mouth, you know. They'd say something stupid about slavery or the Indians or something and he'd bust them right in front of the whole class. Finally this big health teacher we had goaded him into taking a swing at him in front of a couple of other teachers and that was it. They kicked Micky's ass right out of there."

"No one stood up for him?"

"I think Miss Gorham did. Our radical English teacher. But no one wanted to hear it. Kid was a troublemaker, he hit a teacher, end of appeal."

"You didn't try to do anything for him?"

"Jane, what could I do? I was fifteen years old. Don't be foolish."

"I wondered if you might have spoken up."

"It wouldn't have done any good."

Jim rolled over and tried to get to sleep. He wouldn't mind when this weekend was over and he could head back to New York.

Jane faced the other way. She wasn't sure the new job was as good for her husband as he thought it was. It seemed to make him try to be what he wasn't in order to fit in where he probably didn't belong. But he was so tense now that he'd surely take any such suggestion as an attack.

It's hard, she thought, to maintain a balance with someone when you spend your days in different worlds. Her days now consisted of the most basic facts of life—getting the children fed, cleaning their cuts, wiping their bottoms. It could have been any country, any year. They swam, they played, she cooked, they ate, they slept—while her husband was worried about abstractions and illusions, decisions that affected millions of dollars and meant nothing at all.

Monday morning Jim and his family and their two guests said goodbye to Grandma and squeezed into the new station wagon. Lilly and Dick got out at the airport in Portland. They didn't need another ten hours in the car, especially with kids and duffel bags added. Back on the highway, when they crossed the bridge from Maine into New Hampshire, CSNY went off the radio and the Smashing Pumpkins came on.

Jim put on the Jerusalem album. Jane said she liked it. Luke called out from the backseat. He wanted to hear the Donovan tape, "Mellow Yellow" or "Atlantis." Jim looked at Jane.

"Hey," she said, "you're the one who wanted them to spend August in Maine."

## 20

The first A&R meeting of October was full of good news. Press announced that six weeks before the Jerusalem album was to be released they had more than fifty requests for advance cassettes and Lilly had already turned down a Gap ad and a photo spread in *Jane*. The product manager begged Jim to convince Jerusalem to play a few songs at the January National Association of Recording Merchants show, the record retailers convention. Jim defended the band's position that playing conventions was not the sort of thing Jerusalem did.

Zoey said that she might be able to convince Black Beauty to play NARM, show people how good they were, that there was nothing to be scared of. The head of marketing said that was a bad idea. Black Beauty's best chance was for people to hear the music before they got a look at them. "It would be fine if they looked like Lauryn Hill," he explained. "Y'know, that whole Angela Davis seventies sexy afro radical braless Foxy Brown vibe. But these women look like Aunt Jemima in army boots."

Zoey said that was racist and Precious, on the speakerphone, laughed and said, "Lighten up, Zoey. If you heard what the R&B department said when they saw those sisters' pictures you'd have to wash your ears out with Listerine."

Zoey thought to cry sexism but held her tongue. There was nothing to be gained living up to their caricature of her as the angry punkette who didn't understand how the real world worked. She more than understood.

Radio promotion said, "The out-of-the-box reaction to Cokie Shea's single has been phenomenal. There was an opening for something like this and Cokie is driving a truck through it."

Press said, "Nashville is handling print but we're helping out a little on the TV front. I can't tell you how big this is going to be."

"We all know we're taking a big chance coming with these new artists at Christmas," Cantone told his people. "It's the season of megastars, live albums, and greatest hits. But I think our strategy is going to bear fruit. There are still a lot of consumers out there who will want something for themselves after they've bought the box set for dad. We've got a clear field at radio, with print. I think Jerusalem and Cokie Shea are going to change the rules. And we'll all look like geniuses."

There was an empty seat where Bruce Gilbert, the hair band's friend, had disappeared. He went quietly when his contract was up. Booth had offered to do the dirty work but Jim was a man about it. He fired Gilbert himself and let Booth be his shoulder to piss on. With a position open, Jim asked everyone to think if they knew someone who had great ears for pop, who could spot the next Backstreet Boys or, if it came to that, create one. Zoey suggested her twelve-year-old niece.

When the meeting broke up Zoey took a communicar out to Brooklyn, to the studio where Black Beauty was recording. It was in a part of Fort Greene that had beaten back the tide of gentrification. The studio was up a flight of stairs over a Chinese restaurant. It made its living on jingles and radio commercials. It was within Black Beauty's budget.

Zoey greeted Alasha, the leader of the band. Zoey called Black Beauty a band because she could not bring herself to call them what they called themselves, a cultural collective. Alasha told Zoey they were right in the middle of something, but she could sit on the rug between the congas and bass amp if she didn't mind shaking some sleigh bells. Zoey sat on the floor and took the bells like castor oil.

As a matter of principle, Black Beauty would record songs only with everyone playing together in the same room, with no isolation, live vocals, and no punches to correct mistakes. If the feel was right, they did not care about pitch or a stray bum note. They had candles going. They had posters and paintings on the wall. They had notes to themselves stuck to the glass: "i carry my own empowerment" and "when i listen to my sister i hear myself."

Black Beauty played the same song three times and another song once and then the first song again and then a song they made up as they went along that went on for fifteen minutes. Zoey tapped the sleigh bells with a pen. She felt like her back was breaking.

Finally Alasha called a break. Zoey followed her upstairs to the control room to listen to a playback and begged her for the twentieth time to consider working with a real producer. If not for the whole album, at least for the two most commercial songs.

"Z-girl," Alasha said with confidence but no stridency, "I know you want what's best for us. And you know what I said before, if Gil Scott-Heron wanted to produce us, if Me'Shell Ndegéocello wanted to produce us, if Curtis Mayfield came back from the dead and said, 'Black Beauty—I have been sent by the Goddess to help you make your record,' I'd go for that. But all the people on your list are people who make records we wouldn't buy. How can you ask me to let someone like that take control of my passion? I don't let someone come in and tell me how to decorate my house. I don't have someone pick out my clothes and dress me. I don't have a nutritionist who tells me what to eat for dinner. Why would I give up control of my music, the thing that means most to me in the world?"

"I know all that, Alasha," Zoey said, "and I'm with you. But you wouldn't be giving up control. I'm just talking about someone to make suggestions about little things you and I wouldn't even think of. Like, if that chorus came up sooner would it help radio play the song. Or, try this one in a different key and see if it helps you sing it better. Just someone to bounce ideas off. It would still be your music and your ultimate decision."

"That's right, Zoey," Alasha said. "It is our music and our ultimate decision is to do it the way we know it should be. I take full responsibility. If it fails, it's my failure. If this is the only record we ever get to make, at least it will be the record we wanted to make. If I compromised and then it failed anyway, I would never forgive myself."

"But what if the compromise meant you reached a big audience and were able to make lots more albums?"

Alasha looked at Zoey with a hard gaze. "Then we would be expected to keep repeating the thing we didn't like in the first place. And if we got really successful? So big we could do whatever we wanted? Then we would make the record we're making here." Alasha turned to the engineer and motioned for her to raise the fader on the rhythm guitar. "Why wait? This might be the only chance we ever get."

When Zoey went outside it was dark and the communicar was gone. She tried to call another but her cell phone's battery was dead. She paraded up and down the neighborhood looking for a taxi and finally descended into the subway where she spent an hour working her way back to Canal Street.

By then it was too late to go home and change so she dragged herself to the Bowery Ballroom where she was supposed to be seeing the opening act. The show was sold out and her name wasn't on the list. By the time she nagged her way in, the group she'd come to see was over. She slid down to the basement saloon, screwed herself to a bar stool, and ordered a vodka.

Richard Reader, the *Rolling Stone* writer from Jerusalem's dressing room, loomed up to her with a parody of continental sophistication. "*Hell-o*, may I buy you ten drinks?"

She said, "What?"

"Robert Wagner!" Reader said. "*It Takes a Thief.* He was a smooth spy in a dickey who picked up babes in miniskirts."

"With lines like that?"

"Well, the *hell*-o was Robert Wagner. The ten drinks is me."

"Sit down, I'll buy *you* a drink. Joey! Bring Mr. Smooth a screwdriver please. What's up, Richard?"

"I'm writing a story on Jerusalem and I can't get a tape of the album for love or money. Really pisses me off, because I knew them before any label was interested."

"I can't believe *Rolling Stone* can't get a tape of an album that will be out in a month."

"I'm not doing it for *Rolling Stone.* The West Coast editor already grabbed it for himself. That's fine, I'll do the big feature after they break. But right now I want to do something for *22,* that on-line magazine, and I'm getting jammed by your useless publicity department. Zoey, I need you to be a friend here. I need you to get me that tape."

"Oh shit, Richard, I don't know. Maybe they've made a deal for a first-interview exclusive with somebody big. I can't screw that up."

"Zoey, listen, I've done the interview already! Those guys are my friends! I just need the tape so I can write the article like I know what I'm talking about. And I promise, there are tons of copies out there, all the writers who are doing pieces have them."

Zoey finished her drink, and Richard bought the next round. He was flirting with her. Yeah, she thought, like she'd ever. An idea began to form in the back of her brain and the more they drank, the farther forward it crept. After four screwdrivers it leaped from her mouth.

"I want to make you a proposition," Zoey said. Actually it came out "I yanna mick you a preposition," but Richard was more hammered than Zoey and did not notice.

"Shoot," he said happily.

"I have a situation at work that is very delicate. I am being offered big jobs by both Epic and Interscope. Now no one can know that, Richard, okay? If they knew I told anyone, those offers would go away."

"What are you going to do?"

"I need to let WorldWide know that other labels are after me, but I cannot let them know who, and I cannot cannot cannot be seen as putting it out there myself. Will you help me?"

"Will you give me the Jerusalem tape?"

"I will if you will."

"I will if you will."

The deal was struck. Richard suggested consummating it with a trip to his bachelor pad but Zoey said she was having her period. What she wanted to say was, "I'm drunk, not retarded," but the small part of her brain that was still rational cautioned mercy.

· · ·

In the days that followed Zoey learned something about Internet magazines: they may not be any good, have any readers, or make any money, but they sure are quick. Before a week had passed rumors of the offers being piled before Zoey Pavlov took on a life of their own. Friends were calling to ask if it was true that she had lunch with Clive Davis. One website claimed her asking price had topped a million and the bids were still flying.

"Boy," Zoey said to Richard when she handed him the Jerusalem tape, "I wish I was me."

In the third week, Zoey's snare caught a lion. *Hits* magazine ran this item: "Sharks in Armani are circling WorldWide wondergirl Zoey 'No Dog' Pavlov whose A&R nose sniffed out Next Big Thing–tipped Jerusalem and buzz-heavy Black Beauty. Sony, Atlantic, Seagram, and BMG all have hots for black-clad beauty. A million bucks buys a lot of Doc Martens!"

Zoey breezed into the Black Mushroom like Lady Di in a leper colony. Four people were nice to her before lunch. An all-time record.

Zoey noted that Cantone acted like he hadn't read the *Hits* article. What a phony, she thought. He should have the manners to at least ask me. Just by virtue of being my titular superior he should do that.

She glanced into his office on the way to the bathroom and saw he was on the phone, obviously very upset. He had not even bothered to take off his raincoat before he got into whatever grief was making him curse and stammer and otherwise drop the easygoing all-American jock facade.

Well, she smiled, if that's all this accomplishes, it's good enough.

In his office, Jim wiggled out of his coat while passing the phone from ear to ear.

"Dick, will you please tell her she can't do that! It's a bad idea and anyway, it's too late. The album is mastered! It's barely three weeks until it's in the stores. Review copies are out!

"Well, tell her again. No, let me tell her. Tell her she has to talk to me! Is Mack there? Put him on.

"Mack! What is this nonsense? Lilly can't take 'Hard Hearted' off the album! 'Hard Hearted' is the hit, 'Hard Hearted' is our insurance policy, and—by the way—'Hard Hearted' is a great song. What's wrong with her?"

"Jimmy, you need to talk to her," the Scottish drummer said. "She's gone mad about it. A critic wrote that 'Hard Hearted' sounded like a Pat Benatar outtake. Lilly hasn't really experienced bad reviews before. She's overreacting. But you know, she never liked that song."

"Where is she now?"

"She's gone back to her place."

"Okay, I'm calling her."

"She won't answer."

"Okay, I'm going over there."

"Good luck, man. We'll be standing by."

It took forever for the taxi to crawl through traffic from Times Square to the Village. Passing his own street, Jim saw Jane and the twins coming home from nursery school. They were on the corner, talking to old Captain Tim in his folding chair. Jim tried to get the window down to call out to them, but it was stuck and the light changed and the cab pulled away.

Jim took out his new matchbook-size cell phone and punched Jane's number. He'd given her a portable phone for Christmas, but could not get her to turn it on. Today was no exception. He went straight to voice mail and hung up.

Lilly lived in a third-floor walk-up in a blue building on Sullivan Street. Jim leaned on her buzzer. She did not answer. He phoned. She didn't pick up. He paced up and down in front of her building until a pizza man was buzzed in. Jim followed him through the gate. He went into the courtyard and looked up at Lilly's window. The window was open and the lights were on—she was home. He ran up the stairs and hit her door, shouting, "It's Jim, Lilly! Open the door, I saw you in the window!"

Lilly opened the door in sweatpants and a pajama shirt. She gave Jim a look like "What's the fuss?" and turned and walked into the only room. The little studio was spare and pale. It looked like the paintings of Van Gogh's bedroom. The only sign she was upset was the cloud of smoke and the overflowing ashtray.

"Hey, Lilly," Jim said. "The album is gone. It's being pressed. The sleeve is printed. I couldn't call it back now if I wanted to. And, by the way, I don't want to. 'Hard Hearted' is a great song, as valid for what it is as 'Jean Baptiste' or 'Bed of Nails.' You can't let one bad review turn you against your own song, Lilly. There will be other bad reviews, and lots of good reviews, too. There will be fan letters and hate mail and nasty comments and writers who think you're superhuman. You have to accept that none of them know more about your music than you do."

"I don't think that," she said. She sat on her little bed and lit another cigarette. "But in this case, I happen to agree. I never wanted that song on the album, I never liked the way it came out, and the fact that you and the record company think it's the big hit and the song you want to promote scares me to death. I don't want one more person to hear it than has heard it already. I don't ever want to sing that song again. In fact, I never will. I swear to you, Jim, I will never ever sing 'Hard Hearted' again. You can give it to Loudatak or Cokie Shea or one of those other happy hacks."

"Don't the other three get a vote in this?"

"No. They can play it if they want but I'll leave the stage."

"Okay, Lilly. You've made up your mind. I'll see if it's possible to pull back the album. But it will cause a lot of problems. We may not get it out for Christmas. All the press will break without a record in the stores. If I can pull back the album I will, but I am going to have to ask you to do some other things to help us sell the record, things I supported you in saying no to before. I mean, I might have to ask you to play a song at NARM."

"I won't be blackmailed, Jim."

"Thanks. I put my neck on the block for you—for a decision I think is absolutely wrong—and I'm the bad guy. I know this is a tough time for you but if you're going to get through it you better keep a very clear sense of who you can trust."

"Fair enough. Sorry."

"Okay, let me go make the argument for the worst idea I've ever heard."

"Thanks, Jim."

"Where was this review anyway? It's early for press."

Lilly reached behind her bed and pulled up a crumpled piece of computer paper. She held it out to Jim.

"This is it? What is this? *The Velvet Rope?*"

"It's *22,* an on-line magazine."

"Lilly, an on-line magazine? Are you kidding? Nobody will ever see this. This is some fourteen-year-old in his bedroom!"

"It's written by Richard Reader."

"Richard Reader? What—did you tell him you wouldn't sleep with him?"

"Richard has been a great supporter of Jerusalem. He loves our music and he likes the album. He says that 'Hard Hearted' is unworthy of us and I agree with him."

"I'll see what can be done. And please plug your phone back in."

Jim brooded on the subway back uptown. There was nothing more disconcerting than becoming famous. You always had to give people a lot of rope when they were going through that. And the moment before a musician's first album comes out is a time of frightening insecurity, because they have spent their whole life dreaming of something and it's about to either happen or fall apart. They don't know if they are living in their last moment of obscurity before fame and fortune, or if this flash of anticipation and promise is the best it will ever be—after which they face failure and a fast ride downhill.

Jim knew all this. He'd been through it with bands before. But it also hit him that if Lilly was capable of being this much of a prima donna before anyone had heard of her, she was on the road to becoming Ultra-Bitch when she got big. It's always the ones with the highest underground ideals who end up calling long-distance from the back of the limo to complain that the air-conditioning's too cold.

At eight in the morning an exhausted, half-drunk Cokie Shea was standing under the shower of a purple penthouse suite on top of Times Square's Century Hotel trying to scrub from her skin the smell of J. B. Booth. She turned up the temperature until she almost scalded herself and rubbed soap and washcloths up and down her body. The extension in the bathroom rang once and stopped. Was Booth in the other room answering her phone? Was he insane? It could be anyone.

She dried herself, put on a hotel bathrobe, and went into the living room, where he was picking bacon off a breakfast tray and making jokes with the bellboy. He was shoeless, with his dress shirt open and crumbs in his chest hair. The bellboy looked at Cokie, made a smirking little salute, and said, "See ya, Mister B."

"He knows you?" Cokie said when the kid closed the door.

"We use this place for offsites."

"You bring your whores here."

"We sometimes treat our top artists to a suite here. What's the matter?"

"Booth, what's wrong with you? Do you want the town to know what happened here? Are you bragging? Why did you answer my phone?"

"It rang! What are you scared of? I'm here for a breakfast meeting! Everybody knows that. It was your airline calling about an upgrade for your flight home. I said you were in the bathroom and to please call back later. Cokie, relax. No one cares."

She hated herself for letting this happen. Ever since Brazil, Cokie had been avoiding Booth's advances with double-talk and vague indications that she wished their being together were possible but it couldn't happen right now. She arrived here on the redeye from Los Angeles after an endless flight on which her companion, the chief of WorldWide press, began buying her drinks in the business class lounge and did not let up the whole flight. When she finally arrived at her Times Square hotel, Booth was waiting with flowers and champagne. She wanted to either lie down or throw up but he would not lay off. He kissed her, he nibbled her neck, he licked her ear, he had on a cologne that must have been made from pollen.

She put him off for as long as she could but while she could resist his love talk and was not bullied by his anger, she could not handle the sound of him whining and begging. So she gave in, as much to be able to lie down as to make him shut up. He rooted over her like a hungry hog for a while, she made some gasps and squeaks to suggest fulfillment, and he bellowed one obscenity and collapsed across her.

Coming out of the alcohol now, she swore it would never happen again.

Booth stuffed two slices of toast in his mouth and walked to the window. "How do you like this view?" he asked her. "See, there's my office right up there. I got a telescope. I could look in on you."

Cokie looked down into Times Square.

"Do you spy on the strippers at the Pleasure Center?" she asked.

"They're strippers, Cokie, you don't have to spy on them. You can walk right in and see them naked."

"But a famous executive like you could not afford to be seen in such places."

"Couldn't afford is right. They charge twelve dollars for a ginger ale. So I hear. Anyway, this is the new Times Square. The only ones without pants down there are Mickey and Donald."

"The album is going really well," she said. She left the window and sat on the couch. The smell of the bacon made her stomach turn. He came and sat next to her.

"Everything I hoped for you is coming true," he said. "I want you to look at some ideas I've written down. The British label would love to get you to London for a week to shake some hands and do a little press. One day trip to Dublin could mean a number-one album in Ireland. They love country music there, you'd be amazed. I know we've got you booked tight, but I think it's worth maybe postponing the press week in Atlanta to build a bridge to Europe."

"I've never been to England."

"It's wonderful. I've been spending so much time in Europe I feel like I never see you in person anymore. And the phone calls, while nice, lack one important element."

"How's International going?"

"It's going. It's hard work. I'm always on a plane. I got enough frequent-flyer miles to go to Jupiter."

"Too bad you can't get the Gulfstream."

"That's for special occasions. Maybe your visit to Britain qualifies. I think Wild Bill would sign off on that if I told him it was the only way to get you from Atlanta, where you're doing press, to London to Dublin to Paris and home."

"Wait, why am I going to Paris?"

"I want to take you to Paris for a weekend after we do the week of work, Cokie. Not on business, just you and me being Jack and Cokie. I feel like we started something last winter and between the kidnapping and you working on the album and moving to Tennessee and me getting this promotion and spending all my time in Europe, well, I don't want to lose what started all this. I wasn't sure you felt the same way but after this morning, well. It speaks for itself."

Cokie had been saying no to boys since she was twelve years old. She could cut out a man's heart and it would be two hours before he felt the hole. She leaned forward and put her hand on Booth's arm.

"Jack, I have thought so much about this. You don't know how many times I have imagined conversations with you in the night and reached for the phone and forced myself to put it down. I am such a coward. Sometimes I think my heart has a mind of its own."

"Is that a song?"

"Jack, that first night we met and I went back to your apartment, I didn't know who I was meeting. Was this a handsome guy I was attracted to? Or was this a record executive who seemed to really like my songs? Or was this some playboy who used his power to pick up girls?"

"I vote for the handsome guy you were attracted to."

"What happened between us that night—such as it was—felt right at the time. I was a little swept up. But I have to tell you, I worried about it for a long time after."

"Why? I've done everything I told you I'd do."

"Jack! You didn't tell me you were married! Do you think that means nothing to me? Do you think I feel comfortable seeing you and Lois at functions and having to be cheery and chat with her when I know I . . ." She looked for the words. "I am a serious artist, Jack."

"Cokie, honest, I thought you knew about Lois and me. But that's unfair, I should have told you right away. You understand, though, that Lois and I do not have a marriage that most people would consider a marriage. We have a lifelong friendship, she was there for me when I was nothing. But the way we are now is almost like brother and sister. We'll always love each other but we don't have passion for each other, we don't have a romance. All Lois and I have is a history."

Cokie leaned back on the couch. She rested her chin on her knees and wrapped her arms around her legs, holding them tight together.

"That's just way too sophisticated for me, Jack," she said. "I can't hang my heart on a broken chain."

"Cokie, stop talking at me in song lyrics."

"That's me, Jack."

"I want to be with you. I can give you anything you want in the world, but I need it to start with you wanting me."

Cokie understood that the easiest time to dump a man was right after sex. He'd gotten what he came for and his instincts were telling him to run away. So she willed away her headache and nausea and said evenly, "I want you to be my best friend, Jack. I want you to share in my music and guide my career. I want you to be my wonder counselor. But until you work out what's best and most honest in your life, I can't be your lover."

Booth looked around the room like he was searching for a cue card. Cokie said, "Can we be okay with that for now?"

"No, I'm not okay with that, but I have no choice, right?"

"Neither of us do, Jack. But maybe down the line, we both will." Cokie rose, picked up her suitcase, and headed to the bedroom to dress. She said, "I have to be at Edgewater for a tax meeting."

"Call me tonight," Booth said lamely. "About England."

On his way across the street to WorldWide, Booth tried to decipher the last thing she said. "Neither of us do, but maybe down the line we both will." He turned it over and over in his head. "What the frig does that mean?"

It was a bad moment for anyone to set foot within Booth's sonar. The first to make the mistake were Jim Cantone and Al Hamilton.

"J.B.," Hamilton said as they followed Booth into his office, "we have a situation. Lilly Rope has told Jim that if the Jerusalem album comes out with the song 'Hard Hearted' on it she is going to hold her breath until she turns blue. She is absolutely adamant, Jim has been unable to move her, she would rather go back to cleaning ovens for a living."

"Tell her it's too late, the CDs are pressed."

"I did tell her that," Jim said. "She doesn't care. She says she will refuse to ever perform the song and I think she means it."

"So let her not perform the song."

"It's the emphasis track," Hamilton said. "We can't lose it."

"Read her her contract."

"It's not a legal problem, J.B.," Cantone said. "She's ready to pull an Axl Rose on this one. I think we should try to do what she wants. I'd rather lose one song and have her devoted to us forever than shove this down her throat and have to fight for everything else."

"You told her the CDs were already pressed?" Booth asked.

"Yes."

"Are the CDs already pressed?"

"No."

"What do you think, Al?"

"This is the only sure radio track on the album. Don't let it go."

" 'Jean-Baptiste' could be radio," Jim said.

"Maybe on the Bizarro World," Al said.

"Look, I shouldn't have to be involved in this sort of thing," Booth said. "You two are the head of A&R and the executive vice president of the whole company. I don't even remember the song."

"We wouldn't be here if she could be moved," Jim said. "You have to make the call on this one, J.B. And with all respect to Al's position, if we force Jerusalem to have a song they hate on their album we will be blowing a relationship that will produce many hits in the years to come. I promise you, we need to let Lilly win this one."

Booth sighed. He was still trying to figure out Cokie's parting comment. He came back to the conversation at hand. "You two tell Lilly I want to have dinner with her tonight to resolve this issue. Where's my calendar? Yeah, I've got a nine o'clock reservation at Piccolo. I was expecting to have dinner with Cokie but she's got a tax thing. You tell Lilly it will cost us two hundred thousand dollars to destroy all the CDs we've already pressed and it will boot her album into next year, but I have so much respect for her that I will discuss that possibility with her face to face.

"My condition—no manager, no lawyer, no bandmates, no one from WorldWide. I want the respect of her talking to me one to one. That's how adults work out their differences, not through tirades and ultimatums."

"I'll get her there," Jim said.

"Could you get back her publishing while you're at it?" Hamilton joked.

"You two go jerk off, you've wasted enough of my time and now I have to spend the evening with this misfit. Tell her to shower."

They were not out the door when the SVP of press leaned in. "Knock knock!"

"Does the parade of interruptions never end?" Booth cried. "What?"

"Bringing you the weekly roundup. Have you seen *Hits*?"

"I never read *Hits* and I wish you'd help me."

"Better look at this. Zoey Pavlov is apparently a lady in demand."

Booth scanned the Xeroxed article. "Oh, I've never seen such bullshit. She wrote this herself." He shouted to his assistant. "Sam! Get me the presidents of Interscope and Epic!" Then he said to press, "She pulled this same scam with *Airplay* a year ago. Why do you people fall for this crap?"

"It could be true."

"Yeah, I could be *Blueboy* Fox of the Month, too."

His phone buzzed. Sam had found one of the presidents. Booth said, "Did you see this horseshit in the paper about you trying to hire this A&R assistant Zoey Pavlov for a million bucks? If you want her I'll sell you her contract right now for a hundred dollars. . . .

"Yeah. . . . Right, that's what I thought. . . . Okay. . . . Yeah, yeah, I'm thinking about it. I just don't know if Lydya gives a turd about the Special Olympics. . . . Same to you sideways." He hung up.

"On your way out please mention to Sam that I'd like to see Zoey Pavlov. And don't use any more of the company's paper making copies of gossip columns. It sends the wrong message to the staff."

Zoey got the call to see Booth. She took a minute to go in the ladies' room and fix her makeup. Be cool, she told herself. Don't deny the rumors but don't rub his face in it, either. Make it easy for him to be generous. If Cantone comes up, take the high road.

She breezed into Booth's office. He was screwing a lens cap onto a telescope.

"Hi, Zoey! Sit down, will ya? You want some coffee or a soda? Water?"

"I'll take a cup of coffee, J.B."

"Sure. Sam! Get some coffee for Zoey and bring me a decaf tea! You want milk or sugar, Zoey? Sam! Black!"

Booth came around and sat on the couch with her just as he had with Cokie. Was Cokie asking him to divorce Lois? What presumption! What does the woman want? Booth searched himself and found no answer.

Sam put a tea in his hand. Booth came back to himself. He looked at Zoey, who was failing to affect nonchalance.

"Zoey," he said, leaning forward conspiratorially, "I hear you're getting a lot of offers from other labels."

"Oh, well." She laughed too high. "Don't believe what you read in the press, J.B. They get everything wrong."

"They do, don't they. So, Zoey, I guess the money in front of you is getting pretty big."

"It's flattering, J.B., but I want you to know—my first, middle, and last loyalty is to WorldWide. This is where I want to be."

"Gee."

"I mean, I don't want to be naive. I can't afford to walk away from money."

"Who can?"

"But I'm not greedy either. If I could make, you know, somewhere in the same general range of what I'm being offered elsewhere and stay at WorldWide, that would be my dream."

"What are you making now?"

"Just around a hundred."

"Hmm. And the offers from elsewhere are . . . ?"

"Oh gosh, J.B., I couldn't really . . . I mean, these are confidential sort of, I mean, it's all speculative anyway."

"Just speculatively, though, someone told me you were being tempted to the tune of a million dollars."

"Oh, that's way out of line. A million dollars! Ha, no offense, but I'd be out the door so fast . . . No, no. It's not a million dollars." Zoey told herself to play it cool. "I mean . . . it's not a million dollars in one year."

"A million dollars over time."

"Well, you know, time can go on. I mean, time is really long."

"Right. For instance, you will make a million dollars at World-Wide . . ."

"How do you mean?"

It had been a very awkward conversation, but Zoey kept her eyes on the prize and now she began to think there was a prayer of busting open the piñata.

Booth said, "I mean, if you worked here for ten years! That would come out to a million dollars."

Zoey laughed in spite of her disappointment. "Oh, sure. I pay my cleaning lady a million dollars, too. In forty-dollar weekly installments."

"That's a good one," Booth said. He showed his teeth. "Zoey, I like you. I think you're a peach. I'm delighted that you are getting these big offers. And I want you to go."

Zoey stared at Booth with a big smile on her face and waited for him to say something else. He didn't.

She said, "What?"

"I want you to go."

"Oh. Well, as I said, J.B., I love WorldWide. I would rather be here than anywhere else. I can't help what some uninformed reporter writes. I never said I wanted to leave."

Booth stood up and went back to his desk and started reading a piece of paper. He said, "Right. We had this conversation a year ago, didn't we? I read you were leaving then but you're still here. You must be unhappy. I don't want my employees to be unhappy. So go. When it's your last day make sure Cantone lets me know. We'll throw you a little party."

Zoey picked up her coffee and limped out of the room, shrinking with every step.

· · ·

That night Booth played the first side of the Jerusalem tape in his car on the way to meet Lilly Rope at a Noho restaurant. He walked in right at nine, and she was already in the booth. She looked shy and frail, like a little kid misplaced at the grownups' table. Lilly had tried to get out of showing up but Cantone convinced her he had laid down his life for her and if she would not do it for her she better do it for him. She was dressed in black jeans, black sneakers, and a clean white boy's dress shirt, ironed.

Booth was wearing a camel-hair coat that he threw over the back of an empty chair, a charcoal suit from Savile Row, and a blue shirt open at the collar.

"How are you, Lilly?" Booth asked.

"Fine. This is a nice place. I never knew it was here."

"You live nearby?"

"Just up Sullivan. I must have walked by here a million times."

"I want you to try the lobster bisque. Do you eat shellfish?"

"Oh yeah. I had lobster at Jim's mother's house, she made it for us."

"This place is famous for its soups. Let's start with that."

For the next hour Booth asked Lilly lots of questions about her background, her interests, and her songs. He told her how much he appreciated her sitting down with him face to face like this. He said he wanted her to come out to his house in Greenwich for his November Christmas party. He inquired as to whether she had any interest in acting, and implied that the synergy between NOA's movie division and WorldWide might afford certain shortcuts. He told her that all of WorldWide's guns were lined up to give Jerusalem's CD the opportunity it deserved.

"But, Lilly, I must tell you truly. We need 'Hard Hearted.' It is the key that opens the door to radio and retail. Once we open that door you own the house and for the rest of your long life in music you will be in a position to make the calls and choose the songs. You know, the Beatles didn't want to record 'I Want to Hold Your Hand.' John Lennon told me in confidence. Brian Epstein made them do it. That was the real reason Pete Best quit. But that one compromise opened the door for them to make 'Penny Lane' and 'Imagine.' "

Lilly listened to all this with mounting anxiety. She was peeling her paper napkin. She could not look up when she spoke.

"J.B.," she said, "I'm stunned and actually really flattered that you care enough about Jerusalem and this album to spend all this time and bring me to this amazing restaurant and tell me what to order and ask me all these questions. It really makes me grateful—and humble, in a way. And I want you to know I have so much respect for you and Jim and everyone at the record company. I've never met such a nice group of people. The others and I all feel great when we go up there. I owe you a lot and I know that."

Booth sat and nodded. Lilly went on, "So this is completely with respect. Because I know it's my fault for being weak and letting that song get recorded at all. But if 'Hard Hearted' goes on my record, I am going to have to call every editor and disc jockey and record store owner I can and tell them that it's a horrible song and I'm ashamed of it and I didn't want it on the album. And whenever we play live I'll tell the audience that it's an evil song that came from a bad part of me, and that rather than buy our album I would prefer that they borrow someone else's Jerusalem CD and tape it, leaving that song off. I'm sorry. I wish I didn't feel this way, but I do."

"Okay then," Booth said. "The song goes." He opened the dessert menu. "You ever had Neapolitan yogurt?"

If DeGaul were here, Booth told himself, he'd have sweet-talked this pretentious schoolgirl into doing what the company wanted. That's what DeGaul was good for—stroking the talent, schmoozing the press, charming the clients. DeGaul's reputation as the lovable uncle of rock and roll carried real weight, but where was he when Booth needed him to throw that weight around? Back in the Caribbean goofing off.

It was as if every time KFC needed to cut a ribbon, no one could find Colonel Sanders.

. . .

While Booth bit back his resentment, DeGaul polished off a plate of jerk chicken in St. Pierre.

When he first planned the trip it was with the expectation that Webster's Retreat would be open for business, but Roy Nightingale had hit more snags. His wife had moved back to London for good. Roy kept hitting up DeGaul for money and DeGaul kept writing the checks, but he felt less like a soft touch than a sucker.

The two old friends had beaten around the bush all through dinner. When John P. cleared the plates DeGaul talked turkey.

"It's not working out for us here, is it, Roy?" DeGaul said.

"I don't know what to tell you, Willie. The rains came and took out the seeds for the golf course. The help appears and disappears without notice. It is almost impossible to get first-rate materials. But I believe that in time we will prevail. You know how hard it is for me to keep asking you for more and still falling behind. But each painful step brings us nearer."

"Listen, Roy, I've been thinking about this a lot. I have an idea you might not go for right away but I want you to consider it. Maybe the notion of recreating the glory days of colonial splendor is all wrong. All this hassle over the right clay and the proper pea stone is bankrupting us and I'm not sure it will pay off anyway."

"What are you proposing?"

"Hold on to your hat. What if we think about appealing to a broader constituency? What if we kept the hotel and bungalows but made the rest of the plantation into"—DeGaul held out his hands as if measuring a yard in the air—"an amusement park."

Roy stared at him as if he'd just suggested they form a death cult.

"No, listen," DeGaul said. "I don't mean some run-down boardwalk carnival. I mean a state-of-the-art ten-acre area with great rides and carousels for the kids and a bandstand with reggae playing and a Ferris wheel where you can go up and see the whole island. There's nothing like it anywhere in the country. It would bring in tourists from all over, it would be great for the local economy, and it wouldn't be so exclusive, so rich, so white. The people who live in St. Pierre would love it and people with kids would be able to take a Caribbean vacation."

"Willie, you're talking about taking this, this Eden and turning it into Disneyland."

"Not a bit. We couldn't do that if we tried. Have you ever been to the winter carnival they set up in Paris, near Notre Dame? It's beautiful. It's like something from a dream. That's what I'm imagining."

"And I'm imagining the portable house of horrors the barkers roll into Leicester Square."

"Look, Roy, this is a small place. I don't think we'd be capable of making something too big if we wanted to. But I don't want to be so elitist that we price ourselves out of the market. And right now that's what I see happening. I want people to be able to come to St. Pierre and fall in love with it the way we did when we were kids. And whether the baronial-splendor plan is the best way to do that or not, we've gotta face the fact that it's just not happening."

"You're a persuasive man, DeGaul. I will think about all this very carefully. But I would also ask you to give me just a little more time, just until the summer, to fulfill the original blueprint."

DeGaul started whistling the theme from *The Bridge on the River Kwai.*

Nightingale said it was time to retire. He looked sadly at his perfect green lawn and said, "I suppose a small carousel would not be so out of place."

In January when things were slow and everyone was collating their receipts, a lawyer DeGaul had never met appeared in his office to deliver the masters of the first new album in six years from Fagin Doppler, Irish recording legend, critics' darling, and—since his brief post–Live Aid resurgence ended in 1987—commercial sinkhole.

Fagin was slowly working his way through a ten-album deal with WorldWide, a deal that would have expired long ago had some former A&R chief not been seduced by the "Do They Know It's Christmas" spirit to renegotiate and extend Fagin's contract at a brutal (to World-Wide) advance-per-album rate way back when. That generous A&R man had long since been banished, but Fagin still rose every five years or so with another hopeless album and his hand out for another eight hundred thousand dollars that would never be recouped.

"People who think the labels screw the artists," DeGaul once told Booth, "should get a look at Fagin Doppler's ledger."

Like a few other very rich musicians late in their careers, Doppler had only idiots for employees. Partly this was a function of having been swindled by corrupt management early on; he did not want anyone near his money who could outsmart him. It was also because he had been in the business so long that he figured he knew more than anyone he could

hire and didn't like to be challenged. It was also because he had no intention of paying anyone a decent salary, let alone giving them a percentage of his earnings. So he hired dumbbells at lousy pay who were
thrilled to be able to associate with him and did his bidding with fierce
loyalty and incompetence. DeGaul referred to them as "The bodyguard
of idiots."

Doppler's lawyer was a funny-looking little guy with a bull chest, a
Bronx accent, and expensive shoes that didn't match his expensive suit.
He had a single bushy black eyebrow that stretched across his forehead
from left to right and lined up three inches above and perfectly parallel
to an identical bushy black mustache. He looked like one of those drawings you turn upside down to see another face. DeGaul took the package
from his hands and said, "Boy, I can't wait to hear this!"

The bushy little lawyer nodded. "As you know, Mr. Doppler's former
A&R contact at WorldWide, Mr. Andrew Kasdan, is no longer with the
company. In lieu of Mr. Kasdan, Mr. Doppler instructed me to deliver
the masters by hand to you."

DeGaul winced. "I hope I don't lose 'em." The lawyer pursed his lips.
His mustache did a little dance.

"Well," DeGaul said, "let me get J. B. Booth in here, do this up right."

Booth appeared, sweating and buttoning his shirt.

"J.B., this is . . ." DeGaul had no idea what his name was ". . . the
bearer of the new Fagin Doppler album. You guys know each other,
right?"

"Remind me," Booth said to the mismatched man.

"We have not met, sir. I am Liam Roche. I represent Fagin Doppler
for the purposes of this negotiation."

"What are we negotiating?" Booth asked.

"Sir, under the terms of Mr. Doppler's contract you have thirty days
from delivery of his new album to either accept it and pay him the
amount due or notify him by registered mail of any terms for refusal."

"What, is the record libelous?" Booth asked.

"Certainly not."

"Deliberately unprofessional or containing indefensible obscenity?"

"No."

"In violation of enforceable copyrights or containing plagiarized material or otherwise likely to cause irreparable harm to the good name of WorldWide Music, WorldWide Entertainment, NOA, or its vendors or affiliates?"

"No."

"Will listening to it make me fart at a funeral?" DeGaul asked.

"I have delivered the album to you, gentlemen. Will you sign a receipt?" Liam Roche produced a piece of paper from his pocket.

"Sure," Booth said. He grabbed the paper, glanced at it quickly, crossed out most of the twenty lines of text, scribbled his initials in the corner, and printed his name in big block letters along the bottom.

"He went to Harvard," DeGaul told the little lawyer. "He likes to cross things out."

The lawyer left and DeGaul said to Booth, "You listen to it."

. . .

Three hours later Cantone looked out at his assembled A&R staff. He needed help. "Do any of you have any relationship at all with Fagin Doppler?" he asked.

There was only silence.

"I knew him," old Boris Verger finally said with the expression of Custer describing Sitting Bull.

"That's good," Jim said, "because I need someone . . ."

"We got two things in common," Boris said. "I hate him and he hates me."

"Come on, Boris," Flute Bjerke said. "Like he remembers you."

"Oh, he remembers, all right," Boris said. "I sat right next to him at Townshend's concert at the House of Blues and he ignored me all night. That smug bastard holds a grudge."

"Anybody able to deal with this guy?" Cantone asked. "He's been on the label forever, one of you must know him at least a little."

"What's the issue?" Zoey finally asked. "Do you want one of us to A&R his new album?"

"You better hear it before you put up your hand," Jim said. He went to the tape player and turned on a copy of the master delivered to De-Gaul that morning. Fagin Doppler was defying the clock with a bold techno recording full of electronic distortion, industrial noise, random samples from a shortwave radio, and singing by both Balinese and Bantu tribesmen. Doppler's own voice faded in and out throughout the record, intoning lyrics without melody or sense.

"This has your name written all over it, Flute," Zoey said to the passive Bjerke.

"I think we have to reject it," Cantone said. "I guess the guy wants to be cutting edge, but this is just . . ."

"Can we reject it?" Zoey asked the table. "Doesn't he have some absurdly favorable deal?"

"There must be a way to send back something like this," Cantone said. "Legal will work it out. But Doppler is an important artist with a long history. One of you has to get on a plane and tell him in person."

The five A&R people on Cantone's team looked at him with a single expression. It was the expression that said each of them was taking a step backward.

• • •

On Friday morning Irish time Cantone climbed shivering off the overnight flight from New York to Shannon Airport where he rented a car with the steering wheel on the wrong side and careened along narrow cliff roads against oncoming goats to deliver the bad news to a rock star whose face he had once taped to the inside of his locker.

Doppler, who had the confident manner of a country baron and the best hair weave Jim had ever seen, answered his own door and showed Jim around his great stone house with its arched corridors, Dalí prints, and Chinese rugs. He introduced him to a marble room with high ceilings and no furniture and induced him to sit cross-legged on the floor over a tea kettle.

Jim explained, as quickly as was decent, that he had not come all this way to lay out the marketing plan for the new album. The new album was too avant-garde for the American market, and Jim could not justify forking over eight hundred thousand dollars for a recording of such limited commercial prospects.

"What would you pay for it?" Doppler asked.

That question Jim did not expect. He said, "I'm afraid this is not a record WorldWide is suited to sell."

"Come here," Doppler said, "I want to show you something." He rose and led Jim up a once-grand staircase. At the first landing, Jim saw an old man in overalls startle and jump back behind a door. The help must have been told to disappear while Doppler dazzled the suit.

On the second landing Doppler unlatched a small mahogany maid's door and led Jim into a long room, a sort of extended pantry, filled with computer gear and digital recording equipment.

"This is my *Nautilus*," Doppler said, gesturing around the close room. He added condescendingly, "As in Nemo's submarine, not the fitness apparatus. From here I listen to and speak with my best audience. They are not the middlebrow fogies who once filled stadia to hear me karaoke my old hits. These are real music fans, the adventurers, the front edge of what's coming. What Radio Luxemburg was for me, what FM radio was for you, fiber-optic and satellite communication is for these kids. They are out there, they are listening, and they are downloading my new material in unprecedented numbers."

"That's wonderful," Jim said. "But that's a small group of hobbyists who get off on being part of an exclusive club. I'm not sure they are an appropriate barometer of what will appeal to a broader, more traditional market."

"Come over here, Jim. Look at this screen. This is one of sixty-four sites and chat rooms devoted to my work. Look at what these ordinary, diverse, disparate fans are saying about this new stuff. See here: 'I listened to *Purgatory Railing* all night and had the greatest dreams.' And this one answers, 'I'd rather listen to anything Fagin does than the shit on MTV.' These are not some isolated ham radio hacks, Jim, these kids are in the world. Look at this one. No, that's not so good, let's scroll up. Okay, look here: 'This is the only music I've heard in years that I get more out of each time I hear it.' "

Doppler turned from the screen with a tutor's patient pride. "You see, Jim, I've been doing my own test marketing. The audience for this is out there. I have found them for you. All WorldWide has to do is press up the compact discs and think of how to market to this new constituency."

"We can't do it," Jim said. "We make CDs the old-fashioned way and market them the old-fashioned way to an audience that still likes to pick them up and look them over and lug them to the cashier and drive them home. If the new music you're making is designed to appeal to this audience you've apparently tapped into, I will see what I can do to set up a release so that you can market this material to them, using new technology. When you have a more traditional album of songs, we will be happy to do what we do well."

Doppler smiled sadly and looked at his hands. "I suppose I hoped a younger fellow like yourself might not yet have ossified," he said. "But it's not a chronological process, is it? They pick from the ones already in formation."

Jim smiled and said nothing. He followed Doppler out of his cubbyhole and waited while he latched the little hatch behind them. They went down the stairs making small talk about the winding roads and where Jim could get breakfast. When they reached the front step Doppler let his mask slip just a little. He said, "I expect I won't see you again, Jim. You won't last any longer than the others." And he closed the door.

Jim was surprised he didn't feel worse. He felt nothing at all, except a little startled to find himself in the west of Ireland.

. . .

With the time change he was back in New York before the end of the business day. He went to the Black Mushroom and gave Booth the lowdown. Al Hamilton listened in with amusement.

"Sounds like you went to Dracula's castle," Booth said.

"It's sad to see a musician who used to be so great disappearing up some pathetic idea of hipness," Cantone said, drinking a soda to relight his fading concentration. "He feels like he's right on top of things because he's got a handful of fanatics he can eavesdrop on as they talk about him. He's completely isolated and he thinks he's connected and riding the next wave."

Booth said, "The guy should try to come up with one good melody."

"We lived through this before," Hamilton said. "Remember CB radios? Come back, good buddy. What's your handle there, Doppler? Holy smoke, Fagin, we got us a convoy!"

The three men laughed. Cantone was too pooped to feel anything but relief to be home. "I better go see my kids," he said, and dragged himself out of his chair and was gone.

"He's getting the picture," Booth said to Hamilton.

"Yeah, he seems to be fitting in," Hamilton replied.

"You figure he'll be with us when the change comes down?"

"He'll act like he is. Which is just as good."

"You know what's wrong with this business?" Booth asked.

"DeGaul hasn't seen the light and handed over the company to you?"

"We don't have any good stars! Look around! This thing got off the ground 'cause you had Beatles, Hendrix, Stones, Clapton, Aretha, the Who, Marvin Gaye, James Brown, all out making two, three albums a year at the same time. When they slowed down you had the Eagles, Stevie Wonder, Zeppelin, Elton, Fleetwood Mac. Then Michael Jackson, Madonna, Prince. Real stars, stars people cared about enough to haunt the record stores waiting for the next album. There aren't stars like that anymore. Nobody the public wants to line up to see what they do next. Nobody they trust to lead them someplace new."

"Ah, well, that might be so," Hamilton said, as if he were thinking of a private joke. "But I'm not sure the industry is as interested as it once was in investing the time and resources to nurture those sorts of careers. We all want someone else to pick up the flag and lead."

Booth arched his shoulders. He didn't care to have this conversation again. It was Friday night. He had places to go. Hamilton pushed back his chair and rose. He turned off the overhead light so the room was filled with the neon of Broadway below them. "Perhaps the fault's not with our stars," he said, "but with ourselves."

Hamilton went out laughing at his own joke and Booth locked his desk.

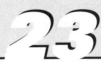

DeGaul was seated next to Lois Booth at a pre-Grammy dinner party at the apartment of a Broadway composer across from the Planetarium on Central Park West. J.B. was nowhere to be seen. DeGaul figured Lois could not be happy about having to make the rounds without him. She would not show it, though. Lois's strength came from being genuinely classless. She was first-generation Irish, which made some people assume she had come off a boat in a potato bag. In fact, her father had arrived in America on the *Queen Elizabeth*. He was a Trinity professor who took a literature chair at the University of Chicago. Her mother was a hard-core soup kitchen placard-carrying Catholic Worker. Lois inherited her mother's passion for charity. DeGaul figured she rationalized being married to Booth by giving away as much of his money as she could get her hands on.

The evening started early. Dinner was served at 5:30 P.M., to accommodate the schedule of those who had to go to the awards show at eight o'clock. The deadline was a blessing, as the hostess was notorious for shoving her idea of entertainment down the throats of her captive audience along with the calamari. By the time the swordfish arrived, a young cabaret star had sung "Send in the Clowns," the ancient chairman emeritus of a once-great record company had made a toast aggrandizing himself for accomplishments actually made in spite of him, and everyone at the long table had listened with a great imitation of attention as the hostess's four adopted children sang the goodnight song from *The Sound of Music.*

"Dinner and a show!" DeGaul said to Lois when the last of the kids was elbowed out of the dining room.

"I'm sure those kids will be better than the entertainment at Radio City tonight," Lois smiled.

"I figure the high point will be the multicultural tribute to disco."

"Or Ricky Martin's Lifetime Achievement Award," Lois said.

DeGaul did not want to ask where Booth was. For all he knew, J.B. had included him in an alibi. It was going to be tough to get through dessert without the subject coming up. He chewed for a long time and looked around the room for another topic. Nothing presented itself. Finally he said, "So, Lois, what are your plans for the new century?"

"I think it would be a good occasion to get a divorce," Lois said.

DeGaul smiled with a goofy look that he hoped suggested, You're pulling my leg.

Lois looked down and smiled tightly. "Did Booth ever tell you about our grand anniversaries?"

"I've heard him refer to that," DeGaul lied. "What does it mean exactly?"

"We met on April seventeenth, 1975, at the kickoff of the bicentennial celebration in Concord, Massachusetts. He was a Marine, I was a protester. He tackled me in a stream as I was running toward President Ford with a tomato. We didn't begin dating until I saw him again in Cambridge the next year. We spent our first night together on July fourth, 1976."

"I didn't realize you were so patriotic."

"By then he was out of the service. He recognized me in Harvard Square. I had no idea who he was. He described my actions at Concord in such detail, I assumed he was one of the protesters." She laughed. "We began our romance at the two hundredth birthday of the United States. You remember we broke up for a while in the eighties."

"He was one miserable dog during that time, Lois. You have no idea how bad it was for him."

"You're a good friend, Bill." Her cheeks were red—with wine, De-

Gaul was certain, not embarrassment. It wasn't like Lois to talk about personal matters so openly, but he didn't mind. "We reunited . . . do you remember?"

"Were we all on a boat?"

"Almost! We were at Liberty Island. We started dating on the two hundredth birthday of the United States and reunited on the five hundredth anniversary of the discovery of America. We always call those our Grand Anniversaries. Now I don't know what we could do to celebrate the two thousandth anniversary of the birth of Christ, but it feels like a cue to call it quits."

"Oh, come on, Lois. You two will be together until the centennial of Sinatra at the Sands."

"I don't think so, Bill." She looked around as if telling a top secret. DeGaul inclined the better of his two bum ears. "You know, Booth and I always celebrated April seventeenth, the day of the protest at Concord, as our secret anniversary. But in the nineties it became this horrible black joke."

"How come?"

"April seventeenth was the massacre at Waco, Texas, and the Oklahoma City Bombing. Our anniversary was occupied by right-wing maniacs!"

"You had it first."

"I don't know, it's all silly, I could never say it to Booth. But I felt like the same poison that had come into our marriage infected our anniversary."

"Lois, my folks were married on Pearl Harbor Day. I was born during the Bataan death march. Every day is the anniversary of something bad and probably something great, too. What you and J.B. have is good. You don't want to let it be jinxed by a bunch of nuts with barrels of flaming cow manure."

Lois smiled. "Say that again, Bill. 'Don't be jinxed by nuts with flaming manure.' I feel like Elizabeth Barrett Browning." They were both laughing.

"Too many Mike Hammer stories. But I mean it, don't give up on J.B. He's a good man. You want me to order him to take some time off so you two can have a second honeymoon?"

"His idea of a honeymoon is going away with *The Wall Street Jour-*

*nal* and flow charts pouring through the e-mail. No, you keep him busy. It's better for both of us."

The rent-a-butlers laid out plates of flan. A big television was rolled in and fired up to a Grammys preshow on a cable station. A black man and a blond woman were standing behind the velvet rope mooning over second-tier singers and first-tier escorts who sneaked looks at the TV cameras out of the corners of their eyes. It's hard to pretend you're ignoring the camera, DeGaul thought, and check your reflection at the same time.

He had a premonition of what was about to happen a moment before it did. While the two TV hosts were interviewing a former Mouseketeer now attempting a crossover into dance music, DeGaul saw Booth and Cokie arm in arm moving through the upper-left-hand corner of the screen. Booth paused, laughing, greeted someone off camera, and then stepped out of the shot.

DeGaul said nothing. Lois seemed to be completely engaged in conversation with the celebrity gynecologist on her other side. Maybe she'd missed it. She didn't let on.

DeGaul was flustered. He stood up and said to the vicinity, "Time to get down to the flea circus." Then he turned to Lois and asked if he could give her a lift.

"Just across the park," she said. "I'm going back to the apartment and watch this on TV. I told the Metcalfs I'd meet them at ten-thirty at Tavern on the Green."

"What, you're consorting with the competition? You're coming to our bash, aren't you?"

"Sure, I'll visit all the parties. Have to see who has the biggest ice sculpture."

"I hear Sony had the actual iceberg that sank the *Titanic* shaped into a perfect likeness of Celine Dion's head. It's floating in Central Park reservoir."

"How will you top that?"

"WorldWide has spared no expense. We've re-created Mount Rushmore in ice cream with my face instead of Teddy Roosevelt. First one there gets to eat my nose."

They said good night to the hostess and went down to the street, where DeGaul's car was waiting. Passing through the park, DeGaul kept running dates through his head and came up confused. He said to Lois, "You and J.B. met in '75 or '76?"

"April seventeenth, 1975."

"He was back from Vietnam already?"

"No, he was about to go. When I saw him the next year he was back."

"He was about to go. April seventeenth. When did Saigon fall? Wasn't it that same time?"

"Just a couple of weeks later. He barely got in and then he barely got out."

"Wait, so how long was J.B. in Vietnam?"

Lois threw her head back. She put a finger to her lips. "Don't question the legend."

DeGaul jumped out at Radio City and let Lois take his car. He made his way to the side door with some difficulty, as the cops were directing pedestrian traffic around barricades and there were still hundreds of civilians with little cameras on the street. When he got to the stage door he realized he had left in the car his manila envelope full of passes and party invitations. It didn't matter. The chief of security recognized him and waved him through.

There was a mob of performers, TV crews, and tuxedoed executives waiting for the few crawling elevators, so DeGaul took a shortcut down the fire stairs and through the Radio City engine room, an expanse of pipes and pulleys that heated the building, raised Rockettes through trap doors, and hid elephant cages when the circus was in town. It was peaceful there.

He reached the other side of the building and was back in bedlam. The Grammys producer, a pig-nosed Welshman with a booming voice, was in a narrow corridor at the edge of the stage having a coronary into a cellular phone while production assistants and women dressed as pixies tried to get out of his way.

"We cannot shorten the Pete Seeger tribute!" he wailed. "We already took out two pieces at rehearsal! There is nothing more to cut! I don't care about Shania right now!"

There was still a voice coming out of the phone when the Welshman placed it on the floor and ground his heel into it, the whole time shouting, "I can't hear you, Gordon, you're breaking up!"

He saw DeGaul and switched to an addled affability, no small trick under live TV pressure, but a talent long-cultivated in one who never knew where his next four-hundred-thousand-dollar job was coming from.

"I'm in a bind here, Bill," he said sadly. "I took on this tribute to Pete Seeger with strong indications that Dylan, Springsteen, and Jewel would show up. Now I'm down to Don McLean and Billy Bragg and the network wants to cut it. I just can't do that to Pete."

"Stick to your guns, Anton," DeGaul said. An elevator door opened and he jumped in.

He came out two floors up in a crowd of heavy metal musicians and seven-year-old girls in Brownie uniforms. The metal musicians were dressed in leather and women's clothes and wore red contact lenses. They were this year's rebellion objects for fourteen-year-old boys, heirs to the great Alice Cooper–Kiss–Marilyn Manson tradition. One wore an inverted swastika as a codpiece. Another was having his most obscene tattoos covered with gaffer tape by a representative of network standards. The leader, who wore a crown of thorns, had his hand down the pants of a woman a few pounds too big for her velvet britches. The Brownies and a couple of den mothers were crowded around the musicians, giggling, having their pictures taken and autograph books signed. Beyond the throng, DeGaul spotted Booth and Cokie.

"What's with those parents letting their kids be part of that?" DeGaul said when he caught up with them.

"This," Booth smiled, "from a man whose kids grew up surrounded by pot and rastas."

"The sacramental herb, mon," DeGaul said. "Anyway, I didn't let them smoke it."

"Bill's kids are amazing," Booth told Cokie. "Straight A's, merit scholars. They take after their mother."

"I'm sure the little girls just see it as Halloween," Cokie said. "I worry more about the band. They'll either end up dead, in mental hospitals, or—if they are lucky—spend the rest of their lives trying to make excuses for being such fools."

"It's all an act," Booth said, "they don't believe in any of it. It's a gimmick."

"I don't think so," Cokie said. "I think those are damaged, frightened little boys. It's good for them to get acceptance but when that acceptance is withdrawn they're going to fall hard."

"I don't know," DeGaul said, "maybe they'll have a fifty-year career. Maybe those cross-dressing mutants are the Tony Bennett of 2045."

"Let's go out front and watch the show," Booth said.

"Are we sitting together?" DeGaul asked. "I don't have my ticket."

"We got a row," Booth said. "Sit anywhere."

Booth, DeGaul, and Cokie planted themselves at the front of the section behind the good-looking hired ovation-starters who make the Grammys seem exciting to people watching on TV. Three sections back and one aisle east, Cantone watched them take their seats. He turned to Lilly Rope and said, "This is a warm-up. Next year you'll be a winner."

"If that happens," she said, "I'm going to send an Indian princess to turn down the award."

Jim smiled. A pig-nosed Welshman was on stage pleading for everyone to take their seats: "Two minutes to live!" he cried.

"Admit it, Jim," Lilly said, "WorldWide's block of ballots next year will be committed to Cokie Shea."

She said it without malice, but Jim felt a jab. "Don't worry about Cokie," he said as the music came up and people ran for their chairs, "she's in a different category."

· · ·

Zoey Pavlov watched the show open on the edge of her mattress in her underwear. She had not asked for tickets. She'd waited all winter for Cantone to follow up on Booth's telling her to hit the road. Cantone had never said a word. She was sure he enjoyed watching her dangle. She had to find a way out of WorldWide. Her contract was up in thirteen weeks and no one from human resources had called about it. She would be damned if she would give Cantone the satisfaction of asking. She'd walk first. She hated the Grammys. She switched the channel to a Fox sitcom about feisty single gals with big apartments and glamorous media jobs in Manhattan. Mack Toomey, Jerusalem's handsome Scottish drummer, rolled over and said sleepily, "Hey, what happened to the Grammys?"

"They're over," Zoey said. "Our side lost."

"That's a shame." Mack ground his teeth, let a ripper, and went back to sleep.

· · ·

Lois was at the Booths' in-town apartment. She kicked off her shoes and found a bottled iced tea. She stood in front of the TV watching the spotlights fly up and down the all-star Grammy audience. On its way to Whitney Houston the camera panned over DeGaul leaning across Cokie Shea to talk to her husband. Lois sipped her drink. She went back to the couch and picked up the remote. She clicked around the channels until she landed on a movie she half-recognized. Jane Fonda, Jon Voight. She wanted to place it. *Coming Home.* She went back to the Grammys. A heavy metal band was parading onto the stage in a swarm of Girl Scouts. She went to the kitchen and found some Mint Milanos. Then she turned back to the movie.

# 24

DeGaul, Booth, and Cantone were in tuxedos in the back of Booth's car, crawling toward the Midtown tunnel and the Rock and Roll Hall of Fame induction ceremony. It had perhaps been a mistake to try to attend the Reebok Human Rights Awards luncheon in Boston on the same day the Hall of Fame had its dinner in New York, but who expected so much traffic going into Manhattan at rush hour? Usually the problem was getting out.

Randy the driver said he knew they should have taken the Triborough. Cantone said he wished they'd taken the train. Booth said if they were so smart how come they were stuck here with a dope like him.

DeGaul said, "Boys, we're sitting in a wide, warm luxury car with a CD player and a little TV. We just left four rock stars, two senators, and a roomful of millionaires and human-rights heroes. We are on our way to a great evening of music that will go on for hours even if we get to our front-row table a little too late for the opening speech. We have money in our pockets and great women who are foolish enough to sleep with us. How bad is that?"

Everyone mumbled. Booth said, "Let's talk business. Jimmy, the Jerusalem album is dead as Abe Lincoln. You don't want to give up on this band, right?"

"No way," Cantone said. "We all talked about building this slowly, letting it happen at a grassroots level. The press has been great, they've got a loyal following at colleges across the country, they've made real inroads in England and Australia. I wish MTV had played the video, I wish we were a little farther along, but no, I think things are slow but on track."

"You're wrong," Booth said. "A little press means nothing. That was just the magazines covering themselves in case the band got big. Not one of those people will be there for a second album. England means nothing. Even if they like something, the second album they say, 'I got one of those already.' Australia—who gives a piss? No, what you got already is not the beginning. What you got already is the best it's ever gonna be. And that isn't good enough to keep this band on WorldWide."

Cantone felt lousy. "What will it take?" he asked.

"I don't know if they should be on WorldWide, truthfully. The girl's cute, but she's a nut. Remember I took her out to dinner to try to get her to keep that song on the album?" He was addressing this more to De-Gaul than Cantone. "One song I knew could be a hit for them if everything went right, and she yanks it off the record. She didn't want to hear about it. Said she'd denounce WorldWide from the stage at every show if I forced her. *Forced her.* 'Here, let me throw you a life preserver.' 'How dare you?' I don't know if it's possible to make up for that kind of mistake now that everyone knows the record's a dog."

Cantone played Booth's game. He said, "But if we decided to try, what could we do?"

"Okay, lookit. First, we need a video MTV will play. No more moody black-and-white slow-motion no-makeup punk band with a toilet in the middle of the room. She's a good-looking girl, she needs to make a video that shows that off. And it's gotta be her in the video, not her three stooges. She's the face, she's the singer, she's the one the audience is gonna care about. Can you get her to do that?"

"I'll try. But we're not talking about making her a bimbo, right? You don't want Lilly in a bathing suit doing the watusi."

"Oh, I wouldn't dream of infringing on her artistic self-image. I just want her looking like, number one, she likes whoever she's singing to, and number two, she's ever seen conditioner."

"I'll try."

"Now," Booth said, "all this is for nothing if they don't have a song radio can play. I don't know, since she wouldn't use the one I liked. Do they have a song on that record or was that thing we did the first video for the best one?"

"No, they have a good song. 'Bed of Nails.' I always thought that was the secret weapon. I guess it's time to pull it out."

"Can I hear it?" Booth called to his driver. "Hey, Randy! You got the Jerusalem tape up there?"

Randy leaned over and rifled the glove compartment and a shoebox on the floor. He came up with the cassette. He put it on and Jim led him to the first song on side two. It was upbeat and Lilly sang it well. The lyrics were a little obscure but the chorus was catchy and there was a goofy "We're an American Band" keyboard hook.

"It's good," DeGaul said.

"It's all right," Booth said. "It's by no means automatic. But if they did a really good video and MTV got on it, it's nothing radio would be unable to play."

"I think I'd remix the song to bring her voice forward," Cantone said. "Maybe shorten the intro to get to the payoff faster. Do a fade during the solo at the end."

"You gotta get her aboard on this," Booth said. "Or there's no album number two."

"I need to talk to you about that, J.B.," Cantone said. "They've got the songs; we picked a producer. I've been hoping to get them in the studio in the next month or so."

"Fine. Get her to do the video we want for this song and we'll accept that as a demonstration of good faith. Otherwise, cut them loose."

Cantone was flustered. "One of the big problems with this band is that they have amateur management. A buddy from the old days, a club owner from New Jersey. The band's loyal to him, but he's the sort of character who shows up for a meeting in old sneakers and a black promo T-shirt. If they had real management, radio would take them a lot more seriously."

Booth looked at Cantone. He was hinting that he'd give one of Booth's management pals this band in return for keeping them alive. The kid was learning. Booth said, "Who did you have in mind?"

"Do you figure Garth Goes would want to work with these guys? Maybe take on the manager they have to deal with the day-to-day, the calls at midnight when the van breaks down. Garth could handle the big stuff, the vision."

"Yeah," Booth chuckled. "Garth's a visionary all right. I don't think so. Garth's got his hands full with Cokie right now, in addition to his stable of greats and near-greats. You sit down with these kids and tell them the facts of life. Tell the manager, too. You can't do anything to entice them into firing him, though. Anyone from a label who tells an artist their manager is a bum walks right into a big lawsuit."

"That's hard. The band counts on me to tell them what's going wrong, and I can't advise them about the most important thing."

"No, you can't. Let them figure it out. Where do you want them to record?"

"Here, I guess, but it's a drag. They're living in their old apartments, they're surrounded by all the scuzzbuckets from the local scene. You know how it is when a band is first signed. Every drug dealer is offering them free samples, every girlfriend is trying to get married, every drunk is borrowing money. I'd like to get them out of New York, but there's no place to go that wouldn't eat up the album budget."

DeGaul said, "I got the answer. Jim, you do what J.B. says, sit down with Lilly and explain she has to really want this or it's going to go away. Don't be pushy, don't be desperate. Just lay it out. 'Here's the options, it's your call.' If she wants to stick with WorldWide and she gives J.B. a video he can use, we take the band out of New York and down to St. Pierre."

Booth and Cantone looked at their leader. He'll do anything for a vacation, Booth thought. Cantone said, "As a break or to record? Is there a studio down there?"

DeGaul was getting excited. "This will be great, take my word! I've been thinking about using that place for recording anyway. Here's a chance to try it out. Who were you thinking of as producer?"

"Michael Krasner."

"What's his story?"

"He's recorded live, in houses, did a whole album in an abandoned church."

"Perfect!" DeGaul said. "He's right on the money for what I'm thinking. We take one of the bungalows at Webster's and turn it into a studio. Let the band set up there with the windows open and the sea breezes blowing through. They can live in the other houses on the grounds. They can play, write, record whenever they want. It's healthy, it's relaxing, it's inspiring. No creeps around, they eat fruit, they swim. They lose all the anxieties and get closer as people and players."

"Montserrat without the volcano," Cantone said.

"Yeah. It's exactly what these kids need to get over the sophomore hump. And if it works, maybe we build a permanent facility down there and use it for other acts. Could become a big ancillary business."

A tow truck with flashing lights came out of the tunnel dragging a Range Rover. Traffic began to move again.

"But she has to do the video for 'Bed of Nails' first," Booth said. "She has to show she's one of us."

• • •

Jim laid out the plan to Jerusalem and their silly manager at a meeting at the Cantone apartment two days later. Jane made hot chocolate and sandwiches and then took the kids to the playground. Lilly sensed what Jim could not say, that making a glitzy video that would probably never get played was payback to Booth for not giving in to him over the song she removed from the first album.

Lilly wanted to go down fighting, but Anthony, Mack, and Dick took the position that they were the ones being asked to make the sacrifice—they were being pushed into the background so Lilly could be brought forward as the star. If they were willing to swallow that for the sake of the band, Lilly should pipe down and be grateful they were so big-hearted.

Lilly turned to her useless manager. He was thirty, snaggle-toothed and unshaven. His breath smelled like beer covering up something worse. He looked pained. "Lilly, WorldWide has done everything our way up to now and it hasn't worked. I think we owe it to Jim to try this his way."

"Okay," Lilly said, standing up and heading to the door. "We'll do the video any way Jim says." She was struggling not to cry in front of these five men she used to trust. She left without her coat.

• • •

Al Hamilton came into Booth's office at ten o'clock at night.

"You're still here."

"I was at a dinner," Booth said. "I came back to return phone calls."

"Jerusalem's making another video?"

"So I hear."

"Have you seen the recording budget submitted for their second album? We're flying a studio down to DeGaul's Caribbean retreat for them?"

"Are we? No kidding."

"You want to sign off on this?"

"Am I a fool?"

"You want DeGaul to sign."

"What a good idea, Al! Wait until next week when I'm back in Germany counting all the money I'm making for the revitalized International Labels Group. Then put it in front of DeGaul and explain that with me out of town, you need him to write his name so the band can get their tickets. He won't blink."

"You hope."

"Hey, it's his stupid idea. The old man thinks it's still his company."

"He's giving you a sword, isn't he?"

"Is he? I wouldn't say that."

"Neither would I."

"Good. Night, Al."

"Night, J.B."

Booth dialed Cokie Shea's phone. No machine came on and no one ever answered. He sat there letting it ring.

Jim tried hard not to rub Zoey the wrong way. He didn't ask her to come into his office. He went to her. She was unhappy to see him. She did not offer him a seat. He stood there and said, "What do you have on for today?"

She read from her Rhino Records calendar: "Conference call with Manus Evans's new attorney; meeting with Loudatak's manager about on-line rights dispute; Black Beauty mixing in Brooklyn; last flight to Portland for tomorrow's mastering session."

"I need a big favor, Zoey. Maybe we can send Flute to Portland and bump the rest of it. Jerusalem are shooting their video and I need you to be there. I just got a summons from DeGaul. I have to fill in for him at some City of Hope meeting."

So Zoey's real work was less important than Cantone's baby-sitting? She was inclined to tell him to jump in the lake, but as she was looking to get out of the Portland trip anyway, and as she would grab any excuse to be there for Jerusalem when Cantone let them down, she relented. "If I have to."

"Thanks, Zoey, you're really saving my neck. There's a Music Express car downstairs. It'll take you to the video shoot in Queens. Great."

Zoey found the black Town Car parked on Forty-seventh Street. She tapped the driver's window and he jumped out and started trying to open the back door for her. She stood in his way and said, "Is this car for Cantone?" Yes yes yes, please I open door. "And you know where we're going, right?" Yes yes yes, please allow me. "'Cause I don't have directions, I don't want to start off with you and find out you don't know where we're going." Hell's Gate Film Studio in Long Island City, Queens, I know very well. "Okay." Zoey opened her door herself and got in. The driver was Russian and wanted to talk. She mumbled single-syllable answers until he stopped.

At the old TV studio she found four big union men in black T-shirts eating Oreos on the sidewalk. A glass door was pried open by thick lines of cable, bound together and running from a truck in the street into the building and up the concrete stairs. The union men ignored her as she clambered up the stairs and onto an old soundstage with the aspect of an airplane hangar. Young women in their twenties moved around the perimeter of the room with clipboards and headsets. A beat-up couch and several folding chairs were placed in front of a black-and-white TV monitor. Near that a makeup artist had spread her powders and creams across a large wooden door resting on three sawhorses. At the end of the room two card tables covered with candy, chips, and cookies overflowed into a big plastic cooler full of Diet Cokes floating in water that used to be ice. It was only noon, but this shoot had been under way since 8:00 A.M., and would not be wrapped until long after midnight. Of all the pieces of modern music marketing, the video shoot was the most depressing.

The center of the hangar was occupied by a sort of plywood fort, from within which emanated light and sound. Zoey found an opening in the wall and entered what was dressed to look like the entrance hall of a New York apartment. A tape of Jerusalem's "Bed of Nails" was playing. She poked her head in and saw Lilly and a man she didn't recognize arguing. Beyond them were bright lights and figures in silhouette. Someone in the shadows shouted and Lilly and the man turned to look at her. Zoey jumped back around the corner. The music stopped. An Englishwoman's voice called, "Someone walked into the shot! Could we please get an AD to stand out there, please! Come on in, whoever you are! Do hurry up."

Zoey walked onto the set. She smiled at Lilly and said, "Sorry." Lilly looked miserable. Zoey passed through what was dressed to look like a bohemian bedroom—an old electric guitar laid on an unmade futon, near a tacky lamp, a plastic record player, and a few secondhand Beat paperbacks in a milk-crate shelf—and joined the director, producer, set designer, and camera crew, all of whom regarded her with something between pity and contempt.

"Zoey Pavlov, WorldWide Music," she said. They shook their heads and went back to work. Lilly and a handsome young man mimed shouting at each other while a bare lightbulb swung back and forth above their heads on a pendulum. Zoey watched for a minute and then turned to a doorway that led into a second mock-up apartment. This one was full of Jerusalem's musical gear. Dick, Anthony, and Mack were sitting on their amps, eating Cheez Doodles and drinking beer.

They greeted Zoey warmly. The three men in Jerusalem were bored and unhappy. They had been relegated to walk-on status in their own song. The concept of the video was that Lilly and her screen boyfriend were to have a screaming, teary argument in the next apartment while lightning flashed and rain fell outside. Meanwhile, in the flat next door, the other members of Jerusalem were a band rocking out. The director—a pale, mumbling Czech who spoke only in whispers and used his British producer as a spokeswoman-translator–ventriloquist's dummy —promised the boys that there would be a great tracking shot from outside Lilly's apartment window over to their window and back. He also said he would shoot lots of pickups of the individual musicians at the end of the day.

"That'll really happen," Anthony said to Zoey.

"Lilly is Huey Lewis now," Dick said. "We're the News."

"Hey, guys," Mack said evenly. "Whatever it takes."

"Is Catalano here?" Zoey asked of Jerusalem's lawyer.

"He was supposed to be," Anthony said. "Where's Cantone?"

"He's supposed to be," Zoey said, and she smiled sadly.

The producer suddenly appeared above Zoey and said, "I'm Lulu. You are from the record company?"

"Yep."

"Perhaps you could speak to your artist. She is having a hard time with Mick's concept. Can you make her understand?"

"Uh-oh."

Zoey went into the other room, where the pale director was getting hot around his turtleneck and Lilly was as adamant as Joan of Arc.

"You tell her it's necessary," the director whispered to Zoey in accented English.

"What's the issue here?" Zoey asked Lilly.

"He wants me to take off my shirt!" Lilly shouted. The male model playing her boyfriend giggled and got hit with eight evil eyes. He shut up and walked away.

"It was in the storyboards," the producer said flatly. "Everyone saw them and signed off."

"The storyboards!" Lilly cried. "A bunch of bad Magic Marker drawings that wouldn't pass as a comic strip in a high school paper! I couldn't tell from your storyboards if I was a ballerina or a gorilla!"

"Okay, you're shy," the director mumbled. He turned to his producer and Zoey. "Lulu and you girl, take Lilly in the other room and look at her bosom. Tell her if it's nice."

"Asshole," Lilly spit. "No one's grading my chest. I'm a musician."

"And I am an artist and this is my art you are treading on," the director hissed.

"I am the artist here!" Lilly shouted. "You are a hired hack making an advertisement for my work, you incredible vain imbecile!" Lulu, the producer, stepped in front of the director like a bodyguard.

"Wait, cool it, time out," Zoey said. "Listen, both you creative individuals. Whether or not it would be artistically satisfying to have Lilly take her shirt off, it makes no sense because you can't show nipples on MTV or VH1 or any of the other places we want to get this clip played. So it's a moot argument. It defeats our whole purpose here."

The director was smoking two cigarettes at once. He seemed unable to find words simple enough for these American fools to comprehend, so after some sputtering he turned to the producer and said, "You explain."

"Lilly's breasts will never be exposed," Lulu said to Zoey, as if Lilly were not there. "He wants her arms folded across her chest like so." Lulu crossed her heart with her arms, holding her shoulders. "We will only see Lilly's naked back and her covering her breasts while she sings to her lover on their broken bed. You understand?"

The director broke in: "It is no more than you would see in a nativity pageant."

"Remind me to come to your church this Christmas," Zoey said. "Lilly, does that make a difference to you?"

"Absolutely not. I will not act like some sex kitten. That is against everything I believe in and everything my music is about."

Zoey turned to the director. "I think she's got you there, boss."

"Don't blame me, then," the director whispered, "when no one plays your stupid video."

"Oh, the stupid part is yours, pal," Zoey said. "The video is mine all right, I'm paying for it. The music, though, is hers and the rest of us are here to help the music or get out of the road."

The director said he would shoot in the other room with the three male musicians while Lilly met with wardrobe. As soon as they were out of earshot, Lilly thanked Zoey for sticking up for her. "Sometimes it's good to have another girl around," Lilly said.

"That director is a headcase," Zoey said. She and Lilly had some tea and then met with the wardrobe woman, who convinced Lilly to wear a short undershirt that showed off her navel.

"I'll give MTV my bellybutton," Lilly smiled. "My nipples are holding out for HBO."

Zoey and Lilly wandered back to the set with their tea. While the director was setting up the cameras for the band's shots, and Anthony and Dick were eating themselves into sugar shock, Mack had taken off his shirt and was on the floor doing push-ups and sit-ups until his muscles popped.

"At least one of you is willing to show off his chest," Zoey told Lilly. Mack, shirtless and sweaty, got behind his drums and pounded them like Tarzan. The director orbited him with a Steadicam, lapping up every sexy sinew.

"I think Mack just wrote the band back into the video," Lilly said.

Zoey was delighted that she and Lilly were buddies again. Jerusalem still had the potential to be superstars, and Zoey had been there from day one. There was no reason to think that, if she were patient, she would not get them back when Cantone finally fell on his face.

"Will we see you in St. Pierre?" Lilly asked.

"What?"

"You know, we do this video, we go to the Caribbean to record the next album. You knew that, right?"

"I knew it was under discussion," Zoey lied.

"Jim's flying down with us and staying a while. It sounds fantastic. DeGaul set it all up. Will you be there?"

Once again Zoey felt the train pulling away without her. "That would be nice," she said.

The members of Jerusalem climbed out of the rickety school bus that had carried them over the broken roads from the airport across the island and stepped blinking onto the grounds of Webster's Retreat. They were like children waking from a dream.

Cantone followed them out of the bus, tired but smiling. DeGaul, who had refused the long bus ride in favor of a hop over the mountains, was already on the piazza with champagne, Red Stripe, and all genres of fruit drinks. Roy Nightingale hung back by the door of his great house, as if waiting to be sure DeGaul's rock band would not bite.

"This is beautiful," Dick said. Like his bandmates', his pale skin looked blue in the Caribbean sun. "Do we have the run of this place?"

"You sure do!" DeGaul said. "You guys are going to christen St. Pierre with rock and roll! Why don't you come up here and we'll have a toast."

Lilly and Anthony walked to the edge of the stream that ran through the lawn to the ocean. The beach beyond the row of palms was white in the sunlight. The waves were climbing to ten-foot crests before breaking just in front of the shore.

"Long way from Sullivan Street," Anthony said to Lilly. She nodded.

Mack did not stand awestruck as the others did. He whooped like Braveheart and ran to the beach, shedding his clothes as he went. By the time he was naked he was in the water. He climbed up a big wave, shouting for everyone to join him.

His bandmates smiled and waved back, but the only person to accept his invitation was a tall, bleached-blond woman sculpted to a pornographer's idea of perfection by the finest Frankenstein plastic surgeons of Hollywood. She was Mack's new girlfriend, Krystal. Lilly, Anthony, and Dick did not bring along plus-ones for what was to be the most important project of their professional lives, and they had tried to dissuade Mack. But he was newly in love and Krystal had a way of not hearing discouraging words. So she came.

Krystal tiptoed to the water's edge on painted nails, peeling off her clothes as she traveled. When she was down to a thong she giggled her way into the water, running backward toward the beach again whenever a big wave approached.

"I see she brought her water wings," Lilly said.

"Does silicone float?" Dick wondered.

DeGaul said, "She's a very healthy-looking girl. What's Krystal's last name?"

"We believe it's Nacht," Dick said. "She's got that Aryan uber-babe thing going."

"Anthony calls her Twenty/Forty," Lilly said.

The keyboard player explained, "She says she's twenty but she looks forty."

Cantone felt bad for the beach bunny, but he was happy to see the band members joking together. As long as it didn't lead to tension with Mack, it was probably fine that Krystal was here.

DeGaul introduced Jerusalem to Roy Nightingale, who was visibly relieved that they were no weirder than DeGaul's other friends. The group drank toasts on the veranda and then John P. arrived with a golf cart to show them to their quarters. Mack joined them on the piazza, dripping, with a beach towel wrapped around his muscular waist. Krystal rolled up behind him with her white silk shirt thrown over her wet body in a fashion statement taken from a Pamela Anderson poster. Everyone raised a glass to a successful recording project and a lot of fun.

As the band and Krystal rolled away on John P.'s golf cart DeGaul turned to Cantone. "Looks like our boy Mack's got his toe in something good."

"I guess," Jim said. "She's about a foot taller than he is, though."

"Yeah, that gal could eat peanuts off his head. I'll bet he's a big man lying down."

"If he keeps running around here naked we'll all find out. I'm going to go unpack."

"Good deal. You're in the same cabin you had last time. You remember the way?"

"Blindfolded." Jim picked up his knapsack and walked off.

Roy Nightingale came up beside DeGaul. "I appreciate your bringing them here, Willie," he said. "But you'll see, it won't be necessary to turn Webster's Retreat into a recording complex. The work is going well now. We'll be ready ahead of schedule."

"This will be nice," DeGaul said. "And if it means WorldWide can throw a little rent money your way, all the better."

Anthony and Dick, the old chums from the cover-band circuit, shared one bungalow. Lilly had a cabin of her own. Mack and the eye-popping Krystal bedded down in a third.

· · ·

One lagoon away, producer Mike Krasner had converted the biggest bungalow into a recording studio. He was sleeping there, with the gear. The theory was that any band member could roll in at any time, day or night, and lay down their inspiration.

Cantone stepped carefully through the maze of cords, wires, and half-unpacked crates in the living room of the recording house, searching for Krasner. He did not find the producer in the bedroom. He called his name and a voice came out of a monitor. "I'm in the echo chamber! Brown door between the studio and the booth!" Jim looked around. If the living room were the studio and the bedroom were the booth, the echo chamber had to be . . . he found the brown door to the lavatory. There was a step down into a small dressing room with a sink and another door into a large bathroom. He followed the wires into a wood-walled sunken shower. There sat the record producer, in shorts and headphones, clapping his hands into a microphone suspended with duct tape from the showerhead.

"The natural echo in here is fantastic," Krasner said. He had vampire skin and a Cousin It mop of beard and hair. The man wore sunglasses in dark Manhattan studios; there was no chance of seeing his eyes here in the tropics.

"So it's going to work," Jim said.

"It's going to be a blast. With some artists I'd worry about leakage and stuff, but we'll make a virtue out of that. These guys are a real band, they've done two hundred gigs this year. As long as their spirit is up we'll make a good record here."

"Great. When's your engineer coming?"

"He's not. I changed my mind. I'm engineer, I'm tape op, I'm tea boy. We're making this record the old-fashioned way. This is Big Pink, man. This is Sly and Robbie."

"That won't burn you out?"

"Cantone, this is a spirit thing we gotta get goin.' Everybody has to feel like they can come in any time and lay down an idea. If we end up with the drummer playing bass and the singer on piano and the bassist sitting at the desk moving the faders and the guy who cuts the grass blowing a harmonica, that's what it'll be. I want this to be Neverland. That's the vibe I intend to create. Anything goes, as long as it's hip."

"Yeah, well, that's cool, Mike, but we also need to make a commercial album on time and on budget. Jerusalem have the rest of their lives riding on this record."

"It will be the best record they ever make because it will be the best time they ever had."

Someone started kicking the bass drum in the living room. Jim and Krasner came out of the shower. Mack, dressed now in white short shorts and sunglasses, was behind his kit, feeling his way around and tightening the heads.

"Rasta!" the producer shouted by way of greeting.

"Hey, Mike!" Mack said. "Is this place the balls or what? I can't believe it! How long you been here?"

"The weekend. I been surveying the sonics. We're gonna make a gem here, Macky!"

"I believe it, man. I can't wait to start. I got some new song ideas I want to play ya, too. Maybe we'll lay down some tracks while the others are off rafting, eh? I'm not just a drummer, you know."

"Mack," Jim said, "I have to ask. You've been in New York all winter.

You've been here half an hour. How come your skin is browner than John P.'s?"

"Tanning salon, Mr. Jim," Mack smiled. "I been getting my u-rays for three weeks so I don't get fried here in the hot St. Pierre sun. The others will be sleeping standing up for the first week. I'm already conditioned. Krystal taught me that."

"She's the next Mrs. Toomey, huh?"

"Don't laugh. She's an actress, a herbalist, a painter, she plays virtuoso flute."

"And she's built like a brick cathouse," Krasner said.

"That's the least of her virtues, mate, believe me," Mack said, screwing in a hi-hat. "But I won't deny it's a nice bonus."

"Nice boners?" Anthony said, entering through the glass doors. "Admit it, Mack. That's why you brought Barbarella along. Meanwhile my wife is back in New York with a full-time job and a baby."

"She could a come, man. Not my fault if you have no romance. Krystal's an amazing woman."

Anthony blinked. "Favorite color: Pink. Likes: horses. Dislikes: People with bad vibes."

"She was born in Sarajevo, man," Mack declared. "Her family was killed by the Serbs. She's like *The Painted Bird*."

Anthony began playing an old Kinks song on the upright piano and Mack fell in behind him on the drums. Producer Krasner plugged in a guitar and whacked out the chords. Jim left the boys jamming and walked to the beach, where he found the unlikely duo of Krystal, in a tiny white bikini, and Lilly, in black shorts and a black T-shirt, sharing beauty tips. Krystal was advising Lilly on a depilatory she ought to check out while Lilly grinned and nodded her head as if she were listening to a talking dolphin.

"Well," said Krystal when she saw Jim, "that's enough girl talk. I'll leave you two to do business." She skittered off to the edge of the water, where she struck a pose Jim thought he might have once seen on a calendar in a garage.

"I understand she was Miss February," Jim said to Lilly.

"February 1981 maybe," Lilly said. They both laughed. Jim was glad to see Lilly happy.

"Listen to this," she said. "I have an idea for a song, you have to help me remember it." She looked out at the ocean and sang Jim two verses of a pretty melody with the refrain, "Then I knew, me and you, we were goners."

Jim told her it was great and meant it. "I really think this is going to be good," he said. "You've got good songs, the band's getting along, and this is a perfect creative environment."

"You're right. If we can't do it here, we'll never be able to do it at all." She turned and looked him up and down. "You've been a good friend to us, Jim," she said. "I know it hasn't always been easy for you, and I don't feel great about every decision either of us has made. But I know your heart is good. If anyone other than you had been between us and World-Wide, we would be gone already."

"Thanks, Lilly," Cantone said. "I feel like we're in this whole thing together." He smiled. "When Mack shot Barney's toe off, you and I were both blasted into WorldWide, for better or worse."

Lilly laughed. She said she wished Jim could bring down Jane and the boys and stay a while. He did, too, but he didn't have that luxury. He assured her it would be a good thing for the band to have quality time with DeGaul. The CEO really was a great guy; once he and Jerusalem had a chance to become pals, the band was pretty much assured of being a WorldWide priority.

Jim said goodbye on the third day, sad to go. In future years he would often replay in his memory that conversation with Lilly on the beach. It was not the last time he ever saw her, but it would turn out to be the only chance they had to settle accounts before everything went insane.

Jerusalem's first couple of days in the Caribbean were spent winding down to local speed. Full of nervous energy when they arrived, they would jog, swim for twenty minutes, lie on the beach for fifteen, checking their watches the whole time, go back to the bungalow, shower and shampoo, survey the pantry, and run into the village three times a day.

By the fourth day, though, they had detoxed from New York and downshifted into the relaxed St. Pierre rhythm. The music flowed, tensions slipped away, and creativity flourished. Everyone swam, wrote, played, recorded, slept, and spent more time laughing than they had in a long while.

They cut the songs they brought with them in record time. Producer Krasner warned them not to mess with those tracks any more—they were done. He called it "knowing when to take the crayons away." New songs poured in from every direction. All four band members were full of ideas, most of which they agreed were better than anything they brought with them from the States. Inspired giddiness prevailed. One sunstruck afternoon they recorded a twenty-minute reggae version of Mr. Jay's anthem "If You're on the Ball and You're in the Groove You Got It Made with Orange-Aid" with Lilly playing bass and Krystal doing a hula dance.

While Jerusalem were building their album, Royal Nightingale was supervising the raising of his landscaped arcadia. Mr. Jay, John P., and Buster served as field officers to a battalion of locals who daily rolled in from the village to hoe, shovel, and sculpt the terrain into an Englishman's idea of Eden.

DeGaul moved around the grounds in perfect contentment. He was concerned about the bank loans he kept covering for Roy, but for once the grounds work seemed to be getting done faster than it could wash away. He knew Jerusalem might be disappointed with WorldWide's interest in their new album, but what he heard sounded great and he was certain Cantone was right about Lilly; she could be a star. He put off going back to Manhattan a few more days. He trusted Booth to cover for him.

DeGaul uncharacteristically elected to stay in with Roy and reminisce when Jerusalem invited him to come with them to the big Saturday-night beach party. The Webster's day workers liked to toast the weekend with an all-night blowout on a secluded beach on the rocky road between the Retreat and the village of St. Pierre. They would build a bonfire, dance, drink, and smoke ganja. It sounded like DeGaul's kind of hoedown, but he told the band he was bushed, then asked John P. and Buster to keep an eye on the kids and get them out of there if things got weird. The people of St. Pierre were the gentlest DeGaul had ever known, but asking drunk young men around a fire to control themselves while Krystal did the topless Lambada was asking for more, perhaps, than flesh could handle.

It turned out to be a great night for a beach party. The moon was full and the waves were unusually high, washing up planks and plastic bottles and other debris. John P. said it meant there had been a storm at sea, they were lucky it had missed the island. St. Pierre's south coast faced open ocean for hundreds of miles. Big storms came out of nowhere and took even experienced fishermen by surprise. It was one reason this beautiful area was so underdeveloped. The ocean here was treacherous.

The locals brought boomboxes and beer. A couple of women roasted eels on what looked like enormous flyswatters and passed them around. The sparks from the great bonfire roared up into the sky. Lilly danced with Buster, Mack made out with Krystal, Dick fell in love with a local girl whose father dragged her home early, and Anthony got drunk and ended up pounding on a log with two sticks.

At midnight everyone had gone tribal and was having a blast, when Krystal stumbled back from a roll in the sand with her Scottish soulmate and announced, "Did you guys know there's a boat over there?"

No one paid much attention. John P. politely asked what sort of boat. Krystal said, "A really big boat, like a yacht or something, on the rocks with a hole in the side. Has that always been there?"

John P. got up and followed her over a couple of small dunes and across a short marsh, where there was a rocky little beach and the remnants of an uncompleted jetty. There was also, now, a thirty-foot schooner—the sort rich people rent for tours—with a hole in its belly, sitting sideways on the crest of a shoal just ten feet from the waterline.

John P. walked into the water and studied the boat. A voice came from inside. It said, "Holy shit!" Except it sounded like "Hoe-lay shite!" It was a Scottish voice.

"What did you find, Macky?" called Krystal from the shore.

Mack's head popped out of the hole in the side of the boat. "You won't believe it!" he shouted. His head disappeared for a moment and came back, like a puppet, holding out two off-white bricks.

Krystal squinted her eyes and said, "Cheese?"

"Not quite, lovely!" Mack said, disappearing again. John P. rushed into the water, ignoring the sharp rocks he stepped on, and made it to the boat. He stuck his head into the hole in time to smack foreheads with Mack, climbing out.

"Look, Johnny, look," Mack whispered. The half-submerged hold was filled with bricks of cocaine, stuck together with god-knows-what paste to carry to market.

"Get out of here now, boy," John P. said. "Whoever was on this boat might come back. We don't want to be here."

"I don't think so, Johnny," Mack said. "This boat's been here a while. I think whoever got off, got off somewhere else. Out on the ocean. No way this boat landed on these rocks with a crew aboard. This ship was abandoned." He laughed wildly. "And I'm in nautical salvage! Law of the sea! Raise the *Titanic*!"

John P. dragged Mack, who insisted on bringing one of his bricks, back to the bonfire with Krystal trailing along behind saying *ouch ouch ouch* over every stone. John would have preferred to head straight to Webster's, but he had to collect Lilly, Dick, and Anthony. He warned Mack to shut up about this and went to round up the others. But rounding up the others wasn't easy. People were spread all over the beach, dancing and drinking and smoking and talking. The moon had gone in, it was hard to see. By the time he got Lilly and Buster away from the group, Mack was talking excitedly to Anthony. Worse, Krystal was waving her hands in the air and pointing in the direction of the wreck to Dick, who was standing in a circle with several of the locals.

John P. saw it coming as sure as a hurricane. Starting with Mack and Anthony, people began to peel off from the party and move toward the dunes and the treasure. He convinced Lilly to wait with Buster in the van, but by then he had to go looking for the other four. When he got back to the shipwreck, every drunken day worker was ahead of him. The boat was rocking under the weight of his grounds crew and their wives and buddies crawling over it and extracting armfuls of cocaine bricks. Mack was in the middle of it. Krystal was standing with her toes an inch away from the water, screaming that it all belonged to her boyfriend.

John P. went down to the water and grabbed Dick and Anthony by their necks. He dragged them back up the sand, shouting at them that if they didn't run for the van as fast as they could they would be picked up by soldiers and buggered in a brig. It was a lie—there were no soldiers coming, and by morning there would be nothing to find but a busted boat. The threat worked, though. The tipsy musicians beat it back to their ride. Mack and Krystal would be more trouble. John P. waded into the surf and met Mack coming in with an armful of bricks. He grabbed Mack by the hair, leaned into his face, and shouted, "Get your woman and run to the van now! Soldiers are on the road with machine guns! No one's getting out of here alive!"

The drummer figured it was a lie, but he had as much contraband as he could carry and when John P. picked up Krystal and threw her over his shoulder, Mack elected to follow them back to the car.

As he shooed them over the hill and toward Buster's headlights, John P. turned and looked back at his community. These people were local color to the Americans, but they were his friends and neighbors. This was the town where he grew up, these were the men he worked with every day. They did not think of themselves as poor, because they had everything they needed to live and no experience of what they lacked. John P. had a quick and vivid premonition of all that changing.

He watched two men from his day crew throw punches at each other over a pile of bricks on the beach. He saw the sister of his brother's wife shoving aside another woman to get a foothold on the boat. He saw the boy who swept out the market digging a hole in the sand and trying to bury a chunk of cocaine.

Buster hit the horn and John P. turned toward the van. He didn't want to see any more.

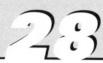

Zoey woke to what felt like a firehose slamming and shaking the window of her apartment. She rolled out of bed and pulled back the curtain. Rain was blasting sideways in sheets, rattling the glass. She stumbled around the small room trying to force herself awake. She went to the tiny kitchen to make coffee and looked through the small, dirty window over her sink. It was a monsoon. She'd never seen rain like this in New York. She looked at the clock. She had just time to make it to her 9:00 A.M. meeting if she didn't shower. She sponged under her arms and around her neck, brushed her teeth and tongue, raked a comb through her hair, and pulled on some clothes.

It took twelve minutes to complete all these ablutions. By the time she did, the rain had stopped and white sunlight was shining.

"That was weird," she murmured. She grabbed a hooded poncho just in case and headed downstairs to the street.

First surprise was that it was remarkably muggy. By the end of the block she had to take off the poncho and carry it. There were big puddles everywhere, and the sidewalks were more jammed than was usual. Zoey paid no attention. She went down the steps into the subway against the tide of a mob of screeching schoolchildren on a field trip. She fought her way to the turnstile through a swarm of people around the token booth, and only realized when she made it to the platform that she was the only commuter left.

She looked around. Three trains were stuck in the station, their doors open, sitting in three feet of water. It was like Venice. A conductor and an engineer in red rain gear were standing smoking cigarettes. Zoey asked if the trains were running at all. "Nowhere," the conductor said.

Okay, said Zoey, that explains the throng going the other way. I better find a taxi.

Up in the street she found a scene out of a Godzilla movie. The avenues were crammed with cars, the overpacked buses were not making any of their stops, and each taxi was full, locked up, and sticking to the middle lane. New Yorkers were shoving one another, fighting over pay phones, shouting into cell phones, and offering bribes for rides to truck drivers.

Well, Zoey considered, this certainly bites the big one. She trudged, sweating, two avenues over and it was even worse. One taxi light came on and a man with an umbrella knocked down a nurse on his way to chase it down the road. Zoey started walking the forty blocks to Times Square. Ten blocks along, a taxi with a single passenger in the back pulled up alongside her and turned on the light.

"Are you getting out?" Zoey asked the rider, placing her hand on the door handle.

"Yes, but across the street up ahead—I have to go to the bank machine."

"Great!" Zoey called to the driver, "I'm getting in." The driver paid no attention—he took advantage of a changing stoplight to swerve through the intersection and across five lanes, Zoey running along behind through the honking traffic.

When the cab stopped she let the passenger get out her side. She started to climb in but a large man with a small girl had already jumped in the other door.

"Sir," Zoey said, "I had this cab."

"Fuck you, bitch! I'm taking my little girl to school!"

"Well," Zoey said, "she's a lucky little daughter to have such a sweet dad." She let the cab go and resumed her long march.

When she arrived at the Black Mushroom, damp and smelly and an hour late, she was relieved to learn that she was among the first people to make it in at all. New York City had been shut down by four inches of rain. What the hell will we do, she thought, when terrorists let loose the swine flu? Maybe she'd be out of the city by then. The way things were going she'd probably be out of the city by Christmas, back working at her old 7-Eleven.

Booth no longer acknowledged her at all. If she called his office, no one called back. She was not invited to any meeting he attended. She was being erased.

Zoey felt her future slipping away, and she did not know how to hold on. She usually pushed these thoughts away, but with all her meetings on hold because of the flood she did not have the usual nonstop distractions. She closed her office door and sank into her chair. All of her A&R subordinates—motley group of liggers and do-nothings though they were—now routinely went over her head to Cantone with even trivial questions. His open-door policy had completely undermined her, and she was not even sure he was smart enough to know it. The Black Beauty album was not released, it had escaped. And though it was showing a little more life than anyone had expected, that was not saying much. There would be no video, no tour support, no bookings on Letterman or Conan. The album was generating some nice press, but that was the fool's consolation. "Nice press" were the famous last words of lost careers.

What scared Zoey most was that she had not found any act she could believe in since Jerusalem slipped away from her. Everything she heard sounded awful, and a couple of the awful acts she'd passed on were already in the Top Ten. Zoey was worried that she was losing her gut, that she could no longer rely on her own taste and instinct to tell her what music the public would buy. When the rest of them realized it, she was sunk.

She turned on the TV. There was a sign of the times. When did record companies start relying on television to break bands, to tell them what was hot? When radio went completely corporate, she supposed. She clicked to one of the video channels and saw her doom. A perky teenage girl with enhanced breasts and jelly-injected lips was leading a bunch of peppy clones in a sexy bump-and-grind that looked like Up With People in a brothel. This was what it had come to.

Zoey felt like the only one who could see the emperor had no clothes. When did everyone decide they wanted to be a Pepper, too? Rock and roll had once seemed like an alternative world, where the freaks got to be cool and the cheerleaders were the weirdos. Now kids thought it was hip to pay money for clothes with corporate logos, to wear their labels on the outside, to march around as sandwich boards. This was not what she signed up for.

Zoey and her mom and her little brother grew up in a huddle in Ann Arbor, Michigan. They never had much money, and after her dad ran off with his best friend's wife they had nothing. She was a weirdo in school, a poor kid with high test scores, leftist politics, and a big mouth. Zoey's mom told her that in the real world her intelligence would give her the upper hand. She promised Zoey that no matter how cruel the creeps in her junior high school were, when she got out in the big world her brains and drive and creativity would make her a big success, and the preppies and pep squad girls who ostracized her would be back in the suburbs full of regrets.

Well, it didn't work out that way. The straights had captured the underground and the gals from the pep squad were the new pop stars. When did everyone decide that looks mattered more than talent? When did record companies begin signing musicians based on their photographs? Where was Zoey the day they announced that transfer?

Zoey found her first community—small and unpopular though it was—with the little group of kids in her high school who shared her love for Talking Heads and Elvis Costello. At the University of Minnesota, she got a job on the student entertainment committee and helped bring Squeeze to her school. She met the band and they talked with her about music like she really understood. It started to feel like her mother had been right. The big world was going to be welcoming.

When college ended she got a job working for a Minneapolis promoter. She convinced him to take a chance on a Cure concert and it was his biggest hit of the year. Zoey became his liaison to the underground. She became friendly with Hüsker Dü, the Replacements, and the Minutemen. The musicians all agreed that she had great ears. She was bound and determined to get a job in A&R at a record company.

Finally there was a crack of hope. Through her musician friends she got a shot at going to New York to work at a major label—but it was in publicity. Zoey took it as a way to get a foot in the door. Publicity is the traditional women's ghetto in the music business, and she arrived at the bottom of the pecking order. Zoey spent her first nine months in Manhattan sharing a one-room apartment in the East Village with two other women and doing tickets, the lowest job of all.

It was a misery, but it was the only way in. Zoey was responsible for taking ticket requests from journalists and other freeloaders, seeing who her boss wanted to service, calling back and saying no to some (lots of recriminations and threats) and yes to others (no gratitude) and arranging for their tickets to be picked up (left behind), messengered to them ("I never got them"), or collected at the door.

Zoey had to deal with ungrateful snots and last-minute demands until an hour before showtime, at which point she would go to the venue to stand by the door with the guest list and be abused nonstop while the music inside went on without her. God help her withstand the contempt pissed on her if she asked some mumbler to repeat his name. Lord save her from the bloody-minded vengeance promised if she made a mistake or could not find someone's name on the hand-scrawled napkin the band sent down five minutes before showtime. God forbid she ever hear the words "Thank you."

But boy did she hear it when the schnorers got offended because their pair of great free seats to a sold-out concert were a section behind the great free seats given to someone they considered less important. Those spoiled leeches would call Zoey the next day snorting derision and expecting her to thank them when they finished their tirade by saying, "I won't mention this to your boss, but make sure it doesn't happen again."

No, she thought. Next time I'll send you obviously counterfeit tickets and let the promoter's hired apes drag you under the stage and beat you with the leg of a chair.

Zoey prayed to be delivered from publicity, but it was a slow crawl up the seven circles. In time she graduated from ticket flunky to baby-band baby-sitter to on-the-road spy, filing progress reports on new acts to headquarters from the back of the tour van. The newly signed groups figured someone from the record company always came along on club tours. In fact, Zoey was sending word back on whether the label's tour support was being spent wisely: "Bassist suicidal, look for replacement now. Singer holding up well, an inflated ego makes a mighty life raft. Manager incompetent, better suited to previous job as head-shop vendor."

From baby bands, Zoey moved up to big tours and spin-doctor status. She knew she had to get off the plane when she heard herself advocating a middle-aged star get liposuction for a *Vogue* spread. At the end of three years of pain and humiliation, Zoey was a vice president of publicity at Ashram Records, a midsized label in the WorldWide galaxy. She was twenty-seven. When Ashram was sucked into the WorldWide mothership in a cost-saving consolidation, Zoey surprised everyone by trading her big title in publicity for a lesser job in WorldWide A&R.

Her former coworkers took it as a sign of insecurity. Some whispered she had swallowed a demotion in order to keep from being laid off. It was neither. Zoey had never wanted to be a publicist and she never stopped looking for a chance to move into A&R. If doing so meant taking a step back, she would take it.

Nine months after she made the switch, WorldWide violated a dozen promises and eliminated the entire former Ashram publicity department as redundant. Her old colleagues might have praised Zoey's foresight, were their mouths not filled with accusations that she had been tipped off in advance and sold out her old friends to save herself.

It hurt, but Zoey took it. They all just lost their jobs, she figured, they have a right to their resentment. And anyway, if they believe I'd hang them out like that I guess they weren't my friends anyway.

Sitting in her office now, Zoey finally knew how they felt. It was tough to keep bitterness at bay. The record business was full of good jobs for insensitive people, but if you loved music, if you cared about musicians, if you rooted for the great artists over the haircuts and boob jobs, it would break your heart.

What happened to moderating hipness, she wondered. Barbie and Ken have taken over rock and roll and no one admits they care. Joe Precious claimed it was because of the fall of the USSR, the scandal of communism, the loss of any reservation about money as the measure of morality. "At least in the old days," he had told Zoey over drinks one night in Los Angeles, "people paid lip service to socialist ideals of generosity and equality. At least there was the fashionable pretense of a public conscience. Now greed is unchained and—even more remarkable —has been bestowed with moral force."

Precious's response was to "use the enemy's strength against him," which to Zoey meant it was how he rationalized milking money out of gangster rap. Like that was not one more manifestation of the selfishness and irresponsibility he was smart enough to recognize but not decent enough to resist.

Zoey's last boss took a lot of credit for her ideas, but at least her ideas got through. Cantone was a whole other deal. He was so happy to be in the frat that it would never occur to him to question the admissions policy. He was the Ken doll given flesh, which is why Booth liked him.

He is the new breed, Zoey thought. He looks good and speaks well but he has never had an original thought in his life. He is a ditto.

Zoey's assistant came in and said, "Got a minute?"

"Got a razor blade?" Zoey asked.

"There's a man who's been calling and won't leave his name. He says he has to speak to you about a serious personal matter. He's on the line again."

"Put him through, I need a stalker." Zoey waited for the phone to ring. Probably another of those first-year Merrill Lynch jerks making cold calls.

The phone buzzed and she said, "Zoey here."

"Zoey, hi, my name's Tim Baerenwald from Calhoun, Brebner, the law firm. Thanks for picking up. Listen, I hope this isn't out of line, but I've been hearing a lot of great things about you from a lot of mutual acquaintances and I wonder if there's a chance we could get together."

"Am I about to be arrested? What are you asking me?"

"No, listen, Zoey. I do some scouting for different entertainment companies. I sometimes put together executives with firms searching for talent."

"You're a headhunter."

"Sure."

"Am I being hunted?"

"You could be. I'd like to get to know you a little. Could we hook up? Outside your office?"

"Hey, you're not going to murder me and stuff my body in a drum, are you?"

"Ha, ha. No, you could come up to our offices. Or we could hook up at the bar at the Century or someplace convenient to you."

"Look, I'm all jammed up today. Tomorrow's bad. How about Monday, maybe early. Like, breakfast."

"Great. Where do you like to go? The Paramount? Four Seasons?"

"I like Hojo's. Times Square. Don't have to worry about seeing anyone in the business."

Baerenwald laughed. "I like Hojo's, too. I'll meet you there Monday at what time?"

"Eight-thirty?"

"Great."

"Hold on, how will I know you?"

"I know you."

Well, Zoey said to herself. Mystery date. Maybe those internet stories are doing me some good after all.

Her assistant came to the door with a worried face. "Anything?"

"Paternity suit," Zoey said, and started returning phone calls.

The Monday morning after St. Pierre found the drug boat no one showed up for work at Webster's Retreat. Mr. Jay and John P. went door to door looking for their day crew, but the crew was indisposed.

Roy Nightingale paced the lawn in circles, chewing his fingernails and turning colors. DeGaul tried to calm him, but it was hard to make a case for cool. For Webster's to be completed this year, everything had to go perfectly. A couple of weeks of bad weather could sink the dream. This was worse than bad weather.

Mr. Jay said it might just be a villagewide hangover. But when no one showed up Wednesday he could not pretend the crew was coming back.

DeGaul offered to pitch in with the simple maintenance—watering the flowers, rolling the tennis court, changing the pool filters. Nightingale was inconsolable. Among the missing, DeGaul noticed, was Buster. The flat-earther appeared Wednesday afternoon and took his usual position on the tractor mower as if nothing had happened. DeGaul said to let him be but Nightingale was determined to play Lord Jim.

"Buster," Nightingale said sharply, "where have you been?"

Buster smiled and looked this way and that. He reached into his lunch bag and brought out a brick of cocaine, wrapped in tinfoil. "I got three more," he smiled. "I buried them in my yard at night when no one could see."

Nightingale was appalled but DeGaul smiled and said, "Let me get this straight, Buster. You dug a hole in your yard and buried three bricks of cocaine."

"That's right. Everyone knows I got them, but when they rob my house they will find nothing."

"Explain this to me," DeGaul said. "Do you have grass in your yard?"

"Of course. I have a green thumb, you know that, you see the lawn here. That's all my doing."

"Of course. So everyone knows you have this stash and you figure thieves are going to come for it. But what I'm wondering is, are the thieves going to see a little mound of new brown dirt in the middle of your perfect green lawn? Did you leave a marker saying, 'Here's where I hid the drugs'?"

Buster leaped from the tractor and ran toward the gate. He turned, ran back, took his brick of cocaine from his lunch bag, handed it to the startled Nightingale, and said, "Hold this for me!" and lit off down the road.

Three minutes later DeGaul pulled up beside him in Roy's van and said, "Hop in, Buster, I'll give you a lift!" Buster led him up the winding hill road to the tiny house where he lived. The lawn was smooth as a golf course, rows of flowers bloomed in perfect lines, and there was a big hole in the middle of the yard. Buster ran to the hole and fell on his knees. He clawed at the dirt for a minute before giving up. He lay down on his belly on his perfect lawn with his face in the hole.

DeGaul genuflected beside him and put his hand on Buster's shoulder. "Chin up, fella," he said. "Let's get back to Webster's before Roy loses your last brick."

For the rest of the afternoon Buster would not speak. He rode his lawn mower, as usual, up and down the grounds, seated miserably on his last bar of coke.

Nightingale watched from the porch. He said, "Bill, this is the end. The drugs are going to kill our dream."

"I'm not half so scared of the drugs," DeGaul said, "as I am of the money. That's what ruins a nice neighborhood."

• • •

That afternoon DeGaul, Nightingale, and Mr. Jay drove into St. Pierre. It was like Las Vegas crossed with the Wild West. They saw Webster's pool boy cruise by in a Jeep Cherokee with the sound system blasting "Johnny Too Bad." They went into the tiny fish shop to eat lunch and looked at prices that would shame the best restaurant in Paris.

Driving out of town they saw one of the missing day crew struggling up a hill carrying a box spring big enough to accommodate a horse on his honeymoon.

"Where do they go to sell the blow and buy all this crap?" DeGaul asked his companions. "They sure ain't picking up Jeeps and giant mattresses in St. Pierre."

"The far side of the island," Nightingale said. "The city."

"That's what I figured. This is very bad, fellas. Number one, they're obviously selling the cocaine to drug dealers in the city. That means those dealers are going to come out here, looking for the treasure chest. Number two, a bunch of rubes rolling into town and unloading that much coke and spending that much dough is going to attract a whole lot of the worst kind of attention."

"The army," Nightingale said.

"I'm thinking worse than the army," DeGaul said. "I'm imagining whatever Bolivian that boat belonged to. Somebody lost a yachtload of cocaine. Assume it was somebody professional and mean. We don't know how it happened and we don't care. But it's a safe bet that if whoever it was hears about a sudden coke boom in a little town just off the trade route where he lost his cargo, he's going to come looking."

They rode back to Webster's in silence. Nightingale got a drink and disappeared upstairs.

DeGaul went down to the bungalows. Jerusalem were recording. He watched them for a few minutes through the glass walls of the living room. Then he took out his portable phone and called Booth.

"Where are you, Bill?" Booth demanded. "You were supposed to be back on Monday! Things are falling to shit around here and we got the DNC fund-raiser tomorrow! Tell me you're calling from the airport."

"I'm not gonna make the fund-raiser," DeGaul said. "I got a per-

sonal problem down here I have to take care of. . . . Yeah, it's a bitch. . . .
Look, J.B., this is going to take a little longer than I expected, but you
hang in there. Cover my ass with the board, okay? The band is sounding
great, by the way. These kids are going to be big. Lots of hits. Did that
'Bed of Nails' video get any reaction?"

"Nothing. Big waste of money. She should've taken her shirt off."

"That's okay. The second album's gonna be the charm. I'm sorry to
bail on the Democrats, but they won't miss me. Slip them a thousand
bucks in an envelope with my name on it."

"Come back to work."

"Tell NOA I'm negotiating a new distribution deal in North Korea.
And look, J.B., I'm easily reached, call me with anything."

"I'll watch your back, buddy. But get home soon, okay?"

"You bet. One more week."

DeGaul clicked off. He knew Booth was hungry. He knew that every
day he stayed in St. Pierre that hunger was fed by resentment. But De-
Gaul believed that deep down Booth had a good heart, and when the
chips were counted it would show through.

He came back to the house to find Nightingale in the foyer with a
suitcase, twitching.

"Going to town to buy a mattress?" DeGaul asked.

"Look, Willie," Nightingale said nervously, "it's over. I see that, I accept it. This has been a grand folly, but if I stay at Webster's any longer I
lose my wife as well as the dream. So having lost one thing I hold precious, I am going home to London to see if it's too late to save the other."

"Aw, come on, Roy . . ."

"No. It's all yours now, Willie. Yours and the banks' and the credi-
tors'. It was always yours, wasn't it? I was riding in your wake, as I've always done. Funny, isn't it, how you could be both the bon vivant and the
business head? For all my earnestness and perfect penmanship, I never
had a tenth of your ability."

"Roy, we all have days like this. You've had more than your share.
What do you say you fly up to New York with me for a week or so, we'll
bring Martha over, and we'll all have a great cosmopolitan time a thousand miles from any seashells."

"I'm quitting on you, Willie. I've already called the solicitors. Everything's in your name now, including the debts and those mortgages you were so good as to cosign. I'm letting you down. I'm running away. It's your dream now, Willie."

DeGaul stood on the piazza and watched his old friend drive away. Geez, he thought, I don't even know where the fuse box is. He walked out and looked at his new domain. "Hey, Buster!" he called to the figure sitting awkwardly in the saddle of his tractor mower, "you already cut that lawn three times!"

# 30

Cantone was in his office going through a pile of tapes. He had put off listening to the A-list demos from unsigned acts brought in by his own department, top lawyers, big managers, and friends of Booth. Now he was trying to make up for lost time, shoveling away at the pile. He sat in a big armchair next to the stereo and rotated DATS, cassettes, CDs, and the dreaded audio-visual demos presented by the representatives of artists more photogenic than musical. "To get this one," the code went, "you need to see the whole package."

In his lap he had a schoolboy's ringed binder. He made a list of names down the left side and filled in his comments. He tried to listen to each tape all the way through but sometimes he had to fast-forward.

The longer he listened the shorter his comments got:

"Gangsta rapper with ANTI-gangsta rap. Send to R&B division. *Could be on to something here.*"

"Boy group à la Backstreet/NSync. White? Second song good. Too late."

"Reunion with two of five original members. No one misses them."

"Hippie jam band. Not as good as a lot of acts who don't sell anyway."

"Female rocker. If Bob Seger were a girl. Too 1998."

"NOT Stupid-smart. Stupid-stupid."

"Puffy copy—bad pitch."

"Britney of France? Sounds like Tiffany of Taiwan."

"John Cafferty imitator."

He came to the next tape and stopped. It was from a musician named Paul Slocum whom Cantone had loved as a kid. He had three of Slocum's albums and had played them every day of eleventh grade. He saw him play at college gigs and clubs around New England. Slocum had not had a record deal in five or six years. He had written Cantone a personal note mentioning the name of a mutual friend in Maine.

Cantone put it on. It was good, it reminded him of home—which made him worry that it was dated. He listened more. It was good. But it probably was not as good as Slocum's best work, which no one bought. The third song was great. He rewound and played it again. This one could have been on one of the albums Jim had loved so much as a teenager. But maybe Jim couldn't trust his own reaction, was bringing more sympathy to it than another listener would. Slocum was old now, forty at least. There was no photo included. Jim read the letter again. It struggled to be cordial, but there was a touch of desperation. Slocum was tugging at his sleeve. Thank goodness he doesn't know what a big fan I was, Jim thought. I'm glad he doesn't know I'm the same kid who used to wait by the back door after the show to talk to him. He was nice enough, then, but pretty smug, kind of condescending. Of course, I was seventeen with my mouth hanging open. He was nice enough.

Jim rewound the tape again. He didn't know how to separate his feelings about Slocum's old records from his obligation to evaluate the tape objectively. DeGaul, he was sure, would like it, but DeGaul was not part of this process. If they followed DeGaul's taste WorldWide would sign Bo Diddley. No one knew that better than DeGaul, so he stayed out of it. Jim had learned that was a sign of real power. When asked for a favor the man close to power rushes to prove he can do it. The man with real power smiles and says, "Oh, I would love to but my people don't let me get involved with that sort of thing! They're afraid I'll mess it up!"

Jim put the Slocum tape in his bag to take home. He knew he'd carry it back and forth for a few days and then empty out his bag and add it to a stack of other undecideds where it would be slowly buried. It would be kinder to Paul Slocum to just say no. But Jim was sure that if there was even a tiny chance of a yes down the line, Slocum would rather be in the pile of possibilities.

Jim wondered if the pressure of his job was corrupting his ability to trust his own taste.

His assistant leaned in. "Booth's on the phone."

She was supposed to be holding all his calls, but Jim was grateful for the excuse. He answered and Booth said, "Go home and put on a suit, we're going to a political fund-raiser in the Hamptons."

"Not that I don't appreciate the invitation, J.B., but I wish I'd known earlier."

"You're filling in for DeGaul. Our CEO can't tear himself away from jungleland for a dinner with the next president of the United States. Stay on the line, Leilani will give you the details."

• • •

Booth hung up the phone when his secretary came on. He got up and walked around his desk. It was just astonishing. A major political event at the home of a top movie producer and DeGaul cancels. Just woke up and decided not to put his pants on. Astonishing.

Booth prided himself on understanding his job. His job was to make decisions that made DeGaul look good. It was not DeGaul's job to agree with Booth or even know what Booth was doing. DeGaul empowered Booth to run his company and rewarded him when he did well. If the company ever started doing badly, Booth would take the fall and DeGaul would keep going. Booth understood that. He had always understood that.

But he was no longer a kid. He was forty-five. To be DeGaul's number two at forty was great. But Booth did not want to be DeGaul's number two at fifty. There is a point when you are no longer on your way, when you have got as far as you're going. Booth knew he made DeGaul look good. He made DeGaul's luxury possible. So far fortune had been with them both. Booth had imagined that DeGaul would eventually step aside, and if he did so while things were good, it was not too much to expect that Booth would replace him. But no hot streak lasted forever. Sooner or later WorldWide's fortunes would dip. If DeGaul chose that day to retire, his job would go not to Booth but to some fresh face.

Booth had never considered that DeGaul might elect to take his re-

tirement without leaving his position. He was spending all his time in
the Caribbean doing God knows what. Smoking hash and waxing his
water skis. How could he be so selfish?

Booth looked at the framed photos on his office wall. He and De-
Gaul with Mick and Keith, he and DeGaul with Princess Diana, he and
DeGaul with Michael Jackson, he and DeGaul on skis in Aspen.

I'm not betraying him, Booth promised himself. I'm making hard
choices to save the company he built.

. . .

While Booth was repelling his attack of conscience, Zoey Pavlov was
many levels beneath him, meeting for the second time with attorney-
headhunter Tim Baerenwald, a youngish man with a longish face and
shortish hair. Their first rendezvous, at Howard Johnson's, had gone
well enough that Zoey agreed to a let's-get-down-to-brass-tacks follow-
up at a diner on Ninth Avenue.

"I have to ask you one thing," Zoey said after they ordered.

"Go ahead."

"You work for Asa Calhoun, right?"

"I don't work for him. We're partners in the same firm."

" 'Cause Calhoun does a lot of work for my boss, Booth, and they're
big buddies and everything. If I agree to use you to explore some other
jobs, Booth won't find out?"

"Zoey, I'm a lawyer. I can't betray a client's trust. Anyway, our firm
does all sorts of work on all sides of different music-industry situations.
If we didn't know how to keep our mouths shut we'd be out of business."

"Fine. Just had to get that straight."

"Great. So here's the deal. I keep hearing wonderful things about
you. And of course, with the situation at WorldWide so unpredict-
able . . ."

"What situation at WorldWide?" Zoey was still counting down the
weeks left on her contract.

Baerenwald leaned forward and whispered, "With DeGaul and all.
The erratic behavior, the rumors."

"Oh, rumors, rumors. DeGaul's fine."

The lawyer cocked an eyebrow. "You've seen him?"

"Listen, I don't want to betray Bill's trust any more than you would mine. Now explain this to me. If you find me a new job, what do you get?"

"Straight to the point, Zoey, I like that. My firm gets ten percent of your first year's salary, minus bonus. Fifteen percent if the salary is over a million."

Zoey felt herself about to swoon like Olive Oyl but she stayed steady.

"How likely is that? Passing a million, I mean."

"I don't want to raise your expectations unreasonably. Some of the most promising positions coming on to our radar now are dot com start-ups that don't pay huge salaries but pay off in stock options. One fellow we put in a seventy-thousand dollar slot a year ago just cashed in his options for four million. Imagine—we took a seven-thousand-dollar commission on that placement."

"Ya win some ya lose some."

"Oh, don't misunderstand me. We're delighted. I daresay he is now retaining us on a steady basis. See, Zoey, our firm needs to stay in touch with the next generation of executives. We want to represent you today because we know you are a good bet to be the J. B. Booth or Bill DeGaul of the future."

"Yikes. Well, okay, then. Take me."

Zoey came back from lunch with a new bounce in her step. She got more good news when she landed back at her desk. Flute Bjerke was in the door with a big scoop.

"Z., have you looked at SoundScan?"

"Why? Did Cokie Shea make it into the Guinness Book?"

"Black Beauty. They sold six thousand albums this week. That's up from two thousand last week. From eight hundred the week before. Did you know about this?"

Zoey tore the printout from Bjerke's hands. "Are you sure this is right?"

"Absolutely, I checked it three times."

"Oh my God. Get me some painter's bands, Flutie, I'm going lesbian."

. . .

Five hours later a car carrying Mr. and Mrs. J. B. Booth, Al Hamilton, and Jim Cantone passed through the gates and up the long dirt driveway of a Long Island estate belonging to a revered movie producer active in Democratic politics. The three men talked about work the whole way out on the Long Island Expressway. Lois Booth read a magazine. They were bearing ten-thousand-dollar-a-couple invitations to a barbecue dinner, country music recital, and moonlight dance to raise money for Democratic candidates for high office in the Empire State and beyond.

They showed their tickets for a second time to a tuxedoed giant at the front door, and joined a party that spilled out from the house's great parlor into the backyard and down to the sea.

"Jim Cantone seems nice," Lois said to her husband after they'd greeted the guest of honor and picked up some lemonade. "Very young."

"He's just what we needed," Booth said. "He is the audience. Never gonna make Mensa, but in his job that's an attribute."

"He has twin boys, four years old."

"Lot of that going around. It's the age of fertility treatments."

The Booths stopped talking then. They had waited too late to have children. Lois had two miscarriages, then they stopped trying. Through it all she never brought up the abortion she had at Booth's insistence when they were first dating in the seventies. But each knew the other kept silent calculation of how old that child would be. It was the biggest of the things they never said out loud.

Hamilton and Cantone were out by the cold ocean, soaking up the schmooze.

"It must be great to live like this," Cantone said as they climbed a short bank that separated the lawn from the beach.

"You'll get there," Hamilton smiled. It surprised Jim. He felt like he was doing so well now, he could hardly dream of more. But maybe Hamilton was right. Maybe this was just the first foot on the stairs. After all, he was just thirty-one.

"Al," Jim said, "you have to get Booth to stop bitching about DeGaul not being around. It legitimizes all these rumors. I know J.B. resents it, but he's got to shut up and support Bill."

Hamilton looked at Cantone for a long time, then he said, "Booth is the best friend DeGaul ever had. You have no idea."

"I'm sure I don't, but the gossip is bad for WorldWide. It's important that everyone know we all stand behind DeGaul." Cantone waited for some agreement. It didn't come. So he said, "If it ever came down to it, I'd stand with DeGaul no matter what happened."

Hamilton scratched his nose. "Noted."

Asa "Kingfish" Calhoun came shambling through the sand carrying a drink that had a swizzle stick and rolling an olive on his tongue. The ocean breeze was flapping the lawyer's comb-over like a flag.

"Hammy," Calhoun said to Hamilton.

"Mr. Calhoun, how are you, sir? Good to see you spending your own money. I understand you still hold out hope for a revival of the Wallace wing of the party."

"George or Henry? No, I'm a Lester Maddox man."

"You know Jim Cantone."

"Hi, Jim, good to see you. Wild Bill still not returned from digging the canal?"

"He's with us in spirit," Hamilton said. "You need me for something."

"A legal matter, if I could steal a moment. Jim, would you forgive me if I keelhauled Big Al for a minute or two?"

Cantone said he was going back to the house anyway and left the insiders to talk.

"Baerenwald's hooked your little punk girl," Calhoun said.

"Fine. Booth wants her out of our hair without having to go through the drama of firing her. She's the type who'd throw herself down the stairs and sue us for unlawful termination. Where are you going to stick her?"

"Maybe an IPO. Lose her in cyberspace."

"Why short yourself the commission? Come on, put her where she can do some real damage."

"You are an unethical prick, you know that, Hamilton?"

"Look who's calling the kettle African-American."

"What did you have in mind?"

"What's the big studio this fellow's involved with?" Hamilton was referring to the party's host. Calhoun reminded him. "Right. They're trying to buy into the record business now. What are they calling the label they're starting?"

"Vision Music."

"Got your finger in there yet?"

"My firm is advising them."

"Of course you are. I say you tell Vision Music you have a hot prospect for their A&R chief, but it's going to be tough. She's a superstar at WorldWide and they won't let her go without a fight. Cost a million easy to buy out the deal."

"They're movie people, Al, but they're not cretins."

"Just a suggestion. You'd take commission on a million instead of a hundred thousand. And we'd be grateful."

"No one in the world would pay a million dollars for Zoey Pavlov."

"Why not? She has no taste or ethics. She could be a big success."

Calhoun looked out at the ocean, his hair sailing behind him. He said he'd mull it over. "You want me to look for an on-line IPO for you, Hammy? Build a bridge to the twenty-first century?"

"I'm already there."

Hamilton felt like it was a hundred years ago and he was in the buggy-whip business. He knew the automobile was coming, but should he invest in electric power? Steam? Wasn't internal combustion dirty and dangerous? You could see the shape of the future and still back the wrong horseless carriage.

"I have enough problems," Booth thought. "Why do the people I employ to help me instead devote all their time to piling on more?"

In the crown of the Black Mushroom, Cantone was bending Booth's ear about why they should make a record with a never-was folksinger named Paul Slocum. Booth had seen this before; the messiah complex. The young executive given the power to make dreams come true with a wave of his wand decides he must use his great abilities for the good of all mankind, like Superman. It was a special form of hubris, Booth thought, that inevitably ended in tears. The young executive would discover his power was not as great as he thought, he could not turn a has-been into a hot property. The has-been, his hopes raised and dashed, would turn bitter and accuse the young executive of bad faith, incompetence, and immorality. Everyone ended up sadder than when they started.

For Cantone it was probably a lesson worth learning, but Booth saw no reason to waste a lot of WorldWide's cash and energy teaching him.

So Booth knew what he was going to say already, but etiquette insisted he had to sit there and listen to Cantone make his pitch before he said it.

"No one was more surprised than me," Cantone told him. "I figured

Paul Slocum was ancient history. But I had to admit that if the same tape had come in by a twenty-two-year-old kid, I'd have been running for a bus to meet him. I very cautiously said I'd like to hear more and the next day the guy sends me twelve songs on a cassette, just him and a guitar, and J.B., they were fantastic. Much better than the studio demo, because there was no cornball production. I mean, these songs were like great Petty or Springsteen. If the Wallflowers had songs like these, it would move ten million. I said I was mildly impressed. I paid for some more recording in a good studio with a couple of young players."

Booth arched his eyebrows. Cantone assured him it was a modest budget and hurried on. "You've got to hear this. Listen."

Cantone loaded a DAT into Booth's deck. The songs were fine, they were pleasant, maybe this guy could get some covers in Nashville. Booth closed his eyes as if he were listening intently. He turned his chair away from Cantone, whose puppy-dog enthusiasm was giving him the creeps. Booth tuned out the music and let his thoughts roam. Why did DeGaul disappear into the Caribbean and make it so easy for Booth to move against him? Wild Bill was not stupid. Was this some sort of feint? Would DeGaul come roaring back into town with both guns blazing when Booth finally struck? Was it possible that Al Hamilton could not be trusted? What was Booth missing?

He realized the music had stopped. He spun around and looked at Cantone, who was smiling cautiously.

Booth pretended to choose his words carefully before he spoke. He waited for the pause to progress from pregnant to poignant. Then he smiled sadly and shook his head. "Jim," he said, "I'm a little surprised. I never thought of you as selfish."

Cantone was set for an argument about aesthetics, and prepared to debate economics, but an uppercut to his scruples caught him by surprise. He said, "Huh?"

"Lookit, I know this is the music you like to listen to when you go home. I respect that. But don't you see how egotistical it is to try to impose it on other people? You're a smart guy, you have refined taste. You live in Manhattan, you go to nice restaurants and the theater. You're richer and more successful than the average American and you have a much-better-looking wife. When you go home to your beautiful downtown apartment tonight, you will put on some rarefied music like Paul Slocum and stare out the window at the skyline while Jane lays out some nice cuisine. Fair enough, Jim. You've earned it."

Jim tried to protest, but Booth's verbal steamroller was going downhill and no fool dared stand before it.

Booth went on: "Your value to WorldWide is the little part of you that is still a hockey jock from the mountains of Maine, that's still in touch with people who watch *Wheel of Fortune* and shop at Sears. Jim, this album is not for them. This album is for you."

"J.B., those people at Sears in Maine or Oklahoma or Utah are exactly the ones who'd love an album like this. They're still buying replacement copies of the Eagles' *Greatest Hits* because no one's making anything new for them!"

"Jim, Jim. Listen to yourself. Sheryl Crow is for them. Jewel is for them. The public doesn't want some old white-haired guy with a mustache who looks like he escaped from the farmer's market. They can get this kind of music from the old artists they love or they can get it from good-looking young acts. But what you're proposing here is that you know more than the public does. It's a very elitist attitude, and if anyone other than you came at me with it, I'd be very disappointed. You, I know you're not a snob. I know you don't mean to impose your taste on other people. But that's what this will smell like, and it won't work. It's totally your call, but I would advise you as a friend and as your biggest supporter within this company, don't blow all your capital on a self-indulgence. It's unfair to all the other people here who would have to work a project without a prayer. It's unfair to Paul Slocum, who has no chance of succeeding in this marketplace. And it's unworthy of you."

Cantone knew he'd feel these cuts later, and think of things he should have said.

He stammered and managed to say, "I know we're set up to move millions of units. But there must be someplace, just once every year or so, to make a record just because it's great. Even if we don't think a lot of people will buy it. There must be room for that."

"See," Booth said, "to me, what makes a record great is that it reaches millions of people. And a record reaches millions of people because it is of its time. Now maybe if Paul Slocum had put out this exact album in

1972 it would have sold millions and won a Grammy. Because then it would have been of its time. But he didn't, and to imagine he could make up for it now is like saying now that we have heat-seeking smart bombs we should go back to Vietnam and blow up the VC tunnels. Too late! It's too late. But listen, you're the A&R chief. If you feel this is something you have to do, I won't stop you."

Jim knew that going ahead in the face of Booth's resistance was impossible. Booth would let his attitude be known. Marketing and publicity would down tools. Paul Slocum's album would be a disaster and Jim's ability to fire up the machine for other projects would be hobbled.

"I'm not going to force it," Jim said.

"Of course not." Booth smiled. "You're a smart guy and you're a good guy. You take the demos home and listen to them all you want. You bought 'em, you enjoy 'em. Just leave the rest of America out of it."

This, Cantone thought, is moral jujitsu. Standing up for doing the right thing gets flipped around to become evidence of selfishness. We are in the era of late high capitalism. Everything has been reduced to its dollar value. A painting is as good as its auction price, a movie as good as its opening weekend, a home as nice as its resale value. And Booth is the master of kung fu.

Booth felt bad for Cantone. So he offered him some good advice: "Jim, nobody knows what's going to happen with the record business in the next ten years. I don't know if people will be punching up music online or over the telephone or through the radiator. I don't know how much longer we few old shops are going to get all the money just because we own the trucks and the pressing plants.

"But I can tell you this—we've had a great run. A hundred years of keeping ninety-five percent of the money and all the rights! Who'd have believed it? How can we complain? If the roof falls in tomorrow, if the means of production go into the hands of the artists, or Bill Gates or Jeff Bezos or whoever the hell it's going to be, just make sure you've got your ass covered. Get your family taken care of. Get yourself an artist who'll make you rich before the bottom falls out. I don't care if it's a Britney or a Ricky or a Sporty or the return of the rhumba. But find something that won't take ten years to pay back your investment, because, honest injun, in ten years I don't know if you, me, or the industry will still be here. You're a good guy. Forget this high-and-inside crap and you go get yourself something that will pay you back fast. Go get yourself a Hootie."

Jim left and took his Slocum with him.

Booth tried to get back to his real work but Al Hamilton appeared. How could a fat man slide so quickly through a crack in the door? It was a mystery.

"You need to sign these," Hamilton said, laying in front of Booth a stack of documents with yellow and red stickers that indicated where his signature and initials should go.

Booth glanced at the papers quickly. They ratified a change that had already taken place, the transfer of profits on U.S. artists in Europe from the American to the European bottom line. This paper change made it look as if Booth had taken European revenues through the roof while DeGaul had let the States droop.

The accounts had already been credited; this was the final formality. Booth knew that Hamilton, probably alone in both hemispheres, understood the implications. This was the pistol aimed at DeGaul's head. Until Booth put his name on the paper, the whole enterprise could be blamed on Hamilton if DeGaul wised up. Once Booth signed, there was no hiding his complicity. He would not sign until he was sure that Hamilton was with him.

"Where is he, Al?" Booth said sadly to Hamilton. "Why isn't Bill here? What am I not understanding?"

"I don't understand either," Hamilton said. "Perhaps we're thick. Or perhaps Wild Bill is acting in a manner that defies logic. Or perhaps . . ." Hamilton hesitated.

"What?"

"Do you suppose he wants out but he doesn't want to say so?"

"I've never known DeGaul to not say what he wants. He's not Captain Subtle."

"Sure," Hamilton said. "What I wonder sometimes is, is he even being honest with himself? Maybe what he wants is so contrary to his self-image that he can't bring himself to admit it to himself. Like the fellow who doesn't want to admit he wants out of his marriage, so he just treats his wife worse and worse until she leaves him."

"What are you, Sigmund Freud?"

"Just speculating."

Al Hamilton did something Booth had never seen him do. He walked over to Booth's closet, opened the door, and poured whiskey into two tumblers. He brought them back and handed one to Booth and drank from the other.

Booth said nothing. He took a swig.

"Here's what's chewing me up, Al," Booth said. "I'm starting to feel like my loyalty to DeGaul is making me disloyal to WorldWide. How long can I keep covering for him before those silly Swedes start thinking he's lost it? God forbid they decide they know how to run this company better than we do!"

"You're the only one who could hold WorldWide together," Hamilton said. "If DeGaul goes, you're the only one the staff and artists would accept as a replacement. Not to mention Wall Street."

"I worry about the stock price, Al. Once rumors of Bill's absence reach *The Wall Street Journal* . . ."

"We're on the defensive. I know. J.B., I have to tell you this. In his heart I don't believe Bill understands how profoundly the economy has changed. Intellectually he knows that the value of WorldWide is in the perception of its value to investors. But in his heart he still thinks it's all about P&L, all about sales. He still lives in the old world."

"It worries me a lot."

"It should. J.B., for all the ups and downs and momentary scares in the financial markets, there has never been a boom time like this. All of the nation's pension funds and retirement accounts have been moved into the stock market in a very short time." Hamilton was moving into professor mode. The liquor. "With stocks going up up up, ordinary civilians take even more of their money and buy more stocks. So now all of us with large public companies are working for Wall Street. You understand that. Most executives understand that. I don't know that De-Gaul truly understands that."

"The Swedes do," Booth said. "They figure out DeGaul doesn't and we'll be working for some albino from the Stockholm salmon farm."

"Which is why we have to secure our positions now. Or we'll be sitting on the beach with Bill."

"There won't be anything left of WorldWide to fight for."

"That would be the worst of all," Hamilton said loudly. "If the empire DeGaul built fell apart because no one had the guts to take his hands off the wheel." He took another drink and whispered, "Everyone will rally around you, J.B."

"I love the old son of a bitch."

"Which is why you have to do it. You have a conscience."

"He's been a second father to me, Al. I just wish he would stand down of his own accord."

"You have a fiduciary duty to the company."

The two men studied each other.

"Let me tell you something that might make you feel easier, J.B. You cannot take DeGaul down."

That stopped the conversation. Booth stared at Hamilton, who took his time rolling the last bit of whiskey around in his glass and drinking it. He continued: "It is beyond your power to take out DeGaul. All we can do is make sure that when DeGaul trips up so badly that even those wooden Indians on the NOA board cannot miss it, when the stockholders start trampling each other on their way to the lifeboats, you'll be the one in position to step in. But you don't have to destroy DeGaul."

"I couldn't."

"Of course. But you owe it to all the rest of us to make sure that if DeGaul destroys himself, you're in place to lead a smooth transition."

Booth thought about this. He liked drinking in the day. He said, "You're a good man, Al. Whatever comes of this, I need to know you'll be beside me."

"Shoulder to shoulder."

Booth pulled the trigger. He signed the papers and passed them back to Hamilton, who made a little bow.

Hamilton said, "DeGaul deserves to get off the conveyor belt, enjoy his wealth while he's still able."

"We should be so lucky," Booth said.

Hamilton gathered his documents and stood to leave. "Hey," he said, "did Cantone sell you on signing his senior citizen?"

"You heard about that, huh? What's wrong with that kid?"

"He's well intentioned."

"I can't make up my mind about him."

"You know what Joe Precious listens to when he goes home?"

"Vanilla Ice?"

"Chopin. Mozart. But he goes out and signs Brute Apache and the Hip Hop Army."

"I didn't know that. I thought Precious was a real street kid."

"He understands the street. He doesn't sleep there."

"Good for him."

Hamilton put away both men's empty glasses and walked to the door. He had his hand on the knob when Booth suddenly called out. "Hey, Al. What happens when all the people who've been putting their retirement funds into the stock market reach retirement age?"

"The baby boom," Hamilton smiled. "The pig in the demographic python. When that python finally tries to shit out that pig, Brother Snake is gonna bust his guts all over the landscape."

"Yeah."

"Get your beach house now."

"Yeah. Get yourself a Hootie."

"Get yourself a Hootie."

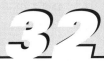

"Where is DeGaul?" Booth asked anyone who came within a yard of him. He asked in the conference room, he asked the mailroom, he asked the Black Ethiopians condemning the white race on the corner of Broadway and Forty-fourth Street. He cornered Cantone in the elevator. "Where is DeGaul? What do you hear from your girlfriend in the Caribbean? Has he gone native? Has he lost his mind? Does he think the CEO of a major corporation can canoe off the edge of the world for weeks at a time and no one upstairs will ask where he is?"

"Jerusalem have been sending me tapes," Cantone said, "and they're terrific. You're going to be delighted. Do you want to come in for a minute and hear something?"

"Like I could give a flying piss. All I know about Lilly Rope and the Jerusalems is that they've now spent their next three album budgets and all their royalties playing beach ball with DeGaul in Surf City. I don't care if they flush their career down the stinkhole but if Wild Bill doesn't come out of there he won't have a job to come back to."

"Could that really happen?"

"If not for me it would have happened already."

Booth's public groaning about DeGaul's absence was spreading through the company. Rumors were flapping around like bats. At the restaurants and nightclubs where the music industry grazed, backstage at the big shows at Madison Square Garden and the Meadowlands, everyone who saw Jim coming asked in low voices what was really going on with DeGaul.

When Jim called St. Pierre—and he was willing to hang on the phone a long time to get through—everyone sounded fine. Lilly and the boys were happier than he'd known them to be since the night he signed them. He got DeGaul on the phone and was surprised by how normal he sounded.

"Yeah, it's going great," he said. "When are you coming down here?"

"I thought maybe this weekend," Jim heard himself say. "Things are slow for once."

DeGaul said great and rang off to take another call. From Booth, he said, which surprised Jim a lot. Since when was DeGaul so easy to find? Since when was Booth able to find him? He called American Airlines and booked himself a ticket through Miami to St. Pierre on his own credit card. He wasn't sure he wanted WorldWide to know he was going.

. . .

Cantone was so tired when he landed at the big airport that Saturday afternoon that he broke his vow and let the Kamikaze Brothers, Chris and Paulo, fly him over the mountains to St. Pierre. It wasn't as scary, he found, if you knew what was coming.

When the little plane skidded to the end of the gravel runway, John P. from Webster's was waiting for him with a van.

"Hello, John," Cantone said. "Mr. Nightingale sent you over to collect me?"

"Mr. Nightingale's gone," John P. said as they started down the winding road to Webster's. "Mr. DeGaul's running the show now."

They passed through the village of St. Pierre, around a broken fountain that Jim had used as a mile marker on his earlier visits. He was surprised to see signs of opulence amid the poverty, including a red Camaro left alongside the fountain, a couple of expensive off-road vehicles parked against the concrete houses, and at least one street kid wearing an expensive leather jacket over cutoffs and a dirty undershirt.

"Is someone making a movie down here?" Cantone asked. John P. shook his head no and said nothing.

They came around a bend in the road between a single-pump gas

station and a pink cement house with a screen door and a DRINK PEPSI-
COLA sign out front. Two heavy men with beards had their car parked
sideways, blocking half the road. They waved at John P. to stop. He did,
a few yards away from them. While the men approached John reached
under a blanket on the floor and lifted a pistol into his lap.

"What the hell, John?" Jim said.

"Shhhh," John P. said. He rolled down his window. One of the men
said hello and John answered him by name.

The man looked at the gun in John's lap without surprise. "I got two
bricks to sell," he said.

"Go to the city."

"Your boss don't want some for his friends?"

"DeGaul is not a fool. Why don't you come back to work, Lee?" John
P. said. "Your children need their daddy."

The bearded man looked at John P. He looked at Cantone, who felt
like he had fallen through the rabbit hole. The bearded man turned and
walked back to his friend. John P. backed up the van and drove around
them.

The gates to Webster's Retreat were closed and locked with a chain.
John P. honked the horn and Buster, holding a rifle, came and opened
one side until they drove through. This is worse than anything Booth
could have imagined, Jim thought. I've got to get Lilly and the band out
of here.

The van pulled up at the piazza of the great house. DeGaul appeared, relaxed as ever, the same charming rover, holding up a cigar and
waving at Jim.

"Cantone! Welcome to Nutopia! Did you meet any scoundrels on
your journey from the airport?"

Mack and his girlfriend, Krystal, walked out of the house in bathing
suits, carrying beach towels. They said, "Hi, Jim!" and "Come in for a
swim!" and carried on down the road.

"Bill," Jim whispered, "what is happening here? You haven't been at
work in over a month! Have you gone mad?"

"Just looks that way to the untrained eye," DeGaul said. "You're not
a snitch, are you, Jim? I can trust you to keep a secret?"

"I'll keep a secret for you about what you bought your kid for
Christmas, Bill, but this is a little beyond my experience."

"Come on, you know I wouldn't do anything bad. This is a charitable enterprise. Great lesson of the twentieth century, Jim. When reason and morality fail, depend on capitalism. We've had a little problem down here the last month. A big load of cocaine washed up on the town beach. All the locals got hold of it and started selling to the dealers in the city. That was bad. What was worse was when they started wanting to see what all the fuss was about and started using. All of a sudden Mayberry turned into Dodge City."

"The town's full of cokeheads?" Jim asked.

"Pretty much. The people without money started getting jealous of the people with money, the people with money got high and got paranoid. Fights, revenge plots, firebombing, robberies. The place went loco.

"At first it seemed like the whole thing was a big laugh. One guy who works here sold a brick and bought a big air conditioner for his house. Trouble was, he's got no electricity! Another guy goes to town and buys a huge bed. Too bad it was bigger than the shack he lives in!" DeGaul's face changed. "But it's not funny anymore. This was a peaceful place. Now you see whipped children and battered wives. Nightingale couldn't take it, he ran off. It's up to me to get these people working again, and Webster's Retreat is the only employer around. Jim, I'm not kidding, this could be a real moneymaking proposition. A recording studio, a hotel, a resort, an amusement park. But if I turn my back now, the whole town goes down."

Jim could only stare at him. "You see why I've been hung up down here?" DeGaul asked.

Finally Jim managed to choke out a few words. "I know you're loaded, but . . ."

"People think a fella earning ten million a year has it made," DeGaul said, "but let me tell you, investments like this can knock a man's portfolio for a loop. And my accountant says the tax benefits are dubious."

Jim thought he'd never met a character like this in his life.

"See," DeGaul went on, "that ten-million-a-year figure, it's a little off, but let's use it for the sake of easy math. First of all, one half of that goes right off the top to taxes and other deductions. All the stuff you see on your paycheck. Federal tax, state tax, New York City tax—boy, that one's a bitch, I must have bought the mayor a new subway line by now—

insurance deduction, dental, medical, retirement, WorldWide optional charity contribution deduction, which ain't optional if you're the guy whose name goes on the dunning letter. On and on. So right off the top, before my paycheck hits my bank book, five million gone."

"You must shelter your money," Jim said.

"Don't believe in it. Bad karma. Always told Booth that. As soon as you start worrying about money it rules you. If you ignore it, it keeps coming."

"Okay, you still have five million a year."

"I'm not lucky like you, you married the right woman. I got two ex-wives and two expensive daughters. I'm carrying the load for them. Take half of what I got left and sign it over to them. What does that leave on the table?"

"Two and a half million," Jim said. He had to remember to ask for a raise.

"Okay, I have a nice brownstone in Manhattan. Nothing too lavish. It would be a middle-class house in most cities. My mortgage, upkeep, and insurance on that and the summer place? Another million. What am I left with to live on?"

"A million and a half."

"Right! A million and a half a year! Gee whiz, by the time you take out tips and taxis . . ." DeGaul spun around and headed into the house, declaring, "I just wish they'd started paying me the kind of money they pay me now back in the eighties. I would be a rich man today."

"Go take a shower," John P. told Jim. "We have dinner at eight."

DeGaul's face suddenly appeared at a window. He called to Jim, "Wait till you hear what Jerusalem's been up to! They're on a real roll! I'm in love with Lilly, I'm gonna ask her if she has a mother my age!"

Jim turned to John P. "Wild Bill." He smiled and shook his head.

• • •

Cantone had never seen Lilly and her bandmates as happy as they were at dinner that night. Everyone was tanned and radiant. The songs they played Jim fulfilled all the promise he'd heard in Jerusalem at the start.

Under DeGaul's auspices supper at Webster's Retreat had shaken off the last vestiges of Roy Nightingale's colonial tradition. John P., Buster, and Mr. Jay shared the whole meal with Jim, DeGaul, the band, the producer, and Krystal, who had adapted to the climate best of all. Everyone pitched in on the dishes. Mr. Jay announced, "Many hands make light work."

It impressed Jim that the same three local men who were now scrubbing plates and drying glasses—Buster in an apron—kept rifles close by to defend their outpost against gangsters. Jane would say they were equally in touch with Venus and Mars.

While clearing the table Jim suggested to DeGaul the depth of Booth's anxiety about his long absence. DeGaul said, "I appreciate that it's hard on him. But you see why I've been unable to leave here right now. I trust you and J.B. to hang in as my tail gunners a little longer."

"You know, Bill," Cantone said, "there are fax machines and phones. I think it wouldn't be so hard for you to just stay in touch with the office while you're down here, let them know you're alive."

DeGaul paused for a moment as if weighing a secret. Then he said, "Well, sure. But it's important to Booth that people see I trust him to run things without me."

When the cleanup was done Cantone went out on the porch with Lilly. He told her the songs were great, she should put on the final vocals and call it quits.

"I know, I know," Lilly said. Jim could not get over how much younger she seemed in St. Pierre. "I guess I'm enjoying the feeling of having most of it done and still having a little to do. I kind of don't want this to be over."

"DeGaul was right about St. Pierre, huh?"

"Part of me wants to never go back to New York, Jim," Lilly said. "Once I'd been down here a little while I realized why it had been so hard for me this last year. I needed to be in a little house in the open air completely alone. At first it freaked me out. It was like *Trainspotting*, you know, I was climbing the walls and sticking my head in the toilet. But when I got lonely enough, I started talking to myself. And when I began talking to myself, I remembered the sound of my own voice. That's what I'd been missing in New York.

"I started writing songs as a way of talking to myself when I was a teenager. They were my comfort and company. Then the strangest thing happened. The very songs I made to make a friend of my loneliness brought me out into the world and drove my loneliness away. It was what I always thought I wanted, so I felt happy, I felt rewarded. Honored.

"When I got real friends and acceptance the voice I used to hear went away. I thought I didn't need it anymore. I did not admit to myself that I missed my loneliness. I missed the voice in my head talking to me. I wrote songs in which I couldn't hear myself. Since I came to St. Pierre, I've got my voice back."

"You're not going to lose it again, Lilly," Jim said.

"Hope not." She smiled and spun around. "Anyway, this has been magic."

On his way up to bed Jim stopped in Nightingale's library for a book to read. While he was going through the shelves he heard DeGaul talking on the phone in the next room.

"Hi, Al. How goes it, man? Good. Listen, I've been reading through these faxes and I think you're good to go on the IPO. I don't know if it'll pan out long term but we can milk a few million out of it before the day traders wise up. Yeah. That international conference call still on for the morning? Patch me in, okay? Don't worry, they won't know I'm there. I'll tape down my mute button. Good. Those Krauts still giving J.B. a hard time? Bastards. Well, you tell him not to let them feed him that guff about local taxes. It's a crock. He should tell them to peel off the taxes into a separate account and put 'em on their company credit cards. That's right—two different lines, one for the warehouse payments and a second for the taxes. Guess which line will suddenly disappear? Right, beat those wily Germans at their own game. Where's J.B. now? Okay, tell him I'll be up for a couple more hours if he wants to call. Great. Sleep tight, man."

Holy cow, Jim thought. DeGaul's been in touch with New York all along. So why is Booth pretending he's vanished? Do all the top brass know this? Am I the only one out of the loop? Do Booth and DeGaul not trust me?

Jim Cantone had a personality trait that many people would call an attribute. He knew how to keep his mouth shut. Always had. He took to heart that nineteenth-century aphorism "I have often regretted my speech, never my silence." And Lincoln's line—better to keep quiet and be suspected of idiocy than open your mouth and remove all doubt.

His discretion had served him well. He remembered the story his high school friend Micky Cowls told him after Micky was expelled. Micky said he ran into Miss Gorham, their hippie English teacher, at a rock concert and she said, "Micky, you and Cantone are two peas in a pod. You are my two favorite students ever. You have the same great spirit, the same spark, the same openheartedness. But Cantone is going to be a success in this world, Micky, and you're not. Because he has one talent you don't have. Cantone knows when to shut up."

Standing in the library, Cantone considered—not for the first time—that holding his tongue had not always been for the best. There were times he might have stood up and he didn't do it and it caused him regret. One time was when Micky was railroaded out of school. Jim heard two teachers talking about it days before it happened. They said, "That little bastard turns sixteen next week and then we'll take care of him." One of those teachers was the one Micky hit. He was sure the teacher provoked it. But how could that ever be proved, and who would believe Jim, Micky's buddy, against a teacher anyway? Especially when the second teacher was sure to join in and say it was all a lie.

So Jim kept quiet, because he didn't have all the facts and he probably couldn't have helped anyway. Just like now.

# 33

In New York, Jim told Jane what he'd learned in the Caribbean. He wasn't sure what to make of it all, but whatever was going on was certainly not what the industry believed. DeGaul was still in contact with WorldWide, or at least with Al Hamilton. Was Booth unaware? Was Booth's job in jeopardy? But he and DeGaul were best friends. DeGaul had just promoted him. Jim didn't know what to think.

Jane said he should go and ask Hamilton what was going on. Jane still believed the truth was invulnerable. She called on Jim to be straight-ahead with all these people. She brought out the best in him.

The next morning Jim perched outside Al's empty office early and waited for him to arrive.

"Cantone," Hamilton said when he appeared with keys and coffee. "You are up with the sparrows. To what do I owe the courtesy?"

Jim followed Al into his office. "Al, I need you to level with me," Jim said. "I'm trying to get a handle on this DeGaul situation. You know, everybody in the industry is pumping me about these crazy rumors."

"You're wise to ignore them."

"I've tried. But here's the thing. Booth is all bent out of shape because he seems to think DeGaul has deserted him, skipped off to the islands and left him high and dry."

Cantone left an opening for Hamilton to speak. Hamilton didn't bite.

Cantone continued: "J.B. has been pretty vocal about this, and it's spread through the whole building. Everyone thinks DeGaul's run away from home. Now everyone in the business thinks it, too."

"You're exaggerating."

"Maybe a little. But here's what I can't factor. DeGaul is in touch with WorldWide, right? He's getting reports, he's going over paperwork, he's on the phone, even monitoring meetings. Doesn't Booth know that? How could he not?"

Hamilton sat for a moment, impassive as a cat. He finally said, "Of course, you've been in touch with St. Pierre. Your band is recording down there."

Jim saw no sense in offering any more than Hamilton. He shrugged.

"Jerusalem are not privy to everything that goes on between the chief executives of this company. Few people are. I wouldn't take much notice of gossip, Jim. It tells us little about what is really happening. As you obviously know."

"So what is happening, Al? My inclination was to go to J.B. first. But you're the man who knows the angles. I didn't want to talk to Booth until I talked to you."

It was a subtle threat, Hamilton realized. A polite suggestion that if Hamilton did not bring Cantone into his confidence, he would spill the beans to Booth. Too bad the boy didn't realize they were Booth's beans. That big Buddha Al Hamilton thought things through for a minute or two, and then sat back and rolled out a lie like Ali Baba unrolling a magic carpet.

"I'm going to tell you the truth, Jim," Hamilton said. He pressed his intercom and said, "Would you see if J.B. can join us, please?"

He told Cantone, "What I'm about to tell you skirts the edges of unethical business practice, but it is absolutely necessary in this situation. Can I trust you to keep what I'm about to tell you secret, even if you're called at some point to testify?"

Jim nodded.

"Okay, then. As you know, DeGaul is grooming J.B. as his successor. I daresay—and Bill plays his cards close to the vest—the day is not far off when he would like to spend a lot more time outside of WorldWide's day-to-day. But DeGaul is a very loyal man, and he does not want to leave you, me, and his other senior staff at the mercy of Sweden's idea of a successor when he goes."

Booth appeared in the door with a look that said, "What?" but something in Al's manner made him come in quietly and listen.

"I'm bringing Jim into our little conspiracy, J.B.," Hamilton said. Booth registered alarm, but Hamilton gestured gently and said, "Please, let me explain."

He spoke to Jim again. "Key to DeGaul's strategy is that the NOA board and all the satellites accept J.B. as chief of WorldWide ILG. We need a year or two to cement those relationships before Bill can even consider handing off leadership here."

Booth read that Hamilton was churning out baloney. He didn't know why and he didn't like it.

"What we have up against us, Jim—by we I mean DeGaul, J.B., myself, and a few others at the top level—is that there is some resistance within the global structure to Bill handing the wheel off to J.B. There are some characters within the broader organization looking for a coup, looking to move ultimate power over WorldWide Music out of this building and off this continent. I can't say more.

"Now, DeGaul has decided that the only way to make sure things go as we all need them to go is for him to put J.B. in the driver's seat now, let Brother Booth demonstrate to the NOA board that we can steer the company successfully."

Cantone turned to Booth, who blinked.

Hamilton continued, "We are, as you now know, in touch with Bill every day. We are keeping him posted on every move and development, and he is warning us of snares in the road. It seems byzantine, I appreciate that. But that is the world we negotiate. If things go wrong, DeGaul is ready to step back into the picture publicly. But if things go right, we might have an easy transition and maintain the WorldWide tradition when Bill decides the time is right to pass the torch. Okay?"

Cantone looked at both men. The story sounded like bullshit to him. It sounded like a comic book. But he would need to play it over in his head a few times before he could shake it open. So he just said, "You guys are operating on a lot of levels, aren't you?"

"It's a drag, isn't it?" Booth said from the couch. "Too bad everybody can't be straight up all the time, but there's a lot of liars out there."

"Jim," Hamilton said, rising from his desk and moving toward Cantone's face, "you can't refer to this to anyone at all, you understand. I don't want even DeGaul to know you figured this out. He'd rip me open. Again, we are in murky legal and ethical waters here. None of us ever wanted to drag you into it."

"You're the next crown prince," Booth told Cantone. He'd worked out Al's scam now; he could have some fun with the kid. "If this should blow up in our faces, we wanted to make sure you were clean."

Jim wandered back to his office to think it through. He passed Zoey in the corridor. She spoke to him first; it was a day of wonders.

"You see the numbers on Black Beauty?" she asked.

"No, I've been out of the loop."

What a liar, she thought, he must be so jealous he's pissing bile. "Some new radio format, Afro-Bohemian, has made them a flagship. They're going to sell a hundred thousand. BET is asking for a video."

"Really? Cool."

"So I have your authority?"

"Yeah, sure."

She ran off before he added any rules.

. . .

Back in Hamilton's office, Booth wanted to know what was going on. Hamilton said he didn't know what Cantone knew, but he sure knew DeGaul was in contact with them and listening in on meetings. Hamilton said he figured Cantone was in touch with DeGaul's hideout because of Jerusalem being down there with him.

"So what do we do with him?" Booth asked. "Should we get the Kingfish to move him out of here and stick him somewhere safe?"

"Why would he go? You practically just promised him the presidency. No, Cantone's not going to be a problem. He's got his future mortgaged to Jerusalem. If this second album is the monster DeGaul and he say it will be, we will have to accommodate him. And you know what? He'll have too much to lose to cross us."

"What if the Jerusalem album flops?" Booth said.

"Then who cares what happens to him? Either way, he's got a taste for the good life. He's not going to blow it to go down with DeGaul."

"You better be right," Booth said.

"I am. I recognize something in that kid. He knows how to keep his mouth shut."

# 34

"We've been dreaming too long," DeGaul said to John P. "It's time to go back to our waking lives." Webster's Retreat was under control. The cocaine had all been sold or snorted. Most of the locals were back at work. Some young men had left St. Pierre and would never return. Some families were broken. DeGaul was hiring all ages and sexes. John P. and Mr. Jay would carry out his plans when he returned to New York. He exhaled ganja smoke and looked down the hill over the canopy of palms at the roof of the great house from which music was floating, and the ocean beyond it, on which two small cabin cruisers were bobbing.

On the larger of the two boats, Mr. Jay was checking oxygen tanks and examining diving masks for cracks and leaks. On the smaller, Buster was assembling fishing poles and unpacking coffee cans full of bait he'd dug before dawn. He tied a fly for DeGaul, who liked to practice casting on the sea. The music from the house was carrying over the water.

Dark smoke had been rising from the kitchen chimney. It turned white.

"You know what that means don't you, Buster?" Mr. Jay called from the other boat. Buster grunted. "We have a new pope!"

DeGaul made it back to the great house, and he joined Krasner, the producer, uber-babe Krystal, and the four members of Jerusalem around a white wicker table. He rocked happily to the music they were playing at full volume through the studio monitors Krasner had dragged up to the house. Jerusalem had finished the backing tracks for fourteen songs and Lilly had put final vocals on three and guide vocals on six more. Krasner had been up all night doing rough mixes and sequencing them together, along with assorted one- and two-man acoustic numbers, instrumentals, and unfinished musical sketches.

The effect on everyone in the company was what the producer hoped: the music sounded great and the musicians were inspired by how much they had accomplished. They knew the work had paid off. Whether they stayed a little longer—everyone's choice—or took the tracks back to New York to finish, they were over the hump. The band had made a breakthrough.

To celebrate, DeGaul had arranged the hire of two boats for an afternoon on the ocean, one for fishing, one for swimming and scuba diving. Mr. Jay, whose lengthy curriculum vitae included qualification as a diving instructor, had been giving the band lessons all week in the cove. Now he was prepared to qualify them as divers in an on-deck ceremony and lead them into the depths.

"Hey, amigo," DeGaul said to Mack, "if you're going diving you better lay off the margarita. Mr. Jay doesn't mess around with that stuff. He'll pull you out of the water like a codfish and lock you in the hold."

"I'm from Glasgow, Bill," the drummer smiled. "We put stronger drink than this on our babies' cornflakes."

"Bill is right, gobber," Krystal said to Mack. "We've been planning this dive all week and I want to be able to enjoy it."

"Okay," DeGaul said, "who's fishing and who's diving?"

"Diving," said Lilly, throwing up her hand.

"Diving," said Anthony.

"Fishing," said the producer.

"Mack and I are diving," Krystal said.

"I'm gonna try both, Bill," Dick said. "If you don't mind I'd like to ride out with you and John P. and fish for a while, but I want to try diving, too."

"Glad to have you, Dick," DeGaul said. "Anthony, is your family going to make it down here?"

"That's up in the air, Bill," the pianist said. "If we decide to keep recording here, they'll probably come next week. If we're leaving soon, no."

"A last toast," Lilly declared, raising her fruit drink high. "To Bill De-Gaul and St. Pierre, where for once everything's right at the same time."

All cheered, all drank, and all made ready for the sea. "All right, Marines," DeGaul said, "let's hit the surf!"

The whole party squeezed into a yellow rubber safety raft and rowed with many jokes and little coordination to where it was deep enough to drop the outboard and putt to the two boats. DeGaul, Dick, John P., and Buster took the fishing boat out a mile and threw their lines over the side.

Mr. Jay dropped anchor within sight of the smaller boat, but far enough away that the divers would not scare the fish. It was a great day on the water, a steady breeze, a few whitecaps but sunny and clear. Mr. Jay took his role as diving instructor seriously. He ran the giggling musicians through their routines twice before he let them strap on their tanks.

DeGaul was on the deck of his vessel casting flies back and forth like Indiana Jones with his bullwhip. The producer, Krasner, was scared to death one was going to land in his long beard, and kept disappearing into the small hold. Dick sat with his line over the side, dreaming of a whopper but happy just to be where he was.

"You know what I think, Dick?" DeGaul said. "I think that when you guys arrived here you would have all gone crazy if you'd had to get up early and spend a day on the water. Now, you're a bunch of laid-back Rastafarians."

"Except Anthony. He's a pastafarian."

"You've all relaxed and it hasn't hurt your music one bit."

"No, it's improved it. Absolutely. Art should be conceived in passion and formed in reflection—that makes sense to me now. No, this has been a great experience. The band almost shook apart in the craziness of touring and sleeping in the van and having to make pressure decisions on no rest. This trip has reminded us all that we got in the band because we like one another. It's been great."

"Hang on to that when you get back to the States."

"We will. I'd like to hang on to this tan, too. The main reason we couldn't have spent a day on the ocean two months ago is that we'd all have died of skin cancer."

The afternoon passed outside of time. They could have been in the water for half an hour or two days. Lilly found that the slow, deep in-and-out of breathing from the diving tank moved her into something like a yoga trance. She followed Mr. Jay through a school of yellow fish, around a boulder that looked like it was made of gold, and toward a coral shelf that seemed to have fallen through a hole from another dimension. She reached out to touch the coral but Mr. Jay shoved her aside. He floated past, waving her away. In doing so he ran up against the coral with his leg. Lilly didn't understand until he came away bleeding. The coral had sliced though his shorts and put a thin gash into his upper leg. She followed him to the surface.

"I'm so sorry," Lilly said when they got into the air and took out their mouthpieces. "Didn't know it was dangerous. Let's get you back."

"No worry, Lilly-Belle," Mr. Jay said. "Cut up on coral a hundred times. Follow me back to the boat. You can't dive alone."

On the deck of the diving boat, Anthony warned Mack and Krystal that Mr. Jay and Lilly were coming back.

"Okay, okay," Mack said. "Last salute to a fallen foe and then the treasure goes over the side." Mack had in his lap a brick of cocaine lifted from the beach the night of the goldrush. He had been saving it for the appropriate occasion and brought it out to sea in his beach bag, wrapped in a sock. He, Krystal, and Anthony had whittled off enough samples while the others were diving to be full of an unearned confidence. With great ceremony Mack carried the remains of the brick onto the bow of the boat, saluted, and dropped it into the ocean.

"Ah," he said as he watched it sink, "if my old mates could see me now."

Lilly and Mr. Jay climbed up the stern ladder. "Mr. Jay's been cut," Lilly called out. "Will someone bring over the first-aid kit?"

They helped Mr. Jay dress his wound with unnecessary urgency. Lilly could read that her friends' moods had been altered by more than diving.

"I'm going over to visit Dick on the other boat," she said. "Who wants to swim with me?"

Mack, filled with illegal bravado, declared he would love to escort

Lilly to the other boat, and even offered to let her ride on his back. Lilly and Mack put on their tanks, flippers, and masks and fell over the side together. Mr. Jay waved a white towel to signal the other boat that they were coming.

The two divers climbed aboard the smaller boat. Lilly asked Mack, who was breathing hard, if he and the others were stoned. He admitted they had done a little blow as a farewell tribute to the great St. Pierre shipwreck. Lilly told him he was crazy to do that and then spend the day diving in the hot sun. They piped down when DeGaul joined them.

"How's the fishing, Bill?" Mack asked.

"The fish are too smart for us," DeGaul said. He was smoking a joint rolled in newspaper. Mack nudged Lilly to say nyah nyah. "You guys come to take Dick away from his misery? I think the poor cat's got his hook baited with doughnuts or something."

"Hey, Dick," Lilly called, "you want to go diving? Mack needs a break!"

Dick relieved Mack of his tanks and went under with Lilly. Mack stayed with DeGaul a while and then announced he was going to swim back to the other boat to make sure Mr. Jay wasn't making time with his girlfriend.

DeGaul said it might be too far to swim after exercising all day, but Mack was full of energy and cocaine confidence. He dove in and DeGaul watched him torpedo all the way to the other boat.

"Man," DeGaul said to Buster, "it must be great to be young."

John P. called DeGaul's attention to the sea. It was flat. The wind had died completely and the air was turning swampy. DeGaul was a little high but he knew what that meant. "Get the kids out of the water," he said, and went below and turned on the radio. He got the news he expected. A severe tropical storm had come out of nowhere and was bearing down on St. Pierre. He told Buster to wave the red flag to Mr. Jay. They needed to get in fast.

Within three minutes Dick had climbed over the side of the boat and was rhapsodizing about the glories of the deep.

"Where's Lilly?" DeGaul asked him.

"She went back to her boat. Everybody's back where they started."

"Okay," DeGaul said, "we gotta get out of here. There's a storm coming."

On the other boat, Mr. Jay examined the changing sky and tightened the bandage on his leg. The bleeding had not stopped, the cut was deep.

"Is Lilly staying on the other boat?" he asked Mack, who was winded from his swim and whose heart was palpitating like it was about to spring from his chest.

"Yeah," Mack answered, shaking. "Mr. Jay, I gotta lie down, I think."

"Okay everybody," Mr. Jay shouted, "grab on to something, we're going to try to outrun this storm."

DeGaul watched the other boat turn toward land. The atmosphere was changing by the minute. The clear skies had turned thick without the sailors noticing, but there was no missing the black shadows moving across what was left of the sun.

John P. took the captain's station, standing at the wheel behind the windscreen. DeGaul sat in the passenger's chair and put a hand on the rail. Buster and Dick each grabbed a corner of the stern. Krasner stayed below in the small hold. John P. turned over the engine and they began crossing toward the shore. The still water started moving against them, first lapping and then slapping and then ramming the boat as it skipped and bounced against the waves.

"We're not gonna beat it," John said quietly to DeGaul. A black wall was spreading across the water ahead of them from west to east. The clouds and rain seemed to have solidified into a rolling cliff.

"Gun it, John!" Dick shouted. DeGaul could see John was driving full-out, but the waves were shoving the boat backward. The dark wall was moving toward them. White light throbbed behind the black clouds. Lightning. DeGaul saw the other boat pass into the storm before them. Their tarp roof was ripped off almost at once. DeGaul watched the larger boat wobble, pitch, and right itself. Then it vanished into the dark.

DeGaul, holding on to the rail as he moved, got himself into the tiny hold. The boat lurched and he slammed into a wall. Krasner was on the floor in a fetal crouch with two flotation cushions over his shoulders. DeGaul regained his feet and found four life jackets. He slipped one on, climbed back to the deck, and passed out the rest. A great wave slammed into the port side, and the boat lurched. Buster's jaw was set as he tied on his life jacket. Dick fumbled with the bindings while trying to hang on to the rail with one hand. DeGaul strapped on John P.'s jacket so he could keep both hands on steering the boat.

The black wall was almost on them. John P. kept gunning the engine. For a moment all resistance seemed to drop away. The boat shot forward into the center of the storm.

The rain hit them with almost comical force. Dick fell on his ass; Buster was lifted off his feet but held the rail tightly. DeGaul added his right hand to John's on the wheel. The waves came sideways, lifting and dropping and lifting and dropping the small craft and trying to spin it around. If that happened, DeGaul knew, they would never bring it about toward shore again. He looked at John P.'s face. He was whistling. DeGaul loved him.

The bow kept its course, the boat did not turn, but now rainwater was pouring in faster than the scuppers could empty it. Water seemed to be coming from every direction, and for a moment DeGaul worried that the bow had cracked. The lagoon came into view. John P. wrenched the wheel against a current trying to drive him east with the wind and tide. They gained more distance than they lost, and the cove opened in front of them.

The lagoons at Webster's Retreat were not deep enough for vessels, but that meant nothing now. A great wave lifted the boat like a surfboard and carried it into the cove with a force and suddenness that even in this circumstance was shocking. The boat shifted sideways and came sliding to a stop in the shallows.

It took a moment for DeGaul and the others to register that they had made it. They laughed and leaped into the churning, waist-deep water.

Mr. Jay and Anthony were on the shore to grab them and share in victory shouts and war whoops.

"You take out insurance on those boats, Bobby?" DeGaul shouted to Mr. Jay. Even as close as he was to vomiting from fear, Dick was surprised to learn that Mr. Jay had a first name.

"All set, boss!" Mr. Jay shouted back. "Everybody okay on yours?"

"I think so. Dick—you lose your sea legs? Where's the rest of your crew?"

"Krystal took Mack up to the big house," Mr. Jay said. "He got pretty spooked, started crying. Where's Lilly?"

The question hit DeGaul like a rock.

"You had Lilly!" he shouted.

"She swam off to visit you! Mack said she was riding in with you!"

The horror hit all the men on the beach at once. The rain was still pounding but the black wall was moving east. The storm would pass soon; perhaps they could get back before she ran out of air. The boats were beached and broken, but maybe one could be hauled out of the sand and dragged back to deep water. Or the yellow rubber raft, it had an outboard. If the rain let up, they might get back in that. Dick ran to the house to radio for help, but this was not the United States, the coast guard would not be dispatched into the storm with floodlights and rescue helicopters. This was a Third World backwater in the middle of a disaster. Dick knew as he ran that there would be no rescue, and he knew that in some way it would be his fault, and he knew that these beautiful weeks of music, friendship, and luxury were not the beginning of paradise for him and his friends, but the end. Still he ran as hard as he could, crying as he ran.

. . .

Lilly was under the water. She had come up once to find the boats gone and a second time to find the ocean in upheaval, so she came back under to breathe.

Panic came and went. She breathed like a yogi, slow and deep. She felt she was outside herself, watching. Her air was turning hot; she tried to save what was left. She took a deep breath, removed the mouthpiece, and held the air in her lungs as long as she could. It felt like a very long time. Then the air burst out of her and she swallowed water and felt a great bubble shove up from inside her and push the water out with a belch so loud it made her laugh. She would have to tell Dick. She then thought she might never get to tell anyone anything and she was struck by pure amazement, not even fear, but stupefaction that this could happen to her.

She heard a song beneath her, no words, just notes, a melody rising and turning, sweet and seductive. She wanted to remember it for later, she hoped it was hers, she hoped she had not stolen it. Then the notes, still clear, split into echoes.

It was, she thought, like someone was walking through a house, turning out the lights in each room as they passed. Fear was turned off, then the instinct to survive, then pain, and then she felt memory itself go dark.

Then Lilly's spirit finished moving through the house, and the last light went out.

# 35

As the hand guiding WorldWide International Labels Group, Booth spent so much time on planes that the flight attendants knew his meal preferences and he had seen every Tom Hanks movie on the personal armrest entertainment center three times. He launched his invasions of Europe on Sunday mornings, when the New York airports were relatively quiet and first class had few customers. He'd land in some foreign city Sunday evening, have dinner at his hotel, and startle his local lieutenants with calls to their homes in which he'd drill them about minutia he read off file cards.

The next morning he'd land at the local WorldWide office earlier than anyone else, throwing terror into whichever unlucky department head arrived to unlock the place. He'd get the janitor to open the office of the second-in-command of that station and be behind the desk with a calculator when the poor schnook arrived at work. (In southern France, the associate director of WorldWide's Riviera station dropped his puffy pastry on the rug when he found Booth in his chair, and then nervously ate it anyway while J.B. drilled him about the possible abuse of local retail rebate coupons.)

Booth made a great show of going through expense reports. He would inevitably find some lowly associate who had charged a lunch against company policy, call him in, and ream him out. As word of this third degree ripped through the building, Booth would disappear with the officer in charge for an hour or two, fake interest in his breathless defense of how well he was doing, convince the grateful lackey that Booth liked *him* a lot but had doubts about his subordinates and rivals, and then—his job done—ride out of town like the Green Hornet, leaving fear and respect behind him.

By late afternoon he would be in a WorldWide ILG capital—Paris, Berlin, Rome, London, or Stockholm—for a business dinner with the big shots. He could count on word of his earlier regional terror strike having preceded him. At these dinners he presented an alternative image—he was thoughtful, philosophical, a forward-looker, a big-picture man. He listened attentively, nodded gravely, and only occasionally presented his comrades with small insights into the great future he saw for WorldWide in the coming new world. It only took a passing reference to, for instance, "how assets will be compiled in postcurrency economies" to make even the smartest executives pause in their chewing and marvel. Whenever he could, Booth tried to arrange to have one NOA board member at these dinners. He was campaigning.

At the end of a long supper in Berlin, an Austrian industrialist who sat on the NOA board commended Booth on his continental cost-cutting and asked if the same measures could not be applied to the American operation, where stories of profligacy were harder to laugh off since profits had started slipping.

Booth looked pained and said with a tight smile, "Well, it's a different business culture." The Austrian nodded. In other words, the USA was still living under DeGaul.

Late Monday night Booth was on a plane back to America, having missed only one business day in New York while convincing the Europeans he was everywhere. Each individual scenery-chewing autopsy of a few travel-and-entertainment receipts would multiply into the myth that Booth had eyes in the back of his head and his finger on every WorldWide artery. Thus the upsurge in WorldWide's European profits was credited not to the change in bookkeeping Hamilton had engineered, but to Booth's ruthless cost-cutting and aggressive example.

Somewhere over Greenland Booth leafed through the magazines he'd picked up at the airport. There was a story in *Time* about the new trend in American pop, the "Afro-Bohemian explosion." There, alongside photographs of Wyclef Jean and Erykah Badu, was a big color picture of WorldWide's Black Beauty with a caption that said, "The purest expression of the new trend, Brooklyn-based Black Beauty, has made an album critics are calling hip-hope's *Sgt. Pepper.*"

The article had a quote from Black Beauty's leader, lavishing credit on A&R visionary Zoey Pavlov, who had battled the corporation to give the band the sort of artist-friendly deal that made it possible for so progressive and conscience-bound a group to hitch up with a multinational conglomerate. The article went on to talk about how Black Beauty's sales were multiplying weekly and all the radio stations were making room for them on formerly frozen playlists.

Booth dug out his phone and called Cantone. He got voice mail. He said, "Better switch on the rockets behind Black Beauty. Let's see if we can make something happen here."

Then he punched in the Kingfish at home and said, "Did you see *Time*? Zoey Pavlov might be worth more than we thought. Maybe you could sell her to those dopes across the street—keep them from being any sort of threat for a couple of years, until they figure out she's useless. Get yourself another big finder's fee and a cut of her signing bonus. Over and out."

Booth stuck his phone in his leather briefcase and looked again at the magazine in his lap. "Hip-hope's *Sgt. Pepper.*" He had to laugh. What a great business. We put all this money and energy into trying to make one thing happen and it doesn't. Then we toss some crap into the street and next thing you know everybody's falling on their knees around it and calling you a genius. It's fantastic. We're all geniuses and not one of us knows anything.

When he ran out of magazines to read he closed his eyes and floated back over the jolts of the last week. Booth had been spending so much time on planes and in town that he had barely been to the house in Connecticut. He'd made it home last Saturday and found his clothes in the bureau and closet of the guest room. Lois explained that she'd moved everything out of their bedroom to have it painted and the wallpaper changed. She moved her things back in when the job was done, but left Booth's where he could sort out what he wanted.

Booth took some time taking that in. His wife had moved his effects out of their bedroom until "he could sort out what he wanted." Lois always did have a melodramatic flair. He said he had to go to a late show at Irving Plaza that evening and he'd stay in the city. Anyway, he said, he was thinking of getting some new clothes.

He had not spoken to Lois since. He had another crisis to deal with. Cokie Shea had a new boyfriend—a former minister named Judge, some righteous dipshit who ran homeless shelters in Memphis and appealed to her messiah complex. That was scary enough, but now she had come up with the insane notion of issuing a special collector's edition of her first album that would replace a track that had references to unmarried sex with a new song about the second coming. This special edition of the CD, complete with lyrics printed in a little cardboard hymnal, would be sold primarily in Christian bookstores.

When he shared this new lunacy with Al Hamilton, the finance captain simply said, "Hell of a distribution network there. Bigger than Wal-Mart."

After three days of being avoided he got Cokie on the phone and would not let her go.

"You know I respect your spiritual convictions, Cokie," Booth said while bending backward to try to ease the pain radiating from his spine. "I don't always share 'em, don't always understand 'em, but I sure have stuck up for them. But I need to warn you as a friend to be careful of getting associated with the religious right. It killed George Bush's presidency and it can sure kill a musical career."

"I don't think this is a comparable situation," Cokie said. She was on a tour bus, driving from Dallas to Houston for a show.

"It could hurt your image," Booth said, "turn you into a cartoon to a lot of people. More than that, I just don't want to see you hurt. I'm worried this guy Judge is taking advantage of you."

"Tom Judge has asked nothing of me," Cokie said evenly. "He has given to me with both hands. If anything, Jack, I'm probably taking advantage of him."

"Listen, Cokie, I've been looking into this character. He's one of these lake-of-fire tent beaters who go around scaring old ladies and little kids. Plus, he's a prolife extremist. You don't want to get dragged into that garbage."

"How do you know I'm not prolife, Jack?"

"I don't care what you believe for yourself, Cokie. Just don't allow yourself to be associated with someone who wants to infringe on the rights of others! I think this Elmer is pro–death penalty, too! Rumor is he supported the execution of some retarded guy in Arkansas. Believe me, I've looked him up. He's slippery as a gut. I'm worried for you."

"I guess maybe Tom might say an innocent baby is not morally equivalent to a convicted murderer. If they were, all you people who are anti–capital punishment would have to be antiabortion, now wouldn't you?"

Booth covered his eyes with his hands. The flying nun was lifting off again. He tried to reel her back to earth.

"Cokie, listen to me. You're now doing what my Harvard professors would call mixing up two different species of argument."

"Well, God knows I never went to Harvard, Jack. And unlike you I am not a night-school-trained attorney. But isn't the term you're groping for *specious* argument? Is that how you pronounce it?"

Booth felt his arteries expanding. He felt like he was trying to hold a sliding truck on an icy road. He breathed in and out. He would not be drawn into another game of rhetorical Ping-Pong with a born-again bimbo. He stopped. He chose his words. He spoke with calm authority.

"Put all that aside, Cokie, and focus on one point: You cannot be antiabortion and cross over to pop."

"I understand you, Jack," Cokie said, and hung up on him.

The plane landed at Kennedy. Randy the driver was waiting. "You talk to anybody, boss?" he asked Booth on the way to the car.

"What about?"

"Lilly Rope is dead. She drowned down in the Caribbean. DeGaul was with her. Apparently he took her out on a boat, they were partying, she went swimming, and he forgot and left her behind."

Wow, Booth thought. He ran through the implications in his head. He felt sorry for the girl—he'd had dinner with her once. He wondered if there was enough material for a posthumous CD. Enough video material for a long-form? Doubt it. It occurred to him as they got on the Long Island Expressway that Cantone was now demolished. He had nothing to hold over anyone. He would have to get on Booth's side in the coming revolution just to hang on.

He wondered if DeGaul had been banging her down there—that

would explain a lot. How do you forget somebody in the ocean? Probably drugs involved. Had to be bad for DeGaul. What was it Hamilton had said? We have to wait until DeGaul does something to destroy himself—then we step in and pick up the pieces. Booth couldn't believe it—after all the little maneuvers and big lies, all the manipulation and nights spent on airplanes and days talking horsecrap to foreigners, it was happening. It was really happening.

· · ·

Jim was at an airport, too. He was in Newark, waiting for the plane carrying Anthony and Dick. He was filled with irrational recriminations. He kept telling himself it was not his fault, but he could not beat back the voice insisting that if he had never met Lilly she would be alive today. If he had not tried to play God, if he had not pushed her into something she didn't want, if he had stood up for her when the pressure came down, if he were not a pretentious fool masquerading as a wise adviser, this girl would not have died. He had no business tearing up people's lives with promises of dreams he could not deliver. She should never have known him.

The plane was late. Jim was climbing the airport walls. He checked his voice mail. He sped past the calls of shock and condolence, the reporter from *The Village Voice,* and stopped on a new call from an unknown number. It was Booth, telling him he'd seen *Time* magazine and to pull out the stops for Black Beauty.

Jim did not understand the reference, he had not seen *Time.* He went to the airport newsstand and bought a copy. He was amazed and happy for Zoey. Black Beauty, the band Lilly had risked her own deal for, was going to have a hit. What a wonderful testament to the dead girl's faith and generosity. Lilly would have been so proud.

Jim dialed Zoey's number to give her the good news.

Zoey Pavlov's phone had been ringing all day. She finally let the machine take it. She had gone out with friends for dinner at a fancy restaurant to celebrate her A&R triumph. In all the excitement she had missed the news about Lilly. Zoey's contract with WorldWide had expired. Once that would have paralyzed her, now it was all to the good. The headhunter had called three times today with ever-sweeter offers.

Hamilton himself had said Booth and he hoped she wasn't going anywhere, but he was still coy about money. To hell with him, to hell with
Booth. Let them beg. She picked up the check for her pals at Balthazar
and finally answered the phone in her jacket.

"Zoey, it's Jim Cantone. I just want you to know, we're so proud of
what you've done with Black Beauty. We're pulling out all the stops.
Booth's told me to spend what I have to to take this album over the top.
You've done a great job, Zoey. You should be very proud."

Zoey listened, astonished. It sounded like Cantone was fighting
back tears. God, she thought, he is literally choking on his jealousy. She
said, "Thanks, Jim, I've got another call," and clicked him away.

She smiled at her pals, who were drinking the last of the champagne
right from the bottle. Cantone, she said to herself. What a weakling.

# 36

The fallout from Lilly's death was felt from Australia, where her long-lost father turned up at the head of a chevron of solicitors, to Stockholm, where the board of NOA asked why the head of the music division was on a boat with a rumored brick of cocaine and a young woman he let drown.

The local authorities were paid off quickly enough, but the internet buzzed with conjecture that Lilly Rope had been murdered because she stood up to the barracudas of the corporation or knew too much about WorldWide's involvement in a St. Pierre–based drug cartel.

*The Wall Street Journal* ran an investigative piece that exonerated WorldWide of complicity in Lilly's death—while raising the rumor in respectable print for the first time—and which explored DeGaul's ownership of the Caribbean retreat where she died. The *Journal* article noted that while it was not illegal for the CEO of a company to send clients to work in a resort he owned and then bill the company for their accommodations, it "created the appearance of impropriety." The piece further suggested that DeGaul had been absent from WorldWide headquarters for months at a time and enjoyed a profligate lifestyle more appropriate for the music business of the seventies than today. Most disturbing to morale at WorldWide, the article contained quotes from anonymous music industry sources inside and outside the label who said that Bill DeGaul was past his day, losing his marbles, and a figurehead whose actual thinking was done by J. B. Booth.

DeGaul put together a package for the *Journal* reporter. He filled a shoebox with St. Pierre sand, a spliff of ganja, and a corkscrew, which he explained in the covering letter was "to get that stick out of your ass." His assistant, Cindy, discreetly removed the joint and replaced it with a bottle of rum.

All of which might have been swept under the rug if NOA stock had not taken a big dip. The movie company was coming off a bad year, the magazine business was in the dumper, and the retail division was going through a restructuring. WorldWide Music was supposed to be the ugly sister who sent home her paycheck to float the family, but the *Journal* article threw a scare into investors.

DeGaul expected to tough it out. He expected he had the friendship and loyalty of his subordinates. He was back in the office every day. He worked the phones until well after midnight. He showed up at industry dinners and tributes. But the New York politicos and upper-class fundraisers quietly dropped his name from their invitation lists. He was still part of rock and roll society, but no longer a sure thing in Society society.

DeGaul gave no sign of caring. He went out to hear music, he went to Yankees and Mets games, he played racquetball twice a week, and he took his younger daughter on a tour of Ivy League colleges.

• • •

While DeGaul and his daughter drove from Yale to Dartmouth, Al Hamilton climbed the clean white steps of a clean white building in the middle of Stockholm. Everyone he saw was blond, dressed for tennis, and smelled like soap. For once, Hamilton felt funky.

He had never been in the home boardroom of NOA. The paint was light blue and the furniture was blond and reminded him of *The Jetsons*. Around a table shaped like a painter's palette sat the board of directors, some of whom Hamilton knew from stockholders' meetings, a few of whom he'd never met, and at least one of whom he had never heard of—a droopy man with a vaguely French accent who seemed to have slid almost under the table and preferred to stay there. After some quick greetings and introductions, the drooping man's head peeked up over the rim of the table and said, "You are the black? I was told they were sending the homosexual."

"We're both here," Hamilton said. It took a moment for the man under the table to get the joke. When he did, he let out a sound like a clock ticking at double speed. Al realized it was his way of laughing. Everyone else laughed, too. The man poked his head up to chin level and said, "Good! I like homosexuals," and then slid back down.

The board members, at least half of whom were Canadian or American, asked a lot of questions about the stock price, the future of packaged music in the face of new delivery systems, and the viability of finding a new format that would encourage consumers to replace their record collections again.

Hamilton gave considered answers when he felt he had something to say, and admitted ignorance of matters beyond his qualifications. After almost half an hour of such swordplay, the board got down to the real subject.

The chairman was a man in his mid-fifties whose native Swedish accent had been softened by a decade in Toronto. "We trust your discretion, Al," he said. "We are struggling with a very emotional issue and we need your guidance. In the last year or so we've all gotten to know J. B. Booth, and he has done a crackerjack job reorganizing and improving WorldWide ILG. The figures are just remarkable. Profits have gone way up at a time when much of our company has not been performing up to stuff.

"At the same time, we see how, as Mr. Booth's attention has moved from the U.S. operation, things have gone very moody. American percentage of revenue generated has fallen precipitously. It makes Booth look good two ways—when he focuses on Europe, Europe booms. When he turns a bit away from the States, the States recede."

For one instant Hamilton flashed on the chance of a double-cross. Maybe he was going to take the fall for the drop in U.S. profits. He knew how he'd respond. He'd show them how the relative ups and downs of Europe and the States were mostly the result of the paper shift of accounting credits for American units sold on the continent. But it was unnecessary paranoia. No one was blaming him. The moment passed without Hamilton having to go for his gun.

"We have some questions for you, Al, and we appreciate your candor. First, is J. B. Booth a man who could ascend to the CEO position for all of WorldWide, including USA, Latino, and ILG?"

"Absolutely," Hamilton said. "Booth could actually do his current job better if the authority were not divided. The current system has within its design some redundancies which make more trouble than they help."

"Very good. Thank you for that honest answer."

"I have a concern." An Englishwoman Hamilton knew to be friendly with DeGaul spoke up. "Candidly, I always saw John Booth as a sort of a dese, dem, and dose character. Forgive my political incorrectness, but does he have the social skills to operate at the very highest levels? We need someone who can deal with NOA's interests in the Far East, India, a whole variety of circumstances in cultures with distinct and sometimes arcane traditions. Would Booth be comfortable sitting in a room like this in, let's say, Egypt?"

Hamilton began to frame an answer, but an American named Jerry spoke first. Hamilton knew this fellow, too. He was meat-and-potato second-generation Philadelphia Irish. If he turned against DeGaul, Booth won.

"I think I can speak to that, Ann. J. B. Booth comes off a little coarse but I understand that to be a bit of a front, a face he uses to keep his image in the rock and roll world. Booth is a very sharp guy, a Harvard lawyer and a decorated military officer. I wouldn't let the rough package fool you."

"Thank you, Jerry, I'm glad to know that."

The chairman asked Hamilton if he would be so gracious as to step outside for a few minutes. He stood and made a little bow and left the room.

When Hamilton was gone the American held the floor, as Americans will. He glanced at file cards on the table in front of him as he spoke: "I think we all know we've got to make a move here. I love Bill DeGaul and I've supported him through some pretty tacky affairs. But we have a young girl dead here. Whether or not she was a talented singer or a star of the future I don't have a clue. She was in Bill's care and she died. Drugs seem to have been involved. It speaks of a sort of lifestyle that has no place in our company or, I think, in our society. If there ever was a time when that sort of amorality was excusable it's long, long gone.

"Factor that in with the fiduciary aspects. How does the market value our music division? Well, we get mixed signals. The overall prospects are stable thanks to remarkable growth on the international level. What's been the catalyst for that growth? Moving responsibility for International away from DeGaul and giving it to Booth.

"What's been the brightest light on the domestic front? This country-and-western singer Cookie O'Shea. Where did she come from? J. B. Booth discovered her and nurtured her and I guess even picked out her songs.

"Put that all up alongside Bill DeGaul's long history with World-Wide, the fact that he's an amiable character and we all like him personally. He's a clever, ingratiating guy. But where is he? Where's he been all year? I don't like gossip and I don't like innuendo. We've made Bill rich enough that I don't believe any of the suggestions that he's been engaged in financial hanky-panky. But it is pretty obvious that his investments in the Caribbean are taking up more of his time and attention than we are. I look around and I have to conclude, very regretfully, that Bill DeGaul has already left us. He's just decided to keep collecting his paycheck."

No one spoke to disagree.

An Austrian man shoved up his hand. "Jerry, I'm with you on all of that," he said. "But I have a practical question. I have always been given to understand that DeGaul commands tremendous personal loyalty among the singers on WorldWide records and from the community of music professionals. What are the possible repercussions if we toss away the paterfamilias? These people are not always the most mature and rational, are they?"

That set off ten minutes of varied and vigorous opinions. The chairman was finally obliged to point out that as none of them knew what they were talking about, Al Hamilton should come back in.

Hamilton had met the Austrian board member before, at a stockholder's meeting in New York. He smiled when he remembered De-

Gaul's assessment of him: "That cat has a head like a flat tire and every time he opens his mouth he lets out a little more air."

Asked about the artists' feelings for DeGaul, Hamilton told the Austrian, "I should not be the one to answer that. I can't say I didn't expect it to come up, though, and I have a suggestion. Some of the most important figures in the U.S. music business are in France right now for the MIDEM conference. I know of two knowledgeable, objective individuals who would be ready to fly here tomorrow to share their perspectives with you, as they have shared them privately with me. One is perhaps the most important music-industry attorney in New York. The other is a prominent music publisher with several artists on WorldWide. Both work closely with DeGaul and Booth. Both also work closely with other major music companies in the United States. They know the whole terrain and they will speak candidly and confidentially."

"Well," the chairman said, looking around. "Bring them to us!"

"There is another key perspective I'd like you to consider," Hamilton said. "But you must bear with me on this. One of WorldWide's greatest stars, Lydya Hall, is in London. She could certainly give you the artists' perspective. But—please, take no offense—Miss Hall would never be comfortable speaking to a whole room like this. If I could convince her to change her plans and fly up to Stockholm, is it possible that the board could select just one or two representatives to meet with her, perhaps at her hotel?"

There was buzzing and then they said yes.

Hamilton went off to make the calls and show how he could move mountains. The mountains were all sitting by their phones, waiting to be moved. The next evening the chairman of the NOA board and the British woman Ann were with Hamilton in a double-decker penthouse hotel suite waiting for their audience with Lydya Hall. What Lydya said to them about Wild Bill made their ears bleed. By the time she got to his calling her in the middle of the night to say that if she didn't do what he told her he'd arrange for her to lose her children as well as her career, the British woman wanted DeGaul horsewhipped and fed to the ants.

At the same time, in the blond boardroom, objective experts Garth Goes of Edgewater Publishing and Asa Calhoun of the law firm Calhoun, Brebner, Jackson & Baerenwald were explaining to the rest of the

NOA board that Bill DeGaul was actually a detriment to WorldWide's business and a figure of ridicule among artists. The only thing holding the company together was the Job-like patience, Atlas-like strength, and Brando-like charisma of J. B. Booth.

Garth Goes flew back to London with Lydya Hall. Asa Calhoun and Al Hamilton went back to New York on separate planes. Hamilton waited until he was over Newfoundland to call Booth and tell him, "*Enola Gay* is coming in."

# 37

The following Monday the chairman of the NOA board and Jerry, the American board member, arrived in New York and fired DeGaul in his office on top of the Black Mushroom. Wild Bill took the news like a trouper. He even had the grace to shake both men's hands. There had been a plan to have security escort DeGaul out of the building, but when the chairman saw how impeccably DeGaul accepted his dismissal, he was ashamed of himself and quietly called it off.

As they awkwardly said goodbye DeGaul said, "Who's got the job?"

The visitors spoke at once. "Booth."

"Ah, the legacy lives on. Does he know yet?"

"He just found out."

"Okay. See you around, boys."

On his way to Booth's office DeGaul ran into Cantone in the hall. "How are you holding up, Jim?" he said. "How are Mack, Dick, and Anthony doing?"

"Not good, Bill. They're looking for people to blame. They're half grief-struck, half guilty, and half in shock that their rosy future just disappeared."

"That's three halves, Jim."

Jim had no idea he was talking to a ghost. He went on about his own problems: "I don't know what to do about the unfinished album. There's good stuff there, I'm inclined to put it out. I suppose we could even put 'Hard Hearted' on it. Lilly will come back and kill me for saying that. The band is distraught. Anthony wants all the St. Pierre tapes destroyed because he sees them as the cause of Lilly's death. Mack wants to finish the tapes himself. I think he has visions of carrying on the band with him in charge and his girlfriend, Krystal, on vocals. Dick is horrified by that and not speaking to Mack. Someone calling himself The Witness is on the internet spreading conspiracy theories. Oh, and the rock critic Richard Reader is peddling a book proposal."

"How are you feeling?"

"I keep thinking it's my fault. But then, as soon as I even form those words I think I'm aggrandizing myself somehow, writing myself a bigger place in her story than I deserve. It's really shaken me up. Even the good memories bring on bad feelings. I can't listen to her music at all."

"What about her parents?"

"Her father's lawyers are trying to seize all the tapes and register a name-and-likeness trademark. Her mother's locked in the bedroom with the lights off."

"Give her whatever she wants," DeGaul said. "She's lost her child."

DeGaul walked down to Booth's office. No one was there. So he went back to his own and called in Cindy, his assistant. She took the news worse than he had. She wept and cursed the unfairness of it all and threatened to use her frequent flyer miles to go to Sweden and give the board a piece of her mind. DeGaul hugged her and consoled her and then he said, "Hey—how'd you get all those frequent flyer miles? You never take a vacation. Cindy! You been getting credit for my flights?" She blushed and nodded and they both laughed.

DeGaul asked what the board members had done when they left his office. Did they go toward Booth's? She said no, they went straight to the elevator and out. Yeah, DeGaul said, I had a feeling. He asked her to put out an APB for Booth. "Try Hamilton's office first. I want to see both of them."

They arrived together. Hamilton said nothing and shook DeGaul's hand. Booth said, "Hey, boss," and awkwardly hugged him.

"You pulled it off, men," DeGaul said. "You are a couple of cold bas-

tards. How are you gonna keep from murdering each other? It's gonna
be like *The Treasure of the Sierra Madre* around here."

"You don't mean that, Bill," Booth said.

"The balls I don't." DeGaul wore a dead man's grin. "You don't think
you could line this all up without a few of the rats whispering to me in
case it went against you, do ya? Shit, boys, I haven't seen so many people
trying to cover their asses since I walked into the girls' locker room."

Booth and Hamilton glanced at each other. Kingfish Calhoun was
dead.

"I guess I'm sentimental," DeGaul said. "I hoped when push came to
shove you'd find your consciences. I guess that's like wishing you'd find
your antlers."

"This is a sad day," Booth said. "Let's not say things we'll regret."

"Yeah," DeGaul snapped. "Like, 'Why don't you come to WorldWide
and watch my back?' Hah! Sorry, J.B. You're just doing what you do. I
can't be mad at a skunk for stinking."

"That's uncalled for, Bill," Hamilton said.

"You're right, Al. I'm out of line. Nobody likes a whiner."

The door opened. Cantone came in. He was too upset to worry
about what he was walking into.

"I'm very sorry," he said. "I need to tell all three of you. Lilly Rope's
father just served WorldWide with a court order demanding all her master tapes, notebooks, demos, and copies of her contracts. How do we respond?"

"This is not the time, Jim," Booth said.

"No," DeGaul said, stepping forward. "Let me speak one last time in
my capacity as CEO of WorldWide Music, incorporating Tropic
Records, a division of NOA. Hey, Cindy! Take a letter!" His assistant tiptoed into the room, blowing her nose in a Kleenex.

DeGaul said:

"Dear Mr. Roper,

"We all share your heartbreak over this terrible tragedy. Lilly was
one in a million. All of us who had the good luck to work with her were
in awe of her talent. All of us who knew her, loved her.

"Regarding your request for Lilly's masters and personal effects. Her
clothes and private possessions have already been collected and sent to

Lilly's mother. Her lawyer has copies of her contracts. Regarding the tapes and professional materials you request, given that competing claims exist from—among others—Lilly's bandmates and Lilly's mom, and given that we are cognizant of your having had no time for Lilly when she needed you and are only now raising your head to pick the meat off her dead bones, please be advised to blow it out your ass.

"Very sincerely yours,

"William DeGaul, Chief Executive Officer."

Cindy began crying again and ran out of the room. He called after her, "Cindy, cc Asa Calhoun on that one, would you please?"

"What's happening here, Bill?" Cantone asked.

"I'm out, Jim," DeGaul said. "I just got handed my walking papers. I suspect the severance package will be phenomenal. Mr. Booth is now CEO. God knows the man has worked for it. Mr. Hamilton will be playing Bonnie to his Clyde. Now, if I can trust you mugs not to steal my curtain rings I'm going to go over to *Billboard* and approve my obituary."

DeGaul walked out of WorldWide like he was stepping away for a quick lunch. He stopped only to sign a blank expense report for his assistant and date it last Friday. "Last chance to live it up, Cindy," he whispered, and he was gone.

# 38

Booth, Cantone, and Hamilton stood in DeGaul's office looking at one another while Cindy sobbed outside.

"We need to control this in the press," Hamilton said.

"I don't think Bill will go public," Booth said, "but he's pretty pissed. Now is the moment he could hurt us, before the lawyers sew up a parachute with a confidentiality clause. For twenty-four hours he can say anything to anyone."

"The board will be preparing a statement," Hamilton said.

"Wrong signal. First word has to come from us. Thing is, anything you and I say will be held against us if DeGaul unloads. I got a three-sentence release all written. I'm clamming up."

Hamilton looked at Cantone. "He could do it."

Booth studied Jim's shocked face. "Why him?"

"Music head, youngblood, face of the future. Nonpolitical. It sends the signal that this is good news for the artists, for the music. Don't put down DeGaul, just pay tribute to the incredible vitality J. B. Booth has brought to WorldWide. Looking ahead to a new era of greatness, taking decisive steps to insure the future. Good for Wall Street to hear this, too. Cantone's well liked, his endorsement of this transition will carry weight."

"You up to it?" Booth asked Cantone.

"I don't even know what happened."

"Which is why I like you talking to the press," Hamilton said.

"The truth?" Booth said. "This does not leave this room. DeGaul screwed up too many times. He was selfish. He wanted all the rewards but he no longer wanted to do the work. The board looked the other way as long as they could, but it got too blatant. The long absences, the weird operation in the Caribbean, the profligate lifestyle and abuse of company funds, it all came to a head."

"You say none of that," Hamilton said.

"Not on the record anyway," Booth said. "It's background. You keep the focus on the positive."

"Make it about J.B.," Hamilton warned. "His success with International, his nurturing of Cokie Shea, the acquisition of Solidarity. He's in touch with the times."

"You up for this?" Booth asked.

"Sure. Just give me a few minutes to gather my thoughts, make some notes."

"You got it," Booth said. "Cindy! Get press on the phone! Cindy! Don't cry, you still got a job."

. . .

Cantone did a couple of phone interviews that afternoon. They went okay. He plugged Cokie and Brute Apache when he talked about the bright new talent Booth was developing. He put off speaking to *Billboard* until Tuesday morning. They went to press Wednesday and came out Friday. He knew that whatever he said to them would become the official WorldWide mantra to the music industry, and would shape the assumptions behind other articles. He had to sweat that one.

It was raining when he left work and he didn't have an umbrella. He arrived home at ten, after the kids had gone to bed. There was a large cardboard box in the middle of the living room.

"Bill DeGaul came by," Jane said. Jim had not yet told her what had happened that morning, and apparently Bill hadn't either. "He left you that box."

Jim opened it. It was full of LPs, old vinyl albums. Jim leafed through them. Dylan, Muddy Waters, Roy Orbison, Jack Elliott, Odetta,

Presley, Everlys, Sam Cooke, Howlin' Wolf, Tom Rush, Slim Harpo, Dave
Van Ronk.

There was a note: "Cantone—where I'm going I won't need these.
Remember where it all comes from. Keep hope alive—DeGaul."

"Hey, Jane," he said. "Is the turntable still up in the closet?"

. . .

The next day when Jim got to work the bomb had dropped and people
were picking through the rubble. Jim looked into DeGaul's office. It was
full of packing crates. Cindy had resigned that morning, but she was
protecting DeGaul's personal effects like a mother cheetah. Booth's new
assistant, DeeDee, was talking to some painters about how Booth
wanted the place redone.

Jim went to Booth's office. It looked like Bloomingdale's stockroom
at Christmas. Gifts, cards, telegrams, flowers, baskets of cheese, baskets
of sausages. "What a haul," Booth laughed. "You gotta love this business.
When you're on top, everybody's your pal. I fall in front of a train? They
won't know me. Hey, Jim—get a load of this." Booth dragged out a half-
unwrapped bicycle. "Look at this! Ron Delsener sent me a bicycle! What
the hell? All I can figure is he told his secretary to send me a stationary
bike and she screwed it up. What do you think?"

"I think you must be the man, J.B. It's like Santa's workshop."

"How're your people taking the news?"

"Fine. You know, they all wonder how it's going to affect *them*. The
good ones see it as an opportunity, the not-so-good ones are scared it's
going to mean they have to deal with someone new."

"Who's not so good?"

"Ah, come on. I don't mean not so good. I mean the geniuses and
the merely brilliant."

"You do those interviews?"

"Yeah, I think it went okay."

"Good man. Jim, this change is going to be good for you. Less bullshit for you to have to deal with."

"Cool."

"Hey," Booth leaned forward and smiled and said quietly. "Screw
DeGaul. It's our turn now."

Cantone called his wife and asked her to meet him for coffee before she picked up the kids. They rendezvoused like lovers at a diner near Penn Station. He told Jane that he was being asked to shovel the dirt onto DeGaul's casket. It was both an invitation from Booth and Hamilton to join their inside club, and a test of his loyalty.

"Like becoming a made man," Jane said.

"I feel stupid," Jim told her. "It was obvious they were setting up De-Gaul, but I didn't want to see it. I should have gone to him but I was too cautious. Now it's too late for him. And these guys aren't sure if they should throw me overboard after him or give me a pistol and welcome me back. Two things I do know—there's nothing I can do to change what was done to DeGaul, and if I cross Booth now I'll be out of a job, maybe out of the business. I have to think about you and the kids."

Jane had been listening seriously, but now she became angry. It took Jim by surprise.

"You do whatever you want," she told him. "But don't you ever use me or the children as an excuse for greed, dishonesty, or weakness."

Jim didn't know what to say. His wife's fury disarmed him. She said she had to collect the kids and gathered her things and left.

Jim went back to his office and asked Helga to hold his calls. The giant secretary was trembling for inside gossip about DeGaul. Jim told her it was a mutual decision based on a realistic assessment of the demands of the business plan over the next ten years. She would have been less insulted if he'd just said, "None of your business."

He locked his door and sat for as long as he could. He finally picked up the phone and called the reporter for *Billboard*. They talked for quite a while.

When they were done he opened the door and went through the stack of pink phone-message slips. One jumped out. Charlie Rose was doing a segment on the DeGaul ouster on his PBS talk show the next night and someone from WorldWide had to be on the panel. Rose wanted Booth, but Booth told press to send Cantone. Jim said okay.

•  •  •

Thursday night Booth came in late and watched a tape of the Charlie Rose show. He had to fast-forward through some State Department drone talking about the Russian economy and a former third-party presidential candidate hawking his new book. The fall of DeGaul was given the last fifteen minutes of the show, after most of America had switched over to Leno or Letterman.

Cantone looked stiff but presentable. He wore a blue dress shirt with open collar and a Prada jacket. The kid had finally cracked the dress code. Also on the panel were an entertainment reporter in a bow tie and a record producer who'd had a lot of hits in the seventies and now spent his days writing bitter letters to radio consultants and the Rock and Roll Hall of Fame.

Booth took off his shoes and socks. He thought about looking for the toenail clippers. The segment started with the host giving the usual tribute-dinner rap about DeGaul's glorious history and how today's ouster seemed to mark a turning point for the record industry; the last of the great visionaries was gone and the accountants had taken over.

"Lordy, Lordy," Booth said to the empty room. "They never get tired of that one, do they? How many last great visionaries will we have to bury before we're done hearing about it?"

The journalist shook his head grimly and lamented how with De-Gaul gone there was no beacon for foundering musicians to swim toward. The old producer was capable of talking only about himself, but he saw DeGaul's ouster as a metaphor for what he said had happened to him—the giants pushed out by the gnats. Booth almost hit fast-forward, but the panel turned to Cantone and Booth clicked up the volume.

"Bill was of another era," Cantone said slowly. "He was what I guess we'll all soon start thinking of as a twentieth-century man."

Right, Booth agreed to himself, he was out of time. Forward into the future!

The host pointed out that DeGaul was not dead, merely fired. Jim smiled and said Wild Bill would outlive them all. Then, to Booth's horror, Cantone started talking about DeGaul as if he were Mother Teresa.

Cantone claimed DeGaul was part of a "beautiful accident," a convergence of music with a generational and social revolution that was born in the fifties, flowered in the sixties, became big business in the seventies, made millionaires and billionaires in the eighties, and came into its decadence in the nineties. By the end of that fantastic run the bean counters were trying to quantify beauty. Loyalty of every kind had been replaced with a panicked sense of "How can I make my million before I get fired?" That was not a world Bill DeGaul accepted or even acknowledged.

That invited the other panelists to pile onto WorldWide and—by the time they were done—J. B. Booth. Cantone just sat there. The record producer even did a little imitation of Booth's Rhode Island accent crying, "Ot? What do I care about ot?" The journalist laughed hard. Furious, Booth looked to Cantone, who merely shook his head and said, "It's unfair to blame the rest of us for not being as good as Bill DeGaul. No one's as good as Bill DeGaul."

Booth sat stunned as the segment played out with more slander and invective. When the tape ended he continued to stare at the humming fuzz on the screen. Finally he noticed the red light blinking on his phone machine. Several messages groaned or chuckled about what would come to be called the Charlie Rose Massacre. The last message was from Hamilton, who said just three words: "Cantone killed us."

· · ·

The next morning bundles of *Billboard* appeared at the Black Mushroom. Booth sat down in his new chair in his new office that still smelled of paint and put his feet up on his new desk. He read the page-one news about DeGaul's resignation from WorldWide. It continued inside. He turned to read the rest of it and was distracted by two related articles on the same page. One was a history of DeGaul's career from Latin America to New Orleans to WorldWide. It read like an inspirational story for boys.

Across the bottom of the page was a column titled "Guest Spotlight" with the headline A GIANT PASSES, AN ERA ENDS. It was credited, "By James Cantone, SVP East Coast A&R, WorldWide Music."

Here's what Booth read:

> I would like to address the concerns of the whole music industry, from artists to retailers to radio programmers, about the viability of World-Wide Music after the departure of Bill DeGaul. Bill leaves WorldWide with a great legacy, but in the long run the only true value of a record company's legacy is that it provide a foundation upon which the fu-

ture can be built. Bottom line: WorldWide's future promises to out-shine its past.

"Gratitude," Bill DeGaul always said, "is the reward for favors about to be received." That's a hard philosophy. Bill rose by it, and some say he fell by it. This has always been a business of personal connections. Perhaps as the music industry is absorbed into the larger economy, personal connections matter less than they once did. Maybe Bill was slow to recognize those changes. If so, he has paid a high price.

Other publications have quoted "observers," "insiders," and "well-placed sources" saying Bill DeGaul was "out of touch" with the mainstream. Could this be the same Bill DeGaul who was seen four or five nights a week at concerts, clubs, and showcases? The same DeGaul whose idea of recreation was to bounce from bar to bar hearing music by bands in whom he had no professional interest? The same DeGaul who prowled the secondhand stores of every country he visited looking for records he could not get at home? Bill DeGaul was long past having to work for money. He lived for music.

The same nameless experts speculate that Bill took too much power to himself and would not delegate. That would be a great flaw in a corporate executive. But how can his anonymous accusers reconcile that with the man who deferred to his subordinates again and again, in decisions about signings, marketing, and planning? If DeGaul took too much power to himself, how can we explain his decision to divest himself of direct control of WorldWide's international divisions and hand their operations over to his trusted lieutenant, J. B. Booth? Those are not the actions of a man who cherished power.

Bill DeGaul inspired trust in artists, business associates, and just about everyone else who ever had the good luck to know him because he was the kind of man the record industry used to be full of but who are now in short supply. He loved music, he genuinely enjoyed the company of musicians, and he was enthusiastic about new ideas. Bill was an entrepreneur. He started his first label—the legendary Tropic Records—because he heard something great and wanted everyone else to share it. Bill always heard what was coming and spread the word. He never lost his love for music because he never lost his love for life.

Booth stopped reading and shouted to the ceiling, "This is the biggest load of pigpuke I have ever seen in my life! Cantone should wear a tutu!"

He read the rest:

Some consultants and efficiency experts would maintain that characters like Bill DeGaul don't follow the corporate flow chart, they ignore the seating plan. If that's true it is a flaw, and Bill DeGaul is not the first record pioneer to pay a high price for it. But we work in an industry that flawed characters like Bill created. They were the ones with the guts and perseverance to go into the woods, down to the delta, across the ocean, or into some loud, dirty bar and react with a human heart that said, "Everyone should hear this music!"

Entrepreneurs like Bill showed how R&B, rock & roll, and other outsider music could be the engine to build multibillion-dollar empires, subordinate to neither accountants or the old entertainment conglomerates. It was a window men like Bill pushed open for a while, and now it is closed again.

Today we are told business must be ruthless to compete in a global market where money, information, and fads can zap from Rio to New York to Stockholm in the time it used to take for a box of records to make its way from the Caribbean to New Orleans. We must move into the future, and great executives like J. B. Booth and the whole WorldWide team are the sort of people who know the new world and see its opportunities.

But when we say goodbye to Bill DeGaul, when we wish him well in his next pursuits and celebrate all the good times and great music gone by, we should not kid ourselves. We should not ignore what we're losing. It's why most of us got into music and what no accountant can measure. It's our souls.

Booth put down the magazine. He noticed that the only photograph of him on the whole page was a shot of him with a bad haircut, standing behind DeGaul at a party for Lydya Hall. The SVP of press stuck her neck into Booth's office while keeping her feet outside in case she had to run. "Knock knock," she said. She was holding *Billboard*. She smiled nervously. "What do you think?" she asked.

"What do I think? I think the little wop sent a drill right up my ass. What do you think?"

"I think we have to let DeGaul have his day and then in a week or two we place some pieces centering around you and your plans for the new WorldWide."

"That's good advice, thank you. Could you please step on glass on your way out? Bye!"

Al Hamilton went into Jim Cantone's office, closed the door, and said, "Start telling me now how you talked for two hours about Booth and they only used the ten minutes you threw in at the end about De-Gaul, after you thought the guy's tape was off."

"Is Booth pissed?"

"Who cares? You're obviously not a man who worries what people think. Why is this under your name? Did you actually write this pablum?"

"No, it's stuff I said in the interview. They edited it down."

"Without your permission."

"No, I said it was okay."

"Did you read it first?"

"Yeah, I saw a fax. It seemed all right. They took out all the contractions and put in words like 'cherish.' They told me they were running other articles dealing with WorldWide's future. They wanted a sidebar about DeGaul."

Hamilton studied Cantone. "I can't make up my mind about you," he said at last. "You seem sincere. But you'd have to be smarter than you pretend to be, wouldn't you?"

"I don't pretend to be anything, Al," Cantone said. "I can't operate on as many levels as you guys can. Maybe I'm not smart enough to remember what I said to who when and how I'm supposed to change it when I talk to who else. That's all too much for me. It's easier for me to just tell everyone the truth."

"Sure. 'I'm so sorry, Lilly, the CDs are already pressed.' "

"Good point, Al. The longer I hang around here the smarter I get."

"Straighten up, boy, or you won't be hanging around here."

Hamilton left. Cantone sunk into his chair. He had to try to find his contract. Zoey Pavlov appeared in his office. That was a rarity. She said, "So what about SoundScan?"

"What? I've been busy. I haven't checked the charts."

Oh, what a liar, Zoey thought. Look at him, he's miserable, he can't stand it.

She said, "You didn't see what's number eighteen?"

"Not Jerusalem?"

"No, although I think they did get a little postdeath blip, didn't they? No. Black Beauty has entered the Top Twenty and is still climbing."

Jim said, "That's fantastic, Zoey. Congratulations. This one is all yours."

She went back to her office, confused. Was it possible Cantone was sincere? He couldn't really wish her well, could he? And if he did—if somehow he always had—what did that mean she had turned into while she was hating him?

• • •

Cantone's piece in *Billboard* set the tone for most of the articles that followed. DeGaul was celebrated as the noble frontiersman whose like we shall not see again. Artists and managers who never got along with him tried to establish their own legitimacy by spinning out warm reminiscences of their days with Wild Bill. One breathless British magazine compared DeGaul's ouster to the voters rejecting Churchill after he won World War II. The consensus was that he took a fall he didn't deserve.

Booth was, of course, diminished. Rather than being seen as the savior, he was the putz who could never measure up. He was, once again, the clown with the bad haircut. He imagined he heard people laughing when he left the room.

"Fire Cantone?" Hamilton asked him from the top of the Mushroom. The blinds were all drawn.

"And pay out his mitigation period? No chance. That little worm is going to learn no one makes his bones on me. He's got a year left on his deal. I checked. That's a long time to dangle. I am going to let him lie awake and wonder. I want HR to remind him that any attempt to negotiate future employment with another label while under contract to WorldWide is a violation of his contract and will be grounds for a lawsuit against both him and the parties with whom he might seek to negotiate. I want Kingfish Calhoun to make sure everyone in the business knows Cantone wears a black mark, and anyone who deals with him is out of the clubhouse."

"It'll get back to him."

"I want it to. Trust me, by a year from now, when we finally let him drop, no one will go near Cantone. Meanwhile, I'll make sure he's assigned to only hopeless projects. He will not be able to get within a hundred miles of a hit. One year from now when we finally throw him out of here without severance, Jim Cantone won't be the brave young man who spoke the truth and paid the price. He'll be a no-talent screw-up who had his shot at the majors and blew it."

"Remember," Hamilton cautioned Booth. "You won."

"It don't feel like it," Booth mumbled.

# 39

Looking back later, it was hard for witnesses to say when Booth's reign began to unravel, when the normal day-to-day threats and antagonisms degraded into steady Hitler-in-the-bunker misery. Even in happy times Booth had routinely ended business calls with the salutation "drop dead," but in his final year the habit of belligerence became an ugly addiction. No one wanted to be around him, and while fear of reprisal and the inclination to toady were the glue that held many business relationships together, a plurality of important people eventually decided, independently, that their world would be a prettier place if J. B. Booth were not in it.

The first hairline crack was Booth's new inability to keep a secretary. For ninety grand a year most executive assistants would put up with Mussolini, but Booth burned through four secretaries in ten months. The head of human resources was heard joking that these vets now qualified for less stressful work as Hong Kong air traffic controllers. Each time another quit Booth expressed loud relief that one more incompetent was out of his hair. The senior staff listened to the tirades and rolled their eyes at each other. Their bigger worry was that Booth seemed self-destructively intent on stifling the career of Cokie Shea, who had sold two million copies of her first album, four million copies of her second, and was boiling with ambition to make the difficult leap from country to the mainstream on CD number three.

WorldWide should have been trying to smooth the path for Cokie; if she made the crossover to pop she could become one of the best-selling stars in the world. But Booth was not helping. He was pouring salt in the wounds of the Nashville office, which did not want to lose its biggest cash cow to New York. Cokie offended the Nashville marketing department by making demands appropriate for a pop act, but unusual in the low-rent world of country. Cokie's case was this: "I sell more records than most pop acts, I make the company more money than most pop acts. Why should I get a smaller promo budget than most pop acts?" She expressed through her new minister-manager-husband the proposition that WorldWide treated country acts in general and her in particular like the embarrassing hillbilly cousins who happened to find oil in their meadow. Word reached New York that along Music Row Cokie referred to Booth as "Mr. Drysdale."

Booth was determined to force a fight. When Crash Cronin appeared at Booth's weekly direct-reports meeting to put forward a compromise Cokie Shea marketing plan, Booth said, "Tell her to ask Jesus for the money," and refused to discuss it further.

Crash limped home to Nashville like a man carrying his own coffin. Eight days later *Variety* broke the story that Cokie Shea was withholding her new album from WorldWide until the label demonstrated its ability to successfully market her music.

The article quoted Cokie:

> I had a wonderful relationship with Bill DeGaul. And I love all the folks here at the Nashville office. But I'm not sure any of those new boys in their shiny shoes up in New York like or understand the country music audience. Like one of my new songs says, "I won't sit at the children's table anymore." As soon as the new team at WorldWide presents me with a respectful promotional plan, I'll give them the album. Until then, I'll be on the road singing my songs for those who care.

Booth reacted like Tojo singing *tora tora tora*. "If the bitch wants a war," he wailed with his door inappropriately open, "I'll send a block-buster down her ungrateful hick foxhole!"

Asked by *Entertainment Tonight* why she would not give her new songs to WorldWide, Cokie smiled sweetly and said, "My daddy always told me, 'Honey, don't cast thy pearls before swine.' "

When that sound bite showed up at the end of Booth's weekly press compilation reel during the Wednesday lunch meeting he drove his fork into the oak conference table with such force that it stayed there for the rest of the day. After Booth ripped through the agenda, rejected all proposals, insulted his subordinates, and stormed out of the room, Al Hamilton turned to the shaken senior staff, pointed to the erect fork, and declared, "Whosoever pulls this sword from this stone will be the new king."

Cantone and Booth remained publicly cordial by avoiding each other as much as possible. There would be a reckoning when Jim's contract ran out, maybe sooner, but neither had the energy to initiate the inevitable death match. Still, after the fork-in-the-table scene Jim had to say something. He might allow Booth to destroy himself, but he could not let him sink the label.

Jim ignored the attempt of the secretary-of-the-week to wave him away and went into Booth's office. He found him with his back to the room, staring out at Times Square.

"J.B.," Jim said. "We shouldn't let Cokie's stupidity pull us into a public pissing contest. Let's give her the press and get us the billing. Let me go down and tell her we'll work out a generous promo plan if she'll shut up and give us the album. It's all PR to her. Let her be a big shot in the papers for a week. Give her a chance to retreat with dignity and we get the record."

"Retreat with dignity," Booth repeated. "That's quite a plan, Jimmy. I send you down to surrender, we capitulate to her idiotic demands, she gloats about it in the press, and we tell each other we won. Sounds like the Smothers Brothers' plan to get us out of Vietnam. Remember that? No, you couldn't. The Smothers Brothers' plan was, we pull out and declare victory! Got a huge laugh, everybody repeated it. We pull out and declare victory. The real joke was, that turned out to be Nixon and Kissinger's plan, too. Almost worked."

Jim said nothing. Booth kept staring out the window, not looking at him. Then he said, "Why don't you just land a helicopter on the roof and I'll re-create my famous advance from Saigon?"

Jim said, "I don't see what it benefits us to descend into a grudge match with a little girl."

Booth turned and looked at him. "This is a business of little girls.

Little girls writing songs for little girls who buy CDs. Boy singers who look like little girls. Businessmen with the guts of little girls."

"I don't need to fight with you. Why are you being so hard on everyone?"

"I am trying to hold my company together and I am doing it alone. The people who should be helping me do nothing. Worse than nothing. They whisper dirty stories to reporters. *The Wall Street Journal* is preparing an article about my *excesses*—including rumors of the affair with Cokie Shea that destroyed my marriage. All of this is based on interviews with employees of this company past and present who smile to my face, take my money, and sign contracts swearing confidentiality. If the incompetents and snitches who surround me were content to merely do nothing for their absurd salaries, I could do their jobs as well as my own and live with it. But doing nothing is not enough for them. They must also destroy the good work others do."

"J.B., you should know I have not been a source for these articles. We have our differences, but I would not say anything behind your back I wouldn't say to your face."

"What do you want, a medal?"

Jim gave up on trying to find any common ground with Booth. He said, "See ya later," and headed toward the door.

Booth kept talking. "I know you're honest, Cantone. You're the most honest person I ever met. That's your vanity. The last temptation is the temptation to martyrdom. That's how they'll get you. Someone will put up a cross and you'll jump on and nail yourself up on principle. Sooner or later you'll fuck yourself over out of pride and egotism." He almost smiled. "But I'm sure you'll have another job lined up when you do."

The latest nervous secretary stuck her nose in the door, sniffing, and said, "Sorry—Kelleher on line two."

"My divorce lawyer," Booth said. Jim tried to get out of the room but Booth told him to stick around.

He picked up the phone, grunted, and listened. "How could she know that?" he demanded. "No one knows about that account! The IRS doesn't know! It's incorporated in Zurich and banked in the Caymans! It's money from my publishing company! How could she possibly know?"

Booth was supposed to have divested himself of his old publishing company when he joined WorldWide. By setting up beards to front the publishing firm, Booth had been able to sign to WorldWide acts whose songs he owned, effectively paying himself big advances from the WorldWide treasury and promoting artists in whom he had a financial interest. It was no surprise that Booth's wife had deduced the arrangement, but if she could prove where the money was hidden she must be Charlie Chan.

"So she wants half of that, too?" Booth sighed into the phone. There was a long pause. Booth said nothing. Cantone watched all the air go out of him. Finally he said, "Do what you have to do," and hung up.

He turned to Cantone. His eyes were red with tears of what? Anger? Heartbreak? Loss? Betrayal? He looked like a man past caring about discretion. He said, "Lois is now blackmailing me. I have to sign over to her all of my foreign investments, tax shelters, and retirement, one hundred percent, or she will go public with arrangements I've made over the years that could embarrass WorldWide and expose me to the mercy of the Internal Revenue Service."

Booth fished in his drawer, found a cigarette box, and lit up a smoke. He sucked it down to the filter before he spoke again. Cantone wished he could pull a lever and fall through a trapdoor, but there was no getting out of this shit pile without picking up a spade.

"My wife wants to see me ruined," Booth said calmly. "She is willing to publicly shame me, destroy my career and reputation, and then see me in jail. She lived with me a long time." He choked out an empty laugh. "She learned a lot."

Jim went back to his office and closed the door. He picked up his phone and called the Caribbean. After a while, he got DeGaul.

"How's life in the big top?" Jim asked.

"It's fantastic!" DeGaul shouted. "Can you hear that music? We've got the world's first reggae carousel! The horses go up and down on the offbeat!"

DeGaul was standing in the doorway of a trailer, looking over the midway of his Webster World Amusement Park. Rastas and baldheads were painting booths, hammering boards, and test-riding the Caribbean's scariest roller-coaster without benefit of seat belts.

"You gotta see this water slide," DeGaul told Jim across the wires. "It's the highest point in the parish! We had to put two red lights on top to ward off airplanes! It's the wildest thing you've ever seen! Fifty thousand gallons of water! TooLoose, this old local, thought the idea was to climb up the slide like a waterfall! He was about thirty feet up when he sees a raft full of bredren plowing down on him! He jumped off and landed in the pool at the bottom! Sixty years old, came out fine!"

"Bill, I have to ask you . . ."

"Get this! We're going to have concerts on the midway with great acts from the whole rock era! I got Bo Diddley booked! Bobby Charles, Jesse Winchester! John Prine and Wilson Pickett are playing the first month! They love it, they get a great family vacation, all expenses paid, and play for an audience that really appreciates them! You gotta come!"

Jim got to the point: "I hear you've been advising Lois Booth on financial matters."

"She told you that? Don't say anything to J.B., he'll have a hit squad on me. Lois and I are old friends. I can't stand by and see her get screwed by that rat-fink backstabber she married. Do J.B. good to lighten his load a little. Squeeze that fat camel through the needle's eye."

"Everybody here misses you, Bill," Jim said.

"Let 'em! I've gone to a better place. When am I gonna see your family down here, Cantone? I might have Robyn Hitchcock booked in March—that's your generation!"

"I'll be there," Jim said. He hung up his phone and checked his e-mail. There was a red alert from the press department that the manager of Black Beauty, WorldWide's best-selling new band, would be quoted in a *Wall Street Journal* article saying that the band had no special relationship with J. B. Booth and that any suggestion Booth made to the contrary was untrue. Black Beauty did not care who ran their record company—they were above such petty concerns.

Jim typed a note back to the head of press: "Blood in the water."

Booth held on through the *Journal* article, even as it spawned me-too pieces in *Rolling Stone,* the *New York Observer,* and *Entertainment Weekly.* Word was around that a reporter for *Esquire* was interviewing everyone in town for a mammoth hatchet job. Someone faxed Jim an advance sketch of the opening illustration. It portrayed Booth as King Kong, bloodied and bellowing and swatting at planes from the top of the Black Mushroom, with a helpless Cokie Shea in his furry paw.

Cokie continued her strike against the company, telling her suburban cowboy-hat audiences that she'd sing her new songs to them for free but wouldn't give them to the corporate bean counters for a million dollars. That line always got a big cheer, although she was actually singing those songs for $47.50 a ticket, plus a piece of event parking.

Booth made one attempt to settle the war with Cokie. He got her on her home phone after midnight and offered her a million-dollar off-the-books cash bribe to cut the shit and come back to WorldWide.

"You're pathetic, Jack," she said. "Do you really think you can make your biggest star a whore?"

Booth went red. "Why not? I made a whore my biggest star."

That was the end of any relationship between J. B. Booth and his greatest discovery.

Booth capitulated to his wife's financial demands and she cleaned him out. He felt okay about it. He told Al Hamilton that if giving up his life's savings meant he never had to see Lois again, it was a bargain. That line got a big laugh every time.

Once he put Lois behind him, Booth was free to publicly date sexy TV stars and fashion models. He took to it with awkward energy. He paraded down red carpets to awards ceremonies and charity banquets with babes on his arm and a smile on his face.

For years and years he had held such women in his imagination while he made love to Lois. They had married back when they were young and broke, before he dreamed of ever having a prayer of women like these looking at him. Booth had not always been faithful during his years of marriage, but neither had he ever before been single and rich. He thought he could finally live out his sexual fantasies. And yet he found, to his infinite sadness, that when he finally got the famous sex symbols he had dreamed of into his bed, he could achieve climax only when he closed his eyes and imagined he was with Lois.

That was what finally broke his heart.

# 40

In the end the only one who was ever going to bring down Booth was Booth. He finished himself off not because of all the enemies, real and imagined, lined up against him, but because of one bad day.

It was two years after he met Cokie Shea, two years after he was kidnapped. It was two weeks before Cantone's contract expired.

He had a cramp in his foot that the doctor said was in his mind. It kept getting worse. All he could do was sit on the edge of the tub in his new bachelor apartment and soak it. He was filling the tub to do that at seven in the morning when his phone rang. A call that early usually meant a crisis in Europe, but in this case he picked up and heard the unwelcome warble of superlawyer Asa Calhoun.

"J.B., we have a crisis—and a solution. You're not going to like it, but it has to be done."

"It's six-fifty A.M. Where the hell are you?"

"I'm in Hawaii. I just left Manus Evans."

"What do I care? You woke me up."

"You know Manus Evans has been suing me. You know he claims I colluded against him while serving as his attorney."

"Well, you did, you snake. You collude against all your clients. That's why we pay you!"

"Shut up, Booth, I'm on a cell phone!"

"What, you think there's someone who doesn't know?"

"Listen to me, this is bad. Evans won't back down. He's irrational, he's out for blood. He's on the juice again and he just caught his third wife sleeping with his drummer."

"Don't tell me. He can get another wife but it's hard to get a good drummer."

"This isn't a joke, J.B. He knows he's fat and old and headed for Vegas. He knows his salad days are behind him. He wants to take us down with him."

"What do you mean us, white man? As his attorney of long-standing I'm sure you remember that Manus Evans departed WorldWide after twenty-one years and fifty million albums for a bold new beginning at Moniform. As I recall, you brokered that deal. I also remember Manus giving a lot of interviews bitching about how WorldWide had let him down and didn't promote his albums anymore and only cared about signing cowgirls in tight pants. That was before his big debut for Moniform entered the charts at forty-eight, slipped to a hundred and two the second week, and landed in the discount CD club before he had even finished a video for VH1 to reject. That would be the same Manus Evans?"

"Here's the bottom line, okay? He has hooked up with a vicious boy attorney from outside the business. This kid has old money behind him and wants to make his name by nailing us."

Booth's call-waiting was clicking. He ignored it and said to Asa, "I still don't get this 'us.' This has nothing to do with me. Go cry to whoever's running Moniform this week."

"It is about us because you have twenty years of Manus's catalog and all his hits. You are the source of all his royalties."

"That's right, I'm batting a thousand and he's out of the game."

The call-waiting kept clicking and Booth kept ignoring it.

"You be quiet and listen to me," Asa said. "I want you to seriously absorb what I am about to say. And don't tell me why it can't happen, because there is nothing you can think of that I have not thought of already. I tell you, this has to be done."

"What."

"WorldWide must raise Manus's royalty rate on all his catalog to sixty percent. No packaging deductions, no cross-collateralization. Sixty percent of a hundred percent on all units across the board, and the label to pay for annual audits at the pressing plant."

"SIXTY PERCENT?" Booth screamed. "ARE YOU INSANE? HAS MANUS LEARNED TO MOONWALK?" The clicking of his call-waiting was beating in counter-rhythm to the shooting pains in his foot. Booth bellowed on. "Even if I had any motivation to want to make Manus Evans happy—which I certainly do not—I couldn't pay him sixty percent! You know that. If any other artist knew we were paying Manus a sixty-percent royalty it would blow the lid off the business for everyone. For everyone!"

"This is the point, J.B.," Asa said softly. "If we give him the royalty he will shut up forever. He'll sign a document binding the deal to his discretion."

"Worthless. Unenforceable."

"Listen to me, Booth! Listen. Manus wants to force a confrontation. He wants to blow up the business. Do you understand what I'm saying? He has been ripped off by everyone he ever trusted, his career is over, he has fifty or sixty million to spend on a very big murder-suicide and he wants to take us with him."

"Lookit, you asslick," Booth said. "I know what he can do to *you.* He's been around long enough, he knows how the game is played. He can probably show you dicked him over when you were supposed to be representing him. I feel bad for you. I really do. If they disbar you I'll give you a job in human resources screwing my staff on their employment contracts. But your problems with Manus Evans have zero to do with me."

"I will make this even simpler. Manus and his rich baby lawyer are going to show a pattern of collusion between me and WorldWide. They will show fraud and conspiracy. They will almost certainly get a judge to agree with them. Manus's old deals with WorldWide, all twenty-one years' worth, will be ruled invalid. His masters and copyrights will be reassigned to him."

"Well, that would be a shame," Booth said. "We still sell his *Greatest Hits* album at Christmas. But frankly, Kingfish, I don't care very much.

WorldWide got everything out of Manus Evans there was to get, and if he wants to take his old records back and rerelease them on Manus Discs from his garage, I will just have to live with that."

"Shut up and think for once. If a court invalidates Manus's contract, it will create an enforceable precedent for every other artist we have shared. Do you understand what I'm saying? All the contracts will be voided! Every singer who has been represented by me or any other lawyer also on retainer for you will become a free agent. Now do you understand why this is your problem?"

Booth was, for once in his life, unable to speak.

Finally he said, "Give him money."

"I don't have that much money to give!"

"You have insurance."

"No, I don't, Jack. No one will give me malpractice insurance."

"Why not? You've got a multimillion-dollar law firm!"

"Because everything we do is malpractice, you idiot! Unfortunately this is the first case I've seen where the victim is too pissed-off to settle and too rich to be squeezed. The only thing he will respond to is the suggestion that he might get sixty percent of all his albums. And his masters. And his publishing back. And he wants to be on the cover of *Spin*, but that one's nothing to do with you."

"Is Moniform willing to do it?"

"Yes, they are in. Of course, they only have two albums that sold nothing anyway."

"If I do this I'm going to delete every one of his albums except the *Greatest Hits.*"

"He thought of that. You can't."

"You go to hell, Asa! You're in on this! You're running a good cop–bad cop on me!"

"Hey, baby. I wish. This is bad cop–bad cop and I'm not calling the plays."

Someone was pressing Booth's buzzer and beating on his door. He told Asa to wait a minute and put on a bathrobe and looked through the peephole.

It was Sheila Ratzi, the left-wing lawyer who lived in the apartment under him. She was on the co-op board and every time Booth wanted to do something with his new property she blocked it. He hated her.

He pulled open the door and said, "What is it, Sheila, I'm in the shower."

"Lie! Lie! Lie!" she said. "All you do is lie! You'd lie about what you had for breakfast!"

"What is wrong with you?"

"I know you're not in the shower because your bathtub has been overflowing into my closet for ten minutes! All of my clothes are ruined! If you don't shut off the water the ceiling is going to come down!"

"Aw shit." Booth ran into his bathroom. It was a waterfall. He forgot he was running a tub when the phone rang.

"All right, all right," he shouted to Sheila. "I got it! I'll mop up!" He started throwing designer towels on the floor. They floated. Booth hated living alone.

Sheila stood there screaming threats of legal action and listing all the ways he was going to pay for this. He closed the door on her. God, Booth thought, I can't believe I was a lawyer. These people are animals.

He went back to his telephone. "All right, Asa," he said. "I'm going to make this happen. But you better make sure whatever confidentiality deal you make with Manus Evans is airtight. Don't do it yourself, have a real lawyer read it. I want you to make sure Manus knows I am doing this as a personal favor to him. No, I don't trust you. You'll tell him how you held me down and got it for him. I want you to have him call me. Tell him that's part of the deal. I want you to have him call me in Switzerland on Saturday so I can put my spin on this. Okay, you dirty, swindling hypocrite?"

"You can't go on speaking to people this way, J.B. It makes people not want to talk to you."

"My dream in life is that people won't want to talk to me."

Booth hung up and went to mop his floor.

• • •

Everything at work was worse than usual. Booth was scheduled on a 6:00 P.M. flight for Paris. Any day leading up to a rush-hour drive to the airport had an extra dose of anxiety. It started to snow. A jet had gone off the runway at Kennedy the night before. If they got off on time, he'd get into Paris at dawn, where he had to get to the other terminal and get on a puddle jumper to Bern, where a driver stupid in three languages would haul his bone-weary ass to a ridiculous Disneyland-style retreat house on the lake at Montreux where Booth would watch his European managers bitch about their budgets while squandering the company's money on champagne boat rides and souvenir music boxes that play "Edelweiss." It was a horrible itinerary. He wouldn't have time to see a single Alp. Booth sat at his desk trying not to think about it.

Nathan, his latest assistant, loomed in and said, "J.B.? Sorry. Someone from Avis is on the phone. They say you never returned the car you rented for the Super Bowl."

"Of course I did. I picked it up at the airport, I returned it to the airport. How do they think I got back there? It's ridiculous."

"They say it never came back. The bill is up to twenty-five hundred dollars."

"It's their mistake, I returned the car. Tell them to call corporate travel."

"Corporate travel says that since you weren't traveling on business they can't get involved."

Booth was screaming at the travel agent when a subordinate of the SVP of press came into his doorway and stood wavering like the rooster on a weather vane. Booth knew it must be something bad if the SVP was scared to bring it up personally. He motioned for the rooster to bring it over. She laid a magazine in front of him as if it were giving her a rash. A paper clip marked a page in the middle. By the time Booth, still on the phone, pushed it open, the rooster had hightailed it out the door.

It was one of the slick magazines that pretends to be for jet-setters but is actually for housewives. There was a spread called "Is She Really Going Out With Him? Gorgeous Women Who Date Gargoyles."

There was a photo of Booth and Cokie at the Grammy Awards. She looked like a supermodel in short dress and high hair. He had three chins, chipmunk cheeks, and his face scrunched up like Harpo Marx. He must have been turning to make a joke to someone and the camera caught him at his worst possible angle. Even in the most miserable hotel mirror in Paraguay he never looked like that.

He folded the magazine and slipped it in his wastebasket. Why bother, he wondered. What kind of person feels good about doing that to strangers for a living? Jealous people, he supposed.

The travel agent asked him to wait and didn't come back. He realized the song playing while he was on hold was "The High Cost of Lovin'" by Cokie Shea. He hung up.

Nathan brought in his paycheck. He opened it and looked at all the zeroes. Booth didn't use direct deposit. For at least a couple of minutes every two weeks he needed to have something in his hands to tell him why he put himself through this.

The check rang another bell. He had not picked up foreign money for his trip. He looked at his watch. It was lunch hour. The lines at the bank would be endless. He grabbed his coat and ran out.

Booth could have sent Nathan to the bank, but since Lois and her lawyer burrowed into his financial records he tried to handle his money himself. He'd set up an account no one knew about in a Times Square bank just south of the Black Mushroom. He could go there, deposit this paycheck, and buy a thousand dollars' worth of foreign currency.

The snow was turning to sleet as he walked to the bank. Inside the lines were as long as he expected. He stood there with the little people. The teller, when he finally reached her, made his life more miserable. Some bank personnel treat you nice when you show them a paycheck bigger than the value of their house. She was one of the resentful ones who was going to demonstrate how unimpressed she was. She insisted that because of the size of the deposit he go over to customer service and get it okayed.

"Miss," Booth said, "you misunderstand. I want to put this money *in* your bank."

"Sir," the woman said with uncalled for nastiness, "you want to put some of it in and take a thousand dollars out. Bank policy is to wait five days for a check to clear before we allow money to be drawn on it."

"Lady, listen. I come here all the time. I do this all the time. If you don't want to let me take a thousand dollars out of this check, just deposit this check and wait for it to clear and let me make a withdrawal from the sixty thousand dollars that's already in the account."

The woman snapped her tongue and said, "You want to deposit this and withdraw a thousand from what's already in the account."

"Yes."

"You fill out a withdrawal slip?"

"Yes. You have it."

"No, sir, you filled out a deposit slip only. I need you to go back and fill out a separate withdrawal slip."

"Why don't you just give me one and I'll fill it out right here."

"I can't do that, sir, you must go back to the counter and fill out a proper slip and then I'll process your request."

"Don't do this to me."

"You can leave the check you're depositing here now and I'll put that in."

Booth stalked away, filled out the form, and got back in line. He looked at his watch. He bounced on his heels. A spasm of pain shot up from his foot. He flinched, it was getting worse. Idiot doctor.

He finally made it back to the teller and gave her the withdrawal slip. She smiled sweetly. She handed him a thousand dollars. He asked her to please change it into two hundred dollars in French francs and eight hundred dollars in Swiss francs. She said for that he would have to go to the special services counter. If she had known he wanted foreign money she'd have sent him there in the first place and he could have done all his transactions at once.

Booth didn't even insult her. He just took his money and said, "It's not my fault you hate your job."

The line at special services was nine persons long. There was one teller working; the rest had gone to lunch. Booth thought he could reorganize this bank in one year.

He felt something hot and wet on his neck. He reached up with his left hand. Something was dripping from his hair. He looked at his fingers. The something was thick and brown. He smelled it. Mustard? He stuck the thousand dollars in the right pocket of his raincoat and reached around with his other hand. There was mustard all over his back. He was confused. He turned and saw a tall Latin kid walking away from the line, toward the exit, with a plastic mustard dispenser in his hand. Booth reached in his pocket for the thousand dollars. It was gone.

He screamed, "STOP! ROBBERY! GRAB THAT KID! HE JUST ROBBED ME!"

Booth ran across the bank. The other customers did nothing to help, they stared at him as if he'd farted. Booth ran toward the door, screaming, "Come back here, you bastard! Stop that thief! Stop or I'll shoot you!"

A bank manager stepped forward and blocked the door as the kid approached. The kid did not resist. Booth ran up at the same time a guard finally arrived.

"This thief just took a thousand bucks off me!" Booth stammered. He was livid, red-faced, the vein in his neck was pounding. "He squirted mustard on me! Look!" Booth twirled around to show both men the back of his coat. Mustard was still dripping from his hair. He was spinning like a lunatic.

The guard seemed to regard this as an everyday event. He said to the kid, "Want to empty your pockets?" The manager studied the people leaving the bank. There were a lot of them. Whatever he was looking for, he didn't find.

"What's the mustard for, chief?" the guard said.

"I'm havin' a sangwich," the kid said. From the pocket of his jacket he produced a hot dog with a bite out of it. The kid squirted a long line of mustard on the hot dog, took a big bite, and smiled at Booth.

"Search him," Booth commanded, "he's got my money!"

"We can't search him, sir," the bank manager said. "We can only hold him until the police get here. Then they'll arrest him and charge him and see if he wants a lawyer."

"Well then, call the police. This punk has my money in his pocket."

"I have to tell you, sir," the manager said, "he probably doesn't. Most likely he passed your money to an accomplice the moment he took it. If he ever had it at all. He's a distraction to let the other one get away."

"Search him!" Booth shouted, reaching out for the kid's jacket, "he has my money!" The guard put out his arm to separate Booth from the kid, who was chewing his hot dog as relaxed as if he were watching the circus.

The guard spoke to the kid. He said, "What do you want to do, sonny? You want to wait for the cops and get fingerprinted or you want to just empty your pockets for this gentleman?"

"I don't care," the kid said. "I got no pockets."

He opened his jacket and held up his arms. He turned 180 degrees around. It was true, there were no pockets in his slacks or shirt. He reached into the two pockets in his jacket and turned them inside out. A few crumbs from the bun were the only contents.

"Maybe it's hidden on him somewhere," Booth said, but he knew it wasn't. He'd been scammed. The cash was gone. And worst of all, he would have to get back in line and go through the torture of getting another thousand or arrive in Europe with no money.

Booth got his francs, finally, and went back to his apartment to shower off the mustard and change his clothes. On his door he found a summons issued for damage to Sheila Ratzi's apartment and possessions. He wiped his feet on it.

He called Randy, his driver, and told him to pick him up on the sidewalk in front of his building at 4:00 P.M. It was going to be torture getting out to the airport in this weather.

In the shower Booth rinsed the mustard from his hair and replayed the insults of the day. What was that nonsense about the rental car from the Super Bowl? He remembered the whole thing perfectly. After the game he went to a dinner and a party. He left late and drove back to the Holiday Inn at the airport so he could catch the first plane home in the morning. He returned the car at the airport and then went to the hotel. How did he get from the car return to the Holiday Inn? Wait, that's right. He was bushed, he'd had a couple of drinks. He decided to go straight to the hotel and return the car in the morning. He put it in a garage. Then he went to bed.

And what did he do in the morning? He was walking through the whole thing in his head. They hadn't given him his wakeup call. He was late, he ran for the plane and made it just as they were closing the door. He remembered it all. He was proud that he made it. He was happy all the way home.

And it hit him: He left the rental car in the short-term parking at the airport. That meant he had a thousand-dollar garage bill clicking away right now as well as a rental-car tab. He leaned his head against the wall. He turned off the shower. He got out and reached for a towel. There were no dry towels. All the towels were piled on the wet floor.

Booth dried himself on a bedsheet. His foot was throbbing. The pain was starting to radiate up his leg. Maybe it's phlebitis, he thought.

He went out to the sidewalk to wait for Randy in the freezing rain.

Booth knew he'd catch a cold with his wet hair. Then he'd get on the plane and breathe recycled air for seven hours. They'd probably seat him next to an ebola victim, going home to die. He shifted from good foot to bad foot on the edge of the sidewalk, trying to get warm. Where was Randy? Probably showing some can-can girl how to work the cigarette lighter.

A tall, broken-toothed homeless man wearing a wool hat, an ill-fitting coat, a cape made from a horse blanket, and cardboard-coffin shoes came and leaned against the streetlamp next to Booth. Booth looked up at him. The man grinned with a deranged leer and shook his head rhythmically, as if he were listening to a Walkman. He wasn't though, he was just nuts.

Booth stepped a foot or two away. The man took out from under his cape a cold can of Campbell's tomato soup. The top was off. The man put the rough rim to his mouth and drank. Soup ran down his chin. As he drank, the man took two steps to his side, sliding up next to Booth again.

Booth glared. The man scratched his crotch and licked his lips. Booth didn't want to give the creep the satisfaction of letting him get to him, but the guy smelled like a cesspool. Booth stepped off the curb and out into the street to look for Randy and the car. He watched the avenue through the sleet. No sign.

Booth turned back and looked at the homeless man, who was laughing. Booth felt his ears turning red. He felt a lump forming in his throat. He stared up at the creep, who was giggling and dribbling and rocking his head and rising on the sidewalk a full foot above Booth in the gutter.

And while Booth stared right at him, the homeless man threw back his head, hawked up a big wad of phlegm, and spit it into Booth's face.

The whole world turned white for a moment. Booth remembered this whiteness. When he was a kid in seventh grade a ninth grader named Red Ionata walked up in gym class and kicked him in the balls. There was a frozen instant when all the feeling drained out of him and his body temperature seemed to drop to zero. And then, in a brutal rush, the heat came back on and pain flooded into him.

The heat came back on in Booth and he turned berserk. Through the spit in his eye he saw the bum chuckling. He reached up with both hands, took the madman's collar, and pulled him violently forward, smashing his own forehead into the bum's nose. Booth didn't let him fall back. He held on to the collar while the bum staggered off the curb. Booth kicked him in the knee with his bad foot. The man squealed and tried to turn. Booth got his left hand behind his enemy's neck and drove him to the ground.

An Asian man came running from a store, shouting. Two passersby yelled, "Hey! Cut it out!" Someone said they'd called the cops and a college kid told his girlfriend, "That is so fucked up."

The bum was on the ground, trying to roll away. Booth wouldn't let him. He kicked him in the side as hard as he could. They were now out in the avenue—sleet came down, cars slammed on their brakes and blared horns and swerved.

Booth stood back and let the man stumble to his feet. The bum tried to run, but his face was covered with blood from his nose and he ran right toward Booth. It was like he was coming at him in slow motion. Booth hauled back and with all the hatred, bile, and humiliation he had ever known, he swung his fist into the oncoming face.

The homeless man stopped short, seemed to give serious consideration to some new idea, and then collapsed in the street. Booth stood over him. All the car headlights shone on him. A flashbulb popped off in the dark. He felt like Ali in the spotlight. He felt like the heavyweight champ. It was J. B. Booth's slow-motion moment of black-and-white victory.

It turned out the homeless man was blind.

He hadn't meant to spit on Booth. He hadn't known Booth was there. He was just hawking a loogie into the gutter.

The press was not kind. The police didn't want to know. Randy couldn't get Booth's car through the traffic backup, what with the cop cars and the ambulance coming in.

NOA invoked the morals clause in Booth's contract to cut him off without even decent severance. No one could remember when a morals clause had ever been successfully used against a major record executive. The last people at WorldWide saw of J. B. Booth, he was a black-and-white picture in the *New York Post* with his hand over his face.

Al Hamilton called the senior staff into the large conference room.

"How's everybody holding up?" he asked. "Shell-shocked? Yeah, that's how I feel. It's been a rough ride, hasn't it? This last year has been very hard, very stressful. I want to commend you all for doing good work in the face of so many distractions.

"Are the conference callers aboard? We're being buried in snow here in Manhattan, so some of our suburban brothers and sisters are not with us. Is everyone on the phone? Roger in London? David in Berlin? Mr. Precious in Los Angeles? Our new compatriot Jen Rosen in Nashville?"

Everyone on the speakerphone said aye-aye.

"I have some news," Hamilton said. "I hope you'll think it's good. In spite of the meltdown of our two top executives, the NOA board respects us enough that they are not rushing to bring in some outsider to replace J.B. I have been invited to act as interim president of WorldWide Music for six months. If the system works well, we may make it permanent. I suppose given recent events I should not tempt fate by using that word. If the board—or I—feel the need to search for a new CEO, I will gladly go back to the job I like best: signing your paychecks."

People laughed politely. Most were relieved to have Hamilton at the helm. Everyone liked Al and—anyhow—the devil you know.

"I don't want to take up a lot of time talking about what's gone wrong and what's gone right. We have a great lineup of new releases. Lydya Hall is putting the finishing touches on—and you know how I hate hyperbole—the best album she has ever made. We will be judged by how well we help that album find the wide, wide audience it deserves.

"Black Beauty continues to be at the spearhead of a phenomenon. We all see the weekly, even daily articles about the new Afro-Bohemian music and Black Beauty is always credited as the front-runner of that form. It is an enormous credit to all of you, to our superb press department, but most of all to Joe Precious and his team who shepherded this project after our dear departed sister Zoey rode her great credit with Black Beauty to greener pastures."

"Forgive me, I have to say this," the head of marketing declared. "I know Zoey discovered Black Beauty and fought for them and foresaw this whole hip-hope craze. I give her all the credit in the world for that. But I just can't believe Bertelsmann thinks she's qualified to be president of a major record label! Call it sour grapes, but I'm sorry."

"I wonder if someone at Bertelsmann is sitting in a room like this saying that about me," Hamilton said. "Listen, Zoey earned her break and she deserves all the success she's made from it. We still have Black Beauty and they are a landmark band. Historical. They have changed pop music for the better. I am happy for Zoey and happy for us.

"In other news, I am delighted to announce that all of the tensions between WorldWide and Cokie Shea have been resolved. Miss Shea will now be recording for her own label, Smoking Gun, which will be distributed internationally by WorldWide. We have also arranged for Cokie to be the musical guest *and* host of the season finale of *Saturday Night Live.* And that same week she will be gracing the cover of *Rolling Stone.* For Cokie Shea, the crossing over has begun."

"Al," Cantone said, "will Cokie's new label go through Nashville or New York?"

"Let's put a pin in that for the moment, Jim," Hamilton said. "You and I should pull together after this meeting to have a powwow about that and several other possibilities."

He talked to the phone box. "David, how are things on the continent?"

"All systems go, Al," Knopft said. "Believe it or not, Loudatak dates for May and June went up this week and sold out across the board. This album of theirs, *Contusion!,* is selling like blockbusters."

The whole room shook their heads and smiled. Hamilton said, "We may have to see if Bruce Gilbert wants to come out of retirement to handle the T-shirt franchise. Roger, what's new in the United Kingdom?"

"Britain has the hots for Cokie Shea," Roger Rose quacked down the line. "She's exploded in Ireland and Scotland. Liverpool and Manchester can't keep her records in the stores. I was going to ask if we could arrange for her to come over and sleep with some very big retailers, but given your new position of authority, Al, I want to make perfectly clear that I myself prefer boys."

Hamilton didn't like that. The head of marketing jumped in and said to Rose, "Okay, Roger, we'll send you down to Germany to service Loudatak."

"Let's cut the comedy, folks," Hamilton said. "Our business is very, very sound. As long as we remember that this is a business, we will all prosper in the years ahead. I want you to know that there will be no more bloodletting. Everyone in this room has job security. Make sure your staffs understand that. I don't want any more rumors and I don't want anyone talking to the press. As that great African-American leader Gerald Ford once said, 'Our long national nightmare is over.' But our work is just beginning. Thanks, everybody."

Cantone got up to leave and Hamilton stopped him. "Jim, let's grab a minute in my office."

They went into what used to be DeGaul's office and Hamilton closed the door. Jim took a chair and Al sat on the edge of the desk. Jim was ready for anything. He knew Booth had been just running out the clock on him, waiting until his contract was up to toss him onto the street. After the shocks of Lilly's death and DeGaul's fall, after humiliating Booth in public, he had no illusions about a second chance. Thank God he and Jane never got around to moving—they had some money saved.

And now, moments before his own contract expired, Booth had bit the dust. Well, why not? It was a random universe. Lilly was dead, Black Beauty were superstars. None of them had any control over anything.

Whatever Hamilton was getting ready to hit him with, Jim would be neither disappointed nor offended. These guys had no power over him anymore.

"You must be glad Booth's gone," Hamilton said. Jim made a mild protest and Hamilton said, "No, no, that's unfair of me. It's been a hard patch to get through, is all. Listen, Jim. I want you to stay on. Same terms, new contract, two years."

Cantone was surprised at how much relief he felt. He'd spent so much time preparing not to be crushed when he was fired that he refused to admit how much he cared. Now he felt like kissing Hamilton, which would be a mistake on a multitude of levels.

Hamilton kept talking as if the reprieve meant nothing to him. He said, "This system of separate-but-equal responsibilities DeGaul and Booth put in needs to be revamped. It's not healthy to have two people at the same rank sharing the same job. It creates rivalries and tensions. We need to work out a cleaner reporting structure. I'm going to ask Roger Rose to start reporting to Dave Knopft. I hope he goes for it, but if he doesn't, frankly, he can go. Roger's a talented fellow, but World-Wide ILG needs one boss and Dave is the one."

"That makes sense," Jim said.

"I see the same sort of design problems with the way A&R is set up. It doesn't make sense to have one A&R chief for the East Coast and another for the West Coast. You and Precious are both huge assets and I want to keep you both doing what you're great at. But from now on, Joe's going to be overall chief of A&R. This is not in any sense a demotion for you. Joe respects you enormously and, frankly, he understands what you do a lot better than I do. I never claimed to have ears. After all, I'm a bean counter."

Jim felt the chill but he stayed calm. He said, "How exactly is that going to work, Al?"

"Same as always. You are in charge of rock, Precious is in charge of R&B. I think we have to address the reality that pop music now is R&B. That's not good or bad, it's just the truth. I look at what Joe's done with Solidarity and the other rap projects he's brought in, I listen to what's getting played on Top Forty radio, it's pretty clear that rock and roll is no longer the center of the universe. Rock and pop are moving away from each other. I think it makes sense to move some of the big pop acts, such as Lydya, to Joe's purview. It's a neater fit, really, than having her in the mix with Loudatak and Jerusalem. And I'm very interested to see if West Coast can handle Cokie Shea's imprint. That would be a breakthrough. A black unit supervising a country-pop crossover. Imagine.

"See, Jim, I kind of want to shake off that old-fashioned black-white thinking. Why should pop be a subdivision of rock? Isn't pop today really a species of R&B?"

"I get your point, Al. It's a done deal. I'm not fighting you."

"I know you're not, Jim. You're a good man. Everyone likes you."

"Will I have autonomy on the rock side?"

"You and Precious work that out. You have my full support. I'm sure he'll defer to you on rock. You know a lot more about it than he does."

Cantone was amazed. He was keeping his job but he was losing his authority. He'd probably even get a modest salary bump. Another two years, another million dollars. All he had to do was not care.

Hamilton leaned forward and said kindly, "Jim, it's a relief. Rock and roll doesn't have to carry the bottom line anymore. It doesn't have to pay for everything else. Let hip-hop take that financial burden and you let rock flourish as an art form. It's a mature style now, like jazz. It doesn't have to carry the company. What a wonderful liberation. Your job now is just to find great music. Let Precious pay the bills."

Oh, man, Jim thought, I'm halfway to the box-set-and-reissues department.

· · ·

Cantone was never so grateful to live in Manhattan as during a blizzard. No car to dig out, no traffic jams, no driveway to shovel. Just the same two blocks to the train and one block home.

On the subway he stared at installment XII of the long-running Spanish-language AIDS-awareness comic strip that hung over the windows between a 1-800-DIVORCE placard and a drug-detox ad. Some people had real troubles.

Jim played back Hamilton's words, his sentence. He wanted to tell himself that rock and roll had been counted out before and had always come back. Of course it would again. But as what? In his gloom Jim reckoned that if rock had finally kicked the bucket it was the fault of him and his coworkers. They grabbed all the fruit and did not water the tree. They had been passed this music in trust, and they'd taken bad care of it.

A piece of a misplaced song came into his head. "How many cabs in New York City, how many tears in a bottle of gin?" It rolled away from him.

If someone had asked him, when he came to New York to join the record business, what would be the most important part of himself to protect, Jim might have answered obviously, "My integrity," or more thoughtfully, "My love for music." But now he thought it was neither. The hardest thing to protect in any business, in growing up, in going out into the world, was your tenderness.

He got out of the subway at Fourteenth Street and trudged through the drifts. It was already dark, and the snow was coming down hard. He squinted. At the corner of his block he saw Captain Tim in his folding chair, across Seventh Avenue. He waved. The old man did not wave back. Jim looked through the storm. Snow was piling up on him. He crossed over to see if the Captain was okay.

Jim sensed before he touched the old man's skin that Captain Tim was dead in his chair. He stood looking down at him. He fought off the desire to walk away. He went into a Korean market and asked the owner to call an ambulance. The owner did, and then came outside and felt Tim's neck and put an ear to his blue lips and opened Tim's coat and hit his chest.

"I don't know if you should do that," Jim said to the Korean. "We should wait for a doctor."

"I am doctor," the grocer said. "In Korea, I was doctor."

Jim didn't know what to say. A doctor gives it up and works fifteen hours a day in a New York market so his family can live in America. He thought of his own father's sacrifices for his brothers. Here he was, making a million dollars on each two-year contract extension, depressed about a new reporting structure.

He remembered a Neil Young song his father used to play on the eight-track in their truck. "Though my problems are meaningless, that don't make them go away."

All these lost songs, Jim thought, tugging at me like ghosts.

Jim and the Korean doctor stood in the snow on either side of Tim's body until the rescue squad came up from St. Vincent's. They helped the crew load the corpse and watched as the ambulance went away. Cantone picked up Captain Tim's deck chair and said to the Korean, "You want this? No? Will you do me a big favor? Will you get rid of it so my little boys don't see it? Luke and Mark? Thank you. Thank you, doctor."

He made it into his building and up the elevator. As soon as he stepped into the hall he smelled Jane's vegetarian pot pie. It was the best thing. The corridor was warm. Three pairs of snow boots were lined up outside his apartment door, dripping dry.

He turned his key in the lock. Luke heard it and yelled, "Daddy's home!" and was on Jim by the time he stepped inside. Jim carried Luke into the kitchen, where Mark was standing on a chair supervising Jane dishing out the dinner and filling up a plate with corn, potatoes, carrots, and peas.

"We're making supper for Captain Tim!" Luke shouted.

"We're going to take him some pot pie, Daddy," Mark said.

"How did this come up?" Jim asked Jane.

"We had to run down to the market to get carrots," Jane said, covering the plate with tinfoil. She even had plastic silverware. "On the way back we ran into Captain sitting out there under a little umbrella. I tried to convince him to go back to the shelter. He said he liked the snow. He looked frozen. I almost asked him to come up here for supper."

"He could sleep in my bed!" Luke declared.

Jane said, "But I had a feeling you wouldn't like that. I knew you had a big day today. So the boys got the idea to make up a hot meal and take it down to him."

"Boy, that's pretty nice of you guys," Jim said to his boys. "I hope you'll bring me a nice hot dinner when I'm old."

"I'll always live with you, Daddy," Luke said.

"Listen, gang," Jim said. "You all are nice and dry now and I'm still all snowy in my overcoat. Give me the plate and I'll take it down to the Cap'n."

"You really want to?" Jane said. "Great, I'll put out ours. Luke and Mark, get your boots on and go with Daddy."

"No, Jane," Jim said. "It's getting really bad out. Snow's turning to sleet, sidewalk's ice. I don't want the kids out again. I'll take this to Tim if he's still there."

"Okay, I guess. Boys, Daddy's going to take Captain his supper and tell him you boys made it! I need you to help me set the table."

Jim walked out of the apartment carrying the warm plate in his gloved hands. He walked a couple of blocks in the snow, looking for someone to give it to. The homeless were no longer so visible in Greenwich Village. Good fortune and police policy had swept them away. After wandering all the way down to the public library in the snow, Jim dumped the dinner in Balducci's trash can and went home with the dirty plate.

"Did Captain Tim like his supper, Daddy?" Mark asked when Jim came in.

Jim studied his little boy's face. He sat down on the couch, undid his wet shoes, and pulled off his socks. His sons climbed up and sat next to him. He said, "Boys, I have never seen Captain Tim so happy as when he opened that foil and saw that dinner. He said, 'Pot pie is my *favorite.*' Boy, he enjoyed that food. He wolfed down every bit. I went into the Korean market and got him some tea and he had an old feast."

"Maybe I should have put in more," Jane said. "He probably hasn't had a real meal in ages."

"Well, listen. That's not the only reason this was a great day for Captain Tim. He told me some big news. Did you know Captain Tim has a daughter?" The boys reacted with amazement. They wanted to know if she was their age. "No, no, she's a grown-up daughter. And get this, she's taking Captain Tim to live with her and her boys down in Florida! This is his last day in New York! That's why he was sitting outside in the snow. From now on, Captain Tim is going to be living by a nice warm bay all year around."

Jane looked at Jim curiously. "Come on," she said, "let's eat our dinner."

Luke was excited about how old Captain Tim's grandkids were and his new home's possible proximity to pirates. Mark said nothing. He climbed down from the couch and headed toward the front door. Jim detached himself from Luke and went after Mark, who was crying.

"What's the matter, sweetie?" he asked as Mark wrestled with the doorknob.

"I gotta go say goodbye to my friend," Mark said, struggling against his tears. "I gotta say goodbye to Captain."

Jim picked up his son. "He's already gone, honey. You should be happy for him. Captain Tim missed his daughter and his grandkids and dreamed of living with them. Now his dream has come true."

$\cdots$

Hours later the kids had gone to bed. Jim was staring out the window at the snow. Jane was gluing together a broken lamp. Jim had hooked up the turntable and was playing one of the Dylan LPs he inherited from DeGaul. "I know that evening's empire has returned into sand, vanished from my hand, left me blindly here to stand but still not sleeping."

Jim thought about the rise and fall of rock and roll. He decided it was a foolish thing for a grown man to devote his life to allegiances he formed as a teenager.

"Was that true?" Jane said. "What you told them about Captain Tim and his daughter?"

Jim looked at his wife and he looked at the snow. They had never lied to each other. Total honesty was their code, for better or worse. But man, he thought, it's such a mean world out there. Why not protect his loved ones to the small degree he was able? So he smiled at his wife and said, "Yes, it is true."

Why was he disappointed that she acted like she believed him?

"I've been thinking," Jane said.

Jim said, "Hmm?"

"When the kids start going to school full time, I might want to sign up for classes at NYU. What do you think?"

"Sure, if you want to. What do you think you'll take?"

"Something useful. Sciences, I think. Biology or chemistry."

"Lots of lab work."

"I'll look at the brochure. You think it's a good idea."

"Sure."

She finally got the pieces to fit and lit the lamp. She put it on a high shelf to dry and she went to bed.

Jim listened to his record and watched the snow. He imagined what was happening at that moment in St. Pierre. He pictured DeGaul tanned, shirtless, and barefoot on the beach in the setting sunlight. He was drinking a Red Stripe with Buster, John P., and Mr. Jay. They all laughed and pointed to the water slide with its blinking red airplane lights on top.

DeGaul took the dare and a big slug of beer and marched across the sand to the base of the huge slide. He put one foot on the first wooden crossbeam and hoisted himself up. He ascended hand over hand as his friends cheered. The higher he climbed, the more he saw. He saw the lagoons and the bungalows and the fairground almost finished. He saw the waterfall that poured out of the jungle and emptied into the sea. He saw Paulo and his brother flying over the mountains. When he got to the very top of the slide DeGaul threw his leg up and pulled himself over. His empire was laid out before him. He raised his arms to his friends below and sat in the warm water. Then he threw back his head and, laughing, rode all the way down.

That is what Cantone hoped DeGaul was doing. True or not, it made a nice picture. And anyway, it was sweet to believe it.